FRUIT FLY

JOSH SILVER

MAGPIE
BOOKS

A MAGPIE BOOK

First published in Great Britain, the Republic of Ireland and Australia
by Magpie, an imprint of Oneworld Publications Ltd, 2026

Copyright © Josh Silver, 2026

The moral right of Josh Silver to be identified as the
Author of this work has been asserted by him in accordance
with the Copyright, Designs and Patents Act 1988

All rights reserved
Copyright under Berne Convention
A CIP record for this title is available from the British Library

ISBN 978-1-83643-147-3 (hardback)
ISBN 978-1-83643-239-5 (trade paperback)
eISBN 978-1-83643-148-0

Typeset by Oneworld Publications Ltd
Printed and bound in Great Britain by Clays Ltd, Elcograf S.p.A.

This book is a work of fiction. Names, characters, businesses, organisations, places and events are either the product of the author's imagination or are used fictitiously. Any resemblance to actual persons, living or dead, events or locales is entirely coincidental.

Every reasonable effort has been made to trace the copyright holders of material reproduced in this book, but if any have been inadvertently overlooked the publishers would be glad to hear from them.

No part of this publication may be reproduced, stored in a retrieval system, or transmitted, in any form or by any means, electronic, mechanical, photocopying, recording of otherwise, or used in any manner for the purpose of training artificial intelligence technologies or systems, without the prior permission of the publishers.

The authorised representative in the EEA is eucomply OÜ,
Pärnu mnt 139b–14, 11317 Tallinn, Estonia
(email: hello@eucompliancepartner.com / phone: +33757690241)

Oneworld Publications Ltd
10 Bloomsbury Street
London WC1B 3SR
England

Stay up to date with the latest books,
special offers, and exclusive content from
Oneworld with our newsletter

Sign up on our website
oneworld.co.uk

Praise for *Fruit Fly*

'This is an incredible book ... tough and raw and merciless but funny and kind at the same time.'
　　　　　　　　　　　Russell T. Davies, writer of *It's a Sin*

'*Fruit Fly* is savage and darkly hilarious. A pointed satire of publishing with flawed, fascinating characters.'
　　　　Juno Dawson, bestselling author of *Her Majesty's Royal Coven*

'Absolutely unforgettable. A raw, visceral triumph that echoes modern classics like *Trainspotting*, *Young Mungo* and *A Little Life*, yet stands entirely on its own. Strikingly original and deeply human – this book will live rent-free in your mind long after the final page. I loved it.'
　　　　　　　　John Marrs, bestselling author of *You Killed Me First*

'Josh has a fantastic, distinctive voice. The writing is as fearless as the characters are fearful. Bold, raw, uncomfortable and very, very funny.'
　　　　　　　　　　　Jonathan Harvey, award-winning screenwriter,
　　　　　　　　　　　　　　　　　　playwright, author and actor

'*Fruit Fly* is provocative, moving and does not so much carry but propels you along a wild journey that leaves you a little breathless by the end, desperate for more. Expertly crafted characters, stomach-punching prose and a stark exploration of real world issues.'
　　　　　　Onyi Nwabineli, author of *Allow Me to Introduce Myself*

'*Fruit Fly* is sharp, propulsive, and deeply humane, a story about people in freefall written with such clarity, dark humour, and compassion that you can't stop turning the pages. It's a novel that subverts our usual narratives about trauma and illness, healing and redemption, a riotous, tender tale of people writing their own rulebooks. Josh Silver's adult debut is a must-read.'
　　　　　　　　　　　　　Seth Insua, author of *Human, Animal*

'Dark, haunting, gripping, psychologically messy, heartbreaking but also darkly funny. An absolute masterpiece.'
　　　　　　　　Kate Weston, author of *You May Now Kill the Bride*

'Compulsive, propulsive, and obsessive. *Fruit Fly* questions how we exploit our most abject identities for the sake of the audience, and what happens when we have no identity to left to sell. Complex characters with sharp voices and hidden motives. A book that keeps you captivated without allowing you to ever get comfortable.'

Genevieve Jagger, author of *Fragile Animals*

For my friend Leah Brotherhead.
With thanks.

'If I were thinking clearly, Leonard, I would tell you that I wrestle alone in the dark, in the deep dark, and that only I can know – only I can understand – my own condition.'

Virginia Woolf
The Hours, Michael Cunningham

Part 1

1

Leo

> Three days no sleep
> Smack's sweet.
> The aftertaste
> I will push away
> As long as I am able.
> But it is coming –
> The crest of its wave on my horizon
> Ready to plummet,
> Ready to drown.
> It is less poetic now.
> More
> A bin lid
> Closing
> On my world of mangled shit.
>
> @Alias22

2

Mallory

As I start up my sixth game of Candy Crush while sat on the closed toilet seat, I have a very clear and rational realisation.

I, too, am a piece of exploding computerised fruit.

That is the extent of me. Here one moment, only to be pulverised into a spray of sweet nothing the very next. Obliterated. Forgotten.

Outside, I can hear the voices of my guests and the music droning on. *Why won't they leave?*

The truth is, if I did explode, I don't think they'd notice. At least not at first. They would pretend that they cared – at my funeral. That I was important to them. That I had made a mark on their lives in some beautiful and profound way. But they would lie.

One of them lied earlier. A woman I have met only once.

'*Mallory is basically Clarissa Dalloway*,' she proclaimed loudly to my kitchen full of arty (pretentious) intellectual types, pointing in my direction with a mouthful of hummus. Hummus I had bought from Tesco and put in the poshest-looking bowl I could find. I'd sprinkled some coriander on top and pretended I'd made it. (I suppose I lie too. But it's different.) '*Clarissa Fucking Dalloway*,' she repeated, whilst pulling a face like the mouthful was precipitating an orgasm. I swallowed my jealousy. I haven't had an orgasm in years, let alone one triggered by Tesco's own-brand hummus. '*Mallory throws the best parties in North London.*'

Today is the first time this woman has stepped foot inside my house.

But I laughed obligingly. And the guests all agreed, crowded round my kitchen island, nodding, a bobbing sea of wire-rimmed glasses, trilbies, rolled up cigarettes tucked behind ears (lobes studded with hoops and dangling crosses). Everyone defying the vape trend because they are too real, too hardcore and altogether too brilliant to care about lung cancer, like their Tate Modern memberships and Birkenstocks somehow make them immune.

Some even clapped. I waved them off, like they were being silly. *No, no. I am nothing like Mrs Dalloway*. But I wouldn't actually know. I have never read *Mrs Dalloway*, despite pretending to be well-versed in the literary greats so often that I've almost convinced myself I have. What is actually true is that I googled the synopsis – like I do with most of the classics – binged on an overview of the themes and style on Wikipedia, mentally crammed in some sentences that sounded important and now just recite them at people. It seems to have worked. I can even quote bits.

She sliced like a knife through everything.

That's a good one.

'Mal?'

I move my finger across my screen with utter precision, slaying five yellow Jelly Tots in a row. I watch them detonate, the vibrations of my phone tingle my fingers in such a satisfying rhythm that I make an audible gasp.

'Mal, are you in there?'

I do have to be careful. Virginia Woolf comes up annoyingly often within the conversations of this wannabe Bloomsbury set, like she has been adopted as some kind of Mother Figure (*she's a style icon, a homeware influencer, just a total fucking mood*). And so, I bought an early edition of *Mrs Dalloway* from eBay for more than the price of an iPad, bent the pages and put it in the downstairs bathroom – where I am currently sat. It is placed for everyone to see: right on top of the pile of neatly (strategically) arranged books on the shelf, next to the peace lily and the bougie scented candle that smells strongly like lavender, perfectly masking the stench of my deception.

You'd think I'd just read the thing.

She felt very young, and at the same time, unspeakably aged.
Another good one.
I can see it in front of me. Its forcibly broken spine.
My lies, bent into unread pages.
We all lie.
'Mal, are you in there?'
Virginia Woolf killed herself with stones in her pockets. I may not have technically read her books, but I do know that much.
'*Mal!*'
It's romantic, isn't it? Suicide. There is something romantic about it. Sometimes. Not always. Not the ones on the train tracks or in the wardrobes with ties and belts. More the ones in the forests or rivers or lakes. The peaceful ones. I think so.
If I admitted that to my guests, maybe they would leave. Which is what I want.
'Mallory?' My husband's gruff Irish lilt through the door. Fuck's sake. 'Mal, Joanie is asking where we keep the Jäger.'
We have Jäger because we are still young and cool. Effortlessly. That's important.
'I'm just in the bathroom, darling.' I never call him darling unless other people are around to hear it. I take my glass of champagne and down the remainder of its contents. I'm not drunk enough.
He is so handsome. So sexy. Everyone tells me. My knees still go weak. They do.
They do.
'I swear it was in the cupboard in the kitchen island?' He is slurring.
'No, it's above the—'
Damn it. I died.
In Candy Crush, not in reality. 'I'll be two minutes!'
I stand and press the flush, for effect. The water runs as I turn the tap, but I don't wet my hands. I just stare at myself in the mirror above the sink.
I look like I belong here.
'OK, love.' I hear a thud on the back of the door. His head?

'OK.' His voice, barely audible through the wood, like his mouth is pressed against it. '…I'm horny.'

This mirror is distressed. That's what the man at Neptune's furniture store told me. '*This is a distressed mirror.*' I have tried so often to find its emotional anguish, to relate. But all it means is that the glass is purposefully tarnished to the point where you can't really see yourself in it at all. I hate this mirror, but everyone says how cool it is.

My mirror is cool, like my house, my husband and our Jäger.

'Did you hear me, Mal?'

Yes, I heard you. Yes, I fucking heard you. 'Sorry?'

'I'm horny…'

Jäger bombs in a three-floor semi, giving him a semi, in Crouch End at ten p.m. on a Friday night.

This is my life.

My life is enviable.

I have it all.

I turn away from my reflection and open the latch on the door. He stumbles towards me, pushing me back in. 'Ronan…'

'We can be quick.' He kicks the door shut behind him with the back of his foot.

'But the guests—'

He nuzzles into my neck, the back of my thighs now pressing into the top of the sink. His face appears in front of me: his intentionally scruffy stubble, ever enduring hairline, heavy brow and bright-green eyes, which are now gone, lost, blurred by a concoction of clumsy lust and unpronounceable Scottish whiskey. 'Baby…' My skin prickles. He never calls me baby, unless his eyes look like this. 'Just quickly…' His fingers graze my jeans, the inside of my thigh. He never does that either, unless his eyes look like this. 'You're amazing.'

I've trained myself not to flinch now. Every time.

I make a small moan, because I know I should.

Thankfully the moan is short-lived, broken off by someone's voice: neither mine nor his. 'Oh God!'

The door has swung open and Joanie is stood there, frozen and flushed, half in, half out, glass of Chardonnay in hand.

Ronan turns his head away from my neck, affording me some momentary relief. 'Oh shit – Joanie, sorry—'

'No! Please – you two crack on!' she says, turning on the spot, hand moving over her mouth, eyes wide.

'Joanie—' I begin.

'God! No. Not at all. *You two.* You two are such…' She stalls. '*Fun.*'

'We're coming out.'

Joanie laughs, like this is all funny. *My life is fun and funny.* 'It's just – people are waiting for Ronan's speech.'

Ronan's Speech.

Why Everyone Is Still Here.

'Ah fuck,' he says, peeling himself from me. 'Really?' He sounds suddenly shy, but Ronan is not shy. 'Do I have to?'

'Yes!' Joanie protests, then lowers her voice. 'You didn't hear this from me, but Theo brought party poppers – bless him – so be prepared for some bangs.'

He shakes his head, objecting, but it's a lie. He wants to give his speech. I know he does, because I have overheard him rehearsing it in the cellar whilst pretending to use the Peloton.

He exhales. 'Fine.'

Since his recent promotion to one of the commissioning editors for the UK arm of Netflix, everyone wants to hear his genius. *He's only thirty-eight. Thirty-eight! Can you believe it?* Even Joanie has more to say to him than she does to me now. There was a time when she called him a walking red flag, but recently she no longer sees the red, just the faded brown of his corduroyed brilliance. (He loves those cords. They cost him so much money but look like he found them in the bin of an old peoples' home. And yet, that's the point.)

He steps out of the bathroom behind Joanie, straightening his shirt.

'I'll be right out,' I say, but as he playfully closes the door on me – making Joanie erupt with her vibrant laugh that I've always loved – I shut my eyes. I wait for them both to fade away, down the hallway towards the kitchen, where the twenty other guests wait to be inspired.

My hands are shaking.

They still do it, all these years later. A tremor, starting from the inside.

This is my life.

Listening to the cheer explode from our guests as Ronan takes his place centre stage by the Smeg fridge (double door!), I look back to the stack of books on the shelf next to the candle and the peace lily. One about Freud, one by Jung, one about dysfunctional attachment styles in adults, a Sylvia Plath poetry collection and a book with a red cover. My book.

I pull it out. The feel of its spine against my fingertips sends a shudder down mine.

The Sunday Times Bestseller

SHALLOW EMBERS

Beneath a simple graphic of a red flame is the author's name.

Mallory Maddox

It's hard to see my name in print now. Not as fun as you might think. Every time I see it, I find myself having to fight a very strong and visceral impulse to throw the book from the window, flush it away or – a more recent one – spit on it. I avert my eyes from the gold lettering, moving them to the puff quote just to the left of the flame.

'A painfully raw yet beautiful debut – a coming-of-age story to be read by everyone. Maddox has it all'

P.K. ANDERSON

I didn't know who the hell P.K. Anderson was back when I wrote the thing, but by God did I find out. I followed her on Twitter, DM'd gushing thanks, asked her to lunch, invited her to my book launch. Some might say I was obsessive, but I think that would be a tad dramatic. It was strategic. My publisher told me that I needed to surround myself with other up-and-coming authors, so I tried to take their advice. We wrote in different genres. Me: intense realism. P.K.: high fantasy. Paula Kate's debut came out the year before mine. Both our stories had a coming-of-age element to them that seemed to appeal to the same readership, Young Adults. Hers was a trilogy about a bisexual teenage boy who develops the telepathic power of foresight that got a six-figure pre-empt and sold in over forty territories. Mine got a ten-grand offer for world rights, but ended up doing well, thanks to some YouTuber called CreIsYourBae picking it for her book club (she loved the cover), and then it 'exploded' on Twitter. I sold twelve thousand copies in one day.

I was twenty-nine.

Seven years ago.

That was seven years ago. And we never did meet, but I guess P.K. was busy.

Since then, she has left her husband, acquired over one million TikTok followers and a huge film deal from Lionsgate (another six figures for the option alone), and is still writing the series to this day: prequels, sequels, spin-offs, the lot – now from her beachfront house in Malibu. She is an inspiration to so many, according to Cosmopolitan magazine. I can't remember the whole article (I got lost in its sea of hyperbole that made my brain want to implode), but in short it described her as '*fierce, independent*' and, '*not that it matters, strikingly beautiful*'.

Seven years ago.

And for me, since then: nothing.

Well, not nothing. My agent dropped me and my publisher pulled my second book. The TV adaptation fell out of contract. I came off Twitter for 'creative reasons': I got sick of blocking accounts that relentlessly asked me *What's the hold up? Why won't you write another? Maybe you can't LOL* because I myself have been blocked.

Writer's Block.

At first, when I would hear that term, I didn't fully believe in it. It sounded like bullshit to me. But as time went on, and I couldn't think of a new idea, I realised that it could become incredibly useful. I used it to leverage an external narrative of creative brilliance: I was so spent emotionally from writing *Shallow Embers* that I needed to give myself a break. To be nominated for the Waterstones Best Debut Fiction Award at twenty-nine takes a lot out of you – and I was the proof.

It worked. For a while. The pain I professed to have gone through was lapped up in the corners of the internet that cared. *The struggle of being this brilliant.*

But the truth is, I had no more.

No more ideas. No more space. Blocked.

Blocked by my stint in hospital. Blocked by what that meant for me, coming so out of the blue. Blocked by the period of recovery time after it. Blocked by the online counselling course I later enrolled in to pretend I was interested in the psychology of other people *for my books*. (Not because Ronan told me to do something useful and I thought I was going to lose my mind being in the house all day running out of money.) Blocked by the clients I now have (three) who I see on a weekly basis, each telling me versions of the same story. Blocked by feeling small next to my husband and his continued success, his rise, throughout the past seven years, to greatness. All of this underscored by a shadowy, persisting darkness, only punctuated by such intense intrusive thoughts that I have wondered if I'm even real. Blocked by his continued asking to have a child.

Maddox has it all.

I look to the other side of the flame, at the second quote.

'A modern-day Virginia Woolf'
THE OBSERVER

More cheers from the other room.

More of Ronan's muffled voice. 'Thank you all for coming!'

I hate this. This life. The people in my kitchen. The disappointment I can feel from each of them. The constant glances of, *Was it a fluke?* I hate the way I write. Or should I say, the way I don't write. I hate the way I speak. The way I look. Floating around with my hair in a messy bun, not because I'm messy, but because I care. It takes twenty minutes for me to make it look like that. I hate how I have become meek.

Ronan says it occasionally. *You've become meek, Mallory.*

Meek Mal.

I can hear him now, his slurred, rehearsed speech beginning. 'I didn't prepare anything. But I'll say a few words…'

The guests laughing. In love with him.

I slide the book – my book – back into its place, hidden between the others.

'It is a pleasure to celebrate this with you. I can't believe it, really…'

'We can!'

'I have been told Theo brought party poppers. Try not to aim for my head – however much you might want to – or you'll have shit TV for the rest of your lives.'

Laughter.

The jealousy spikes and spurs me to grab the tumbler of whiskey he left on the sink, neck it in one, then pick up my phone. Before I can stop myself I am typing into Google.

How to write a bestseller again.

I stop, considering. *Don't be stupid, Mallory.*

I delete the word *again*, and hit enter.

A few professional-looking websites. Some advertisements for writing courses. How To Write a Bestseller: 6 Easy Steps. I keep scrolling down until I see a Reddit blog.

The truth lies in Reddit.

I open it.

Hello! You're probably here because you know you have the potential to write but you are stuck, sick of your current job and/or you want money.

See. Reddit knows. It always knows.

Well, fear not. Here is how to write the next big literary hit!!!!

Trends to follow:
- *Underrepresented voices are very popular currently. So if you've had a shit life, you = winning!!!!!*
- *Crime is good but make it cosy. People want to read about murder next to their fire places drinking red wine.*
- *Fantasy is huge – throw a dragon or two in there BUT make it sexy. Better still, make the dragons sexy. It doesn't even need to be well-written. Just make your lead character a bit weirdly into their fantasy pet that they ride (lol).*
- *Make people cry. People loooovveee to cry.*
- *Dark is good.*
- *Also – always remember: gay is in. Go gay. It's cool now. It sells. However – here is the gold dust – the perfect blend is gay AND sad. You nail that, you're minted. And probs an award winner.*

Thank me later xxx mwah. Happy writing, bitches

The post has been liked over nine thousand times.

I think of Paula Kate and her bisexual boy, responsible for the Malibu house purchase. And for her divorce. I suddenly think of all the other books that are being screamed about from every corner of the internet. Lots of gay going on. Sorry, lots of *LGBTQI+*. I love so many of those books, and I've actually read, not just googled, them. *A Little Life*. Oh my God, I bawled and bawled, and it was *so long*. Come to think of it, some of my favourite films, too. *A Single Man* – so sad, and so *chic*. *God's Own Country*. So raw and so *real*. *Milk*. Sean Penn was breathtaking – he won all the awards. *Philadelphia*, too. One of the greats. Tom Hanks lost so much weight for the role, he was remarkable. *The Hours*. I *loved* that film. The scene where Ed Harris was so riddled with shame and HIV that he threw himself from the window. It made me cry.

Make people cry.

I'm not gay though.

Wait.

Am I?

I am drunk.

But... am I?

Clarissa Fucking Dalloway.

Clarissa Dalloway was a little bit gay. I swear Wikipedia said so. So was Virginia, as a matter of fact. Yes! She absolutely was. And I have been likened to her – *on the cover of my book. By the fucking* Observer.

Everyone was a little bit. Everyone *is*, a little bit, right?

Virginia Woolf was a little bit gay.

My hands are shaking.

I make my way out of the bathroom, down the corridor, towards the laughter at my husband's pre-rehearsed speech, to see no one notice me enter. I am actually shushed by the same woman who called me Clarissa Fucking Dalloway. I stand at the back of the group, banging my hands together like a Good Wife does. I hear myself saying things like 'Darling! You're so funny!' as Ronan makes his jokes, ignoring the thought that drops into my head from nowhere: to take the Sakuto knife sat atop the kitchen island and cause a domestic bloodbath.

She sliced like a knife through everything.

It was a wedding gift, from my mother.

'Well done!' people cheer around me, over and over, as Ronan bows his head, using a spatula as an ironic microphone, and time stops. As quickly as Ed Harris plummeted from that window, something comes to me. I feel an invigorating heat at the top of my spine, right beneath my skull. And with it, I make a choice. One that will change me from this point forwards.

I will not explode.

I will not put stones in my pockets.

I will choose courage, and write.

It comes. Fleeting, yet momentous.

An idea.

An idea for a new book.

Born from the shallow embers of my soul.

3

Leo

Scratchy.
    Scratchy as fuck.
    Don't worry.
    Do not worry.
    Stop picking.
    You'll be playing with your two best mates tonight. Tina and G.
    They never let you down.
    They never let you down.
    They never let you down.
    'What do you want, lad?'
    His eyes are red. He's bollocksed like always.
    Brick. He thinks people call him this because he's hard as nails and we all shit ourselves at the thought of him, but it's not. It's cos he looks like one.
    'Tina and G.'
    Acts like one. Speaks like one. Thick as one.
    One big lump of cement.
    I glance behind him, down past the bins.
    We are alone.
    I flick my fag butt into the gutter.
    'Your jumper looks box-fresh, is it new?'
    I stole it from a charity shop, but Brick does not need to know this. Brick does not need to know anything. 'Yeah.'
    'Nice. Making money then?'
    No time for small talk, Brick. Just give me the gateway to heaven.

4

Mallory

I sit on the bed next to Ronan's unconscious and naked body, honing in on his hairless nipples. Tiny stubs of black peek through their pink circumference, desperate to be seen.

We have never spoken about the fact that he shaves them.

I have sometimes left my Veet out in plain view on the side in our en-suite, because I could see little cut marks on his actual areola, but he never touched it. Ronan doesn't like to be helped. Prefers things to go unsaid. It's safer that way. And yet here are his nipples, all stubbly and grazed, on his smooth and chiselled torso.

He looks dead. Like a dead model from a perfume advert.

He passed out pulling his cords off, mumbling something about bringing the gifts up from the kitchen. I think he was about to ask for sex, but the heavy intoxication of Jäger and adoration mercifully stopped him.

He's so fun.

He doesn't even snore.

I reach down to the carpet and take my half-full (of white wine) coffee cup that I have brought with me for company, sit back up and glug, then, biting the skin around my nail, stare at the armchair in the corner.

I taste blood.

Stepmother's blessing.

That armchair cost fifteen hundred pounds. We did the attic dormer conversion last year because Ronan wanted more space for when we have a child.

We should start a family, when you're up to it, Mal.

I shudder at the memory of what the conversion made me: uncontrollably feral for picking bathroom tiles and hoarding carpet swatches, like my life depended on it. It took months to plan, as I found it an incredible distraction from my boredom. I had a *new zest for life.* (I turned into a homeware lunatic.) I threw myself in, meeting with the architect and the designer, and scrawling through Instagram and Pinterest for effortlessly inspired choices: the colour palate, the correct shade of Farrow & Ball dusky pink (Tailor Tack or Calamine, Tailor Tack or Calamine? It was Sophie's choice for weeks), the William Morris curtains – gold and Incarnadine Red – the Pooky lamps, the Nkuku side tables, the Loaf Jöelle bed in Egg Box Grey, the Soho Home Theodore armchair.

It is so beautiful. Stunning.

This attic conversion is so stunning.

This attic conversion that no one ever sees.

I would say the words *Pooky* and *Nkuku* so many times that they lost all meaning, and I even began to giddily blend them, for short hand. Nkooky, I would say to people. *The new bedroom is practically sponsored by Nkooky!* But what's worse is that they would laugh, because they knew what I meant. And now, in the stillness of the aftermath, all giddiness well and truly gone, every time I see the bed and its headboard in Egg Box Grey, I want to be dropped and shattered across the floor.

I think of P.K. and her husbandless beachfront life. She probably wears Birkenstocks because she actually needs to. Malibu is warm.

This attic, this life, is so stark.

Six-figure pre-empt.

I can't make that as a therapist with three clients.

Not that it matters, but I'm not *technically* a therapist, despite what I tell my friends, and my patients. It's just a little loophole. To many people the word *counsellor* and *therapist* are interchangeable. I took a twelve-week diploma course in Introduction to Counselling from the Online University, and no one has told me I can't call myself a therapist. Everyone else on the Find a

Therapist portals seems to. Ronan said its fine. He actively encouraged it. *Therapist sounds better than counsellor. And anyway, it's all the same thing. They're mostly quacks. And you're a successful author, so people will believe you.*

I open my notes app on my phone, where I have stored the New York Times review of *Shallow Embers*. I practically know it off by heart, but sometimes reading it gives me the memory of a warmth I once felt regularly.

> Maddox's writing has a profound sense of longing, the nostalgia seeping through every sentence. This book not only appeals to the literary market; it's also going to have the screen production companies hot-footing it to snap up the screen rights – it would make for a wonderful—

It never happened.
Why *did* the film never happen?
P.K. got her film, her executive producer credit.
I scan down the review to the bit I'm looking for.

> I can't wait to see what Maddox brings to the table next. I long for something hard-hitting, thought-provoking and brave. I think we can count on her for this. She has an unhinged bravery that more authors should possess. The literary world is crying out for writers like this. Where will Maddox take us? I for one can't wait to find out.

Unhinged bravery.
Not meek.
Blood coats my tongue as I chew harder, staring at the wall. The paint shade is called White Lies.
Ever so slightly grey.
I don't want to be a therapist, or a counsellor. I never did.
I want to write. And to write, I need to see life.
Go gay.

Gay sells.

I look at my phone screen.

I think of Nick. My brother.

Gay and Sad. Gold dust.

I suddenly remember.

I was once called an honorary gay.

Yes. Or should I say, Yas!

I was.

Just like Judy Garland or Barbara Streisand or Madonna or the Babadook. Sure, this was at school, and it was Joanie who said it after I dressed up as Dumbledore on World Book Day. But she was right. I've always been an ally.

I have the background work done. I do think I have a good knowledge of gay things. Case in point: the cool gay men who congregate at the Maynard Arms like me. I've seen them in the pub a few times, actually. The last time was when I tried to get them to dance with me to ABBA, and OK they said no but I could tell they thought I was a rollicking good time. I was drunk, and probably a little sad – so perhaps they related to my inner world. Before Ronan dragged me away, I think one of them actually once called me Mother – which I know is a term of utmost reverence for a queer icon. I know because I was – still am – up to date with queer trends and terminology. Of course I watch RuPaul and Queer Eye. Yas, mama! Slay! (I love Slay, it's so fun.) Granted, I can't quite remember if he said it in the context of being legendary and iconic, or in the context of being dowdy and knackered, but regardless, I felt respected. They liked me. I felt we had some kind of affinity. A kinship.

Ronan liked it when they called me Mother. But I don't think he fully understood. He thinks drag race is exploitative.

I make an almost cartoon-esque hiccup.

I need A Discreet Gay.

Do they exist?

Ha.

See?

They'd find that funny.

Mother is mothering. Isn't that what they say? People like

Lady Gaga? I type into Google: Where to meet discreet gays near me? Hit enter.

The top result is an app suggestion.

Grindr
Meet discreet gay men in your local area

Interesting.
I do not judge.
Free love, right? The progressive, liberated way to be outside of conventional norms. (Although I can't help but immediately think of the Grindr *killer* – there was a dramatised TV show based on him, with Stephen Merchant trying to win awards by playing a gay psychopathic murdering sex-maniac. I actually think he was quite good in the role.)
I hiccup again.
This is fun.
I am also fun!
I open up my app store and type in *Grindr*.
I could just have a conversation or two. What harm could it do? It says it's an online location-based social networking site to 'discover, connect and explore'.
Explore.
Yes. (Yas.)
My finger is going numb now, from the biting, and perhaps the excitement. The excitement of what? A way out.
A new life.
Away from—
'Honey?'
Shit.
Ronan is stirring. I push my phone down by the side of my leg.
When I can no longer hear him moving, I press download.

5

Leo

I turn down the alley, away from Brick.

'One second lad,' he says from behind me. *Shit*. 'Not so fast. This is sixty. Where's the rest?'

I turn back to him. Try to look not arsed. Not bothered. Shrug, like I'm a stupid twat. 'It's all there.'

Looking stupid is useful. Brick looks stupid, and is stupid. He sometimes can't count. He doesn't know that I know that, but I've been told he's one you can get away from, if you move quickly.

'Should be eighty. You trying to fleece me?'

But tonight he can count.

Which is not useful.

'No way,' I say. 'I'm not.' That's not a lie. I don't like lies. They fuck things up. But when I took the money from the man after the deed, I used a twenty at the corner shop to buy a chocolate bar and a four pack of Stella and some chuddy to get rid of his taste. I got some other bits too. Necessary things. And the change is in my sock.

But I need it.

When Brick looks up at me, I know it's time to run.

I fucking hate running.

My life is running.

Cold sweats, stitch in my side, leg still busted from the abscess that messed me up.

I turn and pelt down away from him.

'You robbing chav!' he shouts before I hear the slam of a car door and his engine start.

I just need some quiet.

I run and run and run, away from his engine, feet smashing into the pavement.

When I get to Wood Green high street, I dodge through the late-night stragglers cramming the pavements, through crowds outside kebab shops, hurdling pools of sick, all the way down towards Ducketts Common. It's grim as hell, but should be quiet. No one goes in it at this time. Well, the pigs come sometimes, but tonight I'll be fine. I know how to hide. Always have.

The promise of silence is in the Poundland bag.

Of peace.

I know the shady spots to wait, until Brick gives up, until next time.

I find my favourite tree and kneel down beneath it. It's shaped like a skeleton in the winter and a fully fleshed human in the summer, like tonight. I pull my cap down over my eyes, Adidas camouflage, open the bag and take out the kitchen foil I also bought from the corner shop.

And the pen.

I rip out the ink tube. Throw it. Snap the plastic. Always hurts, but getting better. My hands. My hands are swollen and grimy. Dirty nails. A kink apparently.

I fold the foil.

Take out my lighter.

Centre the crystals perfectly.

Strike. The crunch of the spark wheel, a gateway. The hairs on my arms prickle awake.

Empty plastic pen to my lips.

Inhale. Deep.

Stillness comes. Bliss.

I lie back and stare at the wet leaves.

It's raining.

I hadn't noticed.

It is so fucking beautiful, this park. I've always thought so.

6

Mallory

Welcome to Grindr!
Please upload your pictures!

Pictures.

I quickly google *what pictures should I use on Grindr*, but I already have a hunch that the answer may cause a few minor hurdles for this mini deep-dive into the gay psyche (let's call it that for now), what with me being a cisgender straight woman. I assume I'm not Grindr's typical participant, but I could be wrong. I often am.

An in-depth Buzzfeed article that I quickly scan tells me the photos I choose really depend on how I *align*, but a two-word post at the top of a Reddit support forum helps clarify what is expected.

Male nudes.

Liked by 13,212 people.

I feel a little uncomfortable. Something is telling me this venture is perhaps a tad too voyeuristic, that I'm prying, or even meddling. That dreaded word *problematic* circles somewhere in the depths of my consciousness.

I remind myself of the truth.

This is not problematic.

This is unhinged bravery.

The Buzzfeed article suggests that Grindr is perfect for people who are newly 'out', or simply questioning. I'm simply questioning. I want to learn. I do. Don't journalists do this kind of thing all the time? Learning is important, especially for the privileged. In fact, I think more people should probably be doing this, to broaden their understanding of the experiences of others. For example, I for one did not know that a 'power bottom' is both a sexual *and* a social position, according to Buzzfeed. The politics of hook-up apps are apparently very nuanced.

Ronan groans, turning slightly.

His eyes remain shut, his lips vibrating on a long and extended outbreath.

After our first ever kiss, all those years ago, the first thing Ronan affectionately told me was that I needed to floss and not just brush. My mother never encouraged me and my brother Nick to floss. Just a quick scrub would suffice, she'd say. She was a busy woman and didn't care for materialistic things, like floss. Ronan said it was completely disgusting to live like that, especially in adulthood, and still I'm not sure if he was being serious – it's hard to know sometimes with all his Irish charm – but the outcome is that I now spend an extra five minutes doing it every night. He never mentioned it again.

He hasn't brushed his teeth tonight, let alone flossed.

My mother loves Ronan.

I miss Nick.

Male nudes.

I don't have any of those. Not one.

According to Buzzfeed, I don't actually *need* pictures to proceed with creating an account. I could use a blank profile, but having one means very few people will interact with me because a faceless/bodyless profile picture means I could be a *total nutjob* – and I need people to interact with me or it would defeat the whole point of this venture. I want to give myself the opportunity to talk candidly and openly – to learn – and I don't want to play games. *Straight to the point* is what people on this app appreciate, apparently.

I suppose I could google pictures of a male porn star and borrow them – the actor doesn't even need to be gay, just nude (maybe with a cute bookish quality so he's still got me in his essence?) – but it might take me a while to find shots that look reasonably down-to-earth and not taken in some obvious and tacky studio (I don't mean tacky in a derogatory way – I'm very sex positive of course – I just can't find another word for it). And I wouldn't want to get done for copyright infringement. I'm sure there'll be something about using fabricated pictures in the Grindr small print, and anyway, authenticity is the whole point here. I want to appear as real as possible.

Ronan snorts. I look at him.

Ronan.

Ronan is real.

That's interesting.

He turns again, this time flat onto his back, so everything splays out.

I glug the rest of my wine and, a little clumsily, open my phone and get up the camera app. I pause for a moment, looking through the screen, wondering if this is some kind of abuse. It's not abuse. He's my husband.

Meek Mal.

I begin to take a few (maybe twenty) photographs of him. Ronan loves to be photographed. And he looks good – really good. The lighting is perfect (thanks, Pooky!). And anyway we have in the past (maybe ten years ago) sent nudes to each other, so what really is the difference?

It's funny actually.

The male body.

It looks funny.

Meek Mal does have fun too!

This is bravery.

Unhinged (drunk) bravery.

I open up my photo gallery and half squint at the grid of beige and pink: Ronan's most strikingly made of Tailor Tack and Camomile, but also the other Farrow & Ball shades of flesh that are Setting Plaster, Nancy's Blushes, Shallot… even some accents of purple and red to really set them off! I try not to look directly at them, but it's all there.

Forgive me, gay gods.

I quickly crop a few of them, cutting off his head and penis, then upload them onto my Grindr profile. I pick one of his torso for my Main Picture, making sure his chest is very much visible. He has a great chest. In the photograph, I see it. Chiselled pectorals from his early mornings at the gym. I did buy him some weights once, with my counselling money, as a gift (he once told me his love language was receiving them). But he said mine weren't the right type so they've just sat in the cellar ever since, gathering dust.

He's hard to buy for.

I feel a twinge of guilt as I crop out the background of one of the shots, a picture of us on his nightstand.

Ronan also once told me he would do anything to help me find my feet again, so I shouldn't feel guilt, not really. And this is the kind of thing he would find funny, if it was someone else.

But it's not. This is him.

He can't know.

No one is going to know.

This research project will end tonight. It is a brief fanning of the flames of my creative instinct.

Yes. That's what this is.

The app tells me I have to choose a name while I wait until my pictures have been approved.

I attempt one, then look at it objectively, like I might be an interested customer.

New, 36

No. That might put people off. The age. The naivety.

Intrigued…

No, sounds too cerebral, and let's face it, the ellipsis is a tad lechy.

Want the dirt ;)

No. Sounds like a builder. Which I'm sure is a thing – a vibe

– but I'm not sure I want it to be my vibe. Speaking of, what *do* I want as my vibe? I feel a little flurry of excitement. *I can be anyone.* This is… new. Different.

Am I having fun?

I settle for:

Chat?;)

Nice and simple, subtle, though I wouldn't go so far as to say *classy*. But definitely restrained. And discreet.

I navigate to the Profile Grid tab on the app, and I'm met with an abundance of squares. My hands begin to shake again as drunken adrenaline takes hold of me, infecting my bloodstream. I scan through each one. There's a variety of pictures: some faces, smiling, gentle and happy; moustaches, earrings, beards, crotch shots in boxers, nipples, sunsets, fists, leather. It is so *interesting*, a patchwork of the beauty and complexity of the human experience, where people can truly be themselves. Each profile name gives a brief glimpse of the person behind the square: 24 shy, DNA Injector, £££, Chillin, Timmy, Mr Fugly Slut, Fat4Fem, Masc ONLY, RiceDaddy, Whites 2 the Front, Broke but Cute, Tina, Tina, Tina.

There are a lot of men on here called Tina. There are measurements too. Not just size, but geographical distances. I look at the top row of profiles, the ones nearest to my current location.

My adrenaline peaks.

They are so *close*.

Top4Btm
129 metres away

Perhaps I know Top4Btm. I can't tell since his picture is of an armpit. But 129 metres means he is most likely on this street, or one adjacent.

I don't know all the gay men round here, and have remained in the house a lot over the past seven years, but the idea that this sort of underground *network* allows people to meet, and talk, *honestly*, makes my skin prickle. What a joyful thing. A place where people are free to explore and discuss their desires outside the gaze of heteronormative ideals and societal norms. Without *shame*. Incredible.

Virginia Woolf would have loved Grindr.

Come to think of it, the whole Bloomsbury set would have. Duncan Grant, Maynard Keynes, the lot of them would have had the time of their lives. Liberation and self-actualisation in its highest form.

SxyRodent
348 metres away

SxyRodent is a little further away. His picture is of an actual face. However, sadly, it's one I don't recognise. At least I don't think I do. He has a sort of youthful glow about him – and slight danger in his eyes. He is a little ratty actually, so his name makes sense. Come to think of it, he actually looks about seventeen. I wonder what the terms and conditions say about age. Surely you can just lie about it – that must be a design fault? I wonder if his mother knows he's on here. I could go on Mumsnet and see if there are concerned parents out there, if they are aware. Concerned Parents of Grindr Users.

No.

I cannot control other people's choices. This is the truth I am seeing.

The truth!

CashPig
412 metres away

CashPig looks a little older and is wearing some kind of mask with ears – he actually looks quite cute and playful. I don't want to stereotype, but he is what I imagined I'd find on here. Behind the mask his eyes look a little sad, a wealth of pain perhaps lurking under the pig face. *Make people cry*. I click on his profile to see a list of letters, *tags*, that make no sense to me.

NPNC. RN. UC. WS. NSA.
Discreet.

I spend a few minutes eyeing up some potential conversationalists, seeing if their tags make any sense.

Discreet. Discreet.

So many discreet.
This is *perfect*.
The app suddenly chirps loudly, my phone vibrates and I flinch.

Your picture has been approved!

I look up at the bed, at Ronan still splayed out on it – having completely forgotten he was here. I bat away thoughts of him calling the police and having me arrested for some revenge porn-related activity. (I think it's illegal now. But I should probably check – though his face isn't in the shots, so I should be fine.) I flick the side switch so the phone turns to silent.
It vibrates again, and a name pops up.
Prince Hairy.
Another face.
He looks nice, a little older. Perhaps he is some kind of stalwart, an elder of Grindr, like Elrond, the king of the Elves in *The Lord of the Rings*. He does seem to have a kind of wisdom to his features. A beard and kind blue eyes. I could ask him for some guidance. I construct my opener, remembering all I know about the queer community from my years of being an ally.

Hey Kween! Slay!

I send.
I stare at the screen, wondering if I should have gone a bit further. *Loving the realness, honey! Slay the house down!* I think

they say that. They do – the drag queens – on Instagram. I don't understand it, but it's fun to—
Message read.
Oh, he's seen it!
Immediately.
Now? What time is it? Late.
11:36.
I suppose gays like to party.
No response.
No response.
OK.
I'm panicking.
And drunk.
This was a mistake.
Delete?
Yes.
Delete it.
Delete it.
Oh God...
It's so derogative!
Pretend it never happened. That I was hacked.
Oh, he's typing.
Oh no.
What have I done?
I hate myself—

                                                             Ummm k?
                                                                 slay

Yas!
See.
I excitedly type –

Slay Kween yas gawd!

Pause.
Then delete. Overkill. Over-slay.

Keep it *chill*.
Instead I write –

I love your pictures
Eating it up! No crumbs left

I press send.
A red exclamation mark appears next to my message.
Strange.
I try again.

You have been blocked.

Huh?

For rules around hate speech, please see the terms and conditions.

Hate speech, Prince Hairy?
I *knew* there would be terms and conditions.
My phone vibrates again.

1 NEW MESSAGE

Someone has initiated talking to me.
To me!
I feel immediately and oddly flattered – a rush of serotonin entering my brain, the excitement making me nearly drop my phone.
I click the profile.

Daddy

Daddy's photo is of a face – which again is immediately comforting. He looks mid-thirties, perhaps a little older than me. Kind and well kept. Responsible. In a shirt, moustached, a little mop of hair pushed back. Quite professional, really.

                                            Hey. Into?

Into? Straight to the point.

                                            You here for fun?

Fun.
Yes. This does feel like that.
I see flashing images of me and Daddy becoming best friends, going for coffee and hikes, discussing the nuances of emotional pain. I haven't had time to think about the voice of Chat?;) yet. Who should I be? The slay Kween approach obviously didn't work as I thought it might. Perhaps I'll keep it closer to home, for now. Come to think of it, someone once said I'm practically a gay man in a woman's body. I can't remember if I've made that up, but I'm sure it was at some point during the attic conversion, because of my keen eye for interior design. I think it was one of the cool gays from the Maynard Arms.
Or it was Joanie. Again.
I settle for –

Most definitely

                                            All right Shakespeare

Shakespeare?
Wow.
Woolf, eat your heart out.

                                            You some kind of professor?

Potentially

                                            Hot
                                            You like to be called Professor?

I mean...

Yes

                                             Hoootttt
                                  You a daddy too?

I think perhaps staying with the more mature type is good. Aligning with them. It feels more comfortable. Safer.

I am

                                                Cute
                                  You're a top then?

Despite hearing it a lot, I'm still not *entirely* sure what that means but I'll just say yes for now.

Yes

                                           Perfect
                                What kind of fun you into?

I'm going to stick with the honest approach.

I'm looking to see and understand the real gay experience

OK, that sounded weird.
Maybe weird is good. Maybe it's a thing?
Oh, God—

                                                    Lol
                             I think I can help you with that
                                           Ur hot

I'm hot.
He sends three aubergine emojis.
I can't seem to help myself but reply, with four.
For research.

What have you got in mind?

> T-party

T-party.

As in, an actual tea party?

> lol. Yeah. It's chill, fun. Nice and safe
> Just a gathering of cool people
> They'd like you!
> Nothing to worry about
> Come!

Nice and safe.

Is it only for Dads?

> No, everyone welcome who wants to meet new ppl
> Have a little chill

Oh, that's nice. A way to grow a circle of friends.

When is it?

> now

Oh, wow – *interesting*. A late-night tea party.
Despite the expanding thrill in the pit of my stomach, I cannot accept the invite.

Sadly it's a bit late. I'm up early

> Don't worry it's all good
> Spk soon x

Damn it. I have a sudden sadness that I might never get to talk to Daddy ever again. I feel like a character myself. My own creation. It's almost like when I started *Shallow Embers*, losing myself in other people. *I can be anyone I want to be. The possibilities are endless.*

I realise something.

I feel alive. A yearning pulls, a draw to what is intrinsically me. Creating. Truth seeking.

Telling the truth.

Could we maybe just chat instead?

I stare at the screen, waiting for his reply.

But he doesn't.

When I look up, the coldness of the off-white wall slaps me awake.

What the hell am I doing?

I stand, pacing for a moment, avoiding my panic. I tiptoe around the bed, to Ronan's side, and stand over his nightstand where I see a stack of cards. CONGRATULATIONS! YOU THE MAN! I AM SO IMMENSELY PROUD OF YOU – LOOK AT YOU GO!

My card is there too.

I hesitate, then take it from the stack and open it.

My darling, I am so proud of you.
Thank you for being the rock of this family.
I owe you so much.
Your Mallory.

My stomach twists into an uncomfortable knot. I turn and study him for a moment, snoring gently. After I wrote *Shallow Embers*, he was working at the BBC, with a mountain of debt. We used my advance to pay that off, and then he was headhunted to Netflix. So much has changed.

He looks so gentle in this light. So harmless.

White Lies.

Something flashes on the nightstand, making me jump.

His phone.
I look down to see it is a message from Joanie.

Loved seeing you tonight, babe. Ur smashing it. We are all in awe. Hope Meek Mal gave u some fun in the end ;)

A sudden surge of heat radiates throughout my body. *Meek Mal*. I'd thought it was Ronan's little joke, his charm, saved just for me. He always smiled after he'd said it, in that way that felt like he was being kind, like he really meant the opposite.

It's so warm in here. Rain starts to drum against the window in the roof, and there is static in the air – a pressure that makes me feel sick – until I hear the distant sound of thunder.

It breaks the pressure.

When I was on the psych ward, leaving wasn't an option. I wasn't allowed to talk about it after I was discharged, either. It was good to stay quiet, I was told.

No one really knew what had happened.

But I know.

I know what happened.

I leave his phone on his nightstand, and take out mine. I open up Grindr and find Daddy.

Hi, what's the address?

Yas!

Yasssssssss

53 Priory Rd, Kween

Priory Road. That's literally five minutes' walk away. It's right near our friends Caro and Benji. They work in tech, and are loaded. It's a lovely street.

Nice and safe.

But I can't leave.

Can I?

Do I need to bring anything?

>Just urself

Are people hungry?

>Starving bb
>We're all starving

7

Leo

> *Heaven.*
> *I have gone to heaven in its arms.*
> *Up. Up.*
> *Hugged the whole way,*
> *Now dancing with it in the clouds.*
> *Its lights are so kind.*
> *Its warmth so endless.*
> *The pain is gone.*
> *But then I turn,*
> *and I realise*
> *This heaven is a dirty floor*
> *That I have been lying on*
> *In a heap*
> *With a packet of crisps*
> *Stuck to the side of my face.*
>
> *@Alias22*

It's been ages, I think. Time becomes irrelevant.

Brick must be long gone, being stupid somewhere else. I could stay here forever. I've always felt at one with nature.

My phone is making a noise. I peel my eyes from the sky, feeling the rain dribble down my forehead.

It's Sam. Dunno why he's still intent on calling himself Daddy, the nutter. There's nothing paternal about him. I hate this app. Hate that it's necessary. That so much of my life is on it.

>   You got the T?

Yeah

>   Any left? Lol

Thinks he's funny, Sam.
But I have to be careful.

Yeah course

>   Better all be there

It is

He won't notice. They're all on it already.
I hope.

>   Know where you're going?

53 Priory Road

>   Lots of people coming
>   Stay discreet

Yeah sound

If he knows I've had some of it, he'll freak, so I've got to act sober. But I can do that. That's one thing I've learnt to nail along the way. Eyes straight. Reply quick – short, to the point, no rambling. The red eyes are because of hay fever, or cos I've been crying at my shitty life, etc.

Be there in 20

I close the app and stand. The park sways. The street lamps and car headlights and traffic lights on the road surrounding the park streak into my eyes in all different colours. Like some kind of shitty, trippy piece of art.

I don't wanna go.

But I have to.

I owe him.

And now I owe Brick.

I owe a lot of people a lot of things.

I open a can of Stella and chug it down. I love it.

I'll get Sam some flowers to keep him sweet. There's a graveyard on the way, so that'll be nice and easy.

8

Mallory

Unhinged Bravery.

I'll only be gone for half an hour.

I take a Tupperware container from the cupboard, wrap some leftover vol-au-vents in tin foil and put them inside it. I see an unopened bottle of elderflower cordial amongst the empty cans and half-full bottles of wine that line the kitchen counter. I choose the only sealed bottle of wine remaining.

By the way, I know I don't look like Ronan. I am aware that's not who they will meet when I show up. But I'm hoping they will find it funny, let me in for a quick chat, that they will potentially see me as some kind of Mother figure, iconic for bringing the vol-au-vents to the party. A real-life ally, turning up in the dead of night to feed them. *Mother has arrived!*

I can hear them now.

Give us what we want, mama! Feed the gays!

(And I'll be taking my pepper spray. I have it in case of a home invasion.)

I get my keys from the fruit bowl and tiptoe towards the front door.

Where will Maddox take us next? I for one can't wait to find out.

The lengths we go to as creatives.

I'm going to take the car. The house is only a ten-minute walk away, but down back streets, so I think it'll be safer. Yes, I am admittedly still a bit tipsy (but the adrenaline is making me pretty sharp now), and I've decided the safety it will afford me outweighs the risks. If anything goes amiss, I can lock myself in. Also, maybe I can just watch from the window for a little bit, scout it out. You know, be sensible about this.

Thankfully, once outside, the rain masks my footsteps. I look up to the house, to the dormer window where Ronan is passed out. I could go back in.

I could.

I peer down the street at the houses, every single one with the same checkered tiles leading up to either a baby-blue or bottle-green door, the local aesthetics competition in full view.

I open the car and close it only when I hear a clap of thunder. It is less frequent now. I can sense a calm settling in the air. The release, after the storm. The freedom. My skin prickles awake. I turn the ignition, punch the address into the satnav and begin driving slowly towards Priory Road, wondering if the picnic hamper was too much. Then thinking, no, they'll love a little flare.

9

Leo

The house is full – I can tell from the doorstep.

It's right posh, Sam's house. He's one of those rich people who's hooked. Hooked on the gak, the party, the people. He'll stay awake all weekend like the rest of us, then put on his shirt and tie and go into work, and no one will know. He won't tell us what he does, but we know he's minted. I'm only allowed in cos I get the stuff, see. He doesn't let any old fucker inside his gaff.

Only some of us. The ones he cares about, he says.

Daddy: The Father Figure.

He lets us come and use his couch, his bed, the water dispenser in his massive fridge, his wealthy mates, his lube, and then we leave, having spent no money, sometimes having made it.

As I look at the door, about to knock, the colours in the window pane start to blend together and dance. I feel good. It's kicking in. I realise, as I stare at it, that I have a weird relationship with this door. When I enter it, I feel fucking amazing. But when I feel it close behind me, days later, I want to die. Every time.

But that's not for now.

That can wait.

I knock three times. No one comes. I look behind me, back down the street. Smells good, the rain. That petrichor. It's dead silent, too. If Brick was following, he'd be here by now.

I'm grand.

The door creaks open, and a head appears in the gap. It's not Sam. Someone I haven't met before. Young. Probably younger than he should be, but hey, I'm no Mother Theresa of this stuff.

He's only wearing his kecks, and the skin on his tummy is pale, almost see-through, like uncooked chicken. I can hear the low thrum of music coming from the living room behind him, or the kitchen – sometimes they do it in there, too – and voices. I hate it when it's busy.

'Hey,' I say. 'Leo. Not seen you before.'

'Where have you been?' he asks. Confident, for a new one.

'Sorry, got lost.'

'Lost?'

'Yeah.'

'Looks like you got lost in a bin.'

He looks at my hands. The dirty nails. I look a mess – Sam doesn't like that. He points. 'Why have you got flowers?'

'For Sam. Where is he?'

'You bought flowers for Sam?'

'Yeah. Why?'

He smirks. 'That's sweet. He's inside, but he's busy.' Course he is. This lad thinks I'm jealous, which is funny. He really is green. He's staring at my face now. 'You've had some of the T, haven't you?'

Shit. 'Who are you?'

'Your eyes are gone.'

'Nah, mate. Haven't. Hay fever.' I realise I'm not stringing full sentences together. It's really hitting me hard right here on this doorstep, which is unfortunate, and the lad is frowning at me like I'm chatting utter bollocks. 'Am I coming in then, or what? It's fucking mingin' out here.'

'Where's your coat?'

Who the fuck is this guy? My mother?

'All right, I didn't realise there would be a seven-year-old bouncer on the door tonight.' He looks pissed off at this. I should have just thought it. I hold up the Poundland bag. 'Listen, mate, it's all in here, just let me in.' And give me the G. I'm scratchy as fuck for it, and I'm spinning out now. Will calm me down. Slow me down.

'Is it real?'

'Course it's fucking real.'

'Last time it was rock salt.' How does he know that? 'So Sam sent me to make sure. Can I see it?'

'Not out here, are you fucking joking?'

But he's not listening. The lad's eyes have moved to a noise directly behind us. I turn to see a car pull up on the opposite side of the road. I can't see the driver but it's not Brick. Car's too nice. Volvo XC40, licence plate this year.

Rich.

The car stops, but no one gets out.

Weird.

'Wait here,' the lad says, putting his hand on my shoulder. I flinch when it makes contact with my wet T-shirt, but he doesn't notice. 'I'll get Sam. He can check.'

Fucking check.

I don't need to be checked.

This could go wrong. Sam is good with seeing if things are missing. And I'm not sure I have time to get rid of the tin foil and pen in the bag. Not a good look, that. Bit of a giveaway.

But I shrug and nod – nothing to hide.

He smiles, then slams the door, disappearing inside the house. I look at the flowers from the graveyard and see there's a half-disintegrated card tucked into the plastic wrapping with a message inside.

Daddy we will always love you xxxxxx

Suppose that still works.

10

Mallory

I turn the engine off and peer out of the passenger seat window.

53 Priory Road. Like any other house on the street. I squint through the dark, a rush of excitement entering my system. The rain is stopping now, and I can see the rose bush out front is beautiful, in full bloom. Are those *orange* roses? Very classy. Checkered tiles, dark-blue door and the typical Crouch End orange brickwork. It really is quite swanky.

Before I take the hamper in my hands, something moves behind the rose bush, up on the porch.

There is someone stood at the door.

A man – I think – holding a plastic Poundland bag. Yes, it is a man, but it's not Daddy – or is it? I can't be entirely sure – it's too dark, damn it – but I swear this person is too young to be him. And no moustache or floppy hair. He looks about twenty, maybe even younger: very boyish, with a black Adidas cap, tracksuit trousers, his T-shirt soaked through by the rain, and he's skinny.

He bangs on the door three times.

Where's the boy's coat?

There's something in his other hand.

Flowers.

Oh, how sweet. A quote comes to mind. *Mrs Dalloway said she would buy the flowers herself.* Albeit *his* flowers look a little half-dead, but still, how thoughtful of him. It's late, so he probably went out of his way to get them from the petrol station.

The pepper spray in my pocket suddenly feels like a weight, a heavy reminder of my own ignorance and prejudice that I have carried around with me for so long. This evening will really be a learning curve, as I step into the realities of another demographic. *Why would I have been scared? How is that fair?* Who was it that said a writer's job is to 'step into the shoes of other people'? Did someone say that?

The man bangs his fist on the door again, louder. I watch him muttering to himself, now holding the flowers over his head as a makeshift umbrella. He hisses something into the closed door that I can't quite make out. I wind down the window an inch, in an attempt to hear him. I don't want to assume his mental state, but he does seem a little rattled, agitated, and actually somewhat wobbly on his feet – bless him. He looks a little… dare I say, dirty? It is very wet, the rain—

'Oi! Knobhead!'

OK, that was loud.

My body tenses.

He steps back from the door, then begins to move into the flower bed right in front of the downstairs window, peering through what looks like a lovely set of white wooden shutters. (We have similar – Ronan wants to change them because *everyone* has them now.) He starts screaming at the glass.

'Oi, you pricks! Let me in!'

OK, interesting way to enter a property, but let's face it, I'd be pissed off too if I was standing in the rain for this long. Especially carrying flowers I'd bought for the host. A little rude to keep him waiting.

The shutter blinds lift up momentarily, and a face peers through the slats. I have to lean forward over the passenger seat – straining my eyes – but I can just make out a moustache, floppy hair, a distinguished look. It's him! Daddy! Yes, that's definitely him. He puts his fingers to his lips, silencing the man with the flowers, then gestures for him to go back to the front door.

The shutters snap closed.

I wait, stock still, as the boy does exactly as he was told.

When the door opens, two heads appear. One belongs to Daddy and the other, a blonde chap. Youngish.

But under the porch light I notice Daddy looks a little different. Not that it really matters, but he looks a little older. Come to think of it, he also looks a little angrier than his pictures suggested. His eyes are dark – black almost – but alert, and I watch them begin to dart across the houses, checking the front windows, then over the cars lined up on either side of the road. They land right where I am currently sat. I am about to wave, *Hi! It's me!* when I remember I'm not Ronan and look nothing like him, so shuffle down further into my seat and wait for them to scan right over me. Once he seems content that he isn't being watched, he opens the door wider.

Oh.

What is strange is that neither of them are wearing any clothes. At least, Daddy isn't. The other one is just in a pair of tiny white boxer shorts.

Daddy starts gesturing to the boy with the flowers, pointing at the Poundland bag. *Show me, show me now.* I suddenly bristle, wondering what the man with the flowers *will* show these two men on this porch in Crouch End just before midnight.

I watch, transfixed, as the man with the cap and flowers checks behind him, left then right, before reaching his hand into his Poundland bag. When he lifts it out, he holds it out to Daddy, passing him something. *What is it?* They are trying to be discreet – which is a little ironic – huddling close together and probably blocking out the light, so the item inevitably drops to the floor. They are all bending over, a blur of limbs and other bits frantically flailing as they scramble for it. Three men on their knees in tiny white pants, an Adidas cap and not much else. *What am I witnessing?* I momentarily feel like I am potentially not real.

Daddy suddenly stands up straight. The others follow. When he lifts his hand to the light, I glimpse something held between his fingers. A tiny see-through plastic bag, no bigger than a matchbox. Something is inside it.

Oh, God.

Oh no.

I suppose it could be salt? Or sugar?

Sugar for all the tea?

I immediately look down at the passenger seat where my picnic hamper sits, and sobriety slaps me like an aubergine to the face.

Shit.

I have made a huge mistake.

Daddy and the blonde boy take the tiny bag back inside the hallway and push the door to, so the flower boy is left on the step again, alone. I watch him waiting, scratching the side of his head anxiously, then quickly slip my phone out of the cup holder, turn down the brightness so as not to draw attention to myself through the glass and pull up Google. My legs cramp as I slide further down into my chair.

I quickly type *what is T-Party – gay?*

OK.

OK…

Reddit, where are you? The truth lies in Reddit. *I've always said—*

There. A subreddit entitled:

/r/*gay:* WTF is a T-Party?

I scan to the top answer, liked 421 times.

T is slang for crystal meth.

Oh, shit.

STAY AWAY *from chemsex parties.*
People die at those things.
Do not go to one, you'll need more than Jesus to help you
 get out.

Chemsex?

Jesus?

People *die*?

My brain begins to unravel, a spool of cotton wool, stalling as it catches on knots of panic and clumps of dread and *oh fuck oh fuck oh holy fuck—*

Wait. *Calm down.* Maybe it's wrong. Reddit can be really wrong: hyperbolic and overly dramatic. It's really just people's opinions, isn't it? And those can't be trusted. *Wikipedia.* Try Wikipedia. Wikipedia is far more reliable.

I type in the word *chemsex* (sp.?), trying to stop myself from dropping the phone into the footwell, to see a page actually exists.

Party and play (PnP), also known as **chemsex** or **wired play**, refers to the practice of consuming drugs to enhance sexual activity. This sexual subculture involves recreational drug users engaging in high-risk sexual behaviours under the influence of drugs, often within specific sub-groups. Activities may include unprotected sex with multiple partners during sessions over extended periods, sometimes lasting days. The drug of choice is typically methamphetamine, commonly referred to as crystal meth, tina or T.

> My phone falls from my hands.
> Panic infuses me.
> Existential panic.

Not least because I just turned up to a drug-fuelled orgy with picnic food. And I expected to meet multiple men here called Tina. But also because I have an immediate and disturbingly intense understanding that I don't recognise myself at all. I feel completely and utterly unknowable. It is as if I have floated out of my body, and I'm looking down from above at a woman sitting in a car, waiting to join a homosexual subculture in her Lululemon anorak.

Days?!

How did I get here? I am aware I have a tendency to romanticise and/or fantasise, but usually it just stays in my head. Not this. Not actually acting on the idea of entering a complete stranger's house as a different person from the person I said I was, give the inhabitants buffet food and expect them to love me for it.

How much Jäger did I consume? Who the hell do I think I am? Certainly not the person the *New York Times* reviewer said

I was. *Unhinged bravery* is very wrong. Just *unhinged* would be more accurate.

Someone shouts, loudly. I jump, stifling a scream, hand over my mouth, and turn back to the door. Daddy is there again, but now he is talking agitatedly, trying to keep his voice low as he speaks to the boy with the flowers, trying to pull the Poundland bag out of his hand. But the boy is not letting go. I can just make out Daddy saying something that sounds like *You've fucking had some, haven't you? Give it to me now!* while the blonde one in his underwear folds his arms across his chest, like some ill-equipped security guard. He looks so young. Does his mother know he's here? Where's his mother?

What the hell am I doing?

I am about to turn my keys in the ignition, to leave, when I realise I will draw attention to myself, which I categorically do not want. I'll wait for the porch to clear, then go home. To my husband.

Shit. *My husband.*

No wonder they locked me up.

Ronan cannot know.

He can't...

Oh, God, I feel sick. *Unwell.* My head becomes immediately very light, like there is nothing inside my skull – which perhaps would make sense of how I ended up—

A thud.

I turn my head back to the porch to see Daddy slam a hand into the flower boy's chest so that he stumbles backwards, releasing his grip on the Poundland bag, falling flat on his back on the checkered tiles. A loud crack snaps through the air as his body makes contact.

Was that his *head*?

I'm not supposed to be here. I'm really not. I need to leave.

Will they see me leave?

Daddy begins to hurriedly root inside the bag, pulling out a roll of tin foil, shaking his head angrily (oh God – why does he hate tin foil?), and what appears to be a broken pen. This revelation makes him shout at the boy on the floor, something about him stealing, being a thief and getting the hell off the porch before he has his head knocked clean off. It's becoming loud (why are they so OK with being so loud and so naked?) but Daddy seems not to care at all.

I instinctively pull my hood over my head in an attempt to disappear into my seat entirely – or at the very least camouflage myself, though I quickly realise my coat is the colour of an actual lemon. The blonde half-child half-security guard starts to laugh, then spits directly onto the boy with the flowers – who is still on his back – then calls him words that I am able to lipread without difficulty. *Letch, whore, pussy slut.*

The door slams shut, and the two mostly naked men disappear.

I turn my head – trying not to make too much movement or become some kind of blinking Lululemon beacon – glancing at the other houses to see if anyone else has come out, if any lights have flickered on behind the windows. Nothing. I turn back to the boy. Not moving. Holding the flowers, face up to the sky, rain pelting in his face. *Why isn't he moving?*

Please, just – get up. And leave. *So I can leave.*

He slowly begins to stand. Good. *That's good.* A fleeting relief envelops me with the understanding that I have not just watched a murder happen. I don't really think going into witness protection tonight would be great news (although at least things would be different, and come to think of it, some good material could come from it) but he looks OK, I don't see any blood. After he's managed to make his way onto the pavement – flowers still in his hand – I watch him begin to hobble away, down the street.

Time to leave.

I put my fingers around my keys, about to turn them again, when he suddenly becomes illuminated in a brilliant, white light. It startles me. I half anticipate him to be transported up into the sky by an unknown entity when I realise they are headlights. A car screeches to a halt and stops dead in the middle of the road right next to me. A white BMW with its bumper missing. A door opens, and a man steps out. The first thing I notice is that he uncannily resembles a lump of concrete. Stocky, bald head, set like a brick. Then I see that he is actually holding one.

I try and dodge the thought that *I* perhaps unknowingly took meth at some point this evening. My body is now nearly entirely in the footwell. I can practically hear him breathing on the road right next to my car. There is something deeply unsettling and sinister about him, his voice hoarse, face bunched like a hardened potato, little scars littering the top of his shiny head. Another potential guest to this fucked up chem-picnic?

'Leo,' he says. The boy in the tracksuit hears him, and stops. I watch him from under my hood as he turns and sees the bald man. When his eyes catch the glare of the headlights, they don't appear alive. He squints. A moment of recognition enters them. His face drops and a look of utter terror is injected into his features. His body turns, and he starts to run, limping away in the glare of the beams.

But the man with the scars moves his arm, throwing the brick.

It lands squarely in the flower boy's back.

The thud reverberates through the rain, through the windscreen, right into the air around me, snapping my brain awake. I watch the force of it send the boy flying forward, down onto the tarmac in the middle of the road. I bite down on my finger so hard that I taste blood. The bald man stands stock-still no more than three metres to the left of my car, staring at the boy. I can see the stripes on his jacket, a cigarette burn in his sleeve.

I should scream. Scream for help. Call the police. But when I open my mouth, nothing comes out. My arms won't move. I am paralysed. Paralysed by the doubt, by the thought of being caught here, with them, somehow complicit...

He moves. Begins to step towards him.

Get out and help the boy.

Call the poli—

'Oi. Look at me,' the man says, now stood over the boy's writhing body. 'No one runs from Brick.' Wait, is he actually called Brick? *What is happening?* 'You've fucking had it, mate. That's your last chance. Gone. You're not using me for your gear anymore, do you get me? Now give it. All of it.'

'He took the stuff...' the boy stammers, trying to push himself up. 'He took it into the house. I'll get it back for you, I swear...' He puts his hand up in front of his face, in an attempt to shield himself, but it's no use. The man's foot lands squarely into it, twisting the boy's head so sharply that his whole body contorts across the wet concrete.

I can't stifle my gasp. I audibly scream.

Oh, God – no!

But the bald man doesn't hear, because the bald man doesn't stop. He kicks, again and again, right into the boy's chest, his face, his head, as my own empties, the only thought remaining: he's going to die. *The boy is going to die.* In an instant, my hand has reached and opened the door handle, and I am standing next to my car in the pelting rain. I can see the boy trying to clamber to his feet, to get away, but he can't – every time the man's foot lands into him, he crumples.

'He-hey…!' I stammer, but I can't – I can't seem to… 'Stop that!'

The bald man is now pulling the boy up by his T-shirt, standing him up straight and throwing his forehead straight into the boy's face – again and again.

'*Stop!*' My voice cuts through the rain.

The bald man momentarily pauses, turns… and sees me. My feet move, and not in the direction I anticipate. They progress forward – *towards him* – and I feel the bottle of pepper spray in my hand, extending it out in front of me, pointing it right at his face.

I press the nozzle.

But it doesn't work.

It *works*, but not as I expected, because he has pulled the boy directly between us, shielding himself. A piercing scream as the pepper spray enters the boy's eyes. The man drops him, so he lands in a heap at our feet.

The bald man's eyes scan me. '*Shit, shit, shit,*' I hear myself saying. He turns back towards the white BMW, its engine still running. I drop to my knees, next to the boy on the floor now clawing at his face, two ripe plums for eyes.

Oh, God. Oh holy *God*! I fumble for my phone – *shit* – I left it in the footwell. 'I'll call for hel—'

'No! *No—!*' His voice is muffled, his mouth swollen so much that I can hardly hear him under the noise of the BMW reversing away from us, back up the road, the headlights swinging over us as he turns. I try to catch a glimpse of the licence plate – *remember it* – but as soon as the car disappears, so do the digits.

'Is someone there?' the boy mumbles. He can't see.

'Yes. Yes, someone's here.' He flinches. 'I'll call for help—' I say, turning to the houses. *Where the fuck is everyone?* But, I stop. I can't be seen here. I can't.

'No!' the boy gurgles. 'Please just fucking – leave me… I'll be fine. Fuck! *My eyes…*'

'I'll call the poli—'

'*No!*' he screams, his fingers rubbing into the mangled mess that was once his face.

I can't leave him here. I can't. He can't *see*. His face is pulp.

My brain has completely whited out, like someone has turned a floodlight on inside my head. I can't think. 'I'll take you to the hospital.'

'No! No way. Just fuck off. Please just *fuck off*.'

Lights are turning on in the windows of the houses now. Concerned residents peering through curtains. 'People are coming,' I say.

That's not good. Not good at all. People will ask why. Why there are vol-au-vents in my car. Why I was sat in it for so long, watching.

I can't be found like this. Ronan.

The boy's bloody hand suddenly grips my arm. 'Help me,' he mutters. 'Please… get me out of here.' His voice is so urgent, so intent, that I feel briefly compelled to take him in my arms and hold him.

Sirens.

I hear the distant whine of sirens.

We speak at the same time. 'Shit.'

I take his hand in mine and pull him up, one arm under his, one around his back, and lead him towards the car, helping him quickly navigate his steps. I open the passenger door, grab the picnic hamper, throw it into the back and guide him into the now empty seat. I slam the door shut, and in the moment of utter quiet outside, I look back at Daddy's house. The wooden blinds are still firmly shut. Like any other house on the street.

Lights begin to flicker on in the porches, people stood peering out of doors in their dressing gowns. I pull my hood up and step into the car.

'I'll take you to the hospital,' I repeat, because there is logically no other option, however thin logic feels right now.

'No.' His head is between his knees. 'Just take me home.'

'Can you see yet?'

'No.'

'Where do you live?'

'Turnpike Lane.' The sirens are growing closer. 'Please drive.'

I turn the keys and leave Priory Road, with the boy in the passenger seat.

11

Leo

It burns like how I imagine hell will, when I get there.
    But I can feel all my limbs, so it can't be that bad.
    'Are you OK?'
    Who is this woman?
    Her car smells fresh. Vanilla. New leather. New money.
    'What's the postcode?' she says. She keeps talking. Can hardly hear her for the ringing in my head, but I know she's terrified. Brick was pretty keen. Pretty sure he wanted me dead. Pretty sure he's wanted to do that for a while.
    'Just drop me on the street.' My lips are numb. Feels like I've got tomatoes that won't burst stuck in my mouth. At least people won't recognise me for a while.
    'No – I want to make sure you get home.'
    Fine.
    I'll take what I can get.
    She keeps asking questions, but I don't answer. She doesn't need to know why I can't go to the hospital, why I don't wanna speak to the police, if my back hurts or not. Course it fucking hurts – Brick threw a fucking brick at it. She can take me home, make herself feel better, then be gone. Never see me again. She'll think she's done her good deed, probably tell her posh mates about how brave she was, then get back to her lovely little life. She keeps saying my name.
    The car stops. 'This is it, Leo,' she says. 'I'll take you in.' Her voice sounds like she's stood on the side of a pool and I'm under the water. I'll be sleeping in the bush tonight, behind the bins. I'm not gonna tell her though.

'I'm good. I can see now,' I lie.

I find the door handle and step out of the car onto the pavement.

I wave into the black until I hear her car pull away.

Just wanted my G.

G and T and a weekend of numb.

Instead my eyes are on fire and my lungs feel like they might explode and I'm pretty sure I've broken a bone somewhere, and now I have to wake up.

12

Mallory

I place my keys back in the fruit bowl.

Every noise, every movement is amplified by the adrenaline coursing through my blood as I stand in the kitchen, amongst the unchanged debris of the party, waiting for the dust of my thoughts to settle into something I can make sense of.

It amounts to: *holy shit.*

I hold my breath, listening for Ronan. He's still asleep. He has to be. Nothing has changed. *Nothing here has changed.*

I'm safe.

My phone vibrates, making me jump.

It's Daddy.

You coming or what, sexy?

I am about to delete the app, but stop myself, sliding my phone into my pocket.

I open the cupboard under the sink and quickly pull on my Marigold kitchen gloves. With a bowl of cold water, fairy liquid and salt, I wipe the blood from my coat, using the stain remover where I have to. When it is done, I hang it gently back in the hallway. It should be dry by the morning.

I take out the bleach spray and a reusable wipe, and I begin to clean. I clean the kitchen top to bottom, scrubbing and scrubbing, binning and washing, my eyes alert to every piece of dirt. When I have wiped the last crumb from the counter, I enter the living room and turn on the lamp.

It is so cosy in here. Studio Green walls, a fireplace with an oak surround, candles that I actually burn, wooden floorboards with a beautiful green and gold Persian rug – gifted to Ronan when he closed a huge deal. I walk straight over it and take my laptop from the bottom drawer of the dresser, then sit in my armchair by the fireplace.

The same chair I see my therapy patients in.

I open the laptop, bring up a fresh Word document and begin to type, my fingers working quickly.

Draft 1
Genre: stark realism.
Trigger warnings: sexuality, poverty, addiction and abuse.

Chapter 1

'What do you want?' the man said, stood at the door.
The boy held out the little plastic bag. He had done it time and time again – but this was different, he could feel it in the marrow of his brittle bones. Inside the bag, inside the house, a world that he loved. He needed to get inside. That was all he needed.
'I'll check it,' the man said. 'Wait here.'
The boy nodded and pulled his arms around himself – his T-shirt soaked through by the rain – as the man stepped back into the hallway of the house.
He was a boy, but not a boy. Twenty-something, with the face of a teenager and the stories many pensioners, sailors and raconteurs could only dream of. As he waited at the door, he noticed the roses were in full bloom. He studied their petals, and saw their beauty.
The door creaked open.
'Where's the rest of it?'
'It's all in there.'
'You're lying.'

'No – I'm not.' But he was.
'Fuck you, Leo. You pussy slut.'

No.
I delete.

'Fuck you, Liam. You pussy slut.'
The man slammed the door in his face. As Liam stood staring at it, he knew he had to sell himself tonight so that he could eat tomorrow.
'Liam,' he heard from behind him.
Before he could turn, a heavy weight plummeted into the back of his head. He felt the pavement before he saw it.
He was alone.
He lay on the floor in the rain, waiting for someone to save him.
But no one came.

I move the cursor to the top of the page and type the title.

SLAY

A novel by

M.M. MADDOX

I feel his pull. Leo.
Liam.
My new protagonist. This has invigorated me beyond any creative desire I have had since *Shallow Embers*, the wedding, Ronan. *Ever*.
And I need more.

13

Leo

I tiptoe into my room and close the door, bag of frozen peas in hand.

I eat one.

Breakfast.

I eat a few more. The way the cold bursts onto my tongue is heaven. A bit bitty though. I spit. Green dribble runs down my chin.

If they find out about last night, I'm fucked. I know that I slept in a bush, because I woke up in it. This was actually the right thing to do. I couldn't be seen like that inside the halfway house. That was good thinking. I would congratulate my last-night's brain, but I don't think it really deserves it.

Because I'm remembering more things now.

I remember losing all the ice, and not having any G. Sam and his weird little mate not letting me in. I remember Brick and his fucking brick. I remember the smell of a car, vanilla air-freshener and brand-new leather. A woman. Scared. The bush. It stank. I'm pretty sure someone had thrown up in it before I made it my bed. I came inside about seven, on the change of shift, which was also correct because no one saw.

I'm telling myself no one saw.

Pepper spray? Jesus. At least I still have my phone, and I can see now, even though it stings like sand has been whipped into my eyes from a windy day on a shitty British beach.

I stare at my reflection in the mirror above the sink in my room, the image clear as day. My face is distorted, like a

Picasso. But it wasn't done by Picasso. It was done by a man named Brick.

He tried his best, didn't he? *Fuck me.* Swelling has gone down a little though. I found the peas in the freezer in the communal kitchen. I can feel them going soft as I clench the bag in my sweaty palm. My face isn't as fat, but it is red. I have some make up that I keep for bruises and stuff, but I'm pretty sure it'll just get congealed in the cuts.

My face isn't the thing that hurts, not really.

In moments like this, of which there are many, the anxiety is what gets me. I feel like pulling my insides out through my throat. It tries to eat me alive. It's trying now. Wants to throttle me with its spindly witch fingers, as it digs its claws so deeply into my skin that I keep scratching my neck. It wants to pull me down into the sink and hold me under. It says things, too, sometimes. *Aren't you ready? It's nice and quiet under the surface.*

Is it possible to throw yourself up? I stick my fingers down my throat.

I don't come up.

I retch though, and it hurts my head, a deep and sharp throb emanating out from the centre of my mangled, idiotic brain. There is a remedy. And no, it's not meditation.

I have two cans left, hidden somewhere in a bag by a tree near the bus stop, which I'll get later. But for now I've got to pull it together without my medicine. I scramble in my pocket for the snapped ciggy I had yesterday, gathering up as much of the tobacco bits as I can find – clumped into the creases of my pocket – pour them into a rizla, roll it and open the window. I light the end and half of it disintegrates with the flame, but I have enough for a few drags.

This isn't gonna be an easy one to get out of. There are rules here, see.

Any fuckery, and you're out, and I can't be out. I need to come up with some excuse, pronto. I'll butter up the staff, make them believe me. *I was on my way back from the cinema. Someone attacked me.* They can't disagree with that. Just need to pull on their heartstrings. *I tried running, but I was too tired – too weak – from the detox*. I'm good at that bit. Manipulation. But it's the breathalyser I'm worried about. They do it randomly.

'Leo?'

'Hey!'

Here she is, the morning nurse doing the register, like I'm back at school. They do this every morning, to check we are in, to check we are dressed and looking after our personal hygiene, to check we are sober, to check we are following our treatment plans.

'Yeah?' I shout back through the door, chucking the fag butt out the window, wafting the air around me, trying to draw some of the fresh stuff inside, only to really disperse the smoke more into the room.

'Night shift said you didn't come in before curfew.' It's Kerry. I like Kerry, she doesn't give me grief. Just gives me my meds and leaves me to it. Doesn't try to have any meaningful therapeutic interaction bollocks, like some of the others do.

'Huh? I texted them.'

'No, you didn't.' She's good though. Good at her job. Which is one thing I don't like about her.

'Shit, sorry – I meant to.' I close the window and resort to hoping for the best. She won't come in until I say she can.

'You'll be breathalysed today. You know the rules.'

Fuck. 'Sure.'

'You going to a meeting?'

'Course.'

'Good. Do you want your meds now, or after breakfast?'

Double fuck. The Antabuse will actually make me vomit – it'll only be bile – and then she'll know. It makes you chuck up when there's alcohol in your system and there is no way around it. I came off the Librium two weeks ago at the detox place, so that one's done, but there are others: thiamine shit, folic acid shit, shit to make my abscess better, shit to help the cravings, shit to help me shit, and then the pills for my head. Mirtazapine. Citalopram. Fluoxetine. Can't remember which one I'm on now. At least no antipsychotics this time. Those ones made my dick shrivel up like a sad little leech. The doctor at the detox broke my dick to fix my head. I said they're linked. My dick and my happiness.

'Kerry?'

'Yes, Leo.'

'I was attacked last night.'

In the pause that happens outside the door, I know she's either shaking her head or rubbing her eyes. At least she can. 'For God's sake, Leo. Let me take a look.'

See? She doesn't question me. Not yet.

'OK.'

I quickly scrub my tongue with hand soap, so she isn't greeted by the smell of booze. When I unlock the door, the smell I am greeted with is the one from the weird brown carpet lining the corridor, which hangs somewhere between boiled cabbage and utter hopelessness. It hits me before her reaction to my face does. She raises her eyebrows, eyes wide. I can tell she thinks it looks bad.

'I see' is all she says.

'Nah, it's fine.'

'Fine?' Her gaze lingers over my face. She's trying to see if I'm pissed or high. 'You look like a crime scene, Leo. I'll get the first aid box. You might need to go to the hospital.'

'Wait—'

But she's gone.

I don't think she'll breathalyse me, not yet. I can work my magic. Convince her. This has worked before. Yeah, sure, typically with the older male nurses – and I don't mean to stereotype but it's an actual fact that most of them are gay – who will wink and say: *Well, listen.* Kerry knows I'm gay, but I still think she fancies me. It's the idea isn't it. Someone rotten and rough. Someone who needs you. And I have been told beneath the chaos there is something going on for me. Dunno if it's in my looks right now, but when the charm is really cooking, it distorts people's view of you. I've learnt that a lot.

I step back into my room and wait. It's tiny in here. I'm not complaining. Halfway houses are typically scummy as hell and bad, but this time they gave me a dorm of my own. They said it was because I'm high risk with other people: easily influenced and easily aggravated. I read that in a report once, which felt like a bit of a contradiction, but it's true that both of those things live inside me. I can't deal with other people. I hate them and need them simultaneously. But trying to stay dry right next to someone else who is trying to stay dry is the worst of the worst. I had this room-mate once in a sober house – can't remember when – but he actually was making money by selling mouthwash to the rest of us. Can't believe I relapsed off fucking Listerine. But when you haven't had alcohol for over two weeks, you can smell it through the mint. I necked the whole bottle, and he battered me, and then I ended up somewhere south of the river with nothing to my name but fresh breath.

I preferred the streets for a bit. I lived like that for a few months, and it was actually quite cushty. I found a good shop to sit outside of where the customers had a social conscience. I'd bat my sad little eyes, and some days make enough for everything. Drugs, scran, hostel: the entire triple threat.

Getting here has taken time. It's taken a long time, and I have done well, they told me last week at the detox. I did well there, and I wanted to get sober. *You want it this time, don't you?* they kept saying. *We can see that. We want to help you. But you have to do your part.*

I was trying.

We empathise with everything you have gone through.

I'm very much aware I am not a special case, but something about the way they look at me does make me feel good. They like having people like me that they can talk about in the office, chatting about all the terrible shit that's happened, looking through history notes, wanting to be the one who says the thing that changes my life. I can picture it: when they go home to their families. *There's this one patient – God, I hope he makes it. I feel like I made a breakthrough with him today. He's only twenty-two.*

Kinda gross that I like to think they're doing that. But I think they are.

I heard from one of the other 'residents' that it costs something like three hundred quid a night to be here. Not for *us* to pay. It's public money or whatever, and I'm not moaning but I'm pretty sure I could get a night in a hotel on the Strand for cheaper. I did suggest that once.

I begin to pace, back and forth, wall to wall, looking out of the window. Trying to ward off the spindly witch fingers that are currently attempting to infuse my every pore with their poison. She's my oldest friend – this witch-woman. Been with me since way before Tina and G and Molly and Charlie ever came along. Our co-dependency goes back as far as I can remember. I need her, and she needs me. I feed her. She feeds me. Cos I do stuff when I'm like this. In her grip. Either do stupid shit, or try and sort myself out.

Wonder which will happen today.

I've always preferred female company.

Gotta get Kerry on side. Manipulate the hell out of her so she doesn't stick that fucking breathalyser in my mouth and send me packing.

'Leo?'

Speak of the devil. 'Yeah, yeah.'

She's brought the whole bloody treatment room with her. Gauze and swabs and saline and those little steri-strips that I wouldn't mind her putting on my face, so people can see how bad it is. *Oh, my God, what happened? Did someone hit you? Can I help you?*

'Are you stupid, Leo?'

'Huh?'

She points to my face. 'I said, are you stupid?'

I smile. Cheeky. Cheeky works. 'I got ten GCSEs. Mostly As. Was dead good in school. So, no.' That's a lie, but people like to think fucked-up clever is better than just fucked up. It's more romantic. So much promise ruined, etc.

'You can't smoke in here.'

'I've not—'

She folds her arms. 'Don't try it with me today, Leo. I'm not in the mood.'

'Fine.'

She breathes deep, like she is trying to inhale patience through the whisps of fag smoke that linger around us. 'So what happened?'

'Got mugged on my way back from the cinema.'

'Do you think *I'm* stupid?'

'I did, Kerry.'

She shakes her head again – her favourite thing. 'Sit.' She points to the bed.

I don't protest because I want her to think she's in control. But she's not. She can't be. I try not to groan as I lower my arse onto the bed because I don't want her to check my chest. I think a rib might be fucked, but right now I'd rather not know.

'Take your top off. I need to look at your chest,' Kerry says. Told you she fancies me.

'Oh, go on, Kez, I bet you do,' I reply. I would wink but I can't.

'I know you think I fancy you – but funnily enough Leo, not everyone does.'

I shrug. 'Fine.'

She helps lift the T-shirt off over my head. 'This thing stinks.'

'In a kind of sexy sweaty way?'

'No, in a you've-pissed-yourself way.' Once it's off she throws it in the corner of the room and starts pressing my ribs. I don't dare look down. 'You're bruised pretty badly. So how many of them were there?'

'I'd say like four. Couldn't see them. Little chavvy scrotes.'

'Mmhmm,' she says, in a way that feels a little like *Takes one to know one*, but I don't question her, just let her tear open a wipe packet with her teeth, then pull on a pair of blue gloves.

'Sexy.'

'You're lucky to be alive, I assume?'

That's an annoying thing to say. 'I am.' It's true though, and not just cos of last night. I am lucky, and she knows it. She's annoying me with her tone. Don't like it. Her being smart with me. 'Why are you being shady?'

'I'm not being shady, Leo, I just don't believe you.'

She's definitely been through the system herself, Kerry. Most mental health nurses have. All of them with their tattoos and dyed hair. Hers is black with pink ends (standard), and she has some scars on her arms, all on the top – the wrong bit. If they wanted to top themselves they would have tried an actual artery.

I know what that's like and there's nothing romantic about it. It's just painful and actually a real let down. No one comes. Until they have to. Then you meet the nurses who do this job cos they think they can relate, but end up hating everyone and themselves even more.

'That's shit, that. You're supposed to be on my side.'

'Close your eyes, this might sting.'

She doesn't wait for me to close them. Just takes the wipe and starts rubbing it over my forehead.

'*Jesus Christ—!*'

'It's got dirt in it. Probably from sleeping in the bush.'

'What?'

'You have sick and chewing gum in your hair. Did you know that?'

Smart arse. 'Yes. I did, actually.'

My mind isn't working as fast as it should, damn it. She's sharper than me today. I can feel her picking bits out of my face – sometimes making noises like *Hmm*, and muttering *OK* and *Well that looks a little better*. Next she's sticking those strips above my eye, which I'm actually chuffed about but I make out like I don't want them, and then pressing my ribs again. I keep my eyes shut for the whole thing cos it's just easier not to hate her this way.

'I can't tell if you've broken anything. I'm going to give you painkillers with your meds.'

'Which painkillers?'

'Paracetamol.'

'Eugh. Rubbish.' I was hooked on Pregabalin for a bit. Loved that stuff. It's hard to find though when you need it, especially when the pharmacies keep them behind the counter and there are only so many old people's hand bags you can look through.

'Right, one last thing...'

I open my eyes to see her holding the breathalyser.

'Come on, Kerry. Don't be daft.'

'It's protocol.'

'Do you not trust me or summat?'

'No,' she says.

'Can we do it later? I feel si—'

'No.'

I look at it, and pray to no one that somehow it's broken. I've tried sucking a penny before and it doesn't work – that was a crock of shit. 'Isn't this a two-way street? I trust you, you trust me…'

She shakes her head, pushing the mouthpiece towards my lips. I keep my lips closed. She knows I'm fucked and so do I. I just want to see if that will give her some kind of impulsive change of heart.

'Please, Kerry.'

She looks at the time on her little nurses' watch, like I'm taking up far too much of it.

'Fine,' I say. I put it into my mouth, and blow.

When Kerry takes it out, stands away from me and holds it in front of her – while she waits for my doom to be confirmed – I try to find something to distract her, or make her empathise, or even cry. A story, perhaps… about my childhood? But then I remember she's told me she likes my poetry, and loads of the nurses do actually because it makes them think I have something to offer the world, that I have something to live for. I wrack my mangled brain for something deep, a phrase or a verse – the stuff that gets the most likes on Instagram. The really sad shit. I post it there occasionally because it makes me feel good when I see the likes go up and up, even though it's mostly lies. I remember something someone commented once under a post, saying: *That is the bleakest shit I've ever heard mate – hope you're OK.*

It's the perfect one.

I begin. '*In the haze of the blackness of my soul—*'

'Point three zero.'

Bollocks.

She shakes her head.

'Listen, Kez—'

'Don't *Kez* me – that's over ten pints. Did you use?'

'Of course not.'

'Leo. Tell me, it's important.'

'I didn't, Kerry.'

'Then let me drug test you.'

I'm now standing. 'Are you determined to get me out of here?'

'No, Leo. This is my job.'

I step towards her. She doesn't move. Begging's gonna be next. 'Just let me stay – I promise, this is the last time. I want to get clean. I do. I fucking…' My voice wobbles. Dunno if it's real or not but I let it happen – go with it. 'I promise. I want to be here. I want to follow my treatment plan. This was only a slip.'

She's not even looking at me. 'You know the rules. You're out.'

'I *promise*, Kerry—'

'It's not my choice.'

'I can't go back out there. People are looking for me. And don't you have to send me on to a fixed address? I haven't got one.'

'Use your benefits. Get a hostel.'

'They all do gear in them. Is that what you want?'

'Sadly, Leo – that's the reality you have to face. Go to A&E, you might have broken a bone.'

'Will you come with me?'

'What? No.'

'Why?'

'Because I work here, with people who want to stay sober.'

'*I* want to stay sober!'

'It doesn't appear that way.'

'You know I don't wanna be like this.'

'Have you been taking your PrEP?'

'Don't act like that.'

'Like what?'

'Like you're my fucking mother.'

She turns to me, shocked. 'Excuse me? I care about you, Leo. I care enough to ask if you have taken the drugs you need so you stay safe during sex—'

'Fuck off.'

'Don't speak to me like that. I know your risk profile. It's important.'

'Just get out.'

'Sadly, Leo, it's you who has to get out. You know the—'

'Rules! Yeah, fucking rules. None of you give a shit, do you?

Not really. I'm just another number to you. I work fucking hard at this!'

'Do you?'

'Fuck you, Kerry.'

'Sobriety isn't going to land in your lap, Leo, however much you want it to. And don't give me your poetry or your *hard life* stuff, we've all had it hard. This is on you.'

'Please, Kerry…'

'Go to the hospital, get your face scanned and ask for some emergency PEP.'

'Fuck.'

She shrugs, and I hate it. She won't budge. Won't do what she's supposed to. *Empathise. Feel fucking sorry for me.*

'Will you come with me?'

'No.'

'Come on, Kez. We'll have a laugh. Then come back, make a brew… It'll all be grand—'

'Pack your bag, Leo.'

I pause, weighing up which way to take this. I resolve she's not coming. 'Can you lend me a tenner to get there?'

She picks up the bloody wipes and gauze and turns to the door. 'The script for all your meds will be ready by twelve. This room needs to be cleared out for someone who wants it.'

She leaves. She's back out in the corridor. But before she is out of earshot, I smash my fist into the mirror, shattering it. I hope she fucking heard. It's her fault.

It's her fucking fault.

14

Mallory

'The kitchen looks amazing, did you get up early?'

Ronan is stood at the countertop with his back to me, making a bacon sandwich for himself. My breakfast is a bowl of granola that he made for me and that I prod at, simultaneously pretending to read, at the kitchen island.

'I did!' I say, ladling a heap of acai and granola into my mouth. It's the last thing I want, but I am able to pretend otherwise, swallowing my shame with it. I am wearing my morning dressing gown – silk with paisley print – and my hair is back in its intentionally messy bun. I am clean. I smell fresh. The Yves St Laurent perfume Ronan bought me lingers on my skin. Small pearl earrings that he gifted me for my birthday now hang from my ear lobes. They are subtle, but he will notice. My hands are washed, nails polished, fingers steady. Moving slowly, I casually take another mouthful, trying to mask the speed and quantity of my thoughts. *Does he know? Is he suspicious? He is so perceptive. About this house. About me. Always about me.* But the place is spotless, and so am I. There should be no trace of last night. Any of last night. *He says he knows me better than anyone.*

'How's your granola?' he asks.

He has his bacon sandwich, and I have my granola. Always. He likes routine. 'It's lovely, thank you.' I stuff another mouthful in. It churns to paste. I struggle to swallow.

'Good. I got this new light stuff.' He picks up the cereal box on the counter next to him and shakes it, still not looking at me. It has the words LOW SUGAR plastered on it. 'So it should be filling *and* healthier. And I topped it up with fruit.' I watch him take a bite of his sandwich, the smell of burnt fat making my insides twist with hungover envy.

'Great.'

'Did you enjoy the party?' he asks.

I sense a shift in his tone.

Probing? Suspicious?

'Yes!' I answer brusquely, turning the next unread page of the book that I quickly pulled off the shelf before he came downstairs, to see a glimpse of Shakespearean verse. 'It was great. You did so well!'

Who makes the fairest show means the most deceit.

Oh, Jesus.

'Yes,' he says. 'I did well. Despite you hiding in the bathroom most of the night, on your phone.' I look up. He keeps his back to me, taking a huge bite of his sandwich. Half gone.

I try to make my voice surprised, with a dollop of nonchalance. 'Oh! Was I?'

'Yes.'

'I was just taking a moment!' I say jovially. 'Just needed a bit of time to myself… It can be overwhelming. And it was your night, not mine.'

'What's on your phone?' he says so bluntly that I nearly drop my spoon. *Shit. Maybe I didn't delete them. Did I delete the pictures? I'm sure I did. I must have. I was meticulous last night. Wasn't I? Maybe not. And he looked. This morning. He knows my password because he told me once years ago, in a way that made me never want to change it. He's seen the photos. Of him. Splayed. Naked. Oh, God. I'm going to prison—* 'What's on there that could be better than a night with a house full of lovely people?'

The bounce from dread to relief in the space of two sentences nearly sends me dizzy.

Answer him.

I can't say Candy Crush.

I make my spoon clink against the bowl a few times as I heap some berries onto it, both to gain some control over myself and so that Ronan thinks I am absentmindedly eating and not in the aftermath of an emotional swing so jarring that it nearly gave me whiplash. It seems to work, because he continues chewing. No reaction. When he has finished the sandwich, he puts his plate in the sink and starts scrubbing it gently with the coarse green side of the sponge.

He is meticulous, and always has been. I can't read him, but he is quieter than usual. Not the jovial Ronan everyone knows. There are a few things this could mean. He could just be worried for me. He's not wrong: I was in the bathroom a lot. Perhaps he did go through my phone, and he *did* see the photos, and he liked them? Perhaps he wants more. That would be the best outcome here. He loved the pictures of himself and wants more of them. Maybe some of me? That's the right thing to assume. Isn't it? Whatever the reason, I need to say something. 'I was meditating.' OK. I need to say more. 'I've been using a meditation app.'

'Mal.' His hands stop moving. It isn't abrupt, but there is purpose to his pause, which makes me twitch. He bows his head slightly, considering the state of the chopping board. He slowly wipes it down with a tea towel and places it on the countertop next to the Sakuto knives.

'Is everything OK, love?' I say.

'I want to talk to you about something.'

Oh, no.

I can tell from the tone in his voice, the way he scratches the side of his cheek, the way the muscles flicker in his neck that he is sceptical. I have never said the words *I was meditating* before, at least not in that order, and he knows it. It sounded so foreign in my mouth that I panicked halfway through, making my intonation change so it sounded like I was asking a question. Like I wasn't actually sure if I was meditating. *I was meditating?* Maybe it sounded cute. *Little old me, trying to be wholesome – aren't I quirky!* But my throat was clogged with yoghurt. He's tense. It won't show on his face, but he is. I scan my brain for a casual response to move things in a different direction. 'Don't you have football in half an hour? Shall I get your boots?' But he doesn't answer – he remains hunched over the sink, seemingly deep in thought. There should be no reason for him to suspect. Should there? I was careful. I was quiet. He was passed out. When I went to bed, he was in the exact same position I left him in. 'It's half past ten already.'

He stays motionless.

Don't spiral.

Don't—

Unless one of the neighbours on the street saw me. Who are his friends that live there? Caro and Benji? Oh, God. Maybe they live next door. Or directly opposite. Maybe they've texted him. *Mal was acting erratically on our street last night – are you aware?* Perhaps they saw me hiding in the car. Tin foil, wine, blood. Maybe there was something in the news. *Woman in yellow coat helps boy flee from scene – wanted—*

'I think it's best to clear this up before I go.'

He has cleaned everything up, so it's evident he isn't referring to the sink.

I swallow hard. 'Has something happened?'

He wipes his hands on the tea towel and turns, looking at me in a way that I can't fully decipher. When he steps to the opposite side of the island, leaning forward, towards me, placing his hands on the marble top, he dips his head and speaks gently. 'Last night was out of character for you, Mal. Should I be concerned?'

I nonchalantly turn another page of the book. Which is actually a play. In verse. Which I admit might seem a tad heavy for a Saturday morning. Shit. I should have picked something light and easy. *Normal People. Fourth Wing.* Do we even have those? I didn't look. I doubt it. 'Concerned? What do you mean?'

'I'm not going to lie – you were being a little odd.'

'Odd?' I spit, like this is entirely ridiculous. 'I was just trying to be present.' I smile, and blink a few times in a way that is meant to appear naive.

'That's the opposite of what you were.' He squints, as if attempting to see past my face, right into me. 'We both know your history, Mal. I just need a gauge on the situation. Some of the guests said you seemed distant. Distracted. A little off kilter. Some said rude.'

'Rude?'

'Yes. Is everything OK?'

His face remains still. I can't read it. 'Of course it is.'

'You were very drunk.'

'Everyone was very drunk.'

He frowns. 'You know you shouldn't be drinking like that.' Ronan never looks angry, and he doesn't now. He looks steady. Unrattled. But troubled. Definitely troubled. 'Something feels off.'

'Off?'

'You're being strange.'

'Strange?' I make a small laugh, because at this point I appear to just be repeating his final words – which is not ideal – so I look down at my page again to redirect.

> *Those who can think,*
> *but cannot express what they think,*
> *place themselves at the level of those who cannot think –*

I've never read *Pericles*, and I already hate it. They say it's the worst one, and I definitely agree. 'I didn't know taking a minute in the bathroom at a party could be interpreted as strange.'

'It was a bit more than a minute, Mal. It was more like an hour.'

'Was it?'

'And then in bed, after. You just sat there with your clothes on. I was waiting...' I can feel him staring at me. The back of my neck prickles with sweat, and adrenaline, from the lack of sleep and the rush of what happened. 'You haven't wanted to have sex for a long—'

'*We have sex.*' I say this louder than I'd hoped, his words stinging me into impulse – to swat them away like a cluster of persistent wasps. It comes out too defensively, bouncing off the tiles, making the vein in his temple flicker. To deflect from the suddenness of it all, I smile, and repeat, 'We have sex,' softer this time, smooth and alluring. I try to fill the words with pleasure, but it's hard. It's hard to do that with only three words. I know, because I have tried multiple times before. Different words, but the same lie.

I feel my cheeks heating up. From the shock of it? The reality? We do have sex, even if it's not in the way either of us would like.

Ronan cocks his head, then furrows his brow. He moves slowly when he's like this. Takes his time. I can see in his eyes he is weighing me up. I struggle to hold his glare, so I push my hands over my face, rubbing my eyes. He sighs. I can't tell if it's exasperation or self-regulation or both.

Or kindness.

He steps around the island until he is stood right next to me. When he stops, I suddenly feel tiny. 'You can't be acting recklessly. We both know how that ended last time.' He leans down and gently kisses my forehead. 'Have a nice, relaxed day on your own today. You don't have any clients.' He makes this sound like I have more than three. Like I am perpetually busy. 'I'll be out all afternoon, so you can just enjoy some peace and quiet.' When he puts his hand on my shoulder, I don't flinch.

I know how not to.

'That sounds nice.' I pause, swallowing a surge of guilt that threatens to topple me. 'I'm sorry. I really am.'

He smiles. 'Don't be.'

'I am…' My voice wobbles.

'Hey – look at me.'

'I shouldn't have got drunk.'

'I know. But we are learning. Together.'

'I love you,' I say. It comes out of me instinctively, impulsively again, but this time born of a need so deeply obscured that I don't know where it originates. It escapes me entirely without deliberation or thought. I have a flash of being stood opposite him in the field we got married in – wearing my wellies, his eyes bright in the sun. In sickness and in health, he'd said. We both did.

He points to the book, open next to me. 'Shakespeare on a Saturday? Sounds lovely.' He picks it up, turning it in his hands. '*Pericles*. Interesting. I didn't know you liked that one.'

'It's underrated,' I lie.

'I think *Taming of the Shrew* is underrated,' he says quickly. He then winks playfully, but the brazenness to his words does something to my insides – a sudden injection of cortisol that makes the muscles in my stomach clench. *Fight or flight. Fight or flight.*

Instead, I freeze.

He places the book back down, but stays standing, right next to me. He begins to pat his pockets. 'Oh, bollocks. I've left my phone upstairs. Could you just google the sports club, I think they've changed the start time.'

I try not to let the panic in my body surface, but it sears through my pores. He never leaves his phone anywhere. 'It starts at midday, doesn't it?'

'They mentioned last week it might move because of the new intake group.'

'Oh, right.' He is staying exactly where he is. 'Sure.' I pull my phone out of my pocket. *The Grindr app.* Is it on the home screen? *Shit.* 'Surely they won't have moved it?'

'Can't you just check?'

A film of cold sweat immediately seems to coat my skin. 'Of course.'

I start to punch in the passcode, as he watches each digit, my brain scrambling to remember if I moved the app. *Surely I did.* I was being meticulous last night. Wasn't I? I managed to *write* – to write pages and pages – and I cleaned everything. *Not a trace. My mind was sound. Sane.* Could I have missed this? I know I didn't *delete* it – because I need the profile. I need *Chat?;)* to remain—

The screen opens.

Thank God. It's not there.

And I suddenly remember.

I buried it within a folder labelled wellbeing.

I try not to scream, *Yas! Slay!*

'Let's see,' I mutter instead, navigating to the internet browser. As I type in the words *Crouch End football club*, I can feel something in the space between me and Ronan: an understanding that we both know this is nothing to do with the football club. Not only because the webpage looks like it hasn't been updated in about three hundred years, but because his hand is still on my shoulder. Feeling for any tension in my body. I know this move.

We've been here before. I always forget how suffocating it is. *He knows that I am hiding something.* 'Starts at midday. Look.'

'Ah, yes.' He kisses the top of my head. 'While you're open, did you get any pictures of last night?'

Pictures.

Pictures.

My brain nearly whites out.

'Pictures?'

He laughs, because I said this like it would be the most ridiculous thing ever. 'Yeah, pictures, Mal. I forgot to take any.' He puts his fingers on my chin and lifts my head so I am looking up at him. 'You seem rattled, baby.'

Baby.

Baby in any and every context makes my brain want to be obliterated with the swipe of a finger. 'I'm not!'

I remember all the shades of his flesh. The grid of his body, all splayed. I know I deleted them. I had to. But for some reason now I'm unsure. 'Joanie got loads. I think I was too distracted! By all the fun!'

'And the bathroom meditating?'

We both laugh, but I want to cry. 'Yes, exactly!'

I open the camera roll. I can't look directly at it.

'So that's what you were doing...' he points to the screen.

His finger is pointing to an accidental screen shot of Candy Crush with the word *DIVINE!* written across a fruit explosion. No flesh.

Thank God.

'Oh...' I say. 'Busted.'

But I feel his body relax.

His hand leaves my shoulder as he glances at the grid of pictures. No hairless nipples. No shades of flesh. Just a few of the two us smiling on the heath, some screen grabs of shopping items from whole foods, and excerpts from articles that I pretended to read for my therapy course.

Nothing amiss.

He kisses my forehead. 'I love you, Marvellous Mal.'

He uses that one sometimes too.

It fluctuates.

'I'll get your boots,' I say, standing up from the stool. 'I think I put them on the shelf in the cupboard.'

As he turns to his bag on the floor – neatly filled with folded clothes and a towel – I make my way into the hallway and open the cupboard door that is flush to the wall under the stairs. We modelled it when we moved in. A place we could quickly throw all our things in before people came over to visit, we said. A practical and efficient way to hide our mess. We both thought it was a great idea. We both also knew that I was the messy one, not him. Ronan has been persistently and unwaveringly clean since I met him at the restaurant Pierre Victoire in Soho at a press party. He was wearing brogues, tan trousers, an oversized white T-shirt and a huge, glowing smile.

I stop, breathing slowly.

It's OK.

I am fine.

Wait. That's odd.

My coat, hanging amongst the line-up.

There's blood on it. On the collar.

I thought I had got it all off? A wave of hot panic makes me bite my lip. *Has he seen?* I was writing for a long time, and feeling hazy with the joy and adrenaline of my creative surge until my eyes started closing. I must have been careless.

He never comes in here.

It's fine.

It is.

I stand on my tip toes and reach up to the shelf.

'Love?'

I pull the boots off it and quickly close the door shut behind me, turning to see Ronan stood in the hall with his bag slung over his shoulder. 'Is everything OK?' he says, looking at my face. 'Monster in the cupboard?'

'Ha!'

He steps towards me. 'I'm proud of you. You're doing really well, OK?'

'Thanks. Have fun. What time will you be back?'

'I'll go for a pint with the boys after. Maybe six?'

'Wonderful. House to myself.'

He smiles. When he leaves, and the door closes, my exhalation is ragged. I stand still for a moment, allowing myself to settle. Only when my shoulders drop do I realise they have been raised this entire morning. My body is clammy, and my brain feels like it is stuffed with wet sawdust. I align my thoughts as best I can.

We both know your history, Mal.

When I feel a little less crowded – and sweaty – I go straight to the living room, take out my laptop from the dresser, and sit in the armchair. I open up *Slay*, and begin to scan over what I wrote last night.

I like it.

I do.

It feels… I don't know. Raw. Fluid. Real.

I hate those words. If ever I saw them on the cover of a book as a puff quote, I'd roll my eyes. But I think the opening is strong. And Liam is intriguing. Part of me wonders if I don't need more from him: Leo. I could use my imagination, instigating a whole narrative journey for him by myself. He got me out of the starting blocks. But something tells me to stay close to the truth.

'What are you doing?'

'Jesus!' I look up. Ronan, in the doorway. I instinctively slam the laptop closed.

'Are you writing again?'

'I – no. I was just… What are you doing back?'

'I just walked past your car.' His voice is flat. Calm, but emotionless. 'There's a picnic hamper in the back seat.'

Shit. The fucking vol-au-vents. 'Yes,' I say. *Don't scramble. Look composed.* 'I made one up to take over to Joanie's this afternoon while you're at football. I thought it might be nice for the kids to have some of the leftovers.'

I make sure my face is straight, then meet his eyes.

He blinks. Once. Twice. Thinking. 'You're going to Joanie's today?'

'Yes – I was going to go while you're at football.'

'Why didn't you say?'

'Oh, I just forgot to mention it.'

'You're planning on drinking?'

'Drinking? No, I don't think I'll be drinking again for a *long* time.'

'So why are you taking wine?'

The wine. 'I thought she might like it. Did you want it? I can keep it here.'

'Mal.'

'What?'

'You shouldn't hide things from me. I *need* you to be honest.'

'Of course.'

'Always.'

'Yes.'

He sighs heavily, then scratches the side of his head, looking down. 'OK. Well, have a nice day.'

'I will. You too.'

He turns. But before he leaves – for the second time – he stops in the doorway, eyes still on the floor. 'When I'm back later, I think it would be really good for us to continue our conversation about having a baby. I think it's time.'

'Definitely,' I say. 'I'd like that.'

I don't really hear the words I say, but I know they left my lips because he is no longer in the room with me.

I wait to hear the door slam again, and this time I sit deadly still, biting the inside of my lip, chewing harder and harder, until the ticking of the small grandfather clock on the mantelpiece becomes a blurred and distant noise behind the weight of my thoughts. One thought – repeating.

A baby.

I go back into the kitchen, wash my spoon and bowl, and take my keys from the side.

I look down at the play. *Pericles*. Its gold embossed lettering and brown leather spine. The edges of the pages are brown and tatty. I open it up, flicking through them.

I pause, my eyes lingering on a line of verse.

To be happy means to be free and to be free means to be brave.

Maybe I was wrong about this play.

I get in the car and drive, stopping only at an industrial bin to throw in the vol-au-vents and wine, then continuing on.

But not to Joanie's, like I said.

To him.

15

Leo

Before I bolted, I shoved a piece of broken glass in my pocket the size of a matchbox.

Just in case.

I don't have any things, which is only a fucking good thing, cos Kerry called the police. I had to move fast.

Always moving fast.

Always running.

I stop at the tree.

Find my beers.

Sit and gulp.

Gulp gulp.

Bye bye, witchy fingers.

Fuck me, I feel better.

Now I got somewhere to go. I know a place. I know what I need to do.

16

Mallory

I haven't done this before.

   Clearly.

   I wouldn't call it stalking, but I am struggling to find another word for it. Driving up and down Turnpike Lane searching for someone I have met only once is definitely something. I'm currently going with the term *creative flare*, but the anxiety and the awareness of how this could look (I suppose not far off lunacy?) need to be swallowed in order for me to continue.

   There is context to this.

The context is a desire for freedom.

   Isn't that everyone's context?

   I pull into the side of the road, pushing my sunglasses up my nose. Yes, I am wearing sunglasses. And no, it's not because people do it in films. It is because I feel less like myself in them. Or more like myself. I'm unsure at this point. Regardless of the reason, I turn on the radio. It's 6 Music playing. I hate 6 Music: everything is so plinky-plonky and glockenspiel-y that it hurts my brain and heightens my anxiety. But it's locked to default, because that's what I want people to hear when I give them a lift. So they think my music taste is peripheral and therefore edgy. The truth is, I love the Scissor Sisters and ABBA.

   But that doesn't seem the correct tone for what I'm doing. Which I have established is creative flare.

   I turn the channel over to Classic FM to calm me.

   Dramatic orchestral music fills the car, sending a wave of panic through my body. It is heavy and rousing, intense and loud, which makes me grip the steering wheel. Something strange happens. The music inspires a sudden vision of myself. I am still in the car, I am still wearing sunglasses, but I am in the scene of a film. And I am being played by Saoirse Ronan. She is smoking, rolling the window down and coolly blowing the smoke out of it as she searches the pavement. She looks cool, and strong. Fierce and determined.

And then it leaves, as quickly as it came.

I try to pull it back, but it won't come.

I am a little surprised. Not only because my vision knocked five to ten years off me, but because I – as her – looked so confident. Saoirse Ronan. Strange, I would never have thought her, playing me. I guess she has the right intensity. And she's kind of edgy. A medium-budget indie.

A car honks.

I turn to see someone behind me yelling that I can't park here.

I quickly release the handbrake and move on, heading back down the road, until I see him.

Leo.

Stumbling towards the bus stop, with a can of lager in his hand. He waves at the bus pulling in, throws his can and jumps on at the back door through a stream of people moving out onto the pavement. The bus continues on.

I follow slowly behind, keeping enough distance to allow for the bus to stop. After about twenty minutes, it pulls over outside a row of little independent shops, and Leo alights. When he steps onto the pavement, he turns to look back down the road – towards me – and fleetingly I see his face. It looks swollen – purple-black streaks run from the corners of his eyes down into his cheeks. He puts half a cigarette to his lips, lights it, then begins to walk away – limping slightly – in the other direction. I watch him take a left around a corner, down the side street running off the main road.

I put my indicator on and follow, feeling an odd sensation running down my spine. I'm not sure if it's a thrill, or a warning, or my conscience. But it isn't telling me to stop.

The street is lined with trees and uniformly preened houses. This is Muswell Hill. It's where most people graduate to from Crouch End when they need a third bedroom.

When I get back later, I'd like to talk about us having a baby.
A horn blares.
I swerve.
Shit.

'Sorry...' I mutter, simultaneously realising I have drifted to the middle of the road and frantically waving an apology to the car heading towards me. When it passes – the driver's middle finger firmly raised – I am left feeling only gratitude that I had the foresight to fulfil my Saoirse Ronan RayBan-wearing fantasy. Because people might know me here.

I have to be careful.

I gather myself and place my gaze back on Leo. The soundtrack – sorry, the radio – is now a little more intense. Rising strings. Deep and melodic. The scene before the scene.

I don't think Leo looked when the car's horn went. I don't think he saw me.

It's hard to drive at walking speed, so I pull over and sit at the side of the road for a moment, watching Leo gain some distance down the pavement, before I continue on. I repeat this cycle for about five minutes, until he suddenly turns off the pavement and into the car park of a building.

A church.

Interesting.

I would not have taken this man for religious. His story continues to surprise. And in stories, surprises are good.

The unexpected is what keeps the reader wanting more.

Perhaps he would be played by someone like Timothée Chalamet. But then again, Timmy isn't really rough enough around the edges, and in the film adaptation it might be nice to find a new up-and-comer. Give them a break into the industry.

I make a mental note.

I park on the road outside and watch him hobble through the parked cars, up to a small door on the side of the building. It's not a pretty church – all stone and spires – it looks more like a community hall. Peeling paint, dirty windows and a battered sign that says LET HIS LIGHT SHINE.

Leo stops outside the door, where there are two men smoking.

It looks shifty.

They talk with Leo for a moment and turn to point into the door.

Leo nods and enters.

The two men throw their cigarette butts on the floor, glance around the car park and go inside, leaving the door ajar.

I look at the time. Three minutes past two.

This fantasy is insane.

This is insane.

But it's also exciting.

And it's a church. How bad could it be?

I turn off the engine and make my way towards the little door, keeping my sunglasses on. It's not sunny, but it's bright – and Saoirse would wear them inside, I'm sure.

*

I hover at the periphery of the church hall.

It is not exactly the most cheerful of rooms. Hanging from the walls are tapestries of anxious and pained faces on top of naked bodies nailed to crosses, upset women washing men's feet and a king murdering babies. The ceiling is low and oppressive. The floor is a scuffed dark oak, and there are remnants of what I assume were either children's parties or weddings swept into its corners – popped balloons, cake crumbs and flakes of faded confetti now clumped together into little grey piles. A strong smell of must lingers. Shards of light enter through rectangular glass panels near the ceiling, cutting through particles of dust that float over a circle of plastic chairs directly at its centre.

The chairs are full of people.

Leo is in one of them. Slouched forward, with his cap pulled down, staring at the floor in front of him, where a ring of candles and sheets of laminated yellow paper have been placed. Each sheet has words in aggressively bold type.

EASY DOES IT – KEEP IT SIMPLE – LET GO, AND LET GOD

Let God do what?

I don't think any of those apply to me.

There is something about the way people are sat – very stoically and sombrely – that makes me feel I have entered the set of some kind of Jonestown massacre re-enactment. I scan their hands quickly for any sign of Cool Aid.

'Are you coming in?'

I look up to see one of the men who was stood smoking at the front door glaring at me hopefully. 'Don't be scared,' he whispers, smiling sadly. 'Is this your first time at a meeting?'

A meeting.

Oh. This is *recovery*.

So, less group suicide, more *Euphoria*.

'No,' I instinctively say, without any prior thought. It's a mistake, I know it is, but he can't think I'm unsure. I must go with it. 'No, no. I've been to a few.' A flash of pity enters his eyes. Does he know I'm lying? 'A *fair* few.' I wave my hand, like this is nothing to me.

'Oh? I've not seen you around.' He has a gold tooth. And a gold chain that says HUGS NOT DRUGS.

'I'm new to the area,' I whisper.

'Well, welcome. You're in the right place.' Well, I know that. 'The meeting's starting. Would you like a cup of tea or coffee?'

I look at the little hatch in the wall opposite, where a woman with no teeth and a light-blue *Lilo and Stitch* T-shirt stands, stirring heaps of sugar into a mug of tea. 'I don't have any change.'

The man looks confused. 'You don't need to pay for it—'

'Right!' I say. 'No, I know. I meant – just in general.' Brush past it. 'I'll take a seat in the…' Oh, sweet Jesus, what do they call it? The God circle? The circle of fire? The halo?

I just point instead.

He nods empathetically, like he has seen many versions of me in his time. I try to eradicate his doubt by stepping confidently towards the circle of doom, where the people are now all saying things in unison. There's a couple of empty chairs, and I notice one exactly opposite Leo. I find myself practically frogmarching towards it, heavily stamping out my anxiety with each step, my doubt hidden firmly behind my sunglasses, which I have resolved to keep on throughout whatever this may be. When I sidle into the chair, I look at the person next to me. He is sobbing. I smile sadly, like everyone else is doing. Has it started? Is this the beginning? I glance around the faces of the other participants. I don't want to sound judgy, but they all look a little different to what I thought I might see. It doesn't feel very *Euphoria*.

I place my hands on my lap, as a mark of respect.

OK, so what happens now?

Everyone shuffles in their seats. Some exchange little glances of recognition. There are more sad smiles aimed in my direction.

Suddenly a gong sounds, surprising me. I turn to see an earnest-looking woman with cropped grey hair and sad eyes holding one, hitting it with a wooden mallet. She is sat behind a small fold-out table. I assume this is the leader. She is, to be fair, a little Tilda Swinton-y (in *The Beach*), based on her lacy sandals and pinched features. Perhaps her cult style icon? She looks like she cares about rules – she thinks they are important for everyone. That type. She waits for the *dommm* of the little gong to stop – which takes a painfully long time – then places it back on the table.

She says, 'Hello, my name is Janet, and I'm an alcoholic.'

Everyone speaks in response. 'Hi, Janet.'

Janet continues in her softly spoken but precise and clipped voice. 'In this meeting we go around the circle and introduce ourselves.' Oh, Lord. 'So, I'll start. Hello – I'm still Janet, and I'm still an alcoholic.'

The circle ripples with a laugh that is gentle yet knowing, which is oddly peaceful, but also completely bizarre. I suddenly feel very much like I am outside of the joke and become astutely aware I need to be very much inside it, in order to pull this off. To appear authentic.

I make myself laugh, copying their tone, glancing round the group hoping they notice. Hoping Leo notices. But his head is still down, hiding his face. A woman with a cloud of grey hair, a headscarf and large wrist bangles catches my eye and nods approvingly. I nod back, in what I hope is a gentle and knowing way. I notice she is wearing pink fluffy slippers.

A rush enters my system. God, this is actually *exciting*. I've not felt this electricity, this freedom, since—

'Hi, I'm John, and I am also an alcoholic.' John is on the right of Janet and looks like he is straight out of a Dickens novel. Slender, tall, messy grey hair, wrinkled eyes, wearing a waistcoat, with a trace of dirt on his collar.

'Hi, John,' the group chimes.

I missed that one, but I'll get the next.

'Hi, I'm Pat, and I'm an alcoholic.'

'Hi, Pat,' I say confidently with the rest of them.

Next to Pat is Mia. Mia looks no older than fifteen and has the poshest accent I've ever heard. She resembles a supermodel. Perhaps the daughter of one? That would make sense. In fact, I wonder if there are famous faces amongst this candle circle. The postcode and the demographic might suggest it, not to mention the creative pressure on celebs. It makes perfect sense. I quickly scan the group again. Alas, no one famous. Not even one early nineties pop star. That I know of. Facial surgery does change people these days. Speaking of, Janet has definitely had her forehead done. Maybe we are all in disguise. Maybe I am with my people. Leo looks fidgety now. Picking at his nails.

'I'm Dez, and I'm an addict,' the man who whispered to me says. I notice people look at Dez a little differently, with a little more reverence and respect. I wonder if being an addict – I assume a much more hard-core version of an 'alcoholic' – determines status within a group. No one else has identified as an *addict*. He even holds himself differently. Leaning forward with his elbows on his knees, his brow furrowed. The weight of his addict past on his back – heavier than for the rest of us. I wonder if I should identify as an addict. I do think it holds itself open to a wider interpretation, and is certainly more obscure. I wonder if it will give me more intrigue. It has certainly made Hugs-Not-Drugs Dez more intriguing. He is actually saying more things now, too. About being grateful and recover*ing*. Apparently he will never be recovered, and that's the key.

Fascinating.

Dez is fascinating.

They all are.

Then Brenda speaks. Brenda is just an alcoholic, unlike Dez, but she still seems very wise, in a very wholesome way. She has very pink cheeks and looks absolutely knackered, and like she owns an allotment and gives massive courgettes to her neighbours.

I'm a little jealous of her.

Then Kima identifies herself. Kima looks like a yoga teacher in her Sweaty Betty leggings and vest, with hair that belongs in California. Then Peter and Asha and Sally all tell us they are alcoholics. Sally is interesting. She is seemingly calm and together, wearing a very beautiful dress, and has the air of someone with a very high-powered job in the city. How did Sally get here? She looks a million dollars. Maybe she's not really one, like me? Maybe she just needs friends? (Like me?) Somewhere to go while the kids run riot on a Saturday morning?

Next to introduce herself is another very interesting woman who calls herself Aphrodite. I love the name, and actually it really suits her. She has a tie-dye vest on, short wavy hair and a quality of calmness that seems entirely authentic. I am immediately enamoured. I watch her plump rosy lips – without lip gloss but still amazingly hydrated – as she speaks, going a little off script, telling us that she is a lover of the moon and at one with nature. I don't really understand how it makes her an alcoholic, but she seems to think it does, and because of the *way* she says it – gently moving her hair out of that face with the intensely thoughtful auburn eyes – I fully believe her. I instinctively laugh when she tells us her Venus is in orbit this month and so she's more prone to relapse and is being watchful, but no one else does. No one even cracks a smile. It throws me a little, as I realise I am still grasping the etiquette and response decorum happening around me. It is very left field at times.

But I am a quick learner.

The self-identification of the participants quickly gathers speed until the man on my right, who is still sobbing, says he is called Brian and he is currently a little drunk – he had a can of cider to steel his nerves – to which Leader Janet responds, 'Sorry,

Brian, you can't share if you've had a drink today.' This seems a little brutal, but hey, I don't make the rules, and leads Brian to sob even more, step out of his chair and leave through the front door. I watch him, shaking my head sadly, like I assume other people are doing. When I turn back into the circle, I realise everyone is looking directly at me. Expectantly. Nodding encouragingly.

Tilda appears like her eyes might explode with the anticipation of hearing the name of a new member.

It's my turn.

I glance at Leo. He is still staring at the floor. I suddenly panic that he will recognise my voice. He never saw me – I temporarily blinded him before that could happen – but my voice could cause problems.

Will he remember it?

Perhaps in the blur of last night, he didn't commit it to memory. My voice may have sounded muffled. I am not a doctor, but I am sure if you've been kicked in the head a few times, your hearing could easily be impaired? Also, a lot of the women in here do sound a bit like me. How much can one really recognise someone off voice alone...?

'Hello?'

Oh, God.

Janet.

Leader Janet is speaking to me.

I should change it slightly. Deepen it? Quieten it? An accent? I could go for scouse? I have nailed that one after I watched back-to-back interviews of Jodie Comer, what with being enamoured by her performance in *Killing Eve*.

'Would you like to introduce yourself?'

Oh, no.

In my panic, I appear to settle for croaky. 'Hi, everyone, I'm Mandy.' I check to see if Leo twigs... but he doesn't look up. Am I safe? I don't even think he's listening. Janet is looking at me like I need to complete the oath. Is it an oath? Screw it. 'And I am an alcoholic.' After the drink driving last night, I actually don't think I'm fully lying.

And I didn't go *full addict*. I'm not sure I'm there yet.

'Hi, Mandy,' everyone says at once. Even Leo seems to mumble it, absently.

I did it. I'm here.

'Thank you,' I say unexpectedly. I feel a strange mix of pride and an instant need to remove the attention from myself, so I look to the lady on my left, willing her to speak now. A woman with a fish tattoo on her cheek and a safety pin through her nose. Please help me, fellow alcoholic.

'Is this your first time at a meeting?' Janet's voice asks.

I look back to see she is directing this at me.

'Hmm?' Janet needs to calm down. She hasn't done extra questions with anyone else. 'Me?'

'Yes, sweetheart.'

I don't like that tone.

My heart is banging. I want to stand up and leave. *What am I doing?* No. Confidence. Fuck Meek Mal. *I'm nailing this.* 'Oh, no. I've been doing this a *while*,' I say, extending the final word to make it sound like I've *really* been round the houses – been *through* it in my time – hoping this will elicit the gentle-laughter response to bolster my credibility. And it does. People nod. Some chuckle in an *I-feel-you* kind of way. *I understand that pain.* And as they do, I watch them looking at me, and it is… validating. Encouraging. It feels really… bloody *good*. 'A long, *long* time,' I add, for good measure. 'Possibly the hardest thing I've ever done.'

I don't want to get cocky, but they are all really loving what I am saying. The only time this has ever happened to me before was when *Shallow Embers* was released. It is surprising. But it feels in some way familiar. The buzz, coming back to me, like it has been lying dormant within my gut for seven years.

Did Mandy write *Shallow Embers*?

Is Mandy someone deep inside me? Who is she?

I glance at Leo. He still doesn't seem to be listening – just picking at his fingers.

'Well, welcome, Mandy.'

'Thank you. It's such a pleasure to be here.'

'It's great to have you here. We can't wait to hear you share.'

'Yes.'

Wait – what?

Share?

I nod, swallowing hard.

The rest of the room identifies themselves. (One woman weeps and says she's not ready to use *that word* yet, and when someone tells her *you've got to fake it till you make it*, I feel even more validated and nod aggressively.) As I watch them, I feel myself settle.

Settle into this role. This character.

Mandy.

Who is Mandy? Who can she be?

Mandy is clever and bright – yes. She is also strong, and wise. Collected. No, not collected. That doesn't feel right. She's a little scrappy. She has made mistakes but she has learnt from them. She's a therapist. A good one. She has a giving heart and been through a lot. She has extended her empathy to people who have hurt her. She has lots to offer, and she is interested in the truth of other people. She wants to learn and broaden her horizons. She is confident and does not worry about her husband, because she doesn't have one. She is childless, successful – possibly she will become best friends with Sally – and owns her own house. People respect her. They see her potential, and she continues to fulfil it. She has flaws, importantly, because that gives her a more rounded and intriguing quality. She is *too giving*. Yes – that's it. It gets her in trouble sometimes. That's her flaw.

And then, finally, Leo speaks.

'Hi, I'm Leo, I'm an addict. Couldn't find an NA meeting so I'm here. It's all the same shit anyway.' He sounds very quiet, but also very angry. Hugs-Not-Drugs Dez catches Leo's eye and winks, nodding solemnly. 'And I fucking hate it here,' Leo adds. I lean forward in my chair. 'But I need all the help I can get.'

17

Leo

This hall fucking stinks.

I can hear myself rambling away, and the beer from under the tree is cutting through a bit – I need to be careful. I'm just about making sense. These people don't know me, but they love to act like they do.

I need to make them think I care. Make them think I want to be here for the right reasons, so I can get what I need. When the collection bucket goes round, I'll take what I can from the change. Swift fingers, that's what someone called me once. Sometimes there are rolled up banknotes – especially in these parts – and they're easier to lift. I like to throw a stone in, to sound like I'm paying my bit, but I forgot one today. My leg fucking hurts and the painkillers are wearing off. I need to get that script to the pharmacy, or it's gonna be a rough night.

And I need the money to get to a guy.

Fucking fuck fuck money fuck.

Watching this lot makes me feel sick. I have to keep looking down.

Do any of these yummy mummies know what it's like? In their lives, they think an extra bottle of posh white wine by the back-porch patio heater on a Friday night is the end of the world. Bangles, headscarves, fucking sunglasses inside.

They wake up in their massive houses and shit themselves that they've said something stupid to one of their work mates, then come here to feel the guilt. They love it in these parts, when people talk like this. I can see them all nodding, tears in their eyes. *Free therapy*, I've heard them say. Like they fucking need it.

'Thanks, Leo,' Janet says. She looks like some kind of sex-starved eagle. 'I'm aware you've been before – but in terms of sobriety, would you consider yourself a newcomer?' I nod. Not because I want to, but because that's what they need from me in order to notice me. To empathise. 'Well, we will leave space at the end for newcomers to share, if you should like to.'

'Thanks,' I say.

That won't be happening. I have fifty minutes to endure, and then the bucket will come and I will lift as much as is humanly possible with my dirty fingers then go to Mo's. Or Paul's. Or Jamie's. Whoever's paying the most. Probably Mo, as I haven't showered, and he likes that.

'Right, that's everyone introduced,' Janet the eagle says. 'Please come in and share as you'd like to. You will receive a wave from me when your five minutes are up.'

It's such bullshit all this. All the Higher Power stuff, like some fucking force exists that will somehow suddenly take *the urge* away. People talking about their *serenity*, their *new way of life*, their *ability to find self-confidence within themselves*, no longer needing it from external things. Where do they even find this bullshit?

Some woman called Aphrodite shares about her fantasy addiction. She says she obsesses about people and is let down because they don't live up to her expectations – and she does the same to herself. I hear people *mmm*-ing deeply – *how relatable* – but I don't get up to leave, which every part of me wants to do, to not listen to this self-serving ego-wank. Instead I decide to zone out.

I start thinking about Mo, and pull my phone out of my pocket. People don't like texting in these meetings, they get arsy about it. I've been nagged by the prissy little rule-keepers to put my phone away many times before, but I find a way to hide it between my legs and open his messages. I need money to get to him. Need money for my script. And he likes gifts. He's weird like that. I don't kink-shame – I've seen enough of them – but I do find it a bit fucking weird that he likes me to bring a family-sized bag of Haribo. He doesn't even open the packets. Just collects them all up and puts them in a drawer.

Nutter.

And I need some fags, to help me through it.

Hi Mo. Tonight?

I wait, as a man starts talking some crap about the truth setting him free, the ego and the low self-esteem paradox that he says he grapples with every day. Now he's just saying fucking words. What's his problem? Smashes two bottles of red wine a night in his North London flat? I feel so fucking sorry for him. Then he comes here and gets what he needs. The validation. They all love to bang on about how you've gotta find that for yourself, but I have never heard people loving the sound of their own voices so much as at these things. *We're all the same*, he keeps saying. *Inside, we're all the very same.*

Hey sexy
Yeah. I'm free later

What do you want?

Everything

Fuck's sake.

But also good. That'll be two hundred quid. Can get some decent gak with that, and maybe even sleep at a hostel, if beneath the canal bridge is too busy. Mo likes it alone, which suits me. He just sometimes gets all hands on. Brought out a belt last time.

Fuck it. I'm already a state.

Nice

He does scare me, Mo. I dunno why. It's all so controlled. It feels like he's thought it all through beforehand, planned every movement and almost directs the whole thing, while I just do what I'm told. That's what he likes. It feels like he could snap at any minute, and I dunno what he'd fucking do.

I do want to stop this.

I do.

We are not all the same. The man was talking shite.

> Bring me a present

Course sxy

By present, he means Haribo.

Weirder than the slapping if you ask me.

'Could I share now?' I look up to see the woman opposite me – the woman who is wearing her sunglasses inside like an absolute tool – with her hand in the air. Those sunnies look spenny though. I could do with a pair – I look like a fucking panda. She probably just hates her crow's feet caused by too many holidays in Greece or on some nice Spanish island.

Not all-inclusive either.

'Of course,' Janet says.

'Thanks, I feel fortunate to have this space to share. Should I just start?'

God, she's weird. Like the rest of them.

'Please,' Janet says.

Jesus, what bullshit are we in for now.

18

Mallory

'I relate a lot to what people say about fantasy and delusion and not living in the real world. I was once a creative, you see.' The circle *mmm*s approvingly. Understandingly. As if to say: *of course you are a creative. Of course you feel crazy. It's a tough pursuit.* 'I didn't think I'd ever get to this point. I honestly was in such a bad place.' My God, it's just coming to me, just tripping off my tongue, and they are eating it up. Mandy in full flow. Who even is Meek Mal? 'I never knew how hard it would become, when I started. I was young. At first, it was just fun. There were very few consequences. In fact, it was joyful. I think it's OK to admit that, isn't it?'

People say, 'Yes, of course! We must!'

Wow.

They are absolutely loving it.

Sally is leaning forward, her gaze fixed on me. The Dickensian man is nodding away like he is having some kind of approval seizure. Even Dez – the ultimate addict – is chewing his lip like he is learning something, smiling occasionally at the things I am saying. The church hall suddenly feels smaller, fading away on the periphery of my vision. There is a stillness in the air – a tension that is palpable. I am on a stage, and there is a spotlight directly on me.

Just ride the wave. Don't baulk.

They want it. My audience want it.

I take my metaphorical mic and choose to continue.

Give the people what they want.

'But the longer my relationship with alcohol continued, the deeper its hooks became. And slowly but surely, the effects followed. It was toxic, because I couldn't say no. I needed it for everything. Every decision I made, every emotion I felt. Without it, I had no idea how to live, how to have an opinion of myself. It made me who I was. In its absence I had completely lost my identity.' I pause, taking in the circle, staring at me with their mouths open in concentration.

A raconteur. I love that word.

'But it became such a crutch, something I kept going back to in order to feel safe, or controlled – because I felt so out of control within myself. And there was one time it took me to hospital.' People frown. Upset, perhaps? That works. That's good. They feel my pain. They relate. 'It was very dark. I felt so lost. I had successes in my life by that point – to the outside world I was completely fine. More than fine. But I had this secret. This secret that was eroding me.' I shake my head. 'I chose to look at everything else as the problem.'

I am alive, my brain on fire. Even Janet now looks enthralled. 'There is a metaphor I once read in a book,' I say. I actually wrote it myself in *Shallow Embers*. I wonder if any of them read it? I doubt Leo has. Maybe Sally, or Aphrodite. Oh well, I can't seem to stop myself. 'Let me see if I can get it right.' I pause. 'A bird doesn't consider its next flight. It trusts itself to know it has the power to move forward.'

This nearly cripples them. Their faces contort with the weight of enlightenment.

I check for Leo's reaction. He doesn't look up. He's fiddling with something in his hands. I think it might be his mobile phone.

I continue on, trying to get his attention. I try and see myself through his eyes, and shift my words in an attempt to make them land with him. He's an addict. An addict. I once saw a documentary – I think it was Louis Theroux – about the opioid epidemic in America. Those people were so lost. They had no hope. They slept under bridges. Lost their families. 'I never thought I could get to a point in my life where I would get out of its clutches.'

That's good. The clutch thing is good. 'It is completely insidious. And what was the absolute worst was the monotony of it all. The same thing, day in, day out. The same outcomes, without ever really trying to change a thing. I knew it wasn't what I wanted, but I never did anything about it. Not until I started coming here. I felt like I was drowning. And bad things happened. I was completely under its control. Every day it gave me this pain in my stomach – in my gut. But when I saw the light, when I got sober, it was like a light flickered on, and that's when I knew, deep in my soul, that I needed to be brave. I needed to rise up and take hold of my life. And that, for me, was the moment everything changed.' I look directly at Leo, almost drunk on the adrenaline. 'I think that anyone out there who is struggling should speak up and share. It's really important to share.' I bow my head. 'And I'll end with that.'

No one speaks.

No one utters a word.

But I can tell from their expressions that I nailed it. I completely and utterly mic-dropped. The stage lights come up, and the audience are there, staring – eyes wide. I can't help but feel they are actually fighting the urge to applaud.

I try not to allow the thought in the back of my head that tells me I am crazy and unhinged. Because it wasn't me speaking, was it?

It was Mandy.

Mandy, who knows her way through the world. Who is powerful. Who is clever. Who has something to say.

Mandy, who is seen.

19

Leo

Why is this woman making her life sound like a shit poem?

Jesus Christ, she's laying it on thick.

I glance at the clock. Ten minutes left. I need to fucking *go*.

Come on, just get the fuck *on with—*

'Now it's newcomers' time. Would anyone like to share?' No. No, I do not want to fucking share, Janet. Just bang your little gong, pass the bucket and let's all be on our way. 'Leo, was it?'

Damn. 'Yeah.' Don't tell them to fuck themselves. Say something that they would say. Use the posh voice. Blend in. 'I don't think pressurising people into talking is morally acceptable.' That sounded good.

The room goes still. No. I shouldn't have done that. I really shouldn't.

Hold it in. Bottle the little fucker up. Just get through. Get to the bucket. 'Sorry, I'm just feeling a bit scratchy.'

Everyone nods.

'That's OK, Leo.'

Fuck's sake, *fine*.

I slide my phone into my pocket and lean forward, elbows on my knees, like Dez did, then breathe out loudly a few times, so they can see this is very difficult for me. 'I'm sick of having to have sex to buy a sandwich.' They stare back at me, eyes wide in shock. Right where I want them. 'Sweaty, gross men who just wanna fucking use me.' Mouths start to hang open. I can see their sad little faces. *You can't say that in Muswell Hill!* 'All this happened to me at the hands of people who use me.' I take off my cap, so they can see my bruises. The mess. Sally – the one who looks like she works in a bank – puts her hand to her mouth. 'Ply me with drugs. Take advantage. I can't do this anymore,' I say. 'I just need some help. I've fucked it so many times now. I just think I can't do it. Sobriety. I think I'm the only one who can't do it. I walk down the street and I look at each face that passes me and I think, *I'd rather be you, I'd rather be you, I'd rather be you*.' I'm pointing at them now. I hadn't planned to, but fuck it.

I continue my spiel about being bad and sad and lonely blah blah blah. I don't want to be with these idiots. Time is ticking on – fuck me – I just need to get to the end of this. I try and put a croak in my throat: I can't cry on cue but I can make it look like I'm a sad little vulnerable fucker. It's easy. I bang on about how much I hate myself, how disgusted with myself I am, that if anyone knew the thoughts I had they would want to die too. I end with a bit about how useful these meetings are, how much I need them, just to keep them onside. Then I stop, put my head in my hands and make my body shudder a bit, to say, *This is too much. This is all too much.* They lap it up. I'll end with desperation. 'I need help.'

'It's OK, Leo,' someone whispers. 'Well done for sharing.'

I nod sadly.

Fucking idiots.

'OK,' Janet says in her patronising voice. 'That brings us to the end of the meeting...' And in the blur that follows, all the fucking speaking in unison, the holding hands bollocks, the serenity prayer, there is a ringing in my head. When the bucket comes I manage to grab a tenner without being seen.

Fast fingers.

I make a beeline for the door. Can't be arsed speaking, although I know they'll want to. They like to give me their numbers. Tell me they'll take me for a brew or some lunch to make themselves feel better. Sometimes I'll take the offer if I'm starving, but that's not what I need today.

'Leo?' Fuck off fuck off. 'Leo can I just have a word?'

I turn to see the sunglasses lady stood behind me. She looks momentarily confused. Or scared. But she keeps looking at me.

There's something about her that's off. Making me feel like she can see through me or something. Up close, I can see her hair is a little grey at the roots. Her clothes are clean in a way that annoys me, but I can't deny she smells well nice, like lavender soap. I note her pearl earrings, which I reckon are more expensive than they look. A loose shirt and fitted jeans. And Birkenstocks on her feet, which make me immediately hate her. Dunno why. I nicked a few of them once from a Schuh, made a mint. She's wearing socks in them too. Maybe it's that. This woman's had it easy, I can tell. Seen her type so many times. Not one of the real alcoholics. One of the ones that slept through her alarm a few too many times, and vomited in the bathroom at work. Probably sent here by her life coach.

'Yeah?' I say. I put my dirty hand out to see if she'll shake it.

She does.

Fine. Still hate her.

'I was just thinking about what you were saying – about needing a place to vent. To get it out—'

Oh God, here she goes. 'I don't need a sponsor – I've got one,' I lie.

'No – not that.' She lowers her voice, stepping towards me. 'I'm actually a licenced therapist and I'm using some of my slots to work pro bono. That means for—'

'I know what it means.' These fucking people. I live my life for pro bono, hun.

'Right. Of course. Well, I thought maybe I could give you my number – and if you're interested you could give me a text? We can meet at a café – somewhere safe – I could help you work through what has happened?'

'I'm good, ta.' I turn to leave.

'Or,' she says. 'Or you could swing by my office. I'd be happy to see you as a client. The space is very private and comfortable – it's at my house—'

'I said—' Wait. At her house. At her massive house. 'Sorry. What did you say your name was?'

'Mandy.'

'Right,' I say. Middle-class boring Mandy, desperate to use me to fill the void. That could work. 'Can I think about it?'

'Sure!' she says brightly.

I get my phone out of my pocket to see Mo has texted a rope emoji. Jeez. 'Go on then, what's your number?'

She gives it to me, and I smile. 'Thanks. That's dead kind.'

'Not to worry, Leo. It sounds like you've been through a lot. I'd love to help you process things if you'd like to.'

These people. Rich and stupid. 'That'd be great,' I say.

'Well, I look forward to hearing from you.' She nods, then leaves.

Still in her stupid sunglasses.

I follow behind her but wait in the car park until everyone has left.

Then I take my tenner and go to Mo.

He's weird this time, and it hurts. He wasn't kidding when he sent the rope emoji. I have to close my eyes. Just think of the gak I'll get with the money, and wait.

And when it's over, I go to the hardware store – something I need – then to the bridge, and score.

I get so much into me that I can't think straight.

And I arrive.

Here.

Home.

My own little slice of heaven.

20

Mallory

> 'I'm sick of having to have sex to buy a sandwich,' he says. The church hall falls silent.
> He stands to go.
> 'Please stay,' a woman asks him gently. 'You belong here.'
> He looks at her, his eyes filling with an anger so deep, so guttural, that when he lets out his scream, even the characters in the pictures crowding the walls seem to recoil – his pain too much for the room to take. It ricochets around the circle, piercing each person with its desperation.
> And he leaves, slamming the door, back into the abyss.

I close the draft and open my emails.

Stanley Maier.

Stanley was my editor for *Shallow Embers*. He now works in adult fiction as editor-in-chief. He was in his fifties when I knew him, and he always told me that if something came to mind, I should get in touch.

I check the time. Ronan texted me to say he would be at the pub a little longer than he'd thought, and that I should order a takeaway for us.

I open a fresh email.

Hi Stan,

I know it's been a while, I hope this finds you well.

No. Delete.

Hi Stan,

I have an idea for a new book.

Yes. To the point.

    After some time of being uninspired, I wasn't sure I would ever write again. I have, however, recently found myself in a position where I'm finally feeling creative. I am aware this email is unsolicited – but I'm currently unrepresented by an agency and wanted to contact you directly. I hope you don't mind me getting in touch. I still had your email on file.
    I've been looking into the darker corners of society and have come across a world that I feel has the potential to really capture people's attention and open up their eyes.
    I have attached the first fifty pages. I would love it if you could find the time to read this blind – without any prefacing – and give me your opinion. I will continue writing, as the narrative is slowly unveiling itself to me.
    Thank you.

I look forward to hearing from you,

Mal Maddox

    I press send, wait to hear the confirmation *whoosh* noise, then close the laptop and slide it back into the dresser drawer. I go upstairs, into the bedroom, and pick up a book. I lie down, pretending to read, until I hear the door go.
    'Hi, honey!' Ronan calls from the hallway.
    'I'm upstairs!' I shout back.
    'The Deliveroo guy was outside! I've got the food!'
    'Oh, perfect!'
    I lift myself up from the bed and pull on my pyjamas. I go

downstairs to see Ronan stood at the sink, in his cords and oversized shirt, with his messy hair.

'Hi, baby,' he says. 'How was your day?'

'It was great,' I say, advancing towards him with my arms outstretched. 'I stayed in and read. I feel so much better.'

'You didn't go to Joanie's?' His brow furrows. Shit. 'The hamper was gone from the car.'

'I threw it out,' I say casually. 'It was getting stale. And I just wanted to be by myself today.'

His eyes linger. Then he gently places his hand on my shoulder, the pressure of his fingers making me feel momentarily safe. 'That's great. I'm so pleased to hear it.'

I smile, a real one. 'Thanks for our talk earlier. It meant a lot to me.'

'I'm glad. It did to me too.'

And tonight, we do what we usually do. We sit together on the couch and watch the first few episodes of a subtitled Scandinavian thriller, our legs pressed together on the couch. Every now and then, he will turn to me, and mouth *I love you*, and I will reciprocate. I am not able to focus on the screen, even though I stare straight at it. Instead, I think about us. I think about the time we met, the Airbnbs in the Cotswolds, the music we used to listen to, the joy I felt in those early months, until I didn't. Until it changed. I think about the way in which my mother told me he was the best thing to happen to me, that I was lucky, that he was out of my league.

'Mal?' he says, as the credits of the second episode roll.

'Mmhmm?'

He takes the control and flicks the button so the TV goes black, then turns to me. 'So what do you think?'

'I think it was quite predictable—'

'No,' he says, smiling. 'What do you think about the baby.'

The baby.

To him, it already exists.

His eyes glow expectantly, as I fight the thump I feel deep in my stomach. Right where the baby will be.

'I think yes,' I lie.

'Yes?'

'Yes.'

'Mal,' he says, shuffling towards me, taking my hands in his. 'Mal, you are going to be a wonderful mother. We are going to be a wonderful family. You are so special. You were made for this.'

'You think?'

'Of course. The writing, the counselling – it's all led its way to *this*. You were made to be a mum, to be here, to look after our child.'

It's hard to lie with three words. But I am getting used to it. 'You are sweet.'

We go upstairs.

Afterwards, he places a hand on my stomach, until he falls asleep.

I gently move his arm, pick up my laptop and tiptoe into the bathroom. Sitting on the closed toilet seat, I open up my computer and see the message waiting for me. Stanley Maier.

Mal,

Hi. It's been a while. When I saw your name come into my inbox, I was glad. It fell on an usually quiet Saturday evening, so I was grateful to take a look. I always wondered where you had got to. A copy of *Shallow Embers* still sits proudly on my bookshelf.

I read what you sent. It's good. Very. On trend with what is selling. Digging into the way poverty affects addiction isn't new, but what is refreshing is this look into the underbelly of a dark world for gay men – the 'chemsex' world – a place that clearly holds a lot of trauma. I think it's something people would be interested in reading about – framed as a 'modern boy succeeds against all the odds' type of story. And championing diversity is really important for us here.

Your style is good, and I enjoy the characters. They aren't likable, but that's on trend these days. The plot needs more danger. Can you do that? Raise the stakes, put Liam in real peril. And mine his inner world, his emotional life. He cannot be two-dimensional. It is currently feeling a little that way. If you can get to the core of him, Mal, then we can talk properly.

A couple of other things to check in with before you proceed – namely authenticity. Addiction is a tough nut to crack, particularly by someone who perhaps themselves has little experience. And, of course, writing a 22-year-old homosexual is in itself something to be careful with. I know you have the ability to write whatever your imagination lends itself to – it is just important we have a gauge on where the impetus to write this particular character comes from. Perhaps you have been inspired by a cousin, a friend? All worth considering.

If you could let me know, and send me more of the manuscript by the end of the month, then we can begin our work together in earnest. Feels like this could be a good one to pitch at Frankfurt Book Fair.

In the meantime, if you'd like to send chapters as you go, I'd be happy to read and offer feedback.

Well done.

Best,

Stan

He *likes* it.

Stanley Maier likes my book.

Could this… work? Is my ticket out of here in these pages? In Liam's story?

End of the month. Three weeks. *Three weeks.*

I quickly type my reply.

Dear Stan,

A joy to hear from you, after all this time. And so quickly! I'm so glad you're taken with the concept – I thought you might find it interesting.

When it comes to the authenticity – yes. I have myself been struggling with addiction since the publication of *Shallow Embers*, hence my writing hiatus. However, with the help of twelve-step recovery and meetings, I am now gladly sober.

As you might remember my brother – Nick – died when I was twenty. The reasons behind why he took his own life were always shrouded in confusion and pain, but I have always known his sexuality, and my parents' inability to accept it, took its toll.

I can of course put Liam in more peril. The stakes in this book are very important. I want the reader to understand just how hard reality is for him. He deserves to be seen.

Leave it with me.

More soon,

Mal

21

Leo

Under the canal bridge, there is a lot of piss.

I've found a spot between two puddles. My brain has woken up a bit now. There are others here, there always are. I don't talk to them. I spin the flick knife I got from the hardware shop in my hands, feeling the blade with my finger. Nice and sharp.

I open my phone and get up her number. Not much battery left. I'll charge it in Maccy's tomorrow.

I know it was her. At the AA meeting.

Her from the car. I saw it before they battered me. Parked up behind me on Priory Road.

And then I saw her get into it when she left the church.

I'd love a Volvo XC40, so I don't forget them. Her with the sunglasses.

Rich, and stupid.

Maybe she feels bad about leaving me on the street last night. Not taking me to the hospital. The way her eyes lit up today, when she heard me speak. She loved it. The poverty of it all. Bet her house is massive. The kind of person that has jewellery she doesn't wear. That car, too.

> Hey
> Thanks for giving me your number today
> AA is amazing like that
> I'd love some help if you're offering. Therapy sounds perfect
> Happy to meet at your house, not really got anywhere to go

I pause, then add:

Sleeping under a bridge tonight

And send.

I quickly take a picture of my sleeping bag. Get an angle that makes it look really pathetic and thin.

In this ☹

Then, just like I thought.

>Oh, Leo, that's awful
>I'm so sorry you're going through this
>Yes. I can do that
>When works for you?

Got any time this week?

>This week is perfect
>I look forward to hearing more about you

This woman is crazy.
But I guess many people would say that of me.
Maybe that man in the meeting was right. Maybe we are all the same.

Part 2

Two weeks later

22

Mallory

I am meeting him in exactly four minutes.

It is 14:26 and The Cuckoo Café in Muswell Hill is nearly empty. I chose it carefully, having spent the past three days weighing up my options from the plethora of coffee shops in North London and settling on this particular one for a number of important reasons. Firstly, I knew it would be quiet because it is tucked away, down an alleyway behind a gift shop that sells British memorabilia like Union Jack cushions and nodding dogs. Secondly, I don't know *too* many people in Muswell Hill – certainly not anyone who comes in here (it has a hygiene rating of four out of five) – so I should stay unnoticed. The time I asked him to meet me is also important: 14:30. Too early for the parents with their children on the way home from the (very expensive) primary schools in the area, and just enough time for the lunch rush to have passed. The café website clearly stated that they don't have colouring books for kids, or a play area, which is perfect. I should be safe from the other women my age who I went to school with and now have children to use those things. Lastly, The Cuckoo Café does not have an intimidating atmosphere. Once you're through the giftshop, it opens up into a large café with lots of tables and open spaces, and from what I know of Leo, having followed him for the last two weeks, I know he likes open spaces.

He seems to like being outside. And there are lots of pot plants in here. Hanging baskets.

It would be good for him to feel safe. That would be helpful.

I am sweating.

I look up to see a waitress wiping crumbs with blue roll off my little wooden table straight onto the floor, avoiding my notebook (it has a paisley pattern) that I have placed neatly in the corner.

'Hi!' I say. 'Could I get two menus please?'

She looks about sixteen and appears as if she would rather eat her own hand than give me eye contact, let alone a menu. Her glazed expression must either be from too much vaping (I can see the coloured plastic poking out of her apron's front pocket) or from the avocado-and-boiled-eggs trance she's been put into from scraping plates. Either way, I can't blame her. Her name badge says she's called Chloe, right under the word Cuckoo.

Cuckoo Chloe.

She vacuously points up to the blackboard behind her head. 'It's all up there,' she says with the faintest edge of *I hate you, you're ruining my life*. 'Order at the till.'

'Thanks!' I return, brightly. Without looking at me, nor with any shame, Cuckoo Chloe takes her vape from her pocket and disappears into the disabled bathroom.

I keep glancing at the digits of the clock on my phone. Checking the door. Finding myself cursing under my breath at a mother who enters with a baby in what I know is an incredibly expensive body-wrap-sling-accessory thing, because Ronan once googled the exact same one and showed me. 'You'd suit that colour,' he said.

It was grey.

Two minutes. Leo should be here in two minutes.

I have a few set questions I'd like to ask him. To help, of course. I want him to be OK, and I'm not sure he has been.

I have brought worksheets. I saved them from one of my therapy seminars. They are about impulse control and breaking negative thought patterns. I think it's a good place to start with him.

It's been hard logistically, following him. *Following* might be a bit extreme, actually. More *observing* him. That might be a better way of putting it. Leo is hard to keep up with. And because Ronan is so particular, I worry he can sense exactly when I've been out of the house, just by the way the air feels inside it.

There are many reasons Ronan cannot know, but for now, let's just say: I really don't want to be sectioned again.

He instigated the last one.

I remember him picking up his phone in the kitchen, thinking he was calling his mother by the way he was speaking, only to find out it was *my* mother. Asking her to come and watch me. *Watch me.* And of course she did it. She would do anything he asked her to. She's had a crush on him since the day they met. And when she came, with her herbal teas and lavender pillow mist, I asked her to leave. I dropped a glass in the kitchen, and suddenly the police were there. In my house. Calling me *love*.

Come with us, love.

It'll be safe where we're taking you. Love.

And Ronan and my mother watched. Both of them. Standing by the sink.

I can't have it happen a second time. That time was enough. It was hell. It was worse than death. It was long, drawn-out torture without the opportunity of death to end it all. It just went on and on. White walls and injections.

It wasn't my fault. I know people who get sectioned often say this – I am well aware – but I was an exception. A section exception. I just fell victim to a crappy system and people who apparently cared too much.

So I've had to be stealthy today and exhibit some behaviours that are possibly secretive in nature, and that I do not feel entirely proud of. One being that I bought a pair of leather gloves. I don't know if it's because I need them (no fingerprints) or if it's because I like them and when I put them on, I feel like the exquisite (murderer) Villanelle from *Killing Eve*. I haven't figured it out yet, and I'm not entirely sure I need to.

I look at the cash in my hand.

To pay for this. Lunch with Leo.

Ronan doesn't know about it. The cash. It comes from one particular therapy client of mine: Elaine. Elaine is eighty-three and doesn't like online banking. Ronan thinks I charge her sixty pounds an hour, but I don't. I charge her eighty. The extra twenty gets put in my tampon box in the bathroom cabinet, and the other sixty goes to him, which he puts into our joint Monzo.

Cash is untraceable, like Villanelle.

Also, Ronan does the accounts, and has done since I was in hospital. '*It's fair, and right. In case you become manic again, and spend all our savings.*'

I didn't spend all our savings.

Fine, yes, I did put a deposit down on a boat. But I didn't mean to. Well, I did, but I didn't want to *ride it away into the sunset*, or *drown myself*, as people seemed to think. I just loved the look of it. Wooden, with a big white sail. It was called the Blue Heather. Yes, its actual cost was a quarter of a million pounds, but it was more an *idea* that I was investing in. A fantasy.

It was moored in Wales, on the Gower Peninsula, near where we went for our honeymoon. Ronan and I had spent days on the pebble beaches, hiding in the shade of the cliffs. I remember it well, and think about it often. We had only known each other for six months by that point, and many people had told me to take it slow, to enjoy it as it was. But I knew he was different. Ronan set my world alight.

My mother adored him. She often asked me: '*How have you bagged this one? Hold onto him, Mallory.*'

I met Ronan when I was working as a runner for the BBC, my English degree being put to good use reading coffee orders off napkins while doing relentless trips to Starbucks. It was cripplingly dull, but it allowed me the freedom to write the first draft of *Shallow Embers*. I was drinking too much and lost, the usual early to mid-twenties pain, but I felt from within the chaos that at least I could control my book. I had this ability to lose myself in it that propelled me. I was certainly lonely, I struggled to make relationships that ever lasted longer than a few pints in the pub, and outside of the world I was creating, I felt dull. But as soon as I opened my shitty little laptop and began to write, the world fell away.

On the night of a press party, he was suddenly there, at the bar, looking at me. He was so charismatic, and interesting, and interest*ed*, in me, in what I had to say. I remember his shirt, the way it was untucked slightly at his hip, and how it was a kind of linen the other men wouldn't wear in that office. It looked chosen and thought out, but also effortless. He was stylish, but what really caught my attention was the way he held himself. Totally assured, but not cocky. Just comfortable. At ease.

He told me about his love of books and of climbing, his hatred of the political system, the patriarchy and snobbery. He had this way of *adding* things. Everything I said, he was able to *add* to it. It felt like I was constantly learning. I told him sheepishly I had written a book – I called it a *manuscript* to sound less basic (everyone had written something who worked at the BBC), and I can still remember the way his eyes lit up. He wanted to hear the whole synopsis, the inspiration for each character, the style, the setting, how long it took, how long it was. He seemed genuinely blown away, and it made me feel incredible. We didn't move from the bar stools until the lights came up and the cleaners asked us to lift our feet so they could sweep the floor.

He didn't ask me back to his, but he kissed me by the bus stop. And after the kiss, we both knew I would be going with him. His apartment was mature, the wooden floorboards covered in stacks of novels and memoirs and scripts that didn't appear to be intentionally placed there for aesthetic reasons, but that were simply the product of someone who had piled them up, after having actually read them in a fit of creativity. There were hanging plants and exposed brick walls. It was like a dream.

The sex was otherworldly. I know how lame, clichéd and gross that sounds, but it's the truth. My whole body left the planet, left the reality I had lived for so long: a horrific mix of unrelenting anxiety and utter boredom. At that point in my life, I was only used to blurry drunken fumbles, or sober awkward robotic thrusting. This was not that. With Ronan, it was almost spiritual. I felt his presence, his care, his light. I know, I *know* how that sounds. But everything lit up. He just kept *adding*.

And *I* lit up.

He plugged me in, entirely. And I understood that up until that point, I had been nothing but a dimming corner lamp. Now I was a glaring, undeniable LED strip light.

Naked and ablaze.
He whispered to me as he kissed me.
He said it was as if he had known me for years.
That he had never felt this way with anyone else.
So completely connected to someone.

As he spoke, the parts of me I hated seemed to dissipate. It was better than alcohol, or a line of coke off the back of a toilet seat. It was pure medicine. My fears went. Gone. And I felt whole. He did that.

And for me, that was insanity.

How could my fears just be lifted from me like that?

But it happened.

My synapses were on overdrive. Flooded by so many endorphins that I swear I saw things glimmering. My hairbrush in the morning. The fabric of bus seats on the way to work. Even fucking pigeons.

It all glowed.

And he was so generous. But not in the typical way, nothing showy – buying rounds for the whole room for everyone to see – rather in a way that felt completely authentic. There were things that I discovered. Like when we moved in together, I found a letter from Oxford Brooks University. Ronan was paying his younger brother's tuition fees. Jonah had been through a lot in his life, and Ronan wanted to help. He did not weaponise his brother's pain to make me love him, and that made me love him even more.

There was something in the way he spoke to others, too. He was so confident and assured and charming. His accent allowed him to say even the most mundane thing and make it sound engaging. But it wasn't just the Irish lilt. He was clever, but not alienating. He was inclusive, but not grandstanding. He spoke just enough, but let others speak too. People clung to his every word. I admit, I do remember at times I would feel twinges of jealousy in the pit of my stomach because of the way others would just stare at him, eyes wide, laughing – always *laughing* – but I soon learnt that this was my own insecurity. He had chosen me, and never done anything to make me feel scared or that he didn't love me.

A year after our marriage, two years after *Shallow Embers*' publication and not too long after the hospital, something shifted. Or maybe it was always the same, I'm still unsure. The writer's block was barricading me, and so we explored other career options. The book was still selling, but not in the way it once had. That money had gone to the deposit on our Crouch End house.

I began my online counselling course. Ronan was very encouraging, because of my lived experience. '*That's what will make you so empathetic, Mal.*' He said I lit up when I was reading the textbooks in preparation to begin. He said I looked *happy, content*, the Mal he always knew. That it was because I had purpose. Not Meek Mal, Marvellous Mal. '*You're back. You're here again.*'

But I wasn't.

I couldn't ignore a depth of emptiness that was surfacing, and looking back I still don't know if that's when it began, or if it had always been there. I had an urge within me to return to how things were. For him, and me, to return to how we were, at the Gower Peninsula. When we would buy picnic food from the Co-op and walk along the cliff edge, talking and talking and adding and adding. It was so beautiful there. The clouds looked as if someone had poured a pint of milk into the sky – the way their edges blended and swirled with the colours, blues and pinks and deep purples.

And the sea. *The sea.* It went on and on and on. When the wind stilled, the waves would calm, and the colours would ripple across its surface, and we would dive beneath them. That rush, that cold rush of adrenaline and clarity that came from the first dunk was how the whole relationship felt. Free. Vibrant. Alive. And he would tell me, '*I will always love you, Mal. There is no way that, while I exist, that will ever change. It can't.*' I remember it as a very specific and all-consuming warmth. As Possibility.

I just wanted it back. Because I changed.

Or we both did.

Or neither of us did.

I thought he might like the boat idea.

He didn't.

So, as a consequence, I now hoard cash in a tampon box. Other than the gloves, I have only used it for petrol, and now for this. For lunch with Leo.

I found Leo last Monday. He was indeed living under a bridge. He didn't reply to my messages after the first night, so I was concerned for him. When Ronan texted me to say he would be late back from work because of a deadline, I drove around all the bridges over Regent's Canal – the only canal in the area. And there Leo was, under one in Camden. It was raining and I had to hide – just a bit, and not in a creepy way – my bucket hat pulled down low. This gratefully did not look out of place in an area like that.

I followed him. Sorry, *observed* him. On foot.

He went to see a man, and stopped off to buy a bag of Haribo. A man called Mo.

It wasn't hard for me to find out about Mo, thanks to Grindr. One thing I have come to understand over the past fortnight is how useful that app is for obtaining things, namely information. I followed Leo that night to a flat near the bridge, and when he went inside, I opened the app. It told me that both Leo and a man named Mo were fifty feet away. I pinned both of their profiles. They were fifty feet away for half an hour, and then Leo left the building. He looked a little different. Shaken. I couldn't observe him further because I needed to get home, but I knew I would message Mo.

And I did.

I take a look at the clock on my phone again. 14:35. I catch Cuckoo Chloe half-heartedly sweeping under a table, the scrambled egg congealing in the bristles of her brush. She doesn't care, just smearing it across the floor.

Will Leo come?

He said he would be here. He said he needed help, that he was desperate. He said he wants a sponsor. I had to quickly google that before I replied. I took myself through the twelve steps of Alcoholics Anonymous in about thirty minutes – just in case. The twelve steps are not something I *loved* (there's a lot of apologising), but I now know enough to help him through it, if he wants, which is what a sponsor does.

Finding Mo – or should I say Mark (as he has become in *Slay*) – was a stroke of luck. He is now growing to be a fairly important character in Liam's story. A vehicle for the danger, the *peril* that Stanley asked for. He is the opposition – the *baddie* in layman's terms – and he will give Liam the opportunity for character development and growth. I am still figuring out Mark's intentions and motives, but I am gaining a clearer picture of how he will present.

I get up the Grindr app and look at my message stream with Mo. It dates from last week, after I was hiding (observing) outside his flat. The blue and yellow messaging bubbles are now less terrifying to me, more a familiar form of useful research.

Hi sxy

> Oh hey. Not seen you on here before

I'm new to the area

> Oh yeah? Niceeeeee
> Welcome

You're hot!
🍆🍆🍆

> Thanks – you too. What I can see of you 🍆
> Any face pics?

;) maybe, if you play your cards right

> Hard to get. I like it

What are you into?

> Ha!

That's funny?

>   How new are you?

I'm new to the area, but not to this

>   I see
>   How old are you?

33

>   Meh. I prefer early twenties
>   Twinks

Oh

>   Not that you look old
>   You look good
>   Well your body does

Thanks! Why twinks

>   They're more enthusiastic

Ha!

>   They love it

Love what tho? ;)

>   Depends on what I want

What do you want?

>   Many things

Lol

>   You still there?

    Yes sorry phone died

                                    U a top? Dom top?

    Yes I am

                                                 Nice
                    You can come play if you want
                            Domination nation!
                  But I'd need to see your face first

    What kind of things do you get them to do?

Mo stopped replying at that point.
'Mandy?'
I look up from my phone, back into the café.
It's him. Liam. *Leo.*
The first thing I notice is the trembling. His whole body vibrating so intensely that I feel it move immediately into the pit of my own stomach. Eyes bloodshot. Skin grey. He has his hood up over his head, the cuts that Brick left now less swollen and red, but still there, infection lingering in their edges.

'Leo,' I say. 'Are you OK? Has something happened?' He doesn't answer. He just stands opposite me, jittery, scratchy, panting. Tears in his eyes. I realise I am now stood up. 'Can I get you some water?'

He nods, wiping his nose with the back of his hand. 'Yeah, go on.' As he sits in the seat opposite me, I notice the smell. I do all I can not to gag. His clothes look damp. *Why?* 'Jesus,' I whisper. 'Do you need food?' He doesn't answer. 'Wait here, I'll get you something.'

I make my way to the counter and can't help but scan the occupied tables as I do. Four elderly women playing cards. A man on his own with scruffy hair and a half-eaten sandwich, typing frantically on his laptop. Two teenagers in school uniform – probably skiving – laughing and flicking baked beans at each other. A lady with an anorak and four dogs at her feet, with a perpetually apologetic expression.

'You ready then?' Chloe says, still seemingly annoyed by my mere presence.

'Yes. Yeah. Could I get a...' Damn it, I didn't ask him what he wants. I turn back to the table to see him now sat, holding his head in his hands. Chloe glances over too and raises her eyebrows. 'He's OK,' I say. Then, to avoid any confusion, 'I'm his therapist.'

Chloe couldn't care less. 'Right. So what do you want?'

'Two glasses of tap water, a hot chocolate, an Americano for me and...' I glance at the black board above her head. What would he eat? Anything? Nothing? He looks like he wants to vomit. 'A baked potato with cheese.'

'Salad?'

'Excuse me?'

'*Do you want salad with the potato*,' Chloe says slowly like I'm a dog, or like I'm thick.

He probably should. His face is the colour of the floor. 'Yes,' I say. 'Salad would be good.'

She punches something onto an iPad. 'Nineteen pounds eighty please.'

I hold out the twenty-pound note leftover from Elaine's therapy session. She looks at it like it's an ancient relic, then back to me. 'You not got card or Apple Pay?'

'Oh, sorry, just this,' I say, as cheerfully as possible. 'Keep the change, though!'

I watch her struggle to open the till – something she clearly has never used – take out a twenty-pence piece and sarcastically make an *oh wow* face at it, then put in the pocket of her apron with her vape. 'Very generous.'

I don't have time for Cuckoo Chloe. She hands me two glasses of lukewarm tap water, no ice, and I take them back to the table, sit in front of Leo and hand him one. 'Here,' I say.

'Cheers,' he replies, and I watch him gulp it in one. His fingers are thick with dirt. There are what appear to be dark-green stains all over his damp clothes, and his fringe is stuck down to his head – I presume not a fashion choice. He keeps shifting in his seat agitatedly, glancing at the door, pulling his hood down further, trying to make himself smaller. And the smell...

'You're wet...' I say.

'Canal,' he says.

'Sorry?'

He looks me dead in the eye. 'I got thrown in the fucking canal, OK? Someone tried to drown me.'

23

Leo

I'm half telling the truth.

I was in the canal, but no one tried to drown me. I was trying to pick up a half-smoked fag butt from the floor, tripped over one of those boat tie things, a piece of concrete just sticking up from the fucking floor – cunty little things, those – and landed face first in the water. That's the stink she's trying to pretend she can't smell. The water. I swear people shit in it.

I'm a proper good swimmer, though, me.

In fact, when I was a kid, I went to a secondary school, and I shit you not, it had a pool. It was dead posh for a state. I won a swimming award. Fastest in the year at front crawl. Been fast since I was little. Always quick. That's what my nan said. And she was made up. Chuffed as hell. She told all her mates. Put the little silver plastic cup in her living room on her mantelpiece, then put her change in it, and every week gave it to me for sweets.

It was how I saved for my first ever baggie of weed.

Loved my nan.

'Do you want to talk about it?' Mandy says.

'Not really.'

'We could go to the police?' she says. She sounds and looks completely terrified at her own idea, but knows it's probably the right thing to say. 'If someone tried to *drown* you, Leo…'

'Will you be my sponsor?'

'Your sponsor?'

'Yeah, I need to get sober.' I need to get in your house.

'Slow down, Leo, we can get to that. As you know, I'm a therapist. And I'm concerned for your welfare. Take a few deep breaths and try and tell me what happened.'

Fucking mental, these people. Like a few deep breaths will solve it all. She sounds like one of those meditation apps they tried to get me onto in rehab. Next thing she'll be telling me to do yoga. She probably does it with all her mates, downward dogging every morning with their chai fucking lattes.

I could tell her a thing or two about dogging.

I look behind me, left and right. I need her to think I'm scared. Vulnerable. I make my voice all soft and quiet. She actually looks like she's about to cry – like she's the one who was nearly drowned in a canal. 'I don't know if I wanna talk about it here.'

I want to talk about it in your house. Where your jewellery is.

'OK...' she says. 'OK, maybe we just sit in silence and breathe for a moment.'

Fuck my life.

She seems like she really wants me to breathe for a moment. Fine.

She has her eyes closed. I think she's humming. This is weird. This is very fucking weird but I guess I've done weirder things to get the moolah.

It's going on for fucking ages.

'Your hot chocolate.'

Thank God.

I look up to see a girl with a name badge that says CHLOE, looking a bit confused – probably from all the breathing happening – then passing me a mug with a mound of whipped cream and marshmallows on top. 'Cheers, love,' I say. 'That looks bloody beautiful.' She smiles. I smile back. She keeps smiling. She's got a gap in her teeth. 'Could be a model, you,' I say. 'Billie Eilish vibes.'

She goes red. 'I love her,' she whispers.

Course she does.

'Is that mine?' Mandy says, all shitty, pointing to the coffee in Chloe's other hand. Chloe places it down without looking at Mandy.

'Your potato will be ready soon,' Chloe tells me. 'Do you want extra cheese?'

'I don't have any money—'

'Don't worry, I'll sort it for you.'

'Well, that's very kind, thank you, Chloe.'

'Don't mention it.'

Chloe turns and practically skips back to the counter. Mandy is staring at me.

'What?'

'Nothing.'

If I can't get into her house, her car would be good. Her car keys must be in her little backpack. She's got weird leather gloves on. And a bucket hat. Come to think of it, she looks a bit fucking odd. Not to judge. Just a bit charity-shop. But I think rich people do that. Try to look not-rich.

Her car would get me a good whack. But her house... I could sell the fuck out of it. Get the fuck out of here. Leave. Hide away in some rural British town, surrounded by fields where no one knows me. Live in some nice hotel for a bit. Get strung out in a spa hotel, work out my next move in a sauna, wearing one of those robes and those fluffy slippers.

I lean towards Mandy and whisper, 'I need help. And I'll tell you what happened. But it's not easy to say.'

She places her coffee down, frowning. 'No, of course. I can imagine. Take your time. You don't have to say anything you don't want to. One moment.' She leans down and starts rummaging through her bag. I scan for keys. Can't see them. Then she comes back up with a pen and reaches for her notebook.

'What's that?'

'I'm going to take notes. Is that OK?'

'Notes?'

'I'm a therapist. I always take notes.'

Eugh.

I guess rich people need to feel useful somehow. I inhale slowly, like this is going to be tough. 'OK. Fine.'

'Take your time, Leo.'

I nod. 'I was trying to dodge this man cos I nabbed his pipe.'

She starts scribbling. 'His pipe?'
'Yes.'
'What kind of pipe?'
'His meth pipe.'
She stops scribbling. 'Oh. Oh, I see.' She stares at me.

'I was gonna return it, I swear – and I thought he was fucking sleeping, but he's one of those that never sleeps, just stays in a state of half-dead. You know the type?'

'I mean... Sure. Yes.'

'But he moved faster than I thought he would, and then he got his fucking blade out.'

'Blade?'

'Yeah,' I whisper. She's still not scribbling. 'Was like one of those kitchen ones. You know. To cut onions and shit. Short, but dead sharp. Had it hidden in his sock.' Her lips part a bit. 'I tried to reason with him, but his eyes went black. The meth can make that happen you know. You must know this, right? Being a therapist an all?'

'Um... Yes. I do. I do. Please, go on.'

'Well, he then called out – and I realised he was shouting to his mates. They live there too – you know. Under the bridge. They make these little gangs you see. I don't join them, I'm more of a lone ranger. Anyway they kind of just appeared out of nowhere – from their sleeping bags lining the walls – and started to surround me. I felt sick – didn't know what to do...' I make my voice go really, really quiet. 'Dunno, Mandy – must be some kind of a trauma response from childhood. Fight, flight or freeze, innit. I tried to run away, but I froze. I wish I hadn't. I fucking wish I hadn't. Cos next thing I know, the man lunged at me with the knife. It went right past me – here.' I point to a rip in the side of my hoodie where I snagged it trying to hurdle a metal fence once. 'See how close that is?'

'Jesus,' she whispers. 'Very close.'

'The force of his body slamming into mine made me fall into the water. And I can't...' I put my head in my hands. 'Sorry, this sounds so pathetic. But I can't...'

'It's OK, Leo.'

'I just feel so fucking stupid.'

'You can't swim?'

Bingo. 'No.'

I suddenly feel tears in my eyes. It must be the comedown. *Let them fall!*

'Oh, God, Leo. Don't cry. I'm so sorry.' I feel her place her weird, gloved hand on my forearm, right on my stinky shit-water sleeve. Her jumper pulls back a bit, revealing a spenny-looking bracelet. Tiffany's. I know Tiffany's. It's got little pendant things hanging off it. Her husband is rich, then. Maybe he has a city job. A banker. Do they have kids? Doesn't seem so. Maybe they lost one. She's clearly needing something or she wouldn't be here. 'How did you get out?'

'I didn't. He followed me in.'

'What?'

'I was trying to get up to the top to breathe and then his body was just next to me. And his hand. His hand went on the top of my head and started holding me under water for ages. Thought I was a fucking gonner. And he was laughing. And all those fucking mates of his were laughing. Saying no one would notice if I was gone.'

'*Oh my God—*'

'It was like he was enjoying it. Kept letting me come back up for air, saying, *You're dead, pussy. You're gonna fucking die under this bridge…*'

Her mouth is now fully open. 'How did you get away?'

'Kicked him in the nuts.'

'Right – yes – that was a great – a great idea…'

'Then managed to take hold of a rope that was lining the wall of the canal, dragged myself along it. Climbed out when I couldn't see them anymore. Must have been dragging myself for about an hour—'

'Jesus, Leo – that's awful. They didn't follow you?'

'Dunno…' I look at the door. 'I mean, they might've.'

She turns to it herself, her eyes widening. 'Are you sure we shouldn't…'

'The police won't do anything. They never fucking do when

it's people like me. They don't wanna get involved. They'll say I'm lying. That there's no proof.'

'No. No. You're right.' I hear her relief. 'So where will you stay now?'

In your spare room, Mandy? 'Dunno, I haven't thought it through. I'll find somewhere.'

'What about a shelter? Aren't there any—'

'Yeah. Yeah. I'll find one.' I pause. 'Just need some fucking money.'

'Are you on benefits?'

'No address.'

'Can you use your previous hostel?'

'They won't let me.'

'Right.'

'I want to get sober. I have to. I nearly died.'

'Yes.'

'I need all the help I can get.'

She leans back, taking all this in. All this stinky, fuck-head, addict mess. Her eyes start darting from side to side, then she picks up her pen and starts scribbling away. I try to read it. Can't make out her handwriting, but I swear I see the word *pussy*. She scratches the side of her head with the back of her pen.

'So, will you be my sponsor?'

She looks up. 'Hmm?'

'You've done the twelve steps, haven't you?'

'Of course. Yes. But…'

'But what then?'

'They say it's best for men to sponsor men, and women to sponsor women.'

They do say that. 'Not if you're gay.'

'Sorry?'

'That rule is there to stop you fucking your sponsor.'

'Oh. Right.' She goes red. Course she's a prude. 'That makes sense.'

'And I don't want to fuck you.'

'Right, no.'

'Definitely not.'

'That's good to know. Thank you, Leo.'

'And I'm assuming you don't want to fuck me?' She pulls a face. Can't hide her shock. Maybe she does though. I point to her wedding ring. 'Happily married?'

She looks down at it. 'Oh! Yes.'

'So... Be of service? Help the newcomer? Go to any lengths? It'll only help you too. They say that.'

'Yes. They do.' She nods. Starts twisting the ring with her fingers. 'I'll need to think about it.'

'Ask God?' I say.

'God?'

'Your Higher Power?'

'*Right*. Yes.' She looks a bit panicked.

'What's your Higher Power?' I say.

'Um... The sea.'

'The sea. Cos it's big?'

'Right. Yes. And it's...' She pauses. 'Enough about me, Leo.'

'You said you'd help me.'

'I feel I'm better suited to help you as a therapist.'

'I can't pay.'

'I said you didn't have to.'

'What are we gonna talk about? If we're not doing the twelve steps?'

She chews her lip for a moment. Then she goes back into her bag and pulls out another piece of paper with printed stuff all over it.

'What's that?'

'A worksheet.'

'A what?'

'A worksheet.'

'I've just nearly been murdered, mate, I dunno if a worksheet is gonna cut it.'

'No?'

'I'm not six.'

'It's helpful.'

'How?'

'It can help you figure out how you got to this point. If you want to get out of this, we need to look at why you got into it. The root cause.'

'Sounds like something you cook with.'

She looks flustered. 'Fine. I don't even have to be your therapist, just someone offering you some support. But if you don't want it – stay like this.' She stands, suddenly different.

Careful.

Pushed it too far.

Stop pushing it.

'Wait. Wait, please, Mandy. I'm messing. Let's do your fucking worksheet. Please, sit back down. I wanna do it. I want your help. Really. And I'm grateful.' She eyes me up and down. 'Your gloves are nice,' I say.

She softens. 'Thank you.'

'So if you're not my sponsor or my therapist, what are you?'

She shrugs. 'Best mate?'

'Funny.'

'Fag hag?'

Her mouth drops open. 'Can you say that?'

'Probably not. I like it though.'

A small smile flickers on her lips. She clearly likes it too. 'Slay queen,' she says.

'Fucking hell,' I say. 'No. Abso-fucking-lutely not.'

'Sorry, is it not OK to say that?'

'Sure, if you're seventeen, or a drag queen, which I assume you are neither?'

I mean, what do I know.

She could be.

She could be anything.

Because she's not Mandy.

Her name is Mallory Maddox, and she's an author.

Interesting, that. Innit?

24

Mallory

Fag Hag.

I'm not complaining. If that's what he wants to call me, I'm fine with it. In fact, I would never say this out loud, but it makes me feel a bit like a Spice Girl. Fag Hag Spice. They always needed a sixth member whose trademark was being progressive and socially aware.

I turn the worksheet over and push it towards him.

POST-TRAUMA GROWTH

He stares at it for a moment, and I see the muscles in his face twitch, like he is battling to stop himself from saying something.

'It's just a timeline of what has happened to you.' As I tell him this, something jars within me. A fault line shifting, two tectonic plates, their edges grinding together. Guilt and shame? I can't help but hear Stanley's words in my mind. *Mine Liam's inner world, his emotional life. He cannot be two-dimensional. It is currently feeling a little that way.* 'It's so you can figure out your patterns, and then you can try and stop them repeating.' Those two tectonic plates grind harder. 'Isn't that what you want?'

I'm helping him.

I am.

This is good for him.

Win–win for both of us. Yes.

'Right,' he says. 'Yeah.' He looks to the door, then to the counter. To Chloe, who is scrolling on her phone, vape now in her mouth. There are still a few people dotted around the tables. The two truanting boys continuing to flick things at each other and finding it unspeakably hilarious. The old ladies not uttering a single word, just earnestly placing down their playing cards. 'Do you think we can do it somewhere more private? Didn't you say you work from your house? Can we go there?'

'Maybe we should get to know each other a bit more first?' I suggest. If we can avoid my house, clearly that's for the best. But I need him to feel safe, so he can open up. *So I can help him.*

I feel panic begin to rise in my chest. *God, what am I doing?*

'I just don't feel safe here, that's all. I don't want all these people knowing my shit.'

He looks genuinely scared. I suddenly feel my cheeks redden. Is this what a normal therapist would do? Out-of-office work? Maybe they would, in an emergency situation. Yes. If someone needed *urgent therapeutic care*, they would do this. And that's what this is. Urgent Community-Based Therapy? He said he was desperate.

If you can get to the core of him, Mal, then we can talk properly.

I push the sheet further towards him. 'We might as well make a gentle start? Since we are here? Just fill it in. No speaking needed.' He stares at it. Then looks up at me with what I can only interpret as a glimmer of what seems to be *embarrassment* beneath the hardness of his features. Wait. Oh, God. *Of course.* He can't write. Just like he can't swim. 'Or you can talk, quietly, if you'd prefer?' I add quickly. 'I'll just make a few notes, if that's OK?'

He nods.

I open my paisley-patterned notebook to see a page of doodles from my last therapy session with Elaine. I quickly turn the page, angling it off the table slightly so he cannot see, and quickly scribble *Liam can't write!*

He pulls his hood over his forehead a bit, crossing his arms on the table. 'Where do I start?'

'Why don't you tell me about when you first wanted to get sober. When was it?'

'Fucking years ago.'

Fucking years ago, I scribble.

'Do you remember the events that led to it?'

'No. That's the point.'

'Right. Well yes, that makes sense.'

'Just kept waking up not knowing where I'd been. Or what I'd done.'

Waking up not knowing where I'd been... 'That must have been scary.'

He pauses. 'Did you never have that?'

'Me?' I lean back, thinking. Thinking like a therapist would think. 'I have definitely woken up wondering how I'd arrived at where I was. Many times. Many.' Wait. And how an *addict* would think. Shit. I wipe my nose with the back of my hand, trying to look like Hugs-Not-Drugs Dez might. 'Lots and lots. Face down. Gutter. You know the story. I know exactly what you're talking about.'

'Fuckin' horrible, innit.'

'Horrible.'

'All the fucking trembling. The anxiety. The blackout fear. Wondering who the fuck you've been with, how many. If you've got some STI, if you've been in a fight, if you're gonna get the police coming round... Why there's blood on your T-shirt and you can't find the cut – so it must be someone else's – why there's sick on your T-shirt, why there's no T-shirt, no trousers, no shoes. Where the fuck they all went and how the fuck you're gonna get new ones.' I just nod, and scribble. Nod. Scribble. Nod. Scribble. *STI, HIV? No trousers, no shoes...* 'I was clever, you know. At school and stuff.'

'I don't doubt it.'

'I got eights in English.'

'Oh!' Interesting. I quickly go back to the top of my page and cross out *Liam can't write*. Actually, this is better. It's useful. Liam is *clever*, but flawed. It might be a bit cliché, but I do like that he could be good with words. Something he could regularly use as a strategy for manipulation. And the reader will empathise more with this scenario, surely: his potential stolen by his struggle with addiction. Yes. *Good with words...* 'Did you do your exams?'

'Nah. I was smoking pot by then.' *Potential stolen.* See? 'But in classes the teachers said I had a very *active imagination*.' Interesting. They said that about me too. 'I have ADHD. My brain moves rapid fast. Not when I'm high, mind.'

ADHD.

I underline it twice.

And then put a circle around it.

I hadn't actually thought about Liam's mental health diagnoses. I mean, addiction, of course. But the deeper roots of other conditions could be a useful delve into his psyche. How does ADHD develop? I can't remember – I'm not sure I actually know. Does it develop? I must look it up. *LOOK UP ADHD!* 'Have you been diagnosed with that?'

'Nah, but I know.'

'You know?'

'Yeah. Self-diagnosed from Instagram.'

'I see.'

'Was proper bad in school. Got kicked out of a few. Bad concentration.'

'Tell me more about your behaviour.' My hand is beginning to hurt from writing so fast.

'My behaviour at school?'

'Yes.'

'I got in loads of trouble.'

Come on… Give me the good stuff. 'What for?'

'I just pissed about.'

I don't know if *pissing about* is what Stanley was after. 'Anything in particular?'

'What do you mean?'

That's a good point. 'I just wondered if there was anything that happened at school that might have led you to feel unhappy.'

I stop. Hoping to God this isn't too much, I start writing the word *unhappy*, over and over again. Scratching it into the paper.

'I guess.'

'Can you remember what? Did you have friends?'

'At school?'

'Yes.'

'Course I fucking did.'

'You were popular?'

'Me? Yeah. Snogged all the girls. Lots of the boys.' Oh, great material. This could be quite *humorous*, actually. Liam needs a bit of light relief. Liam snogging people behind the chapel, exchanging cigarettes. 'And a few teachers.'

I look up. 'Teachers?'

'Yeah. Actually shagged one of them in a store room.' He says this so casually that I nearly miss it. 'Mr Preston. Proper fit, like.'

As I look at Leo, his words landing, something shifts. I see him as a boy at school. Vulnerable. In need of support. Manipulated. And I immediately feel sick. 'That's... not OK, Leo.'

'What?'

'Leo, I just think...' *What am I doing?* This boy needs proper therapy. Not me. 'Have you spoken to anyone about this before?'

'What, snogging everyone at school?'

'No, I mean about Mr Preston.'

'Why would I do that?'

'Because...' Because it's not OK.

'What about your parents?'

'What about them?' He starts tugging on his sleeves.

'I just think, maybe...' I stop. The tectonic plates – the fault lines – suddenly part. It is as if they leave a chasm, and I'm teetering on its edge. I realise I have absolutely no idea what to say. I am incredibly out of my depth. And if I fall, it looks very, very deep. 'Leo, I'm not sure...'

I put down my pen. Close my notebook. 'I think maybe we should stop.'

This does something to Leo that I didn't expect. Not at all. He stands up, immediately, and for the first time since I've known him, looks blank. Like there is no plan, no way out, no answer. 'This was a fucking stupid idea,' he says. Then something lands in his eyes. A blackness. Like he has inserted it, stopping me from seeing beyond. 'I need to get home. Can I have a tenner?'

Home. The bridge. He calls the bridge his home.

'I don't have any change. Please, Leo. I'm sorry – I didn't mean to upset you.'

'Nah.'

'I didn't mean to—'

He thrusts his hand across the table, so it is an inch from me. 'You giving me the money or what?'

'I don't have any.'

For a split second, I see his fingers tense, and my immediate instinct is to flinch and raise my hand in front of my face. But he just drops his arm to his side. 'Crazy bitch,' he says. And then he is moving towards the door.

'Wait, Leo—'

I am up, behind him. 'Listen, perhaps doing it here was a bad idea. You're right. I can find somewhere more secluded?'

He smashes the door open, out onto the alleyway, right into the back of a lady. She stumbles, throwing him a middle finger. 'Dick!' He storms on, not turning to her as she carries on, 'What the hell? Not even gonna *apologise*? Oh my God, what is that *smell*!'

But he keeps moving up the cobbles.

'Sorry,' I mumble, passing her. 'Leo!'

He doesn't turn back, but I hear him. 'Fucking leave me alone.'

And then we are at the top of the alley, turning off it and onto Muswell Hill Broadway. 'Leo, wait—' But the pavement is packed with people waiting at the bus stop, pushing past one another, and it's difficult to follow him through the melee, weaving between the bodies to keep up. I'm not even sure what I'm pursuing him for – I have no idea at this point – but he seems so angry, at what I said, and I want to – I don't know – *apologise*, to stop this, to delete everything and— 'Leo!'

He stops dead. Turns to me. 'What? I don't get it. What do you want with me?'

'I just… I want to help you…'

'You fucking—'

'Mal?'

A voice behind me. A voice I know well. Oh, God.

Oh God, no.

I turn to see Joanie.

Staring at Leo. Then at me.

Standing next to her two six-year-old children, eyes wide.

'What's going on?' she says. 'Is this person bothering you?' Her nose wrinkles at his smell.

She looks at me for an explanation, quickly pulling her children away from Leo.

An image of the text she sent to Ronan flashes in my mind. *Meek Mal.*

'*Mal?*' Leo says, looking at me. 'Who's *Mal*?'

Oh God.

'Who is he?' Joanie continues, pointing at him now.

'He's...'

Time seems to momentarily stop.

Can I tell her I know him from AA? I absolutely cannot tell her that. *Can I?* Can I convince her that in the past two weeks I've become a raging alcoholic? Or do I say client? That's breaching patient confidentiality, but he won't disagree so it's possibly the only option I—

'I'm her boyfriend,' Leo says.

I look at Joanie to see her face almost slide off her skull.

'He's not,' I say. 'Leo, please.'

He shrugs. 'What am I then?'

Joanie looks like she is going to combust. Her children are staring at him like he has descended from another planet. 'Yes, who is he Mal?'

Meek Mal.

'This is Leo,' I say. 'He's a client of mine. I'm helping him.'

I see a smirk cross his lips.

'I'm fucked in the head,' he says to Joanie, tapping his forehead.

I can't read her. She pulls at her children so they are directly behind her.

'I'll speak to you soon, Leo,' I say, trying hard not to sound too pushy, but desperately hoping he will take his cue to get the hell out of here. But he won't take his eyes off Joanie. He's doing that stare he does. The one that looks like he might bite your head off.

'You got a tenner?' he says.

'Excuse me?' Joanie spits, offended. 'No, I do not.'

'Fuck you then.'

Before I can tell him to stop, he turns, right into the path of an elderly woman stood patiently waiting for the bus. She must be in her seventies, wearing a little purple fleece.

Before she can step aside, he lunges at her.

It happens too quickly for me to stop him.

Leo grabs hold of the old lady's handbag. She tries to keep hold, but he pulls so forcefully that she lets go, sending her backwards. The shock of the noise that follows makes me feel instantly sick. The deep thud of her back on the concrete.

And he is gone.

25

Leo

I had to.
    I had to do it.
    Old women carry cash. Everyone knows that.
    Someone should tell them to stop.

26

Mallory

'Get him!' Joanie yells. '*He assaulted her!*'
In the commotion I can hear someone else shouting, 'He went that way, get him!' but I can't seem to move. My feet are stuck to the floor as people begin to crowd around the lady.
The lady on her back.
The old lady, flat on her back.
Oh, shit.
Joanie is kneeling down on the pavement next to her. 'Can you hear me, sweetheart?' she is saying. 'Are you OK?' She's frantic, rubbing her arm, putting her face near hers. 'My name is Joanie and I'm going to help you.' But the old woman is groaning.
There's a bit of blood on the pavement.
It's from the back of her head.
Oh, God. Oh God.
Oh fucking God.
'Mal, what are you doing? Call the police!'
'Right!'
I pull my phone out of my handbag, open the screen, tap on the phone icon and dial 999, but for some reason, I don't hit call. Before I know it, I am holding the phone to my ear regardless, and saying, 'Hello?' to Absolutely No One. 'Yes. Yes. I need the police!'
'And an ambulance!' Joanie shouts.
'And an ambulance!' I say into the phone, again, to No One.
'Who was that guy?' Joanie says to me. 'Do you know him?'
I shush her, as if I'm trying to hear No One on the other end

of the line. 'Yes, my name is Mallory,' I say into it. 'Someone stole an old lady's purse...'

'He *assaulted* her!' Joanie yells at me.

Why is she here why is she here why is she here? 'Right – right. He *assaulted* her—!' I say loudly. *What is happening?* 'We're on Muswell Hill Broadway... Sorry? How long? We need someone *now*.'

I pace around a bit, as if waiting for the answer, trying to collate my thoughts. This was a bad idea. A very bad idea. I should never have come. What the hell am I wearing these stupid gloves for? Who the hell do I think I am? Getting that stupid fucking worksheet out. I should have backed off. Had some fucking boundaries. I'm insane. I am actually the Clinical Definition of Insanity. I will probably get locked up. I probably deserve to be. 'There's lots of blood coming from her nose! But she seems OK!'

'She does not *seem OK*, Mal!'

Shut up, Joanie, I'm on the phone. 'She seems a bit shaken...'

I turn away from her to see her twin children, Crispin and Layla, stood staring at me – like two perfect porcelain dolls – in their school ties and blazers, bags hoiked up to their ear lobes. Looks of utter terror plastered on their six-year-old faces.

Hi, you two! I mouth, waving. Then point to my phone. *Just on the—*

'Mal!' Joanie shouts. 'What are they saying?'

This is an actual nightmare.

I look back at her, to see someone else kneeling at the kerb next to her. A man with a hoodie on and a blue lanyard. 'I'm a nurse!' he proclaims loudly to the crowd, which is growing in size by the minute. 'Can everyone step back, please.' He has his arms up, like it is a crime scene. Which I suppose it is. 'Space, please!' He turns to the lady, perched on the kerb. 'What's your name?'

'Brenda.'

Brenda's voice is shaking.

I'm so sorry, Brenda...

'I'm going to help you,' Nurse Man says. 'I just need to look at your nose – hold your head back, please.'

While I continue to fake-talk to the fake-police, I realise I haven't really stopped to consider that they won't actually turn up. That no emergency services are going to come, whatsoever. Which is going to be a problem, a big problem. I look into the crowd, hoping to see someone else on their phone, frantically asking for an ambulance, but they don't seem to be, because they are all pointing at me, saying things like, *That lady is doing it – she's calling them, don't worry*. And I can see Joanie squabbling with Nurse Man, still faffing with the woman, now trying to actively force her hands off her face. 'You might have broken a bone!' she is yelling. 'You're not supposed to move!' But Nurse Man is looking very annoyed and saying things to Joanie in an assertive tone. Joanie begins to full-out scream back at him, *'Don't tell me what to do! I am first-aid trained!'*

I turn to the person next to me. 'Hi,' I say, to the face of a man with kind eyes and a beard. 'Can you call the police? My phone just died while I was on to them.'

'Of course,' he says. He seems nice. Normal. The right person to make the call. Not me. The opposite of those things.

'Thank you so much. Oh. And an ambulance.'

'Yep.'

'Great. Thank you.'

I back out of the crowd towards the wall, watching him talking to actual people on his phone.

OK.

OK.

This should be fine.

This is going to be fine.

No one will know I knew him. Did I shout his name? Did I? I can't remember. How far behind me was Joanie? Did she hear me?

I find Crispin and Layla, and stand with them, cowering together in a shop doorway. 'Well, this is all a bit scary, isn't it?' They just stare at me.

'Where's Mum?' Layla says.

'She's helping the lady,' I tell her.

'Did you know the man who hit her?' Crispin asks.

Pipe down Crispin. 'No – I didn't.' Then, 'Did you?'

He glares. 'I don't associate with people who would do that kind of thing.'

OK, so I forgot how precocious these two are. 'No. No, of course. And *good*.'

'He's mean,' Layla says.

'Yes,' I agree. 'Very mean.'

'Mum!' Crispin says, his face lighting up at the sight of her emerging from the crowd. He throws himself into her arms.

'That man is a power freak,' Joanie mutters, then, 'Come on, let's get away from here. Every mother and her son now wants to chip in. She's fine.' She waves her hand dismissively, like it's all become a bit of a farce, and takes Layla and Crispin by the hand and begins to frog-march them down the street, away from the throng of people, only stopping when she reaches the little front lawn of a nearby church. I follow along obligingly, matching her frog-march – because I am not really sure what else to do – but also trying to concoct a plan, a reason for why I am here… 'Let's just sit for a moment,' Joanie says, pointing to a bench. 'Catch our breath. Crisps, Lay – sit, please.'

They do. Like little robots. I worry a little about them, because they hardly have a personality between them. Joanie puts her hands on her hips and inhales deeply through her nose, pacing in circles. 'Well.'

'Well,' I repeat.

She stops and looks at me. 'Mal. He's really a client of yours?'

'Yes. He's a client.' It's strange that I'm so able to lie to her face. We were once so close. There was a time when she knew me well enough that she could interpret every wrinkle of my nose, every narrowing of my eyes. But now, she is looking at me like I am someone that she can no longer decipher. And I see her the same way. As a stranger. Someone I don't fully recognise, with two android children that I know nothing about. I don't know her. Not really. But she knows my husband, apparently. She texts him. Calls me Meek Mal *to him*. She used to think I was funny. Clever. Bright. 'He needs help.'

She shakes her head. 'He just seems so…'

'What?'

'*Dangerous*, Mal.'

'I don't think he meant to hurt that woman,' I say.

She nearly laughs. The sort of breathy half-laugh that means I'm being ridiculous. She raises her eyebrows. Folds her arms. 'Well, we must have been watching two very different things.'

'Maybe.'

She looks annoyed at this. Like I should be agreeing with her. 'Does Ronan know?'

There's an edge to the way she says this. Like it's some kind of winning shot.

'No.'

'Well, don't you think he should?'

No, Joanie. And get the fuck out of my marriage. 'He would only worry.'

'With good reason, no?'

No. Not good reasons. 'I'm bound not to tell anyone,' I say, although I'm not sure how true that is, especially if the police are going to be involved. But it sounds legit, and it's all I've got to keep her from telling him.

She nods. 'I see.' I can feel my hands shaking. These fucking gloves. 'Yes. I guess that makes sense.'

'I'm fine, Joanie. This is my world now, and I am managing it well.'

'You sure?'

'Yes.'

'You're never up this end. Why didn't you just meet him somewhere nearer to home?'

'I don't want him to know I live there.'

'Hmm. Makes sense.' Why has she chosen today to be both a nurse and a detective?

'I'll go back and talk to the police,' I say.

She nods.

I nod.

We don't hug. We used to.

I leave her and her two android children on the bench.

But I don't go to the police.

I go straight home and adjust things, so the air will feel the same inside the house as when I left.

Cool, and calm.

When it does, I open my laptop and begin to write.

27

Leo

Under my bridge I fan out the wad of cash.
 Nearly one hundred.
 But that woman…
 Shit.
 I type into Google:
 Muswell Hill news
 old woman dead
 old woman falls dead Muswell Hill Broadway
 Nothing. Thank fuck. Jesus.
 The anxiety. That fucking dark witch is coming.
 I need them all tonight. G, Tina, Charlie and Molly.
All of them dancing together in my brain. Big blackout party in the synapses. But I'm not going near Mo. The shit he's making me do these days is psychopathic. The other night he made me eat a goldfish while he jacked off in the corner of the room. He told me to lick its eyeballs first. Fucking mental.
 Who walked away with the money, though?
 Me.
 But tonight, I don't need that. I need release. I need oblivion.
 I open Grindr.
 Thirteen messages.
 The usual suspects chomping at the bit. The fucking creeps live on this thing. I dunno how they have the time for jobs. Some of them are teachers and doctors and shit. Bored out their minds. Want a little thrill in their shitty lives. I am their fantasy.
 I won't lie. I do like that.

Shane43
Hey sxy, seen you about

KingStallion
Heard you're up for a good time – is this Leo?

PNP 2NIGHT BB!
Leo there's a party tnite get your cute ass down

FREE NOW?
Fancy givin a blowie mate?
you're the best out there
as long as ur not talking
which you won't be
lol
PS not paying tho XXX

I'm Grindr famous.
Fuck my life.
There are starred ones, at the top of the chat list. Those are the ones that have the good drugs. Tommy's messaged – Tommy is nice. He's a dealer who makes his mint on Grindr. Not even a bender. He's got a wife and kids and just makes his money here. Pretty clever if you ask me.

*

TOMMYTIME
Leo
just to let you know lad –
When you get something in your pocket
I've got the good stuff
Hope ur alive ;)

The good stuff means coke that sends you to the gods. It's not too spenny either.

                                            Got some pocket mate

> What else you got
> Where you at

He lives in Camden too. Big old town house. Can't nick shit from Tommy though. He has connections and I ain't fucking with that. When I asked him what he does he said he works in 'business'. That's all he said, but I got the impression it's not a job in the city. But what do I know. I met his wife once. She was friendly, but her face looked a bit like it had been pinned back at her ears, and her lips came out two inches further than they should, so she looked like an angry duck.

Free now
Meet u at the corner
How much you got

> 100

Yeah got a nice night for you mate
;)

I drag myself out from my little corner that I've made under the bridge. It's quite snug, if I do say so myself. I got some nice wooden crates from out the back of the Sainsbury's to use as a mattress and nicked a quilt from the Oxfam. Pretty fresh.

I do feel bad about the woman by the way.

The woman I took the purse from.

I feel fucking awful.

> Coming now mate

Shit. I don't have a change of clothes. And I need to get into his car, but I fucking stink.

I make my way through the market and swipe what I can. A tie-dye T-shirt, some joggers and a woolly hat, cos to be fair, I'm fucking freezing. Can't find any shoes. Fuck it – Tommy will have to deal with these. I pull the new clothes on behind a wall and dump the rest – probably for some other fucker to pick up and wear.

When I get to the corner, his BMW is waiting.

I tap three times on the side window, hear the doors unlock, and open the passenger door.

'Hold on, back seat, mate.'

I do as he says.

When I'm in, I feel like I'm in a movie. I wanna shout: *Driver! Take me to the airport! Got a flight to Barcelona leaving and I can't be late!*

Instead, I say, 'Sorry my feet stink, Tommy.'

He says, 'Jesus, Leo. Keep them away from the seats.'

He drives around the roads for a bit, then pulls in behind a row of industrial-sized bins. He turns and holds out the baggie.

'What's in it?' I say.

'Heaven,' he says.

'All at once?'

'Yep.'

I hand him the cash. He has one of those pens that checks it's real. 'All good, mate,' he says.

'How's Deb?' I ask.

'Fucking wonderful.'

I open the door and get out.

I can't wait long enough. The itch is too intense.

And I can't stop thinking about that woman's face. The one I nicked money from.

I open one of the bin lids, see it's mostly empty (except for some bags of dead vegetables stuck to the bottom) and hop inside.

Close myself in.

Get my phone torch on.

Nice. Nice.

I crush the contents of the baggie and eat it in one.

I dunno when it hits.

I dunno.

But it does.

Everything goes pale. And soft at the edges.

I watch the inside of the bin for hours.
But I feel something inside me.
Fucking gnawing at me.
You can face it.
Mallory Maddox in her weird fucking gloves. What's she up to?
I just… I want to help you.
I just… I want to help you.
I just… I want to help you.
Her voice on loop, filling the bin.
Fuck it.

Hey Mandy – I'm sorry
Please can we meet again

I stare at the screen, waiting for her reply.
Nothing.
Nothing.
Nothing.

Promise I'll keep it chill
I want help

I do.
I fucking scared her off, haven't I?
I lie back and get up my Instagram account to drown out the noise. It's a piece of shit phone, but I got some guy to pay the contract for me if I see him once a week. The screen reflects me back to myself, using a bag of old potatoes as a pillow. It'll do. I navigate to my profile page.
@Alias22.
Got four thousand followers, me. Never shown my face on it. Just my little poems. Lol.
I write this stuff when I'm high and people love it. *Chav poetry.* That's what people comment underneath.
This shit is the real deal.
True life on here!

Be grateful everyone! This lad got the truth.

I quickly type something in my notes app, then screen shot it and post it to the grid. It's harder to do than it sounds because my phone currently looks like an anime cartoon. Pressing the bits I need to seems to take forever, like I'm moving through marshmallow.

I then watch the likes rack up and up – each one, each little heart, an injection of dopamine into my already dopamined brain. But it's not enough. Never is.

Even with the spelling mistakes, it gets over 2,000 hits.

My hand vibrating with each one. It feels fucking fantastic.

I AM A POTATO

Head is black
Like a dead potato.
Those little holes they get
Are all over me
Going deeper than they look
Rotting the inside
Of my brain
My stomach
My soul
Heading to the core
But
They don't reach it
The core stays intact
where no one looks
It remains
Pure, untouched potato.

@Alias22

28

Mallory

The lampshade above my head – one of the three hanging over the kitchen island – is shaped like an upside-down pasta dish. Lots of people have them, so I was reluctant, but I loved the colour. They're not actually from Pooky, but John Lewis. The outside is pewter – a sort of rustic grey-brown – and the inside is a shiny copper. That was important when I chose them, because it makes the light muted, and slightly orange. I wanted to get the tone perfectly correct, to match the Hague Blue of the kitchen cabinets. The orange and blue combination is so satisfying to me. Sometimes I just stand and look at the scene. *This looks good*, I think. *This looks so good.*

Ronan mentioned the other day that he thought it looked dated, and perhaps we should change it.

I look at my phone.

21:00.

He will be back soon.

I think about texting Joanie. But what would I say?

I quickly draft a message.

Hey hon
Spoke to the police, gave description
Good to see you today – sorry I was a bit all over the place!
Shall we get coffee soon?
M x

But I don't press send. I realise that someone secure in themselves – in their story – would have no need to.

I scan over the end of *Slay* – open on my laptop on the counter in front of me.

> 'You're dead, pussy. You're gonna fucking die under this bridge.'
> Liam's head was held under the surface, thrust down, again and again, water filling his nostrils with every inhalation.
> This was it, he thought.
> There was no way out.

I close the document and hide it in a folder on my laptop entitled patient notes – confidential, then bring up my emails and quickly compose one, galvanised by my creative surge after today's events.

Hi Stan,

Just to let you know I'm making headway with the book. I feel I am mining Liam's pain, his trauma and his getting closer to understanding his past. It's quite a journey to go on with him, but I think it feels authentic. I'll let you decide.

I feel I should expand a little on your desire for the book to be rooted in authenticity. As I write, I feel more and more that my brother Nick is with me, and even begin to visualise his face as Liam's. I'm not sure yet if I would be willing to talk about him publicly – should it get that far! But yes. It's really been an emotional journey for me, understanding the pain he went through.

I wanted to send just a little more to you – a few more chapters, as you said. Let me know what you think.

End of next week I will have the first half over to you. More soon!

Mal

I attach the file entitled Chapters 1–10: slay: draft 1.

The front door clicks.

Ronan.

But I don't startle. I am prepared. I calmly press send, wait for the *whoosh*, close the email tab and get up my notes from Elaine's therapy session last week, which are already waiting for me on the desktop. Ronan doesn't shout. Usually it's *Hi, honey, only me!*, but this time, nothing, until the slow tread of his shoes moves through the hallway.

I am prepared.

I take my tea and sip. My mug is half empty and lukewarm, as it should be. Like I have been here for hours.

Which I have.

Nothing is amiss.

He stops in the kitchen doorway, briefcase in hand, a silhouette framed by the hallway light behind him. 'Hey.' He seems quiet. In a mood? Could be. Or tired. Nothing more. 'What are you up to?'

I stretch my arms up like a cat waking from slumber and rub my eyes. 'Just typing up my patient notes,' I say. 'You must be hungry.'

'I am.'

I can't see his face, so I stand and make my way over to him. He looks a little drained, but this is not unusual. His eyes are their typical green, but ever so slightly dull. *Just tired*. He is back late. *He is just tired*. I put my hand gently on his chest and kiss him on the cheek. He smells like soap, with the faintest hint of neroli from the diffusers in his office. I've never been, but he told me the company puts one in every room and that the smell has become so constant that he no longer notices it himself.

'I thought I'd make us something easy. Pasta?' I remain next to him for a moment, watching him.

Did Joanie text him?

'Sounds good,' he says, his voice slightly gruffer than usual. Sometimes he will have a cigarette if he's stressed, but I can't smell it on him. There is a flicker, though, of something, in the way his jaw is clenched. Suspicion? No, because he kisses my cheek. Begins to take off his coat and shoes. He is just tired. *He knows nothing.*

I was sure the first thing Joanie would do after I saw her would be to get straight on the phone to him. Apparently she likes to do that now.

But he doesn't seem to be aware.

Does he?

Maybe she was too distracted by her little robots, Topsy and Turvy.

He turns back into the hallway and opens the cupboard to hang his coat. I move beyond the kitchen island to the sink and take the Le Creuset pan that I have already placed there ready, fill it with fettuccini and boil the kettle. I can hear him taking his time out there, placing his shoes on the shelf.

That's not unusual. He often does this.

'How's the deal going?' I call to him, taking the courgettes I have pre-washed and left on the chopping board. Using the potato peeler, I begin to strip them into long, thin strands.

'It's nearly over the line,' he says back. Not too much effort in his voice, but again, not unusual.

'Oh! Amazing! What is it again?'

'I told you, hun.' Is he annoyed? I hear him move back into the kitchen behind me, but I don't turn. 'It's the book rights we've been fighting for.' I can hear him moving around the kitchen as I keep my back to him. I hear him open the drinks cabinet and the pop of a cork as he opens whiskey, then the *glug glug* of it into one of the crystal glasses my mother gave us. 'Sony, Amazon and Warner Brothers are all putting in huge bids, so we had to give a really solid pitch to the author today, showing her that we could sell our vision, offer her an executive producer position, blah blah – basically give her a feeling that she would be involved creatively, even though we don't want her to write the screenplay.' The drag of a stool from under the island. His sigh as he sits on it and takes a sip. 'She's too heavy-handed, and the book is actually a bit of a fluke if you ask me. I don't think she's a good writer – she's actually a shit writer – but it's a great story, that I know I could make better. But I ultimately need to make her feel like she's in control. I don't think it'll be that difficult.'

'Wow,' I say. 'Must be some book.'

'Bids for the option are going over 100,000. For the option alone. It's a big play.'

'Do you ever feel like it's all just people showing their bollocks off?' I say with a little laugh. Gentle. Fun. Because *he is so much fun.*

'That is what is happening, yes.' He doesn't reciprocate my tone. 'But we have to have the bigger pair.'

He seems serious. That's fine. He can be.

'What's it about?' I say, moving to the fridge to take out a lemon and the feta. 'The book?'

'It's called *Killing Me* – about a girl who is used by a gang to smuggle drugs across county lines.'

'Oh yes, I remember. It's not even been published yet, is that right?'

'Still not even been announced. It's become hot property early. We want it.'

I try to hide any hint of jealousy. 'Sounds *edgy*.'

'It is. But it's more than that. The protagonist is struggling with her sexuality, and her identity, and it's about her breaking free from the gang, and herself. It's got a good personal journey. That's important, it's what people want. It's good. Very.'

'Character-led.'

'Character-led is in!' he proclaims. I hear him gulp, then the pop of the cork again.

'Well, I really hope you get it.'

'Me too.'

A pause, while I cut the feta into chunks. It crumbles between my fingers.

'How are your patients?' I notice his tone shift slightly. This is because he says the word *patients* with an overladen sense of importance, and I immediately cringe. We both know the people I see are rich women who have minor anxiety about their very privileged lives and just need someone to vent to. We both know I am hardly qualified. We both know I am no doctor. That I am no trauma psychologist with an overbearing and intense workload. But I can feel from the way he says it that this is exactly what he wants me to be.

'They're OK,' I say. 'I saw Elaine yesterday.'

'She still moaning about her roses?'

'Ha. Well, yes. A little.'

'And what about the other two? Lillian and Penelope?'

He really shouldn't know their names. I should never have told him. But for whatever reason, I did, and now he knows more about their lives than their own husbands do. 'Seeing Lillian tomorrow. Penelope is on holiday in Spain.'

'Oh, that's right,' he says. 'Are you putting the lemon on after?'

'Hmm?'

'I just know it's better when the lemon goes on after. Not in with the courgette and bacon.'

Bacon. Shit. I forgot the bacon. 'Yes, I remember.'

He taught me this recipe.

'You seem a little stressed,' he says.

This is also not unusual. He says this to me a lot. *Everything is fine.* 'Just a long day of reading notes and thinking which way to go with Elaine,' I reply, replicating the tone of importance he's used. I wince at the notion that I actually have any clue which way to take her – or that she even *needs* taking anywhere – hand-holding her through the difficulty of worrying that the money she has in her savings account isn't accumulating enough interest.

I stir the water with the fettuccini and watch the pasta begin to soften. 'She's very vulnerable and I want to help her,' I add. I push down the top of the pasta so it too is under the bubbling froth.

'Well, I'm glad you do,' he says, with the faintest air of concern, or sarcasm, I can't tell which. Maybe I'm imagining it.

I drain the water and add the courgettes. Sprinkle in some fennel seeds.

'I get frustrated with the team,' he says. 'So many of the numbers people just keep butting their heads in – saying stupid shit that doesn't have any bearing on what the writer wants to hear.

She needs to be guided, not told *We will give you anything you want*.'

I add more olive oil. 'Some people would probably like to be offered whatever they wanted.'

'That's not how it works, Mal. These people don't know their arse from their elbows – not really. And it's my job to *show* them what they want.'

I start ladling the pasta onto two plates. 'I see.'

'Some of my colleagues are complete morons. Had to bite my tongue from telling one of them to shut up when he asked the author if she'd thought about her dress for the premiere. Idiot.'

I squeeze the lemon juice on top, just as Ronan said. 'He sounds like one. Hopefully she will see through it and hear what you have to say. I'm sure she did, and I'm sure it was enough.'

'I hope so. We find out tomorrow.'

I crumble the feta. Done. 'Want to eat in here?' I say, holding a plate in each hand, turning to him for the first time.

He nods. 'Where else?'

There is something. I suddenly see it in his features. His expression. Something underneath it all. It's enquiring. Probing. Like his hand on my shoulder when he asked me to show him the photos on my phone.

'Good point,' I concede, putting a plate down in front of him. He doesn't look at it. Keeps his eyes on me. 'You're staring,' I say. 'Is everything OK?'

'Yes, sorry, I just thought you had something on your...' He points to his own upper lip, referring to mine.

'Oh!' I wipe it with the back of my hand. Nothing.

'No, I think it's just the shadow of your...' He pauses. 'Oh, have you not bleached your moustache?'

This sentence comes as such a slap, such an icy blow, that I have to look down, my cheeks burning with embarrassment. 'Oh God,' I say quietly. 'I haven't for a while. I'm sorry – is it really noticeable?'

'It is,' he says. 'But don't worry. It's just me.' He pauses. 'I'm a little worried you're not taking care of yourself, Mal.'

'I am... I just forgot.' I turn back to the cutlery drawer and take out two forks. When I hand him one, I try to seem unphased, nonchalant, but he can see the cracks now. 'Sorry.'

He takes the fork. Silence.

He stares at me.

I hate it when he does this.

'I think maybe you should give me your phone for a few days, Mal.'

'What?'

He places his fork down on the table next to him, his eyes still fixed on me. 'Why were you in Muswell Hill today?'

Oh, shit. *Shit shit shit.* 'What?'

'And more importantly – how was that not the first thing you told me when I got back?' His stare doesn't falter.

'Ronan—'

'One of your new patients?'

Shit.

'Joanie called me.'

Fucking Joanie. 'Oh, did she?'

'Yes. Why didn't you tell me you had a new patient?'

Fuck. 'Patient confidentiality.'

'That's not held you back before, Mal.' His whole body is completely still, eyes locked, not allowing me to look away, nor allowing me any space to manoeuvre out of his vision. 'And someone that assaults old women, no less?'

'Wait—'

'I'm concerned.'

'You don't have to be.'

'How can I protect you if you're not sharing these things with me?'

'I'm not supposed to—'

'He doesn't sound safe. This *Leo*.' Shit. 'He doesn't sound like the kind of patient you can handle.'

'Why do you want my *phone*?'

'Because I think you need a break. I think you are becoming stressed. And today sounds like quite an intense experience, and it might be good to take a bit of time away from everything.'

'I'm fine.'
'And we both know what happens when you become stressed.'
'I'm not unwell, Ronan.'
'You said that the last time.'
'I'm not.'
'Mal.' He stops. Waits. Staring. 'What kind of marriage are we in if we don't share everything with each other? Isn't that what love is?' He stands. Moves around the island towards me. Places his hand on my shoulder. I don't flinch. I am stuck to the floor. He speaks more softly now. 'We both know that you're vulnerable, Mal,' he says. 'I love you. I *know* you. You can be triggered quite easily and it sounds like a triggering event. Just take some time for yourself.'
'Ronan—'
'You don't know what's best for you, Mal, we're agreed on that.'
'I think—'
'You were out with a young man who assaulted an old lady and you decided *not to tell me*?' His voice is still quiet.
'It doesn't warrant giving you my phone. No. I promise – I am keeping myself safe.' My legs. *Don't give way. Please stay standing.*
He is staring. Calm. Nothing changes in his face. 'Fine. But I'd like you to turn on location settings and share them with me. Just so I know where you are.'
'But—'
'And I'm going to take your car keys.'
'What? Ronan – this is ridiculous. I need my car.'
'It will help you reset. I can order you in some nice Ocado food. You can cook. Be at home. Sounds nice, doesn't it?'
'I...' My brain whites out. All I can do is try to remain standing upright and keep my eyes on him. We stay like this, in this exact position, for what feels like an incredible amount of time in which no other person, no other room, no other conversation exists. 'OK.'
'Good.' He exhales, shaking his head. 'Good, Mal.'
I nod. 'OK.'
I watch him pick up his fork, twirling it in the pasta. He puts it into his mouth, then looks up at me. 'There's no flavour.' He

places his fork back on the table, then leans down, lifting up his briefcase. He opens it, and holds something out to me.

A book.

I can see the title.

Getting Ready for Parenthood.

I take it. 'Thank you.'

'I'm going up for a bath, I need an early night.'

'OK.'

'Our phones are still linked – aren't they? So I can see your location? Don't look so scared... It's just so I know you're OK, Mal.'

I nod. 'Yes. They're still linked.'

'Good.' He kisses my forehead. 'I promised when we got married I would do everything to protect you. And that's what I want. I love you, Mal. See you in bed.'

'Yes,' I say. 'Sorry about the food. I am.'

'It's fine. I'd already eaten.'

'Right. Sorry.'

'Don't be sorry. Oh, and I'm going to send you a link to a fertility app I found. We can share it, so we both know when your ovulation period is.'

He turns and leaves.

I hear his footsteps up the stairs. One flight.

Two.

The opening of our bedroom door.

The pipes in the wall gurgling on.

I grab my phone.

Open up messages.

Find him.

> Hi Leo
> Just seen this
> Same time tomorrow?
> I can meet you at a park near my house
> There's a bench that is very quiet
> Priory Park – Crouch End

Yeah. OK

Nice. Thanks

                                                Don't worry
                                            Glad you're safe

29

Leo

Bin juice. All over me.

My headache wants to split me open. I wonder what would fall out of me. Probably not far off what I'm already sat in. Liquid, dark and sticky, like bile. A congealed concoction of dead veg, fag ash (with bits in it). Shards of glass. Of regret.

I like to say I don't regret anything, but in moments like this I don't believe myself. My anxiety – that spindly fucking witch – robs that from me. She's on me like a hound today. So close I can't breathe properly, nails dug in so deep that I feel like she *is* me. She's fucking brutal. Evil.

Insidious.

I like that word. I get it. Some things just spread, and I'm not talking about rashes. Those clear up if you treat them. I would know. So would all the nurses at Dean Street STI clinic, where they all call me Liability Leo – *Liability Leo's back – What is it this time? – There's access to counsellors if you need it, we suggest you accept the referral*. I'll have to go again, probably tomorrow. Kez was right – she had me clocked. I haven't been taking my PrEP.

At least I have a bit of charge on my phone. I pull myself out of the bin and walk to the park, my head throbbing like a cunt the whole way.

Priory Park.

This park is annoying and I can't put my finger on why. Maybe cos it's not actually a park. More like a fucking garden. All pruned flower beds and the grass is mown. There's not even a shitty swing set in sight. It feels like it's private. Like something exclusive. For residents only.

It's pissing down too.

I thought I wanted her to help me, last night, when I was in the bin.

Silly little bin brain was very wrong.

What I actually want is to score again.

What I can't figure out is what *she* wants. It's weird. She doesn't fancy me. I don't think so, anyway. She might. Fancy a bit of chavvy-gay. Lots of people have that fantasy. They like the danger, cos their life is so dull. Or I've thought maybe she's a journalist doing some shitty annoying Panorama-thing about the state of young gays these days, but she didn't record anything. I don't think. And I honestly don't think she's brave enough to do that shit. Everything reads on her face. It's all over her. I can see her fear. Smell it.

She's here.

I see her yellow coat first.

She was right. The bench is out of view, surrounded by a load of overgrown weeds. If her coat wasn't so fucking bright, I'd not've spotted her. She has her hood up, hands in her pockets like she's hiding, but she's flashing like the sun.

She's well fucking odd.

I move until I'm in her eyeline. She sees me and waves, like she can't quite help herself. Then she looks left and right, checking, like she overdid it, which she did, cos she's the least subtle person I've ever met.

I cross the mown grass towards her and push my way through the weeds. 'You all right, Mandy?' I ask. 'You look a bit mental.'

'Hi, Leo,' she says, all quiet. Her eyes are red. I reckon she smokes pot, you know. Loads of these bored rich types do.

'Sorry,' I say, sitting on the wet bench, 'for yesterday.' My joggers are fucked from the bin juice. Maybe she'll take pity on me and buy me some new ones.

'Don't worry.'

'Was she OK? The woman?'

'I think she will be fine.' She doesn't seem sure.

'Did the police come? Did you have to talk to them? It's fine if you did. If you wanna grass me up.'

She turns away from me, looking off into the park. 'I didn't speak to them,' she says, still quiet.

'They'll probably find me, then I'll be out of your hair.' Speaking of, it looks a bit dishevelled today, hanging down under her hood. 'Not got your notepad today?' I say. 'Thought you might have brought some extra worksheets for me for being such a twat.' She doesn't smile at this. Still doesn't look at me. Playing hard to get.

'You want to get out of this mess, right?' Her tone is a bit harder. Bit more, *I'm in charge*. Ha.

'Of course I fucking do.'

'Then we need to get into the proper stuff, Leo.'

She sounds like she's about to cry. 'Proper stuff?'

'Yes.'

'Right. Like what then?'

'The stuff you didn't want to discuss yesterday.' Now she turns to me. Steady. Calm. 'I think sometimes it's hard to face the past. But we have to, to move forward.'

'Is that on a magnet on your fridge?'

'No. It's the only way to get out of this mess.'

All right. Straight in with the dramatics. Maybe she was an actor once. A bad one. No shade. 'So, what… You wanna know about my childhood?' She nods. Jesus. Getting stuck right in. 'Was nothing special.'

'I'll need more than that. To help you.'

I can feel the scratch, the itch, starting in my chest already. I need to score soon, and I need something big to sell. 'I grew up with my mum. Never knew my dad.'

She leans forward a little. Maybe she *is* wearing a wire. 'What happened?'

'I don't fucking know.' She shifts on her arse, impatient now. 'OK. Fine. *Fine*.' I exhale. 'My mum was raped, so I didn't know my dad. All I remember is being lugged around with her until the services took me off her when I was seven. That good?'

'Yes,' she says, real quick. A bit too quick if you ask me.

'Right.'

'Well, no – not *good*, Leo. But, it's good that you're sharing. Thank you.' She squints, thinking. 'I'm so sorry.'

God, really? 'What for?'

'That's a lot.'

'Is it? I dunno – how the fuck would I know any different – and I was only a kid so it wasn't a big—'

'Slow down,' she says, putting her hand gently on my arm. 'Slow down. Take your time. I'm so sorry this happened to you. And your mum. I'm really sorry.'

I shrug. 'It's all right.'

'You mustn't have felt very safe.'

I shrug again.

She waits, frowning and squinting like she really cares. I dunno if she wants me to keep going or to stop – I can't tell – but it's cold and I'm getting scratchy as fuck and can't bear the silence. I decide I'm gonna just keep going. 'She was called Cherie, my mum. But loads of people called her Cherry, cos Cherie seemed too posh. She also had ginger hair, so it kind of worked. Lots of freckles too. I remember that. I just have memories of her face, in loads of different rooms in different parts of London. The rooms would change but the freckles wouldn't. She was well tough, my mum. And not in a wanky emotional way – I saw her beat up a few men. I must have been six when I saw her knock a man's teeth out.'

'Why did she do that?'

'Because he was a cunt and was trying to feel her up,' I say. 'She had taken me to the job centre with her – he was there in the waiting room. He was stood at first, then I just remember he was sat in the seat next to her and I was on the other side – and he was making her laugh a bit. He kept saying things to me like *Hello, fella, very handsome, aren't you? Do you take after your dad?* And when I said I don't have one, he smiled. Had grey teeth. He told my mum he could help her get money – they started whispering and he grabbed her leg. She then elbowed him right in the face. Blood spurted everywhere. Security dragged my mum out – the man told them he was assaulted, and she wasn't allowed back in that job centre. So every Saturday we had to trek down to one that was miles away, and she couldn't afford the bus so we walked. I liked the walks though. Thought it was fun at the time.'

Mandy waits for a minute, rubbing her hand across her cheek, thinking of the right thing to say. *Can we just get this done?* 'She does sound tough.'

'Yeah, she was. But then things got out of hand. I don't remember loads of it – might have blocked it out – but they started keeping me in at school. My mum wouldn't turn up to pick me up and stuff. I remember one time she did, we got home and she stuck a needle in her arm. And there were all these men in the flat. Men I didn't know. Their eyes were all fucked and some of them just wandered around naked.'

'Christ...'

'Nah, it wasn't like that. They didn't do anything to me. I would just leave and sit in the park, keep going back to check if they'd gone. When they had I'd let myself in. She gave me a key. I was six and she gave me a key. Mad that, innit.'

'It is a bit.'

'Then the neighbours must have called the police, cos I didn't see her after that. Got told when I was about fifteen by my foster parents that she had died. They just said it once, in one sentence, and that was it. They said, *Cherry's gone.* There was a funeral but I didn't go. I was too busy getting fucked up by that point.'

'I see.' I don't say anything else now. My fingernails are digging into the bench. The wood is soft. 'Sorry, Leo. That's a lot to deal with. No wonder...' She stops herself.

'No wonder I'm a fuckhead?'

'I wasn't going to say that.'

'I started drinking first. Loved voddy immediately. Was probably nine when I had my first drink. Would only do it at night at one of my foster placements – the dad was a massive alchy himself, so it was easy to steal. Then tried coke first at about twelve, loved it. Some guy down the road would just give it to me cos he thought it was funny, making me do weird shit like dance and steal the neighbour's dog. Took Mandy when I was fourteen at a mate's party. Thought it was all right but I was pretty bouncy anyway so it just made me feel up-up. Think it was the same time I found ket – which was good I suppose, felt more in control which was all right, but I think I was also a bit addicted to the chaos. And then at sixteen I found meth. And that was it. The holy fucking grail. Got its claws into me. The parties started.'

'T-Parties?'

'Yeah, that's it. Just a total mess of people fucking and getting high, no one wanting to fall asleep cos they don't want to wake up and deal with themselves. So that's been going on since. I got kicked out of about six schools, went to a PRU, spent some time in a nut-house – can't remember how long but that's how I found benzos. They keep me going, take me off it when I need to come down. Loved them… But then when I've got nothing in me I can't do it. Can't be in reality. Hate it. It's like my body wants to just move away from it. And I'm done. I'm fucking so sick of it.'

She stares at me, eyes wide, all wet with tears.

My phone starts vibrating in my pocket.

'I'd like to help you, Leo. I really would.'

'Go on then.' I feel myself getting tetchy. 'We gonna go back to yours and do some worksheets or summat? It's grim out here.'

Whoever this is won't stop calling. Pissing me off. Probably Mo. Or Tommy asking me if I had a good time.

'I think maybe we can find another café, if that's OK? Just for now?'

Fucking hell, really? After all that?

This crazy bitch.

I pull out my phone. Check the screen.

Shit.

Mum

Great fucking timing.

I shove it back into my pocket.

Did she see? Fuck, I hope she didn't see.

'Who was that?' she says.

I stand. 'I gotta go.'

'What? What do you mean?'

I take off, round the side of the park, and wait. I wait for her yellow jacket to guide me, at a distance, down the road. I'm hidden behind a car and I watch her take her keys out and go into one of the big houses. Fuck me, it's massive. She looks back towards me, but she doesn't notice.

She goes in.

I take out my phone. Search my contacts.

Mo.

I need Mo.

Hi Mo – can I come over?

He replies quickly. Always does.

>Steady boy, it's still early

Yeah well. I need to get out my head

>Party? (party-hat emoji) And money?

Yeah

>Fine. Yes. Come over. But you're in trouble

Of course

>Of course what?

Of course, sir

>That's correct
>You're in real trouble tonight, Leo
>Do you understand?

Yes sir

He's a fucking lunatic.
But people have said that of me.

                                      You'd better be prepared

30

Mallory

I hear the door go. 'Hi, love! I'm home!'

Seven o'clock. Bang on time.

I've left Ronan dinner downstairs. The air is still. The place is spotless. My phone has been here all day. He will have checked and seen my location at the house.

I am prepared.

'Food's in the kitchen!' I yell back.

'Thank you!'

Like nothing happened.

We do this. Pretend.

'Just reading in bed!'

I *am* reading. Not the book he got for me, which I have placed next to me on the duvet.

I am reading an email from Stanley Maier.

Hi Mal,

I've read the first ten chapters, and all I can say is, wow. I am frankly blown away.

I hope you don't mind but I shared it in-house, I couldn't help myself, and honestly the entire office is raving. We LOVE it. And the title. *Slay.* So dark, yet funny. Perfectly on brand for this type of social commentary.

A few minor notes – we need more of Leo's past now. And certainly more interaction with Mark. What a dark and sad and unsettling underbelly of society – one I think many more people will be intrigued to hear about. Our head of sales, Pam (I hope you don't mind, I knew she would be intrigued and she just loved the title so much), said she feels this story is both 'necessary' and 'urgent'. High praise indeed.

She is someone to impress – so good job.

I don't want to get your hopes up, but I do have a feeling I can get this over the line at our acquisitions meeting at the end of next week, and the budget is currently strong – this deserves recognition in that respect.

Keep going. Can you get me the next five chapters by next week? I think that should be enough. And a synopsis, so we can get a sense of the ending.

Welcome back, Mal.

It's a joy to see you flourishing like this.

Warmest regards,

S. x

I pull my laptop closer to me, re-reading the email over and over again. Part of me thinks it isn't real. That it can't be real.

But it is.

It's here. In front of me.

The words fill my body, and in doing so, I feel more space, somehow, inside me.

And he even signed off with just his first initial. *With an 'x' next to it.*

Hi Stan,

Wow, thank you so very much for your kind words. I will endeavour to have the next five chapters to you by next week, and have a lot more to say about Liam's past. And of course, Mark. A creation born from reflecting at length on how to authentically represent a trauma cycle.

Leave it with me.

And please, thank Pam! Maybe one day, if this happens, we can all go for a drink together!

M. x

Before I press send, I realise that this is also an opportunity for me to actually meet new people. To form my own friendships. Pam sounds amazing. I can see her now, in a throwback eighties power suit – purple, cool – with high shoulder pads and red lipstick. The clashing colours are dazzling. I suddenly have a vision of me saving her in my phone as Publishing Sis Pam!, with a love heart, and it fills me with such a buzz, the excitement so warm that I actually close my eyes.

'You OK, Mal?'

Ronan is at the door of the bedroom. I'm not entirely sure how long he has been stood there.

'Hi, yes! Just doing more work.'

He nods. 'Good. That's good to hear. You stopped seeing that patient?'

'Yes. Of course.'

'Good. I saw you've been in all day. Has it been nice?'

'It really has. I feel replenished.'

I pick up *Getting Ready for Parenthood*. I have bent the pages and folded down a few. I see him glance at it. A flash of warmth enters his expression, and he leans over the bed and kisses me on the forehead.

'I'm going to have a shower.'

'OK,' I say, and kiss his cheek. 'The book's good.'

'It is?'

'Yes. Really gentle, not stressful.'

He nods. Smiles. 'I love you.'

'I love you too.'

I watch him turn into the en suite, dropping his trousers on the floor.

When he shuts the door, I quickly take my phone out to check for messages from Leo and see the Grindr app – hidden in my wellbeing folder – has a notification symbol.

I open it.
Mo.

> I'm having some people over this evening
> Gonna be fun
> Might get a little wild
> If you wanna join in?

Interesting.
I start to type back.
'Love?'
I look up, the en suite door is open and Ronan is stood, fully naked, with a backdrop of a steam cloud behind him. It's like something from a reality TV show. A mix between *Stars in Their Eyes* and *Naked Attraction*. 'Yes, hun?'
'We're running out of this amazing shower wash. Do you want to use the Monzo to order us some more?'
He's so handsome. He really is.
I can see why people say it.
'Of course! I'll do it now.' He never asks me to order stuff unless things are feeling settled, and he's not concerned.
'Thanks, love.'
He lingers for a moment in the doorway.
Naked.
'Do you want to join me?' he says.
'Hmm?' is my instinctive response. 'I was going to buy this soap. It's Aesop…?'
He shrugs, then wipes his hair out of his eyes. 'We could… You know…' He then glances at the baby book. At the bent pages that I haven't read. 'You've come off the pill now, haven't you?'
'Yes,' I lie.
He smiles, then squints.
Sexy. *This is sexy.*
'Hello,' he says mischievously. 'Did you check the app?'
'What app?'
'Someone's *ovulating*.'
This is not sexy.

'Right. Yes!'

I slowly begin to stand and move towards him. I have learnt to detach. I don't know when, but it happens. I will deal with the shame later. Or tomorrow. Or next week. Whenever it decides to land.

Which it does.

And I am kissing him on the mouth, and he is pulling off my clothes. He drags me with him, into the shower cubicle, through the Crittall glass door. He grabs my face with his hand and says, 'I love you, Mal, you know that, don't you?' And I moan in response. And then I leave. I leave my body and it is as if I am watching us from above. A tile-eyed view, from above the shower faucet. It doesn't look painful, or difficult. I look like I am enjoying it. I certainly sound like I am. It is over quickly. And then he is stepping out of the glass box, wrapping a towel around his waist, and into the doorway, where he turns to me and says, 'You're so beautiful.'

'So are you,' says the Mallory beneath me.

And she stands under the hot water for about a minute, not moving.

Move.

I am back inside myself, stepping out of the shower, and moving to the sink. I start to brush my teeth, then go back into the bedroom, where Ronan is already dozing.

31

Leo

Mo's room is dark and cold.

I never see the rest of his house. The candles are lit. Incense is burning somewhere and it smells like lavender or some shit. But the bed is bare. No duvet or pillows, just a mattress with a sheet on it. That's not how it usually is.

'Here,' he says. White powder, fat as slugs, lined up on top of a book. I read the title before I put the straw to my nose.

THE POWER OF NOW
ECKHART TOLLE

I think it's ket. Or coke. Or meth. Or the lot. He does do that sometimes. Mixes them. I think he thinks I don't know. Or that I don't care, which would be true. His hands, holding a credit card, cut through the powder. I know his hands well. The veins in them, the way they move as he lights his cigarette. They have this thing about them. Makes me sometimes think they have a personality all of their own. They remind me of Jafar from *Aladdin*. All long and twisty. Was my favourite film, that, growing up.

'Leo, get on the bed.'

I'm swaying.

I prefer it when I sway. Things begin to blend into each other. Can't tell the difference between the beige curtain and the beige floor. Right now, they are all one. The mattress smells like it always does – clean. It's fresh. He is clean, Mo – I'll give him that.

'Leo, sweetie?'

He calls me that, like I'm one of his Haribos.

'Sorry, yeah. Yeah. It's just hitting me.'

He is currently faceless. Two studs for eyes in a blur of beige. More beige. Beige, beige, beige.

Handcuffs.

'I told you you'd be punished tonight. What are you?'

'Bad,' I say.

'Yes,' he agrees. 'What else?'

He wants more. 'Pathetic,' I try.

'Well yes. But something else.' I shrug, because I have no idea. 'My toy.'

Oh right. 'Your toy,' I repeat.

I feel my arms gripped together by the metal.

But now I'm not really sure when that happened. Time has gone weird.

'On the bed, sweetie.'

It's got one of those metal frames, you know the type. Looks dead cheap but actually pretty solid.

I lie down on the mattress, face first.

'Turn over,' he instructs.

I do. 'Can I have more?' I say, on my back. I just have my boxers on. I didn't shower. I guess I could say I don't shower. He doesn't seem to care, Mo. Surprising.

In fact he likes it.

'Sure.' He moves away from my vision, and I stare at the ceiling. It's got that pattern on it. You know – the swirls of plaster that your grandma had. 'Here,' he says.

I lean forward and snort off Eckhart Tolle.

Is that how you say it?

Ek – Heart – Toll?

He's holding a knife now.

I see the knife but I am also numb – that helps. The knife is power play, I'm pretty sure, but this time his eyes look different. I feel the cold metal against my chest.

'No moving,' he says.

I am boxer-less. 'Where's my kecks,' I say.

'No talking either. I have a surprise for you.'

He disappears. Well, I think he does. I just lie with my hands above my head tied to the frame for ages. Can hear noises. But it's all fucking swirling. I see things move – shadows, moving shadows – and there are voices. They are in the room.

Am I in the room?

Or oblivion?

I want it.

But these people are here.

It doesn't seem like earth.

One of the voices is next to my head calling me chavvy scum.

Then there's another voice calling me babe and slut.

I don't really know how many. There are at least four sets of eyes.

They are men.

I can see the hair on their forearms and feel their thighs against my thighs.

I'm being pushed over and over, but there isn't really proof of that cos I don't feel anything

just the shifting of my body.

but I want to chuck up my guts.

I turn my head and try to.

Someone grabs me by the hair.

Pulls so hard it feels like my neck might snap.

and I can't really breathe.

I can't fucking breathe.

stop

fucking stop

'*Fucking stop doing that – I know what you're doing—*'

Stop—

Please—

there is no noise coming out of my mouth now. Something is in it.

A sock.

They are laughing.

'*My toy. My* fucking *toy.* I pay for this piece of shit.'

Snorting from Eckhart Tolle.

I can smell the cigarettes and cum.

I am on my front somehow.
When did that happen?
My face is in the mattress
'Yes, sweetie, that's it.'
I am starting to feel something now
Yeah
OK
I can feel that.
that fucking hurts
get the fuck off me get off me get off me
'Bite down, sweetie.'
more powder up my nose.
More.
More.
More.
Tastes good.
Hurts.
But.
Wait.
My arms are free.
and I am not in the room anymore
How the fuck did that happen?
I am outside.
I'm outside and it's cold as fuck.
Hits me like a train.
I don't have my shoes.
That's weird.
Because I do now have my clothes on.
in my hand there is something.
in my hand I think.
It's money.
Yeah it is it's money.
About two hundred fucking quid.
Amazing.
That's fucking amazing.
Buzzing.
Actual buzzing somewhere.

Think it's in my pocket.
but I need to lie down.
there's something running down the inside of my joggers.
it hurts.
it fucking hurts.
I find some grass.
dunno how.
I lie down on it.
I have a packet of Haribo.
I eat them all.

I start moving down the road. Walking. Running. Always running.

My body feels weird.
Very fucking weird.
Like floppy but also not.

People moving away from me on the pavement holding their noses.

Fucking rude.
'Fucking rude!'
I'm fucked.
I'm fuckerooed.
My toes are all cut up think I stepped in glass.
Things are starting to hurt.
On my body.
And inside.
I can't let myself feel it.
No fucking way.
No.
No. I don't want to know.
I don't want to wake up.
I don't want to go to sleep.
Hospital.
But the police will find me.
Can't go to the clink.

I fucking can't go there. But maybe it's better at least I'll get clean. But maybe I won't?

I always find a way.

My feet are moving me.
I'm going past that park.
That park I was in earlier.
I know where I'm going.
Know exactly where I'm going.
I open my phone.
00:42
It's not what time I thought it was but I dunno.
I dunno anything.
I get up her name.
Mandy. Fucking Mandy.

I ned help
PlZ cn u help me
PleaSE
I can't do this aynmore
If oyu don't help me ill tell people
MALLORY
I'm outsid ur house

                                                                     What?

Gonna ring the doorbell
MALLORY MADDOX

                                                                     Wait Leo

Hello MALLORY MADDOXXX
RINGING THE DOORBELL IN
3
2
1

32

Mallory

'Step back.' He doesn't. 'Leo – *step back*.'

Flecks of my panicked spit fly into the night air between us as I hiss at him, frantically tying my dressing gown around my waist, checking back through the open door and up the staircase. *Did he hear? Did Ronan hear?* He stirred. He did. When the doorbell went. But he's had whiskey tonight. Please God, let him be too drunk to wake. I pull the door, so it remains open just an inch – I forgot my keys, shit! And my phone, *shit* – and turn to face Leo, my bare feet cold on the porch tiles beneath me. 'What the hell are you doing here?'

'Hi, Maallee.' He's slurring. Stumbling. Flopping about. All angular limbs and no centre of gravity, grabbing hold of the wisteria trunk that's climbing the front of the house to steady himself, then swinging around it. It snaps in his hand. 'Oops.'

'Leo – go to the pavement.'

'But...' He scratches his head. Under the porch light – blaring over us like an all-revealing halo – he is almost completely translucent. The veins beneath his pale skin are a poisonous, electric blue, creeping up his neck. He looks like he has just been dug up from the depths of the sea. 'It's nice here.'

He is filthy. And loud. Too loud. '*Leo, please.*'

'What? You invited me.'

Did I? I may have done. Oh, God. 'I did not.' I haven't been careful. Not at all.

'Um yeah, you did.'

'Leo—'

He trips over himself, landing on his knees with a low thud. It happens instantly, but also slowly, as if his body or his brain is on half speed. Or the two are disconnected from each other, unable to programme together. He kneels for a moment, then looks at his hands, frowning. 'I'm bleeding.' He is. I can't tell where the blood is coming from, and apparently neither can he, but it is definitely all over his palms and fingertips, now being pressed into the tiles. Evidence. Evidence of his presence at our house. 'That's weird.'

'*Leo, get up.*' I try to keep my voice calm, but the thickness of anger and panic squeeze at my chest. Attempting to lift him, to move him, to get him off this porch *immediately*, I pull at his arm, his shoulder, but he remains a dead weight. I glance up to our bedroom window, to Ronan. Light still off. *Please be asleep. Please.* 'Leo, let's just—'

'Can I come in?' He's dribbling. Foaming. A white trail of saliva-paste hanging from his lips, all the way to join the sticky mess of blood beneath him. It swings as he turns his head to look up at me. *So much evidence. So much body fluid evidence.* 'Everything fucking hurts.' He starts to crawl towards the partly open door.

This cannot happen.

If Ronan wakes—

If Ronan sees—

A reflex moves me, making me grab the collar of his hoodie and yank. He chokes, spluttering, but stands. 'Fuckin HELL that hurts!' It's wet. His hood. Sweat. I think it's sweat. It's *warm*. But I keep my fingers clasped around the collar as I move around him and pull, hard, so he begins to stumble along with me, down the pathway towards the front gate.

Let's just get out of the front garden.

To the road.

Then I can think.

But I can't. Think. I need a plan. An immediate plan.

One is not coming.

I drag him until he is out of the glow of the porch halo, into the half-light of the pavement. I don't stop manoeuvring him down it, away from the front of our home, but not wanting to place him directly in front of the neighbours. When I find a compromise – we're shielded by the Arkells' perfectly overgrown bush between the two houses – I let go. He rubs his neck. Bruises. 'Fucking hell, you're brutal,' he croaks. *Did I cause those?* 'You're insane.' No – I can't have. They are dark, a few hours old at least. *Aren't they?*

The sight of them instinctively makes me want to pull him into me.

He spits.

'Leo.'

My brain threatens to collapse. I almost lose my balance as it teeters like a block of worn and fragile rocks. I suddenly remember the Jenga set Ronan got me for Christmas. It was a stylish one. Each piece engraved with our initials intertwined. His way of making me engage with him in a more playful manner. He said I was isolating myself. Losing myself. Becoming too serious. Too meek. It was expensive – I googled it. From Liberty.

He can be so sweet. So protective.

What have I done?

Will the neighbours hear?

They can't—

'Mallory Maddox,' Leo growls, still rubbing his neck. *He knows my full name.* 'Nice ring to it.' He laughs a strained and hollow croak. 'Fucking nice house you've got yourself. Must be minted.'

'No,' is all I can think to say. *What do I say?* 'I…' The porch halo flicks off, the sensor no longer detecting movement, plunging us into a merciful state of relative darkness. I feel a momentary relief that both our sins are no longer so starkly on display. The road is so quiet. So still. So safe.

Think, Mallory, think.

He smells indescribable.

I haven't thought this through.

Any of this.

Reckless. I've been so… this whole thing… and if Ronan…

'Got a tenner?'

'How do you know where I live, Leo?'

'Followed you.'

'You *followed* me?'

His glazed eyes sharpen their focus on me. 'You're a funny one, you.'

'I...' He knows. He knows I've been watching him. 'I am not funny.'

'Just returning the favour.'

'I don't—'

'You're a liar.'

'I am not.'

'Do you have a bath?'

'A *what*?'

'A bath. I could do with one. I'm completely fucked.' He's not wrong. He could do with a bath and he is completely fucked. But now, so am I. *How much does he know?* I glance over my shoulder, up the road and back down it. *Will the neighbours see him?* They'll start asking questions – *questions are not good*. 'Bet you've got one of those stand-alone ones with swirly feet.'

'No.' We do, actually. 'You're not fucked, Leo. You're not. You just need...' Oh, God, what does he need? 'A good sleep.' He croak-laughs again. '*Shh*. Please – let's – let's just...'

'Ow, fuck.' He suddenly clutches his head and sways. I reach for him, taking hold of both his shoulders in my hands before he falls.

'Leo, what's happened?'

Do I actually want to know what's happened?

He looks like he's about to vomit all over me. 'Easy, Leo.' I could order him an Uber? But I'd need my phone... I could drive him back to his, to his... I want to say *home* but what I really mean is *canal bridge*, and I'm not even sure there'd be a postcode for that. And I'd need my keys. *Shit*. 'Listen, Leo—' I stop, because I see blood on his joggers. Drip marks. Running down the inner seam. 'What happened?' I can't help myself. For him. *Him*. Not the book. 'Who did that to you?'

He glances down, following my eyeline. 'Oh.' I feel his body make a small shudder. 'Didn't realise. Sorry.'

'Where's the blood coming from?'

'It's not mine.'

'It's not *yours*?'

'Well. Might be.' Jesus. 'Doesn't matter.'

I glance back up to the bedroom window. Mercifully, the light is still off. 'Give me your phone, Leo. We need to call you an ambulance.'

He pulls back, taking a step away, releasing my hands from his shoulders. 'No way.' His voice comes out differently. Lower. More assured. The most sober he has sounded since he turned up on my porch. Even, in a way, since I've known him. 'No ambulance. No police. No.' He lifts his hand out in front of himself, into the air between us. *Stop*.

'But… what are you going to *do*?'

'I was hoping you'd have the answer to that,' he says. 'It's why I'm here. I'm fucked, Mallory.'

Please stop saying that. 'It's the middle of the night.'

'Yeah.' He drops his hand. 'And you are going to help me.' He seems very sure about this. Very, very confident that this is what will happen.

'I… I can't, Leo.'

'Why not? You told me you'd help.' I did. I did tell him that. 'I just need a hundred quid to get me into a hostel for a few weeks. So I can get my shit together.' He lowers his voice. Narrows his eyes. 'There are people after me, Mallory.' People *after* him? Oh God.

I suddenly feel…

I don't know.

Something at the base of my skull.

An unusual buzz.

Visceral. Vibrant.

And I realise.

I feel *alive*.

Like I am here. Living. Right *here*.

And it is completely amazing.

This world is amazing.

'Who?' My voice trembles. 'Why are they after you, Leo?'

'Cos I've done bad things.'

'Bad things? *What* bad things?'

He shakes his head. 'I don't have time. Are you gonna help me or not?'

'I—'

'Can I kip here for the night?'

'What?'

'On your couch?'

'Leo—'

'I'm low-maintenance.'

'I don't—'

'Keep myself to myself.'

'But...'

He steps back, eyes suddenly dark. 'What the fuck is wrong with you? You said you were a sober alcoholic whose *primary purpose* is to *help others*. That we should go *to any lengths*. This is me needing those fucking lengths.'

He looks like he might cry. 'Yes, but I have a family, Leo.'

He smirks. 'No, you don't.'

'Excuse me?'

'You have a husband. No kids.'

How does he know all this?

Why is he bleeding?

'Who hurt you, Leo?'

'Why do you want to know so bad? Huh? What's in it for you?'

'What's *in it* for me? Nothing is *in it* for me, Leo.'

'Then why are you obsessed with me.'

'I'm not *obsessed* with you.'

I stop. He stares. I don't know what else to say.

Oh my God. He's right.

Isn't he?

Obsessed. What a horrible word. Secretive. Dirty. Used for someone who is *not OK*. Who is *unbalanced* or *deranged* or—

'Well?'

'I...' Get your shit together, Mallory. Get rid of him. *Now*. 'I want to help you. I do. Of course I do. But you need medical attention first. I can't do that here. So let's just call an ambula—'

'Mal?'

Not Leo's voice this time.

But one I know very well.

When I turn to find Ronan stood behind me on the pavement, it takes me a moment to register the reality of what I see. For a split second, nothing makes sense. It is an odd sight. One that makes my stomach drop and the buzzing in the back of my head reach fever pitch. Not least because Ronan is here, stood in nothing but his boxer shorts. But also because he is holding my special hardback copy of *Pericles* in one hand, and my mobile phone in the other.

It's open.

My phone, not the book.

And I can see the Grindr app glaring back at me from the screen.

Aubergine emojis, Ronan's hairless nipples, all.

33

Leo

He looks mad as fuck.
    Is he gonna hit her with that book?
    He's gonna chuck it.
    At her?
    He is.
    He's gonna—
    'Ow!' Lands square in the front of my head. '*Piece of shit.*'
    'Who are you?' he says.
    'Better question – who the fuck chooses a book as a weapon? Posh twat.' I grab my nose. 'Prick. Better not've fucking broke it.'
    He doesn't seem to give a shit. Just turns to her. 'What did he mean when he said you're *obsessed* with him, Mal?'
    I could answer that. But my brain is banging, ears are ringing, thoughts all juddery. Can't tell if it's the drugs or the book or what happened earlier. *What happened earlier?*
    Fucking Mo—
    'Mallory?' He's got his face in hers now. Hissing. Trying to be quiet. Bits of spit flying. *The neighbours. Can't piss off the neighbours.* But she doesn't answer him. Just stays dead still. Looks like she's about to fucking implode. '*Mallory?*' It's like she's stuck. He puts his hands on her arms. Shakes her. 'Mallory – what is going on?'
    Is she gonna cry?
    She is.
    She's gonna—

'Oi!' I shout. At him. Because the book to the face did something to me. Made me feel all... *awake*. Made me all *ragey*. I fucking love rage. Blocks everything out. I get off on it. Makes me wanna fight. I wanna tear someone apart. Fuck them up bad – break their jaw and rip their skin with my teeth. *Fucking Mo*. But he's not here so it's gonna be this man. Posh Fucking Ronan. 'Nobhead.'

He turns right to me, glaring, so I catch a proper look. Curly floppy hair. Tall. Fit. He's shredded. Stomach muscles like a cheese grater. Might put up a good fight. I'm in the mood. I'm in the fucking mood now. 'Come on then!' I shout. 'Let's have it!'

'Ronan – the neighbours...' Mallory says.

'I'll eat your fucking head!' I scream. Dunno why. Think cos he's just staring. Reminds me of that man from *American Psycho*. There's something weird in his eyes. Something I don't like. He's not scared. That's it. That's what I don't like. And arrogant. Reckon he loves being out here without his clothes on. Getting a posh-person thrill in his kecks in the street in the middle of the night. Can tell all his mates about how he saved Crouch End by lobbing a book at me. Absolute hero. His skin's all bristled. Oh, would you look at that. He shaves his nipples. 'Come on, you piece of twat!'

'Get off this street – *now*.'

He's kinda hot.

'You pussy!' I think I'm screaming – can't really tell. It's like my head is in a vacuum cleaner now, the noise just bouncing back at me. *Everything hurts*. I don't wanna think. I wanna fight. 'Come on!' Getting my lights blown out will help me *not think*. Would be good if he knocked me clean into oblivion. 'Let's fucking have it!'

I'd like that.

Think I'm gonna fall over.

'This is ridiculous,' he says. He's all calm. Makes me even more mad. Think he's Irish. The Irish love to fight, don't they? *Why won't he fucking fuck me up? Smack me?*

'Smack me!'

I throw a fist for good measure. Doesn't collide with anything.

Stumble a bit. Oh – a bush. Nice. Bouncy bush. Bounces me onto something hard.

'Ronan, please – let's just go inside.'

The two of them are all blurry now – can see blotches of black clouds everywhere – think the meth is doing something weird. Might have been a bad batch. Can just make him out, tapping the screen of the phone in his hand.

'We can't just leave him here, Mal. I'm calling the police.'

Jesus Christ.

Not the fucking police.

Can't have that.

'Wait – stop.'

Am I on the floor?

'I'm dialling.'

'All right, nobhead, I'm going,' I say. 'Prick.' I am… I'm on the floor. Looks like I'm gonna be crawling out of here. The book's here. The one he threw at my head. Cover all swirling gold letters and blue. I pick it up. Heavy. Might throw it back.

'Oi!' I scream at him. Wait. No. I could sell this. I turn and point it at her. Mallory. The woman who's obsessed with me. 'You said you would help me.'

The man looks at her weird. 'Mal?'

'Leave it. Let's go inside, Ronan.'

Mal and Ronan. How fucking quaint.

'She promised.' I try and sound sad – I do – but I think I'm about to throw up.

'Hang on…' Ronan jabs his finger through the air at me, still looking at her. 'Is this your *patient*? The one Joanie saw you with?'

'Yes,' she mumbles.

He looks suddenly fucking appalled. 'How does he know where you *live*, Mal?'

'He followed me.'

Oof. Snitch.

There's something weird with these two. I can't see straight but I can see that much. Ronan steps towards me, clenching his fist now, balling it up like the bad man he wishes he was.

'Careful,' I say. 'You come any closer I'll snap your neck.'

I am aware I am on the floor, yes.

But I could.

Come on rage – let's have it.

He stops. Leans down. His face in mine. He just stares. For ages. His eyes scanning me up and down. Maybe he fancies me. I am definitely a fantasy for this type of person. I'm not getting gay vibes though, despite the abs. I've been wrong about it before, mind you.

'You all right, mate?' I say. 'Want a blowie or something?'

He growls. Sexy. 'Don't ever come near this house, or my wife, again. *Do you hear me?*'

'She said I should come visit,' I say. 'Not my fault.'

He steps away, and I sit up.

I watch him pull at her wrist, moving her into him – like protection. But the way he does it is weird.

Makes me say, 'You're a mopey little prick, Ronan.'

He looks at me. Mad as fuck. *Get my name out of your filthy chavvy mouth.*

She looks at me. Scared as fuck. *Don't, Leo.*

Like a little kid.

'All right – fucking fine.'

I turn and move away, crawling down the street. Fucking still got the book in my hand. Weird.

'He's a rabid animal,' I hear Ronan say behind me.

I look back. 'Prick.' But he's not there.

I hear their door slam shut.

Rabid animal.

Kinda like it.

Kinda hot.

But I'm still gonna knock his lights out.

I crawl back up the road. To just outside their house on the pavement. I must look fucking brutal. I'll break the window. Shove this book down his throat. He'll love it. I'm about to go down their little path, but I stop, cos I see them. They're in their front room now. I can just make them out through the glass – the glass I wanna smash. They have those posh wooden blinds that no one closes. He's holding that phone and saying things to her. I can't hear, but I know she's crying. Proper crying.

He's scanning through the phone with his finger. Saying things. Looks like he's calling her mental. She's trying to grab it, but he's pushing her away.

My head. My fucking *head*.

Then she's on the floor. I can see the spit flying from his mouth. He looks mad as fuck. He grabs her wrist. In that way he did out here before. Pulls her up off the floor and out of the front room.

Dunno where to.

Dunno if I want to know.

My *fucking head*.

Oh – shit – I'm gonna vom.

I try walking back down the road.

Make it a few streets.

Need to sit. I need to…

Hospital.

No.

There's a car.

I sit behind it.

Cos I think I'm gonna pass out.

I feel sick.

I'm gonna be sick.

Oh. Yeah. There it is.

Sick. Sick all over me.

Just wait.

Just wait a bit.

Vom a bit. Wait a bit.

Inhale the air.

Night air.

Oh, that's nice. Nice for my brain. I gulp it down like it's vodka.

With it come the memories.

bed sheets the men Eckhart Tolle

Was that tonight? Those men?

How many were there?

I don't wanna think.

Fucking no – I don't wanna remember.

No no no.
hands tied
No no no no no.
La la la la la la.
I've still got this book. This stupid fucking book.
I flick through it.
It is pages thick.
stuff up my nose
READ THE WORDS, LEO.
The words swim.
It's all poetry.
Shakespeare, this.
I liked one of them. At school.
Think it was called *Titus*-something.
Andronicus.
Everyone killed everyone. Everyone was very mad.
What's this one about…

To be happy means to be free
and to be free means to be brave.

This one is shit.
Bullshit. Such bullshit.
my toy
I start ripping the pages out with my teeth.
Rabid animal.
I spit them out on the floor. The floor is wet.
I don't wanna wake up tomorrow.
I really really do not want to wake up tomorrow.
I need my mates. Tina and G.
I remember! I've got money! Ha!
I made a mint tonight.
I'll call Brick. Fuck it.
I find my pockets.
Wait.
Where is it?
Where's the money?

Did he pay me? He did. I remember. I had it.
Fuck…!
No.
Have I…?
I've dropped it.
No.
NO NO NO NO.
Gotta get to the canal bridge
Get home
Get home
That's it
How many men were there?
That's
It
I'm bleeding
I need to look
I need to see
I can't fucking
It's all down my legs
Fuck
The witch is coming with her spindly fucking fingers
To tear me apart
Inside out
I can't look.
I don't wanna
the clouds are parting
It's wearing off
The meth
It's slipping away
I need it back
I need it back
I do not want to wake up
Never want to wake up
Where's my fucking phone
Where…
Here.
Some fucker will let me have a few bumps

I can pay them back
Scroll through the contacts.
I'm trying to find someone
Under the bridge now
It's fucking freezing
Where is it?
Brick
Cam
Fat Fred
Mental Matt
Mo
I don't have many
Sam. There's Sam.
My first boyfriend.
I was seventeen
Mum.
There it is.
Mum.
Fingers won't fucking type!

Pls help me mum

Stare at it
Fucking
Fucking pathetic
Delete it.
Tomorrow I don't wanna wake up.
The water.
The water.
Yes.
I need something to weigh me down.
Stones.
Put them in my pockets.
Can't find any.
Pretty sure the meth'll make me heavy.
Get in the water.
Time to go.

Oof it's cold.
Grim.
Nothing poetic about it.
I guess this is it then.
The end.

Part 3

Two weeks later

34

Mallory

'Morning, sweetheart, would you like a cup of coffee?'

Ronan stands in the open doorway of our bedroom. His voice is soothing. His arms are hanging loosely by his sides. His hands are placed gently in his pockets and his eyes are soft in the morning light. It is still dark outside, but the glow of the corner lamp (a Pooky special with a William Morris shade: a swirling pattern of birds and berries) highlights his frame. Crisp shirt, beige chinos, mop of curly hair pushed to the side. I can sense he is a little sleepy, but he looks ready. Ready for the day. I can feel his quiet confidence, which I have always envied and admired, emanating from behind the tiredness. That steely inner resolve. That grounding rock.

My rock. Unshakable.

He looks incredibly handsome. I have always thought so.

I have.

'Morning, darling.' I glance at the clock on my beside table. 6 a.m. He has asked the exact same question at the exact same time for the past two weeks. 'I can do it,' I say, stretching my arms up above my head, catlike. I almost purr.

'No,' he says. 'Stay where you are. You need to rest.'

He's right. He always is. 'Are you sure?'

'Of course I'm sure.'

He steps slowly towards me across the carpet, stopping when he reaches the bed, and leans forward to kiss me on the forehead. As he does, I smell his signature scent: Ronan's favourite Le Labo aftershave. It's so recognisable as *him*. Expensive, but worth it.

Strong, but inviting. There is a depth to it which feels endless – almost dark and smoky – elevated by fresh floral and woody notes. A hint of iris. It is very comforting. Wholesome.

I inhale again.

It's almost addictive.

I smile and make a small *mmm*. 'Good morning, handsome.'

When he reciprocates, smiling back, I see how white and straight his teeth are. They give the gruffness of his features a commercial appeal. I have always told him he would have been a great model. He will roll his eyes at this suggestion. As if being a model is beneath him. As if there is more to him than just his looks, and it is offensive to think otherwise. He is right. There is so much more to this man than the way he looks. 'It's going to be a great day,' he says gently, perching himself next to me. His voice has been so gentle recently. He pushes a strand of hair out of my face, tucking it neatly behind my ear. 'You always look the prettiest in the mornings.'

The light makes him look so *soft*. That's what I wanted when I picked the lampshade. *A soft glow*. The Strawberry Thief pattern has always been my favourite, and it was the right choice, although I was unsure whether to go *with* the fringe or *without*, and it took me a good few weeks to decide. I ended up opting for *without*, because the fringe was just too kitsch and, let's face it, *granny-ish*. As so many Instagram homeware influencers have astutely observed: there is a fine line between chic and granny. But if you get the balance right, you are revered as a boho delight.

Enviable.

It's all about the colours, I think.

'That's a lie,' I say, looking down. Shy. Embarrassed. But grateful. 'I look all puffy.'

'You don't,' he whispers. 'And I never would.'

He never would lie.

I nod and take his hand, kissing the back of it. 'I have lots to do today.'

His eyes brighten. 'You do! That's exciting.' It is. 'How many chapters do you think you'll get done?'

I lift his hand in mine, pressing his fingers against my cheek. 'I don't want to jinx it, but I think I could get a good four thousand words down today.'

He almost laughs. And not because he doesn't believe me, but because he's *proud. He is proud of me.* 'You're on a roll.'

'Well, I'm inspired.'

'I'm just so...' He stops, biting his lip. He wants to say something, but isn't sure.

'Go on,' I say quietly.

'I'm just really proud of you, Mal – you're turning a corner.'

'Thank you.'

'After...' After everything. 'I can't wait to read it later.'

'Good. I can't wait for your feedback.'

'It's so good, Mal.'

I pull a face, an embarrassed wince. 'Do you really think so?'

At this, he shoots me a look: *We are not going through this again*. Firm, but tender. 'Yes. It's brilliant. And you know it is. You are in your element.' His eyes trace me up and down, taking me in.

The version of me he adores.

Settled. Calm. Correct.

'Thank you.'

'You have become yourself again.' I try not to look away. It's hard, but I manage. 'Right, I'll grab your coffee.'

'Thank you.'

He furrows his brow, shaking his head slowly, as if looking at something he hasn't seen in a very long time. Something he lost that has returned to him. Something he thought he would never get back. This is affection. This is Ronan's affection.

'Magnificent Mal,' he says.

When he gets up to leave, the slats in the bed beneath the mattress groan, as if trying to say something. To interject. To break the calm. To remind me that there are cracks, out of sight, waiting.

I lie still, until the pad of his socks on the carpet disappears down the stairs. When he is gone, I instinctively turn to take my phone from the bedside table. But like every other morning for the past two weeks, I remember that I no longer have it.

'Oh, and I'll bring up your tablets!' he shouts up from below.

'Thanks!' I reply, with a cheery eagerness.

He has it.

My phone.

He has had my phone since the night on the porch, two weeks ago.

He saw everything. Grindr. The pictures I took of him when he was asleep. The conversations with *Daddy* and *SxyRodent* and other men. My overzealous use of the aubergine emoji. All of it. And in the lounge, right after Leo ran away with my copy of *Pericles*, Ronan stood in deep silence for a moment, eyes wide.

I have never seen him quite like that.

The anger beneath was surfacing. That wasn't exactly new. But first: the utter confusion and terror. He looked at me like I was someone he had never met before – an intruder in his life. A lunatic, just escaped from the asylum. He kept his distance, staying at the other side of the room.

'*What is this, Mal? What is happening?*'

I had no excuse.

I had nothing. I panicked. I had to plead guilty. I had to plead complete insanity. I had to tell him about my secret writing project. About *Slay*. About Leo. About the creativity I was finding through this boy for a new book. That I had met him at a T-Party. That a T-Party is not a tea party, despite what one might think. I told him all of it.

'*You've been following a drug addict sex worker – for inspiration?*'

'Yes.'

'*So he's not a client?*'

'No.'

'*He's a random stranger?*'

'Yes.'

'*Do you know how dangerous this is?*'

'I mean—'

'*You've been lying to me.*'

'Yes. Yes, I have.'

'*How can I trust you?*'

'*Ronan—*'

'*You know what happened last time you acted like this. Are you becoming unwell?*'

'*No, I—*'

'*Tell me what's happening then. Because it is very hard to see otherwise.*'

So I told him the truth. I told him that for a while I'd felt like I'd been drowning in my own mind – that I'd felt numb and stuck and small. I said I wanted to write again. That I hated being a therapist/counsellor. And that I'd felt trapped. This wasn't the life I'd imagined. That I'd needed something to make me feel alive again.

He laughed. He laughed like I was stupid. Like I was a child. He said I was naive. That I was living in a fantasy world, which was entirely self-centred.

'*Can you hear yourself?*'

He said it was important for him to understand what had been going on in my mind for the past few weeks, and asked me to show him what I had written. I sat on the couch watching his eyes scan over the laptop screen, over *Slay*, utterly disgusted. His hand went to his mouth. He nearly cried. It was the first time in years – since the time he almost didn't get his promotion – that I saw tears in his eyes. I listened, as his words flooded over me. '*This is disturbing.*' '*Why are you writing this?*' '*It's sick. It's twisted. Who is it even meant for?*' '*There is something seriously wrong with you.*'

When he put the laptop down, he stared at me, genuinely terrified. He said I was unrecognisable. I again tried to explain. I again tried to tell him that I didn't think I was very happy. That I wasn't sure my life was as I wanted it to be, and that perhaps I was trying – in some way – to escape.

He looked so angry.

'*Escape what? Your life is incredible. Enviable.*'

I didn't know what to say.

'*I'm calling the doctor, Mal.*'

I begged him not to tell anyone. I begged and pleaded and said I'd just got a bit carried away with myself and that it didn't need to be a big deal. He took out his own phone – mine was in his pocket – and googled the crisis line, because it was the middle of the night and he didn't think going to A&E would be appropriate in case we saw anyone we knew.

He put the phone on loud speaker and told the lady who answered what had happened. He told her how unsafe I had been. How very, very worried he was for my welfare, and now for his. She sounded young-ish. Maybe early twenties. I could hear she was chewing gum. She kept asking to talk to me, but he said I wasn't able to come to the phone – which I suppose was correct. By this point I was crying on the floor and my voice wasn't coming out right, it was shaking so much. My brain was stalling, malfunctioning, as I was trying to piece together what I had done. How anyone could see any sense in my actions.

No one could.

I knew it.

Ronan told the crisis-line lady that he thought I was exhibiting manic symptoms, and that this had happened before. I heard her say, '*Well, people do odd things – it doesn't make them psychotic*' – which I was grateful for. But Ronan told her it was more than odd. That I was putting my life – and his – in danger. The crisis-line lady said she needed to assess me and so he reluctantly held the phone out in front of my face and told me to speak. The lady asked me a few questions: my name, my age, what day it was. She asked how I was feeling and I said I was fine. Ronan interjected, saying I wasn't fine in the slightest, telling me I needed to be honest, for my own mental health. That my mental health depended on it. The crisis-line lady asked me if I had a history of mental illness. So we spoke about my prior admission, which is when the words *mental* and *health* began to make less and less sense. We said them so many times that they lost all meaning. They became mush. I might as well have been saying *banana* and *rabbit*. *My banana rabbit took a turn for the worse seven years ago. My banana rabbit has been stable since then, but I have felt a bit numb. My banana rabbit was definitely not OK back then – but this feels different.*

She asked if I was scared. I said I wasn't sure. And then she said jovially, '*Don't worry love – so many people have the odd menty-b, we'll help you through it.*'

I said, 'Menty-b?'

She said, '*Yeah: mental breakdown.*'

This made Ronan rage. '*How dare you?*' he snapped. He said he would report her for making light of the situation. But I appreciated what she'd said. It made me smile. And she probably had a very valid point. She apologised, saying she was trying to help me feel a little calmer, and that it came out wrong. Ronan said he was going to make sure that she lost her job. *If this is the state of the banana rabbit system these days – no wonder so many people die.*

She apologised again. He asked how he could complain, and said he would like to put it in an email to her manager. She said OK, and gave him an address. She then continued with the assessment. She was nice, I thought. Friendly. Chatty. She did make me feel less stressed. *People do odd things – it doesn't make them unwell.*

I told her what had happened, and agreed that it was a little bizarre, but that I was a creative. Sometimes I did things that might be out of the ordinary, but this was just my imagination. I was an author, and I was undertaking creative research for my next book. She asked for my name.

When I told her, she gasped.

'*Wait – oh my God – Mallory Maddox? The author Mallory Maddox?*'

It was an incredibly strange moment.

'*Yes, that's me.*'

'*Oh my God – I've read your book!*'

She told me that she loved it. *Shallow Embers*. That she read it when she was in her teens and it helped her *so much*. This was the point that Ronan snatched the phone away from my face and told her that she was inappropriate, and that to be discussing herself and using phrases like *menty-b* during an assessment should get her fired. He would make sure of it. He asked her if she really *truly* believed she was good at her job, because he thought she was despicable. She apologised again and told him to add it to the complaint email.

He said he would.

She said OK.

She asked me some more questions, about my mood, my perception, if I was hearing voices, if I was suicidal. I said no, no to all of it. She told me to call back if my mood dipped, and to speak to my GP about upping the dose of my SSRI, or perhaps changing to another medication.

She asked me if I felt like Ronan could take care of me.

I said yes.

She said OK.

And then Ronan hung up.

He took my phone, and I haven't seen it since.

I am lucky.

I am lucky because my phone doesn't have direct access to my emails on it, so Ronan won't be able to find the conversations I have had with Stan. He would have to log into the browser, and he doesn't know my Yahoo password. I'm not even sure he is fully aware the account exists.

After the banana rabbit phone call and the mention of a menty-b, he was so angry. He told me it would be best for my mental health to delete any evidence of *Slay* from my laptop. He said it would be best for everyone. That if anyone found it, they would think I was insane and deeply disturbed, and that wouldn't be fair to me. And that this boy – this random *drug boy* – was clearly very dangerous. Any link to him could be seriously bad for us both – but particularly him, with his high-profile job. He handed me back the laptop and told me to delete it in front of him. He stood over me as I used the mouse to drag the document into the trash and click ERASE ALL.

It went.

In a second. It vanished. And as it did, I felt a sudden coldness. An emptiness. A real sadness. A longing to go back. Loss.

But I heard him sigh. Relief.

'*I'm not sure you should have this either, Mal,*' he said, pointing to the laptop. '*It's clearly not healthy for you at the moment. It's making you write out some very dark parts of your brain that I don't think you should be accessing.'*

He wanted to take it.

I tried to protest. *'But what about my clients?'*

'Are you serious? You can't be seeing your clients while you're like this.'

But I knew I needed to keep the laptop. It was imperative. I remembered that I had a duplicate copy of *Slay* saved in a file titled CLIENT WORK. Knowing I had that copy was the only thing allowing me to breathe normally. I craved the story I was discovering. The idea of having no access to it made me feel vacant. Without it I felt blank. Nothing.

Meek Mal.

And the deal. Stanley. The money. I wasn't sure what I needed more: the feeling the book gave me as I wrote it, or the future it could afford me.

Could I have both? They would come hand in hand.

So I scrambled, attempting anything to get him to let me have it.

'I need to keep writing, Ronan. It'll help me get better – I promise. I need the creative release. It will keep me steady. I can completely see how that particular story wasn't good for me – it was awful – and it will never see the light of day. But I need to write something.'

He shook his head. *No.*

But then I had an idea. *'What if I write a new book? A different one.'*

He didn't like it. *'No – no more writing.'*

'Wait – wait – listen. Give me a minute.'

I told him I had been thinking of writing a *romance* novel for a long time. No *darkness*. No *sadness*. Just life-affirming love and joy. *'Just what the world needs right now. Just what I need right now.'*

He stopped. *'Go on.'*

I said that writing something *positive* and *uplifting* could really help me. Help change my mindset and bring me back to a place of stability. I spent ten minutes cobbling together a plot (not dissimilar from our own story) about a woman who was lost and afraid and underconfident in her abilities. Then she meets a man. The man she falls in love with lights her up. He makes her feel alive again.

He scratched his chin. '*I like this.*'

'*Yes?*'

'Yes. So – the love interest helps her. Helps her find herself. Helps her find the side of her that succeeds.'

'*That's a great idea, Ronan.*'

He said, '*This book seems much more appropriate.*'

Then he said he liked the idea of us working *together* on it. He could give me *notes*.

And then he came up with a title.

The Air Between Us.

He thought it sounded punchy.

I smiled. '*Wow, I love it.*'

'*They didn't promote me at Netflix for nothing.*'

I agreed. '*You're brilliant.*'

He paused, considering. '*OK. If you turn off the passcode on your laptop – so there's no secrecy.*'

I agreed. Absolutely.

He watched me do it.

And so I have my laptop.

And so now, for the past two weeks, during the daytime, I have been writing my new contemporary and uplifting romance: *The Air Between Us.* And every night, I read what I have written to Ronan. (We are tentative, but are currently comparing it to commercial hits such as *One Day* and *Normal People*.) Ronan tells me it is wonderful. That it is brilliant. That Netflix might even love it. '*Who knows – maybe I'll put in a good word.*'

But none of this is the truth.

None of it.

He is lying.

The Air Between Us is awful. The concept, the writing, the characters, the title. I've never hated anything so much in my entire life. Two-dimensional, thin, clichéd and worst of all: boring. It is deeply *boring*. Embarrassing, in fact. I know that Ronan knows it too. I know that he thinks it's terrible. That it will never sell. But he lies, intentionally, to keep me writing it.

To keep me sane.

To keep me correct.

But every night, after he has fallen asleep, whiskey-heavy, I go into the en suite with my laptop, sit on the closed toilet seat, get up the hidden *Slay* document and write the book that I know *will* sell. The book that will give me what I need. My ticket out. Of this. This domesticised, softly lit, William Morris cell.

This meek numbness.

So, I am now writing two books. Which is ironic, given the writer's block I experienced for the best part of the last seven years. With *The Air Between Us*, it feels like I am wading through mud. Reaching the four thousand daily words' goal seems insurmountable, and sometimes I have to google things and copy-and-paste them into the document to bulk it up. Sweeping descriptions of countryside settings. A whole page dedicated to the structure of trees. (Ronan said he loved it. Because it was dreadful.)

With *Slay*, it is different. I can type whole paragraphs, one after the other, and they just flow. I think of Leo, of what he told me, the way he acted and held himself. I don't even feel the need to go back and edit. It just feels so easy, because there is no *thought*. I enter a space that feels *other*. Removed. Limitless. There is such a strange feeling when I resurface into the reality of the bathroom, having spent hours in a completely different world.

I ache to have it back every time.

I wonder if P.K. Anderson's fingers hurt this much from typing so fervently, or if her eyes burn, like mine do, from staring so intently at the words on the screen as they pour out of her.

I am currently three quarters of the way through. All I need now is the ending.

And I have realised that when it comes to the ending, I am a little blocked. Not *blocked* blocked. But I just need to understand what happens to Liam… Where the story will end, in a way that feels authentic. And for that, I need Leo.

Tricky. Considering everything. But I have a plan.

The day after the night on the porch, Ronan called the police and asked for their advice. They told him to put a security camera up on the front of the house, in case Leo returned. Ronan loved the idea. He ended up choosing a video doorbell that detects motion on the porch, just like the halo light does. He has been working from home for the past two weeks – to look after me – and today is his first day back in the office. If I leave the house, it will alert his phone.

He knows this.

I know this.

We both know this.

But he is going back to work today. Which means I have a window of opportunity. I can get out through the back door and go to the bridge. Try and find him again. I won't need my phone. The bridge is in walking distance.

My excitement peaks. *Just to make sure the story is correct.*

And of course, I want to check he is OK.

Over the past two weeks I've had to embellish a little bit without him. Invent some things. Just a few details. To heighten the tension, to provide emotional depth. At times I have wondered if these additions read as genuine or realistic. Without Leo it's been more difficult to feel confident that they are authentic to Liam's character. But I think it's good.

In fact, I know it is.

Because Stanley agrees.

More than agrees. He loves it.

Wow.

He typed this just a few days ago.

You're really pushing this forward, Mal. It's deeply moving, and shocking. Keep going.

So I did.

I kept pushing it.

And last night, finally, he told me he was ready to submit it to the publisher. I thought I might have to finish the whole thing, which I was worried about doing without seeing Leo again. But he explained that if a concept is strong enough, sometimes a publisher will accept a submission on a *partial*. This means that he is going to submit the first two thirds of *Slay* – tomorrow – with just an outline of the final third. He thinks what we have is good enough to get an offer, and that we might even hear a financial figure before the end of the day. All we need is a strong ending.

Tomorrow.

He forwarded me the email from the editor – Gina – at the publishing house. I quickly pull my laptop out from under the bed as I hear Ronan in the kitchen below, and re-read it, enjoying the fluttering sensation in my chest.

Stan,

Jesus Christ – you do deliver. I thought maybe you were getting too old for this (!) but *Slay* is SO fresh. This is very, very exciting. It's so bleak – but also somehow so funny? Tell M.M. Johnstone we can't wait to read what happens next. She has a real handle on what the market is after. Amazing amazing amazing – relevant, urgent and necessary. I'm sure I'll be in tears at the end.

Best,

Gina

Three *amazing*s from Gina. Each time I look at them my brain floods with an organic ecstasy, heightened with each repeated word. Three hits in one. It almost makes me audibly groan. The way she hasn't even separated them with commas, because she was just too excited to type properly.

Relevant. Urgent. Necessary. Only the best books get called those three words all at once. I don't even think Sally Rooney's books were called those things. Maybe only books like *To Kill a Mockingbird*, and the Bible.

I did that.

M.M. Johnstone did that.

I asked Stan if we can use a pseudonym for this book. He was reluctant at first. Said it wasn't necessary. But I explained I wanted a fresh start, and to move on from the YA days of *Shallow Embers*. I wanted to appear more *mature*, and a little mystery goes a long way. The name M.M. Johnstone seems to work. Johnstone sounds reputable enough and I think the double letters sound serious and intentional. Like P.K., it has a nice ring to it, but it's not too pretentious. Stan agreed.

> This is the beginning of something for you, Mal.
>
> All I will need is the outline for the ending – can you get this to me for tomorrow?
>
> Trust yourself. Your instincts are on point. Or should I say, M.M. Johnstone's instincts!
>
> I didn't want to tell you this, but I have had an indication of their pre-emptive offer. It is £70,000 for a two-book deal. And I think I can push them up. Submit the outline for the ending, and we will make this happen.
>
> Well done – you're nearly there!

£70,000.

I nearly fell over when I first read it. It is *more* than enough.

A deep warmth floods through my blood, awakening a thrill in the pit of my stomach. *This could work*. A mental snapshot of the future invades me. In it, there is no husband. There are no children.

I am alone.

And I am by the sea.

Not in a suicidal way. In a *I will live out the rest of my days by the ocean* way. In a P.K. Anderson way. Although – no. The snapshot is less *California sun-kissed chic*, and more *rural country bumpkin*. I want to keep it British. I want to keep it *woolly jumpers and a dog*.

A dog.

Yes.

A German vizsla. One that runs along the beach while I sip

my coffee that I have bought from the café on the headland. Rain-soaked, wind-battered. Warming my hands by a log fire before a day of writing. Am I in Wales? I could be.

I could.

The Gower. I loved it there.

All the coves. All that *space*. I could swim in the sea every day. Rent a little cottage, whilst drafting the sequel to *Slay*. I could start an Instagram account and upload pictures of the waves, or a bench overlooking the shore, with captions like: *Not a bad view for a day of plot construction*. P.K. Anderson would comment with a single love heart from across the pacific. A small acknowledgement, a secret code of affirmation that I have joined her club. One of freedom. Liberation. Creativity. Unhinged Bravery.

The Gower.

I love it.

This time, Ronan is not there. I could *reclaim* it. That's what people do – isn't it? – when they are healing. They reclaim things. I will heal by the sea.

As I reread the emails, the buzz in the back of my brain erupts again. I have been chasing it for the past two weeks. I feel *alive*. I feel *in control*. I hate to say it, but I feel *powerful*. Should I hate to say it? *M.M. feels powerful*. I have surprised myself at how good at this I am. How good at pretending.

It's not lying – I'm not *telling lies*.

It's planning.

It's *survival*.

But I have to be careful. Incredibly careful. It's not been easy. Ronan has taken more than just my phone. He has taken my bank cards. For my safety – of course. Last time I was unwell, I spent a lot of our money on unnecessary things like the deposit for the boat, and I agreed we didn't want that happening again. But then I panicked. I didn't know how I would receive the payment from Stan (should it come to that). Then I remembered an old Monzo account I set up years ago for groceries. The card is in the bottom drawer of my bedside cabinet.

I am all set.

I am in control.

There is a part of me that feels indestructible.

'You want oat milk?!' Ronan shouts up from the kitchen. 'We're out of almond!'

'Yes, please!'

I push the laptop back under the bed, listening to his feet padding back up the stairs.

'Here you are,' he says, reappearing in the doorway, soft in the light, just as before. He is holding a mug of steaming coffee in one hand and three tablets in the palm of the other. They are vitamins, and my anti-depressant. He hands his cargo to me, careful not to spill liquid on the bedding.

This bedding was two hundred pounds. I could do with that money now. When I spent all my money making this attic conversion a *safe space*, I didn't realise.

Or I did, and chose to ignore it.

I will not ignore reality anymore.

He tuts. 'Oh shit, I forgot water.'

'Don't worry, I'll take them with the coffee.' I smile.

He smiles back.

I am about to place them on the bedside table, to take later, but he puts his finger in the air and says, '*Aah*' in a way that makes my skin prickle. *Aah*, meaning *No. No – take them now. While I'm here. I'm keeping you safe.*

I place them on my tongue, take a sip of the coffee and swallow. It is too hot and burns the roof of my mouth. 'Perfect,' I say. But he doesn't move. He continues to look at me. There is something happening inside him. He is nervous. Nervous to leave me. 'How are you feeling about your first day back in the office?' I add, casually.

'I'm feeling OK.' He looks at his watch. Nearly time to go. 'More importantly – how are you feeling?'

'I feel great Ronan. Really.'

'Good. I was worried.'

'I know.'

'I don't like leaving you.'

'I know, but I'm fine.'

'I have something to tell you.'

I stop. A jolt of anxiety threatens to destabilise me. 'Oh?'

He looks serious now. Very. 'I'm hoping you'll be pleased.' He looks at the floor while he says this, which suggests the opposite might be true. *What is this?* 'I just wanted to add another layer of safety to your day – now that I'm going back to work. And I think you'll be happy.'

Another layer of safety?

'Oh! That's kind, Ronan, but you really don't need to go to all this effort – I'm in a much better place now—'

'I've invited your mother to come and stay.'

I feel the room tilt. 'Oh!' Oh, God. Oh no. 'You've been speaking to my mother?'

'Yes – I thought it was important to keep her updated.'

'Oh, right! Lovely! When is she arriving?'

'Today.'

Shit. *Shit.* I underestimated him. He is too clever. One step ahead. 'What time?' I try to push through the dizziness. The sudden lack of balance. The residue of the sideswipe. 'Today, did you say?'

'I think this afternoon. Does it matter?'

'No – I mean…'

'You'll be in regardless – I told her to knock when she arrives. Oh – I just said your phone is broken – hope that's OK?'

'How much have you told her?' Something bitter emerges in my throat. I don't want to clear it, in case he thinks I'm upset or angry or sad. God forbid he thinks I am sad. 'It's just that I thought – I thought perhaps we could deal with this on our own – just us, together…'

'I haven't told her any specific details.'

'Oh – OK that's—'

'Just that things have got bad for you again. And she's worried, Mal.'

'Mum can be like that. She doesn't need to be.'

'She said she isn't surprised, either.'

I pause. 'Sorry?'

He slowly sits, perching at the end of the bed. I stare at the little mound of my feet under the duvet, and with him looming over them, I notice how incredibly small I appear in comparison. The meekness has seeped back into my being. 'Well – she hasn't heard from you in months, Mal, she assumed something was going on.' He reaches to take my hand in his. I let him. His skin is soft. 'She was worried we were breaking up.' He smiles sadly. *How could we let her think that, Mal?*

'She can be very dramatic.' I let him link his fingers between mine. 'So she's – what? Coming for just a few nights?' I wonder if I can push back the outline for a few days – give myself some time…

'We both thought a week would be good.' A *week*? I feel a sudden claustrophobia closing in at the edges of myself, knowing that his presence, and hers, in this house, in this space – together… *again* – will suffocate me. 'Just until you start seeing your clients again. And your mother can help you get there with that.'

'Right. OK. And she'll stay in the spare room?'

'Well – I'm not sure we should give her the couch – and I don't think she would want to get in here with me!' He points to the bed, smiling, because he has made a joke. But *we both know she would fucking love that, Ronan.* 'Yes, the spare room.'

'It'll be good to have her.' I smile.

'Good. I think it will be good for you to reconnect. She's bringing some work with her, so shouldn't be hovering around too much.'

That's what happened last time. She hovered. Watched. Monitored. His little helper. 'That's great. I'll set up the spare room today.'

'Great. I'm glad you're up for it. It'll be useful for you to have someone, while I'm not here.'

'Yes, thank you. That's great.'

'Right, I'm off.'

'Have a great day.'

He nods. 'You'll be OK? Until she gets here?'

'I'll be fine.'

'I hate leaving you.'

'I know. But I'm doing so much better.'

'I just don't want you going down the same road as Nick.' The sudden mention of my brother's name sends an electric snap through me, the reverberations landing like thunder. 'It'll be good for your mum to see you're doing better. She's been through so much with you both – we can try and keep it light – keep it fun.'

Keep it fun. 'Yeah, I'd like that.' He kisses me on the forehead, like I am a sickly child. 'It'll be really nice for you. I love you.'

'Love you too.'

When he leaves, I sit in a heat of panic.

My mother.

I won't be able to go out.

I won't be able to see Leo.

To talk with him...

Where is he?

Ronan's keys jangling, the door opening. 'Bye, love! Could you order an Ocado delivery? Use the joint account!'

'Sure!'

'And give the place a clean!'

'OK!'

As the front door slams shut, a sudden realisation engulfs me. The panic is about more than having to write the end of *Slay* on my own. It is also because I was hoping to see him. To see Leo. To know that he is OK. To know that he will make it, in the end. That he will live.

35

Leo

Drowning myself didn't work.

Clearly. Cos now I'm here. On this packed train, stood outside the bogs, in the middle bit between the carriages, surrounded by everyone on the fucking planet it seems, sweating my tits off. And everything's shaking. I can't tell if it's the train or me. It's too fucking hot and my brain feels like it's been pulped, or put through a shredder, which is just as well, cos I can't let it think about the last two weeks. I don't want to think. I don't want to remember. If I remember, I might throw up. Or die. I could die. And I don't want to die anymore.

I don't I don't I don't.

Just need to block it out, till I get there. *Just need to get there.*

'Scuse me, mate – watch it.'

'Sorry, sorry.'

'You're banging into me.'

'Sorry.'

Need to get there need to get there need to get there.

The snapshots keep coming. Pushing into my mangled mind, cutting through, flashing like strobes, burning, ingraining themselves into my pathetic neurons.

men, zip, dirty nails, slap, blister, gag, mask, mirror, clock, heartbeat in my neck, hands, men, vomit, couch, grass, hands, neck, blue, red, blood, blood, men, men, men—

Stop it.

Him. In the water.

No.

I hate myself I hate myself I need a fucking *drink*.

'Fuck. *Fuck*.'

No.

No more no more no more.

I'm sweating. I am sweating so much. Feels like hot wax pouring over my skin. Shadows are flickering. The withdrawals are coming. I can feel them like poison emerging in my blood. I just need to get there. When I get there, I can withdraw safe. Two stops left. But I gotta sort myself out, and to do that I need to get into the toilet, but there is currently a child inside it with his mother. He is bawling in a way that sounds like he is in deep pain. Dunno what's going on, but I understand it. I fucking get it. I feel it in my bones. I empathise. I do – we are the same, you and I, small child – but I need you to leave the bathroom now, so I can go in. Not to piss. There's no fluid left inside me. I need to change. My clothes. My whole being. Need to look presentable, or this isn't gonna work. And I really need it to work. I want it to. I do.

I do I do I do.

I can't do it on my own though. I can't. There's someone who will help me.

My *head*. 'Shit.'

'What did you say?'

'Nothing.'

This guy looks so angry…

I'm twitching. I can feel it.

No more oblivion. There's nothing in it. *There's nothing in it for me.* I've got everything I need. It's all in the Sainsbury's bag on the floor between my legs.

It's all here.

It's all here.

'It's all here it's all—'

'Dude, are you insane?'

'Sorry, really.' I am. I am I am I am.

I look up. Every face on the carriage has got headphones, or they're staring into phones. Bored, but fine. I see no pain. None. I'd give anything to be any one of these fuckers. Any single one of them. *Just give me your shitty boring life, please.* Anything over this. It fucking hurts. The truth is fucking painful.

It's fucking horrendous.

My instinct wants to take me from it. Which I admire, I do. It's kind, to want that. But it wants to be high forever. It wants nothing more. It's wired that way. Itching to be out. Dying to be up, up where I can look down and see all these people are just bored fucking ants, fucking molecules, blobs, that mean nothing. It wants to float above them all in a state of bliss and say, *I'm better than you, all the way up here.*

But it's not bliss. Not anymore. Because now even the high hurts. It's not working. It's stopped.

They're fucking right. The people in those groups. Those stupid groups with their candles and circle of chairs. Reality is the answer. I think that woman said it, in that film, *Dune*. The one who knows everything. *Fear is the mind-killer. I will turn the inner eye to see its path. When the fear is gone, there will be nothing. Only I will remain.*

I suddenly picture myself as Timothée Chalamet with his electric-blue eyes, sobering up on a desert planet, becoming an omni-powerful god, standing at a podium being applauded by adoring disciples.

For a moment, it soothes me.

I dunno if I can do it. I dunno if I have what Timmy has. The strength.

I don't know.

'Fuck.' *I don't want to die I don't want to die I don't want to die.* Do other people do this? Repeat this shit to themselves over and over? I've nearly chewed my fucking fingernail clean off. The pain is good though. I need it. '*Fuck.*'

The man pulls a face. He's disgusted. I know I stink. I know I look an absolute fucking state.

I want to live I want to live I want to live.

I turn away from him, keeping my head down, trying to shrink myself, staring at my feet, which have no shoes on them, just socks. They are difficult to hide. And I'm only just noticing right now that they are very fucking dirty, and also very fucking wet. I think it's water. But it might be blood. Not sure. All browny-red like rust. It's hard to tell.

Nearly there.

I push myself into the wall, keeping the bag between my legs. My entire life in a Sainsbury's bag. How poetic. Timothée Chalamet didn't have to deal with this.

'You all right, mate?' Another man this time. Too close. Where are all these fucking men coming from? There's nowhere to go.

'Huh?'

He smells well nice though. Nice eyes. 'You all right?'

'Yeah, I'm fine. I'm fine.'

'You sure?' He's looking at my feet. My shoeless feet. 'You don't look great.'

'I'm sure.'

I suddenly want to cry. I want to cry and put my head on his shoulder. I want him to put his arm around me. To tell me: *It's all right. I'm here. I'm gonna help you, lad. You're so beautiful. Under all that, you're so lovely, I see it. I do. Anyone who doesn't see it is a fucking fool. You're the most beautiful person I've ever seen*, then kiss me, in front of everyone. And he doesn't care, and I am filled with warmth and love and kindness. I need that. That's all I need.

'Mate – are you staring?'

'Oh.' Shit. 'No. Nothing.'

I see his girlfriend next to him, holding his hand. She smirks, but looks concerned. Concerned that I will steal her source of warmth.

I smile. I think. I dunno. My teeth hurt. 'Sorry.'

Snapshots.

hands, men, grit, salty sweat, needles—

Please fuck off please just fucking fuck off— Where's my Lucozade bottle? *Shit.* I look at the man. 'Have you seen my Lucozade bottle?'

'Your what?'

'It's urgent.' Fuck, fuck, fuck. 'I need it. My Lucozade bottle. I fucking – I had it – it was right—'

'The one in your hand, mate?' Oh. It's here. It's in my hand.

It's here. Thank fuck. Alka-Seltzer's in there. Must hydrate. Must. I swig. My face doesn't feel like my own. Feels like its melting off me. 'You good?'

'I'm great. No worries. Thanks. Found it.' I hold it up. Show him. 'Just waiting for the toilet.'

'Someone's in it,' his girlfriend says.

Yes, I fucking know.

I fucking know someone is in it.

I want to split my head open.

Two stops left. Nearly there. Nearly fucking there.

I'm ready.

I am.

She will be fine. She said she would help me. I can't text her and tell her I'm coming because my phone is fucked. It shattered, along with my soul.

Maybe this is a bad idea. What if she doesn't want to help anymore?

She might not.

But I'm running out of them. Ideas. They are becoming very fucking sparse. I can't go back to Mo's. Or the canal. Absolutely cannot. Not after what happened. The police will be crawling all over it soon.

Shit.

I feel like a helium balloon losing its gas. Sad and withered. Everything's been very fucking hazy recently. I think at one point I was on a canal boat with a man named Paul, but I can't be totally sure. Got a lot of scratches. And I'm pretty sure my nose is broken. Hurts like fuck. Dunno when or how that happened. Annoying cos I can't put the gak up it, so I've had to resort to rubbing it on my gums and shoving it up my—

'Are you going in then or what?' The man. I look up. The toilet door is open.

'Sorry, yeah, sorry.'

The mum is pushing her way out into all the people, child in her arms, still crying. I want to do that. Cry like that. Absolutely let the hell out of me.

People make space. Move for her. I duck inside the toilet

before anyone else can. Press the button to close the door. Press 'lock'. I hear it click.

Silence.

Fuck, everything is turning.

Everything—

Fuck me.

I put the Sainsbury's bag down on the floor, close the toilet seat and sit on it. I think the kid was sick. There's sick on the floor and my shoeless feet are in it.

I get it. I understand.

It wasn't my fault. What happened. It actually wasn't.

I dunno what to do.

Get your shit together. That's what you need to fucking do.

I stand up and start to strip. Pull off all my clothes. T-shirt first, then jeans, boxers, socks. I catch myself in the little mirror above the plastic sink. My body looks like one of those Tim Burton characters. Heroin chic. I try to pull my socks off but they stick to my feet. I don't wanna look but I have to. Toe nails broken. Not too bad. Not too bad at all. Thought it would be worse, where I injected between them. No infection.

That's good. That's really good. I'm doing good.

Fully naked, I go to the basin – avoiding the mirror now – shove my hand under the soap lever and push it. Empty. *Of course it's fucking empty.* I turn back behind me and root around in the bag. I know it's in there somewhere. I nicked it from the corner shop – *where the fuck is it?* There. Hand sanitiser. I squeeze it onto my palm – as much as I fucking can – and start to rub it all over my body. All over my face, my fucking nose – ow, *fuck* – over the blue splodges on the insides of my arms, in my hair, scrub my tongue with it, over my feet, up my arse. Stings like fucking hell, but feels like I'm getting the evil out. Cleansing. Sanitising. Does that mean: *to make sane*? Fucking hope so. I can almost feel the alcohol from it seeping into my system, a slow release. I want to drink it.

No. *No.*

I'm good. I'm doing good.

New me.

Sparkly me.

I open the Sainsbury's bag and pull out the shirt and trousers I nicked from the Oxfam. No underwear, but that's fine. A tie. Forgot I did that. *Well done.* That was clever. See, I can be clever. I must give myself some credit.

Fuck. My head is—

'Hurry up in there!'

Jesus fucking Christ. Sounds like the devil.

'Two seconds!' The kid took ten minutes at least. I pull on the new clothes. They smell dusty. They're a bit big, a bit oversized, but I can work with that. And they're covering everything, which is what I wanted. Now for the shoes. I pull them out of the bottom of the orange bag. Swiped these from Camden market, from one of the stalls. I actually like the guy, so I hope to pay him back one day.

I push my feet into them – they look well nice – ball up my old clothes, place them into the empty bag, then shove the whole thing in the bin on the bathroom wall. It's got a little metal flap thing, so I have to use my foot, kicking it till it's all the way in. Then it's gone. Any evidence of the last two weeks – goodbye.

Yeah. That's it. Good.

I stare at the mirror.

I look all right, actually.

Suavest I've looked in a long time. Suit a tie, me.

She'll let me in. She has to.

'Hurry up – I need to see your ticket.'

Fuck. The ticket man. 'Coming!' It's always the men. Fucking empathy issues.

I neck the last of the Alka-Seltzer, scrub my tongue with a big blob of the hand-sanny – for one final oral clean – then open the door.

'Hello. My ticket's on my phone and it's died.'

The man narrows his eyes. He stares at me. It's weird. He looks like a cartoon character, like he's been made by Pixar, with his uniform and big friendly belly. 'Off at the next stop then, mate.'

'Yeah, that's fine.' It's where I'm going anyway.

All part of the plan.

He looks at the phone in my hand. 'I'll have to call the transport police. You can pay them at the station.' He gets his little walkie-talkie out.

'What?'

I can see the man with the girlfriend looking at me. He's glad this is happening. Happy. Like it's the right thing.

'Please, mate – don't do that.'

He presses the button on it. 'Can I get assistance at the station please...'

How do I stop this. *I just need to get there.*

I can't tell if he's gay. Might as well try. I mouth at him, *If you let me off, I'll give you a blowie in the bogs.* Then I wink.

He frowns. 'Excuse me?'

'Nothing.'

Someone talks to him through the speaker. Muffled voice. 'You need the police, Nigel?'

Nigel. They're all called Nigel.

'Yeah, please.' He's still staring at me. He definitely saw what I said. I reckon he is. Everyone is a bit gay. The train is spinning a bit. There's no room in this fucking carriage.

'Sure you don't want a quickie?' I hear someone laugh. But I'm not being funny.

He speaks into the walkie-talkie. 'Yes, police please. At the station.'

Jesus fucking Christ.

More running then.

'I'll pay,' I say. 'Chill. I'll charge my phone at the station and pay. OK?'

He stares at me some more. 'I need to make sure you get off.'

'Don't worry, mate. I'm not staying on this train any longer than I have to.'

He stands in front of me, staring, until the train slows. He definitely fancies me. Intrigued at least.

Fuck. Finally.

The doors open.

'Bye, Nigel.'

I squeeze through the bored, plugged-in people, and through

the gap in the doors before they've fully opened. My feet fucking hate me as I run down the platform, hop the fence at the bottom of it and bolt down the road.

I need her now. Just need her. I don't want to be sweating when I get there. I need to look like I want help. Which I do. I actually do.

All the roads, all the houses look the same. I can't remember which one it is, which is weird.

When I find it, I slow down. Walk, arms out, so the wind dries the sweat patches.

Then I see it. The house. Fucking hell.

I can see her through the window in the front room.

Shit. I walk up the little pathway, seeing the rose bushes on either side – don't remember those – and press the bell. I straighten my tie. Pull the shirt down. No creases. *She will help me. She will.* I check my reflection in the glass panel. I look good. It's fine. I'm doing good. This is the right thing to do.

I can hear someone moving down the corridor. Can hear other people. I think they've got guests. Was not planning on that. Not at all. Not sure this is a good idea anymore…

Bail?

The door opens.

Too late.

'Leo? What are you doing here?'

Fuck. I nearly lose my breath. There she is. 'Hi, Mum.'

36

Mallory

It is 6 p.m. and my mother still hasn't arrived.

This morning I cleaned the house within an inch of its life. I had to move quickly, because I had a lot of writing to do. But I can't lie and say I didn't love every moment of it. Something about scrubbing dirt gives me so much pleasure. Like I am scrubbing the inside of my mind. The whole place smells amazing, and I am well aware you could eat a meal off the work surfaces. The floor, too. You could eat off the kitchen floor.

Ronan will be happy. My mother will be happy.

I need these people to be happy.

After my cleaning frenzy, I ordered the Ocado delivery then blitzed through my word count for *The Air Between Us*, with help from Chat GPT. ('Write me three thousand words of two people having blissful sex' apparently didn't abide by the terms and conditions. So I had to go with 'Write me three thousand words of uplifting romantic conversation on a park bench between a desperate woman and a strong man.' I think Ronan will buy it.) And now I sit at the kitchen island, where I have been all afternoon, attempting to construct my reply to Stanley with the outline for the final third of *Slay*. But the document is currently only four sentences long:

Outline of Final Third: *Slay*:

Liam will make it. He will get better. He will get the help he deserves. He will find his inner strength.

This is all I have.

Isn't it?

Where's the *plot*?

What would Leo do? I need the end to be punchy and climactic. *Surprising.* Is this too meek? Too resolved? Or is this what would actually happen? It doesn't *feel* very Liam, despite what I want to happen. *Trust yourself, Mal*, Stan said. *Your instincts are on point.*

Are they? Can I do this without Leo?

I have no choice now.

What did Gina say? *I'm sure I'll be in tears by the end.*

She seemed so hopeful about this. It is an odd pressure to feel: the need to make someone cry. I hover my fingers over the keyboard and attempt to locate memories of people crying – and why they were.

I can't remember either of my parents crying. Or Nick. I cried a lot. A lot a lot. But that didn't make other people cry.

Ronan never cries. Tears welling up, yes. But actual crying? I have never seen.

A memory surfaces. When I was doing my counselling course, one of the modules was about psychoanalysis and childhood. Freud and Jung. (In fact, a large portion of the course was about childhood, which I found surprising and also a little annoying, if I'm really honest. I have never been a big believer in going into the past. I was hoping I would be learning logical and practical skills to teach patients to break thought patterns, or pragmatic tools to help them regulate and see clearly in the moment. That's what seemed to help me when I was in hospital. The psychologist – a lady named Jan – gave me a workbook with CBT worksheets and told me to use them whenever I got overwhelmed. Journalling. Box breathing. Fact checking. These tools really helped me.)

Me and the other students were told we would Zoom (it was all online) and that it might be quite *intense*. We should prepare a painful memory from our childhood. I chose falling off the swing. It was basic and felt a bit like a cop out, but I knew I could hide with it. When the Zoom started, everyone was a little tentative, but as people shared, it got incredibly emotional. People did not talk about falling off swings – far from it. People talked about moments they were abandoned or hurt or even abused. And there were tears. So many tears. Not just from the people telling the stories, but from those listening. People empathised and related. Each person's story felt like it could have been a part of every listener's. What I noticed was really poignant were the moving forward segments, when despite something awful happening to someone, they had succeeded in spite of it. That's what the therapist who ran the Zoom told us: when people overcome their difficulties, it is very powerful.

Powerful.

The end of my book needs to be *powerful.*

I close my eyes for a moment, listening to my instincts. *Perhaps Liam needs to revisit his past, and he works through his unresolved trauma. The abuse he suffered.*

Yes.

This reflection on the past will bring tears. We will understand why he is the way he is. *Empathise.*

This is the way to go.

This is the way to go to make Gina cry.

I excitedly place my fingers on the keyboard, and begin to type.

Outline of Final Third: *Slay*:

Liam will make it. He will get better. He will get the help he deserves. He will find his inner strength. Throughout the final third of the book, Liam continues to fight against the pull of the chem-sex world. We see glimmers of hope as he attends twelve-step recovery meetings and develops strong relationships with healthier people. We a see a version of the young man he could be: kind, considerate, outward-looking. He meets a therapist in AA, who generously spends some time with him. He becomes a little bit obsessed with her, desperate for the kindness she offers. But she is able to recognise that his past may have a lot to do with his current behaviours. She urges Liam to explore what has happened to him – a lot of which he has blocked out, or – as we, the readers, know – has chosen to forget. Liam realises his need to confront this past trauma. He decides to go back to his home town – a rundown council estate.

    By the sea.

(I would never admit this to anyone, but I actually don't know if they have council estates by the sea. But it's great: a lovely emotive setting. Really sad. The sea can be a metaphor for Liam's turbulent past, etc. etc.)

When Liam arrives, his dad tells him of the harm he suffered at the hands of his own mother. The mother made Liam's life hell. She neglected him as a child, and exposed him to physical and emotional abuse, from herself and others – and then she died, leaving Liam abandoned and stranded. Fighting for himself from a young age. This causes Liam to understand that he has a lack of self-worth which attaches him to people who treat him badly. He decides to confront Mark, the man who has had a hold on him for so long. He forgives Mark for all wrongdoing, and joins forces with the therapist that has helped him. The book will end with the two of them – together – opening a therapy centre, helping those in need.

I pause, and re-read the email.

This should make her cry. Shouldn't it? There is the promise of *hope*. A glimmer of *light* at the end of something that has been, let's face it, pretty brutal. This could offer a cathartic release.

Tears.

(Is a therapy *centre* a thing? I mean… I'm sure it can be.)

I look at the clock. 18:30. I don't have long. This needs to be it. I swallow hard and press send, half squinting at the screen as I do. I can't quite look at it go.

What if it's shit?

But what if it's not?

Tomorrow, I could hear the *yes* I've been waiting for. As Stanley said, I could hear a financial figure by the end of the day.

Six-figure book deal.

Beach-front Malibu life.

I close my emails and log out of Yahoo. I have never been someone who prays, but I catch myself looking up at the ceiling and saying, 'Please make this work. Please, please, please, let it be enough.' Who I am asking, I have no idea. But I can feel the rising current of nerves pulsing somewhere inside me, making the back of my head and my neck begin to shake.

I need to calm down.

Often, when I need to calm down, I will watch *The Hours*. Or at least some scenes from it. In the film, Leonard – Virginia's husband – seems so lovely. The actor who plays him gives him such a beautiful quality of compassion, thoughtfulness and understanding. He seems stuck, unsure how to help his wife. How to contain her. The scene at the train station, when Nicole Kidman cries, is my favourite. I can recite the whole thing. It's incredible. Nicole Kidman is incredible. When he calls her ungrateful, her response gives me chills.

'*I am living a life I have no wish to live. How did this happen?*'

I sometimes say it to myself in the mirror.

'*You cannot find peace by avoiding life.*'

I open YouTube and type in *train scene The Hours Nicole Kidman*, but before I can press play, my heart jumps.

Keys. The door.

I look at the clock. 6 p.m. No knock. Not my mother.

Ronan.

He's back. He will have known her train times. He will have known he would be back before her, and wanted to keep me guessing all day. I close the browser tab, pull up the document of *The Air Between Us* (in all its copy-and-paste Chat GPT glory) and take a sip of my herbal tea.

The door slams shut. 'Just me!'

'Hi, darling!' I shout. 'I'm in the kitchen!'

No reply.

'She's not here?' he says, entering the kitchen, phone in hand, not looking up.

Something's off.

'No, not yet!'

He is still not looking up.

'Is everything OK?' I say through a yawn (a fake yawn, one that I have manufactured to appear unbothered and at ease). Why wouldn't he be? He chews his lip, tapping intently on the screen, not answering. 'Would you like a beer, darling?'

He keeps tapping, shaking his head at whatever it is he is reading, then places his phone, a little too hard, down on the top of the island. He rubs his eyes, as if pushing something back into himself. 'Yes, I need one. Work has been *a lot*.'

A lot.

'Oh, no – I'm sorry,' I say, rising and making my way to the fridge. I try to remain as gentle and as small as possible. The bottle opener is already out on the side. I take one of his special IPAs and crack it open. When I turn to hand it to him, he has moved. Now he's stood in front of my laptop, leaning forward, staring into the screen. 'Was it nice to be back in the office?' I ask. 'The team must have really missed you.'

'You've done 3,812 words,' he says. He must remember yesterday's word count off the top of his head. I have underestimated him. 'Not quite your target.'

'I know.' I pass him the bottle. He keeps his eyes on the screen as he takes it. 'But I'm really happy with what I've written.'

He nods. I watch him roll his shoulder a little as he scans through the document, trying to loosen a knot. 'I'll look properly later. Is everything done?' he says. There is something in his voice that spikes my awareness. Its flatness. 'For your mother?'

'Yes. Bedding washed. Pillow mist sprayed.' I smile. He doesn't. 'Ocado delivery done. Dinner prepped. Wine in the fridge.'

'I saw that on the receipt. Not for you, I hope.'

'Sorry?'

'The wine.' His tone is cold, the warmth of this morning completely evaporated. He isn't even pretending. It makes me immediately on edge, throwing my intuition off balance. I can't tell if I should try to close the distance between us or make it larger. It is as if broken glass has been scattered across the floor: one wrong move and he will be alerted to what I have been doing. That I am still lying to him. 'No – of course not for me. For Mum.'

'Good. You can't be drinking.'

'No.'

He takes a sip of his beer and exhales. Finally he meets my eyes. 'We lost the deal today.'

A sharp heat moves through my body. 'Sorry?'

'The deal, Mal.' His voice is hard. 'Getting the rights to the book.'

'The book?' *Which book? He told me the other day...* Shit. I should know...

'Jesus Christ.' He shakes his head. 'Yes, Mallory. The book I have been working to acquire for the past four months. We lost it. Today. Sony took it. And they offered less money. It's not good.'

He turns away from me, rubbing his face again. There is a density in the air. A volatility. Something I have not felt for a long time. A pressure inside him, moving out into the air between us.

'Oh, Ronan – I'm so sorry.'

'I just...' He glares out of the Crittall double doors, into the garden. 'I just hope it's all worth it,' he says under his breath.

'All of what?' I immediately wish I hadn't asked. I know what. Here. Him. Looking after me.

'I had to meet with Theo after it fell through. He wasn't happy. At all.' Theo. His boss. The big boss. *Oh, God*. 'He told me he thinks that me being away from the office for the past two weeks has contributed to the loss of the project.'

I watch him chewing his lip. Agitated. Restless. 'Oh.'

'Yes,' he says quietly. '*Oh*.'

'Well,' I say gently. 'I thought you being at home had been working out OK... They didn't say anything? I thought they encouraged it. Surely it can't be the only reason?' I ask hopefully. As I watch him picking at the label of the beer bottle with his thumb nail, I remember the book. *Killing Me*, about a girl who is used by a gang to smuggle drugs across county lines. He said the author was too *heavy-handed*. That she was a *shit writer*. 'If I remember rightly, you said the money people made an error on the Zoom call with her – that they came across too strong? Could it not have been something to do with that?'

His slides his thumbnail through the wetness of the label on the glass, drawing a line straight through it. 'Maybe.'

'Ronan—'

'We can't both be jobless, Mal.'

'Well, we won't be. This won't affect anything. They love you there.'

'It affects everything. I have worked so hard.'

'But—'

'Mal, stop.'

'I just—'

'Mallory – *stop.*' He slams his fist on the countertop, silencing me. The shock of it nearly winds me as the echo ricochets around the starkness of the kitchen. I hold my breath, unaware of what to do, or how to respond. He keeps his head down, looking at the marble, his fist still clenched.

'Ronan…' I say tentatively. 'I know things have been a bit stressful…'

He shakes his head, making a thin, condescending laugh. 'Things have been *a bit stressful*? Jesus *Christ*, Mal.'

'I know. I know I've been a lot to handle—'

'You have this incredible ability to make everything about you,' he says. 'Today was important. For *me*. And because I've had to be here, I lost something that was extremely important to my future. To how other people view me. I need you to see that. I need you to recognise that your actions have consequences. I am trying to be responsible for both of us – but it's not easy. I can't hold your hand through everything, Mal. I know that's what you need, but you have to start to look after yourself. I am sacrificing too much.'

I take a tentative step towards him. 'Ronan, I'm sorry.'

'Try and put yourself in someone else's shoes for once.'

'I really truly am sorry.' I reach my hand out, to take his. Gentle. *Careful*.

He pushes it away. 'Don't. I'm not in the mood.'

'Ronan, please.' I try to take it again, but he grabs my wrist, hard. 'Ow – Ronan—'

'I don't want you touching me.'

'Ronan, let go—'

'Hello?' Mum's voice. Through the letter box. From the front door. 'Ronan? Mallory?'

He lets go.

Turns toward the sound. 'Get the door,' he says quietly.

'Hi, Mum!' I shout back. Voice shaking. Steady. *Steady*.

In the hallway, I catch my reflection in the circular mirror on the wall. Make sure my hair is messy in the way it should be.

I pull open the door. 'Hi, Mum!' Bright. Cheerful. That's what she appreciates.

'Hello, Mallory.'

37

Leo

'Could you pass the gravy, Leo?'

I'll be as clear as I can be right now: I've not got a fucking clue what is happening. It's like the beginning of a low-budget horror film. I'm sat on this chair, and we're all squeezed around my parents' dining table on a Monday at five p.m. Them on one side, and their weird neighbours – John and Jean – on the other, everyone eating a chicken dinner, while I enter withdrawals.

This was not what I had in mind. Not at all. There was going to be hugs and tears and hourly lorazepam and a warm bed and *Thank God you're home!*

Not this. I forgot they all do this on this street. Visit each other and eat chicken.

'Leo?'

Not to point the finger, but John and Jean have fucked up the plan. Now I have to act normal and pretend I'm fine, and not like I'm about to throw up on the table. Not like I've just arrived after nine months of ghosting my parents, wearing no socks or underwear, with no moisture in my mouth, sweating like a twat, itching like a bastard, cos I feel like there's mites under my skin. But like I was *just in the area* and wanted to *pop in to see how everyone is*. I panicked. Cos of John's and Jean's judgemental stares.

'*I've just come from work*,' I said, because I've been wearing a tie. Thought it made sense.

'*Oh! How lovely!*' they said.

Mum and Dad didn't say anything.

Now the new plan is to wait till John and Jean leave, and then

I can talk to Mum and Dad. Be honest. That's what they appreciate. Honesty. That's all they've ever asked for. And I'm ready. I am.

I am I am I am.

'Leo?'

What did he want? Oh, yeah. Fuck. 'Gravy. Yes, John.' John looks like he is made out of Play-Doh and has the personality of a straw. *Where the fuck is it?* Jesus. *Gravy.* What a weird word. *Oh.* It's next to me. Right next to me. 'Here you go, John.' I pick it up but I'm shaking so bad that the gravy is wobbling. Sloshing about. Steady. *Steady now.* Then something mad happens. A little face appears in the skin that's formed on the top of it. A gravy-skin face. Looks like it's about to sing me a song – its mouth keeps opening. Like something from a Disney film. That's nice. Wait. No. It's getting strange. Eyebrows are forming. Angry now. Very angry. Evil. The devil. The devil just arrived in the gravy. 'Take it.' Fucking take it, John. Take the devil off me.

'Cheers, lad.'

It's hell. I've come to my parents' house for help and the devil's in the fucking Bisto.

'Well, this is nice,' I say, swallowing down some sick. 'How are you all doing? I didn't expect to see you all. Nice surprise.' I can hear myself trying to sound like some kind of very busy and important business man.

In a stolen shirt.

'It is a nice surprise,' Mum says, in a way that makes me want to cry. I can't tell what she and Dad are thinking. They won't let me be here if they think I'm high. Which I'm not, but the withdrawals might give recent habits away, and then they won't like that either. I've done this before, many times, but not in front of John and Jean.

'It's lovely to see you, Leo,' Jean says, smiling. 'Your mum and dad said you've been doing well.'

I can't look at them. Not directly. My eyes are stinging. It's the comedown. I swear. Making me wobbly as fuck. I can't cry. Not here. 'Yeah, I've been doing really good, thanks, Jean!'

She nods, then starts pouring herself wine. Fucking torture.

'Would you like some, Leo?'

Mum and Dad look at each other. 'No, I'm good, thanks, Jean.' She nods. She's fucking testing me. I know she is.

'Oh, that's right.' Pretending she forgot. 'You don't do that anymore, do you?'

'No.'

'How long's it been?' she says, filling her glass to the top.

Fuck's sake. 'A while.'

'That's good, lad,' John adds, swigging on his Guinness. 'Some people just can't, can they.'

I shake my head. 'No.'

'Some people are just better without.'

'They are.'

'Everyone has their time to let loose, then it's head down, isn't it? Glad you're there, lad.'

'Thanks.' I hate this. But I think I'm steering them off.

I can smell something strange. I dunno if it's me – sometimes you can smell meth through sweat, I swear you can. Or maybe I'm just pranging out, and it's the meat. The meat looks like it's sweating too. 'Chicken's great, Mum.'

'Good.'

She knows.

She knows something's up.

But she will understand. She always does.

But this time she looks different. There's something in the way she's picking up her peas with her fork. Tired. Like a tired little bird. Broken. I can speak to her properly after dinner. Tell her. Tell her everything. Mo. The men. All of it. Not yet though. Clearly. When these two have gone back home. Because if I let on, they will talk. Everyone on this cul-de-sac loves to talk. No one ever ventures further than the petrol station, so they need some fucking drama – they wanna know the dirt on each other so they can tell everyone else, but say it wasn't them that said it. *You didn't hear this from me but…* It's that, up and down this fucking street like a disease behind the net curtains. And I have definitely provided some valuable cul-de-sac gossip in my time, for people like John and fucking Jean. Which is probably why

Mum had her breakdown last year, but I cannot think about that right now. Just gotta look like it's all fine.

'It's really nice, Mum. Is the stuffing M&S?'

'Aldi.'

'Oh, you'd never know that, Liz,' Jean chips in. 'You'd never know at all. They do such good-quality stuffing these days.'

I don't like Jean, but I actually agree with her on that.

'Wish I knew you were coming, Leo,' Mum says, all quiet. 'I'd have made more.' She sounds so sad.

'Thought you liked surprises,' I reply. But we all know she hates them. Her nerves can't take it anymore, not after everything.

'It's good you came,' Dad says.

He looks different, too. Dunno how. Thinner. More strained. Grey, but also see-through. Like water in a pan after the cabbage has been on the boil.

'The potatoes are well nice,' I say, but I haven't had one. I've not eaten in three days cos I can't fucking stomach it. But she will clock me if I don't, so I pick one up with my fork, trying to hide the shakes, shove it my mouth and chew. Turns to a paste. I can't swallow.

Think I'm gonna vom.

'Very good meat, this, Liz.' John again. Small talk about what is directly in front of them is all he and Jean are capable of. 'Is the meat M&S, Liz?'

'No – it's all Aldi, John.'

'Well, you wouldn't know at all.'

'No, you wouldn't.' Jean again. These two are absolutely fucking fascinating – can make a whole conversation out of absolutely nothing. But I do not have head space to think about that right now. Just gotta get through this fucking dinner.

Silence.

Why is there silence?

Can't stand it.

It might make the devil come back.

Someone say something.

'So, what's work at the moment, Leo?' Not that though, Jean. Don't say something to *me* – talk about fucking stuffing again.

Jesus. But there's something probing in her tone, and she keeps glancing at me, little flashes of her eyes. She's got a good bullshit antenna, has Jean. I can almost see it coming right out the top of her blow-dried head, furiously blinking every time I speak. Cos what she really means is, *Do you actually have a job?* 'You look nice in a tie, Leo.' And what she really means is, *What are you hiding?*

It's an art, being shady. She's very good at it.

'Oh, thanks, Jean!' I say, as bubbly as I fucking can. Gotta throw her off. I think she's about sixty, although you can't really know what age she is. She's still blonde. She's had Botox – her forehead doesn't move – but she would never admit it. 'Yeah, I've come straight from work, Jean, yeah.'

'So, you got given the afternoon off?' She's a fucking sleuth.

'Yeah, I did, yeah.'

'That's nice.'

'Yeah, they're nice like that.'

'What is it you're doing?'

'I work in a marketing agency.' That'll do. No one knows what happens in one of those.

'Oh – very swish. Which part?'

'What do you mean?'

'Which part of the agency?'

My brain can't keep up. 'Just on reception for now.'

There's a pause. A horrible pause. Her antenna is gonna explode. Then she says, 'Well, it's lovely to see you using that degree of yours.' The room is spinning. Every fucking person sat around this table knows I didn't finish that degree. 'You'll be running the place before long.'

'Ah, I dunno about that.' I need to deflect away from me, because I think I can see shadows moving around the walls and I am scared I will say something stupid, like I think the devil is here. 'How's work for you, John? Still roofing?'

'Yeah – still going.'

'Sure you're not too old yet?' Everyone laughs, cos it's what we do. We laugh when it's fucking unbearable.

'He'll keep going till he breaks his back, this one,' says Jean, lovingly, which is weird.

'Good for you, John.'

'Hard work is important,' John says, which sounds fucking pointed if you ask me.

I hold onto the table edge. It feels like the room's gonna collapse.

'Well, it's good to see you looking after yourself. Not giving your mum and dad grief anymore.' Fuck off, Jean. *Fuck off fuck off—*

'Ha! Yeah.'

I still don't dare look at Mum and Dad, so I stare down at my hands on the table cloth. My knuckles are all red and scabby. Could be scabies. Wouldn't put it past myself. God, the silence is awful.

'Any nice boyfriends on the go, Leo?'

Jean, you're obsessed. I can hear in her voice that she's trying to sound all breezy, and like she's all fucking progressive and interested in the life of a *young homosexual these days*. But she wants more. I know that I'm fascinating to her. That to her I am the truth of all gay men: fucking mental. She wants me to break. To spill everything all over the floor for her to gobble up and regurgitate to her bored friends over her garden fence.

'Nah, not at the moment, Jean.'

'Well – the lads of London should be so lucky.'

I make a big laugh to stop myself sticking my fork right into my scabies hand. 'Just taking some time for myself, Jean.'

'What happened to that lad?'

'What lad?'

'Sam.'

Oh, fucking hell. I feel my chair tilt. Did it tilt? 'Sam?'

'That's it. He was nice.'

'We all liked Sam.' Yes, we all liked Sam, Jean. We all liked Sam until Sam stopped liking me because I cheated on him with seven different men.

'Ah yeah, I'd forgotten about him.' I hadn't. I fucking loved Sam. I really did. I brought him to my dad's birthday at the connie club three years ago and everyone thought he was my saviour. He had a proper job and was a bit older than me and was really fucking handsome and also very fucking kind. Not *nice*. Sam didn't care if people liked him. He was just a kind person. I hardly drank that night. Didn't feel like I needed it. Cos at that time he was my drug of choice. He filled me up. Got the dopamine hits I needed. Until I didn't. Until it wore off. Then I couldn't help myself. 'I hope he's doing well,' I say.

'I'm sure he is – he was very together. And you looked happy when you were with him.' What Jean really means is, *You currently look like shit.* 'What else is going on for you, Leo?'

Got gang-raped, Jean.

Here to ask my parents for help.

'Not much to report.'

She looks disappointed. I suddenly see something on the mantelpiece behind her head. The framed picture of me, Mum and Dad on holiday in Malaga when I was about six. I feel a twist of dread and anxiety in my stomach as I look at it. They both look happy.

And I do too. The kid version of me. Smiling like that.

He has no fucking right to.

I should tell him. Tell him there's sweet fuck all to smile about.

Then something weird happens. His face moves. Distorts. The devil arrives in his eyes. In my eyes. He's trying to say something – through the picture.

I can hear him.

He's speaking. '*I am your inner child.*'

'What the fuck?'

'You all right, son?' It's Dad.

Dad, please fucking help me. 'Sorry, yeah. I just need a sec. Need to make a call.' I stand up, scraping my chair, and go straight past the table, through the hall and into the kitchen, pushing the door shut behind me. *Fuck, fuck, fuck.* I'm covered in sweat.

Dripping.

I just need to fucking breathe. Well, what I actually need is a lorazepam but I don't know where Mum keeps it. I need to sit down. No. I need to—

Fuck fuck—

'*I am inside you.*'

Oh my God. *Oh my God.*

I need to—

I see the vomit before I even feel it coming up. Right into the sink. It's bile with bits of fuck knows what. My soul, I assume. The immediate euphoria is incredible. A moment, a split second of relief, from myself.

Then it comes again.

And again.

Hurts so fucking much.

'*I'm not going anywhere.*'

Get out of me, you fucking cunt.

But nothing more. Dry retching into the basin. I'm making noises like I'm being exorcised. Which is what I want. Which is what I need. But they're gonna hear.

Get your shit together, Leo.

I open the cupboard beneath me and find the bleach, pour it all over the bile. Find a fork and use the back of it to push the bits down the plug. I run the tap on cold until everything is gone, then stick my head under it for a second.

I look at the fridge. They still have my GCSE results pinned to it with a magnet. From five years ago.

One **9**
Four **7**s
Two **6**s
Two **5**s.

I lift it up. Underneath, another piece of paper. A letter, from the head teacher.

Dear Elizabeth and Gary Fuller,

We are pleased to report that your son Leo was amongst the top ten percent in the country for his A-Level English creative writing exam

The edges are all tatty and brown, with finger prints and bits of old food stuck to it. I run my finger up and down it. I can smell the paper. Smell the school. Still lingering. I loved that class.

I feel a jolt. Fucking mental. I see it play out, right in front of me. The fridge disappears and Chloe Fucking Bridgewater is there, taking my notebook out of my bag and reading it to my Year 9 class. I tried to grab it back, but missed and grabbed her arm. And she shouted that I was abusing her, which made everyone laugh, but also look at me funny, like maybe I was. Like maybe actually I was that kind of person. That it might have made sense. Cos I wasn't weird in a creepy way, but people called me – what the fuck was it? – Man of Mystery. Yeah, that was it. I liked it cos it was sort of romantic. A bit edgy and cool and peripheral. But I had no idea what was under it. The mystery. Just a mess of absolutely no fucking clue. I knew I was gay and that was fine, but it also wasn't, not really. I didn't know what kind of gay to be, so I just decided to be *mysterious*. Inside, though, I was moving at a million miles an hour. I was on lightning speed, and I really just wanted people to think I was fucking interesting. So when she read out the poem and said it was lame and gay as fuck and boring, I felt like that inner bit of me was revealed. And all the mystery disappeared, so actually what was there was just really fucking shit.

I push my fingers into my eye sockets to try and get rid of it, but it won't go. It wasn't even that big a deal. It wasn't – not really – but it was just this moment that I realised I gotta go harder, do more shit, get more from people. I always wanted more. More of what they gave me. It just fucking activated me. My brain. Dopamine. I got it from funny, rude, charming. And I was. I was those things. I managed to claw my way back into their eyelines and, a few years later, Chloe Fucking Bridgewater said, *You're sound, you*, and I thought, yeah, fucking hell, I've made it – I'm sound. I'm sound. She could have called me a twat and I would have believed her.

I didn't know how else to be. I had no fucking clue. So I just believed her words to be true. I stopped writing poems cos it was lame. But then when the exam came around, I thought, fuck it, no one is gonna read this except the examiner, and then I did well. And when I read the letter – this letter – in the school hall on results day, I nearly fucking cried, cos I thought, fucking hell, all that shit in that notebook was me. And I'd just binned it. Cos of Chloe Fucking Bridgewater. Who now has four kids and two French bulldogs and lives at her mum's while she waits for the baby daddy to get out of the clink, but he's a semi-pro footballer so *they'll be minted soon.*

The poem she read to the class was called 'The Waves'.

I turn away from the fridge. Wanna fucking rip the letter up in some poetic and dramatic way and shove it down the sink with my bile. But I don't. I don't cos no one will see me do it, so what's the fucking point. I dunno if I can deal with this. I feel spores of shame and disappointment seep into me like black mould. Or seeping out of me – dunno which way they are going. I don't even have an excuse for this shit. The way I am. I wasn't raped or fucking abused. I just wanted to appear a certain way and then it went too fucking far. I've fucked it all up. I've fucked up my entire life, and theirs too. I know it. They know it. John and Jean fucking know it.

I need to go. Leave. I can't do this to them anymore. I'm a fucking disease. As I go to the back door, I see something on the countertop, next to the fruit bowl.

A bottle of whiskey. It's got a little blue sparkly bow pinned to it. A gift.

Ah, fuck.

'*I'm still here, baby boy.*'

Fuck off.

Fuck off.

Fuck off.

I need silence. I need it. My instinct moves me, and I pick up the bottle and unscrew the top. I can smell it. Fucking liquid paradise. I put it to my lips, and gulp. I gulp and I gulp and I gulp.

Oh, my God.

I feel the devil retreating. The whiskey burning it away. There's nothing like it. The power this stuff has, to remove me. To take me away. I love it. *You've never let me down.*

'What are you doing?'

I turn. *No*. Shit. 'Dad.'

He closes the door behind him. 'Is that the whiskey?'

'What?'

'In your hand, Leo.'

No, no, no. 'No.'

'No? Leo. It's in your hand. I can see it.'

'Dad...' I put it back on the counter top. 'Let me explain. I don't even want it.' I watch him rub his hand over his face. Shake his head. 'Dad, I came here to sober up. I came to ask for your help.'

He looks at the tiles. 'I suspected.'

'What?'

'You look awful.'

'Something bad happened.'

'It's always bad, Leo.'

'I know. I know – but I wanna get clean, Dad. Properly this time. I just need a bit of help.'

He doesn't speak. Doesn't move. Then, 'Money?'

'I don't know. Yeah. I mean, I suppose. What do you think? We should talk about it properly. That's why I came here. I wanted to tell you I think I could do rehab properly this time. I really fucking do. I want it, Dad.'

'How?'

'What do you mean?'

'How do you think we're going to get the money for that?'

'I dunno.'

'What do you think we're going to do? Remortgage the house?'

'No. Course not—'

'Again?'

'Yeah – no. I don't want that.'

'So, what? Why are you here? What are you asking for if you know we can't do that? I genuinely want to know what you think is going to happen here.'

'I just...' Fuck. 'I just need it to stop, Dad.'

'How many times have you said this? Stood in this kitchen and said these exact words?'

'This time's different. I really wanna get clean. I'm ready. Because something really bad happened and I'm scared that—'

I stop because he's staring at me. Right in the eyes. Feels like I'm being skewered. 'You know what I noticed at the table?'

'What?'

'Your mum can't even look at you anymore. She's scared of you. She's scared of her own son.'

'Dad, I know I've taken the piss—'

'She thinks she ruined you. She blames herself, you know. What did we do?'

'What do you mean? This isn't about you—'

'No. It's always about you.'

'No, sorry – I just mean…'

'Try and put yourself in someone else's shoes, for once.'

'Right.' Fuck. 'I'll go. I was going to anyway. Don't wanna put this on you or Mum.'

'I think that's best. Come back when you're ready to be honest.'

'I wanted to be. I did, Dad.'

'Not with us. With yourself. You live in a world of lies. You don't even know what's real anymore.' I want to ask for a benzo – I think Mum has them upstairs – just to take the edge off, but he looks like he's about to cry. 'I'll tell John and Jean you had to go back to work.'

'Yeah,' I say. 'Yeah, OK.'

I wanna hug him. Feel his warmth. It's all I want. It's all I've ever wanted.

All those men

Just wanna hear him say, *You're beautiful under all this, son. You're wonderful. You always were.*

'Can I say bye to Mum?'

'I don't think that's a good idea.'

'Right. I'll be off then.'

'Right.'

I can't look at him. I unlock the backdoor, go round the side of the house, into the gulley next to the garage. I used to sneak out and smoke Benson Hedges Dark Blue inside it. They never cared, not really. I was fifteen then.

This fucking place. It gives me a pain in my chest. But that's not it… It's in my soul. Never felt this kind of pain before in my life. It's in the centre of me. Right at the middle.

It's been there as long as I can remember. I try to detach, to move from it, but it won't go. It's so fucking loud. That buzz, that thing that comes in waves.

Can't go back to the canal. Can't go to Mo's.

The police. The police will fucking get me.

Running out of options. One left.

Mandy. *Mallory.*

She said she would help me.

She promised to.

If I show up… Honest – not out of it… She might let me detox at hers. She has spare rooms – her house is huge. She'll have lorazepam cos she's that kind of person. But there's something else she has. She wants something from me – I know she does. It's like she wants to be my mum. There's something in her. Like she has warmth that she doesn't know where to put. Like it's all stored up for someone that isn't that mad husband of hers. And I think she wants it to be me. Cos I think she gets me. I think she sees the person I am. I do. I think she likes me.

She sees me. She knows who I am. Under all this mould.

Maybe I can put my head on her shoulder and cry.

I feel like she'd like it. Like she'd want it.

I'd like that.

I'm fucking crying.

I start to run. If I don't run, I'll implode. It's a blur. Everything is moving past me but it doesn't feel real.

Back on the train, back in the bogs, hiding from the ticket man. Hopping the gate at Crouch End, and down the streets with the massive houses in orange brick. Through the park, to her street, where I stop. I can't go in like this. I need to sleep.

I need to lie down first.

I go down the little side street, behind the row of houses, and see a run of bins. I move down it, keeping low, until I'm outside the back of her garden. Even the bins are fucking posh. Cobbles and ivy everywhere.

I pull myself up over the wall and take a look. It's a long

garden, with a patio by the back of the house. Everything's dead quiet. I dunno if I can go in. Not yet. If he's gonna be there, then that is a problem.

Wait. There's a shed. A fucking shed.

That'll work. That'll do.

I pull myself over, quietly, landing down between some rose bushes. I need to fucking sleep. I don't want to be all jittery and fucking mental in front of her.

I scan my eyes over the garden.

I creep along the edge, watching the back windows. Can't see anyone inside. Not yet. The shed isn't locked. Course it's not. I pull open the wooden door. There's nothing in it, not really. Some old paint cans and sheets. I push the door shut. Sit down on the floor.

Vomit isn't coming.

Just need to lie down. Need to sleep.

But my brain feels stuck. Stuck on that fucking picture on the mantelpiece. Can't stop thinking about it. Mum looked like a totally different person back then. She looked so happy. Now she doesn't.

She doesn't look the same.

38

Mallory

She looks the same.

Stylish. Neat. Her hair remains a silvery grey, cropped short, her lipstick a subtle shade of red – not overpowering, but enough to be noticeable. A refined statement. Her clothes hang perfectly around her small, angular frame. An oversized trench. Black boots and tidily fitting trousers with a dead-straight crease down the front of each leg. She is holding the handle of her suitcase in one hand and an umbrella in the other. It isn't raining. The umbrella is the same shade of peacock blue as her nails.

'Is there a camera on the doorbell? I didn't want to touch it in case it exploded.' Her voice sends an age-old warning into my bloodstream. She's here, she has arrived and she is using the *accent*. The accent I forget about (or choose not to remember) until I hear it: altered to remove any trace of evidence that she grew up on Druids Heath council estate, in deepest Birmingham. Her posh accent. A deflection from the truth.

Exactly how she likes it.

But I know the truth. I know that the clothes she is wearing have been meticulously chosen from Vinted. The nail varnish from Amazon, and the umbrella from a charity shop. She will have spent weeks looking for the perfect one. No one would guess. But I know. I know my mother. She is brilliant at it. At appearing how she wishes to. They said something in AA... *Fake it till you make it*. And she is living proof that you can.

'Oh, yes – that's just another one of Ronan's gadgets.'

'Fancy.' She takes a few steps back from the porch, moving her eyeline up the exterior walls of the house. 'I forgot how beautiful it is.'

I wait, watching her take it in, attempting to calm the adrenaline that has come with me from the kitchen, now ringing in my ears. I hone in on the top edge of what appears to be a wilted tissue, sticking out of the top of my mother's coat pocket.

She would hate that I can see it.

I can still feel Ronan's fingers around my wrist.

'You look well,' I say. 'You look really great, Mum.'

'Thanks, you too,' she says, still looking up.

I find myself glancing behind her, to where Leo stood two weeks ago covered in blood. Part of me wonders if I will see him around still, crouching, hiding behind a car. Part of me wants that. For him to disrupt this. To make it go away.

Mum's eyes lock onto something and narrow. 'Is the wisteria trunk broken?'

'Oh, yes,' I answer, shrugging. 'I'm not sure how.'

'That's such a shame – it won't flower.'

'It's cold, are you coming in?' She looks at me, eyes widening a fraction at the sharpness in my tone. I smile to offset it. 'It's so nice to see you!'

As she advances towards me, the heels of her little boots clicking on the pathway, I hesitate, wondering if there will be a hug or a kiss on the cheek, and I can see she is wondering the same thing. Undiscussed, we opt for a jolty hug, with a pat on the back. 'It's nice to see you, too, Mallory,' she says into my ear. I fight a shudder. I can smell her. Lavender soap. She has used that soap since I was young. I impulsively squeeze my eyelids tightly closed, in an attempt to shut down the memories that threaten to flood my consciousness with the scent.

When she lets go, she moves past me, into the hallway, leaving her suitcase on the step. 'Did you repaint in here? It looks *bigger*. Oh, Mal, it's *so* nice.' She straightens out her coat sleeves.

'Go through,' I say. 'I'll bring your bag.'

I close the door with my foot and pull the bag along the tiles on its wheels, following her down the hallway and into the kitchen. I was wrong. She does look a little different. She looks – dare I say it – *older*. It's not in her features, but in the way she moves. More timidly, trepidatiously, which jars slightly with the way I've always thought of her. She's in her sixties now, but it's the first time I've ever really seen her as *ageing*.

She would loathe that.

'Stacey!' Ronan's voice bounces off the work surfaces. 'Oh my God, you look – *amazing*! Is that a new coat?'

'Ronan!' I hear the Brummie slip out as she careers straight towards him, arms open. Her poise slips. It sometimes does when she's excited, angry or taken off guard. This is the former. 'It is new! Sweet of you to notice.' From the kitchen doorway – where I linger momentarily – I see him practically pick her up into a hug, so her feet nearly leave the floor. When he releases her, she is giddy, like a child, light-headed at a theme park.

'Here, take this,' he says, handing her a glass of wine from the top of the island.

'Oh – I shouldn't, it's only six o'clock.'

'You absolutely should,' he protests. His eyes are glinting. He's undone his tie and his top button. He looks so handsome. 'How was the journey?'

'The train was incredibly busy,' she says, taking the wine, posh voice resuming. She lowers its volume. '*But thank you so much.*'

He winks at her. 'Don't mention it.'

Mum takes a sip from her glass, then makes a pleasurable groan. 'Oh, that's lovely – *just* what I need—'

'Don't mention what?' I interject, pulling the suitcase down the step onto the herringbone kitchen floor so it clunks loudly, alerting them to my presence.

Mum turns, a little startled, as if she had forgotten I existed. 'Oh!' She glances playfully at Ronan in a way that makes my jaw clench. 'Oh – whoops. I wasn't meant to say.' She mouths to him: *Sorry.*

'Sorry for what?' I look at Ronan. 'What?'

He smiles back at Mum in a way that is so secretive, so coded with the nuance of a gated-community in-joke that it makes me imagine throwing the suitcase at him. His head splits open, blood pouring over the marble countertop, and Mum is desperately attempting to stem the bleeding with her little wilted tissue.

She turns to me. 'Ronan booked me into first class.'

'Oh!' I say.

'It was incredibly kind of him.'

'We couldn't have you standing by the toilets for two hours,' he says, winking again. He winks a lot around my mother.

I make myself busy, pushing the suitcase against the wall. 'That's so nice – I'm glad.'

When I turn back round, Ronan is right in front of me, his hand out, holding a glass of what appears to be tomato juice. 'Here, darling.' He kisses me on the forehead, then places his hand gently on the base of my spine. When he removes it, a tingling feeling remains in the exact place he touched me.

'Oh, lovely – thank you.'

Everything is lovely.

And everyone is polite.

'Are you not drinking at the moment, Mal?' Mum says, in a way that sounds more like an allegation than a question, then takes a large gulp of her wine.

'No – no. Not at the moment…'

'I suppose that makes sense.'

I nod. 'But please, you enjoy it!'

She smiles – *I intend to* – then turns on the spot, looking at the walls, the pendant light hanging from the ceiling. Still giddy, eyes wide with awe. 'God. It always feels like I'm on holiday when I'm here.'

Ronan laughs loudly. 'Good! That's exactly what we want. Mal, take your mother's coat, for God's sake!'

'Yes, of course – Mum?'

'Oh, thank you.'

'Get comfortable, Stace,' he says.

In the moment that follows, I watch my mother's face change, just slightly, into the smallest wince. It would be unnoticeable to anyone else, but I see it, because I have seen it before. The wince is not directed at Ronan, but at herself. She hates her name. She hates being called *Stace* even more than *Stacey*. And for as long as I can remember she has made a point to correct people. But she has never corrected Ronan.

To her, both versions are 'common as muck', but at least *Stacey* is a little less – for want of a better word – basic. She has worked so hard. All her life. She has worked so hard to appear *not basic*.

She slips her arms out through her sleeves and hands the coat to me, eyes roaming around the kitchen. 'Have you painted the hall, Ronan?'

'Ah – yes, I did, about six months ago. It's just a slightly lighter shade.'

'It makes the place look bigger. If that's possible. Well done you.'

He nods. 'Thanks!'

I picked it.

I picked the slightly lighter shade.

I notice that in the time it took me to open the front door, Ronan has lit the candles. The ones we save for important people. The Diptyque set in their earthenware containers.

'You'll have to see the dormer conversion,' I say, 'I had so much fun designing it.' I hear my own voice, altered slightly, almost morphing into hers. Competing.

Already competing.

'Oh, wonderful,' Mum says, not taking her eyes from Ronan.

Is she tipsy already? She has always been a lightweight to both mid-priced white wine and Ronan's magnetism. I just can't tell which it is that is getting her high.

As I take her coat back into the hallway and begin to hang it in the cupboard, I hear eruptions of her laughter behind me – at a pitch and frequency that I know is completely authentic. He is so good at making her laugh. I've never known anyone to do it. Around others – me included – she has always been so serious.

There is something else in her pocket. Along with the wilted tissue.

I pause. I don't want to look, but my hand seems to reach down without any consideration or desire to gain approval from my brain. I glance down at my palm, half squinting, as if whatever is in it will disturb me less through a blur.

A half-empty packet of Polo mints. The foil twisted at the end where she has opened them.

The feel of the foil against my skin sparks something, a broken circuit in the back of my mind, making me shudder as it ignites. Mum used to curl the end up like that after giving one to me and Nick on the mile-long walk to school every day. This was when we lived in Tottenham. We moved to Tottenham from Birmingham when I was four and Nick was six. I can't really remember Birmingham, but it was a nice house, and we had a good life. I think Mum was happy there. We moved because Dad left, and she found out the truth about him. We moved to a tiny, rented two-bed in a huge building that stuck up into the sky like a stack of brown Lego blocks. We knew no one.

A fresh start.

I hated that place.

Mum did too, but she never said it. I don't remember us having a single guest for the entire time we lived there. Mum wouldn't allow us to invite friends over from school.

Buried memories continue to surface.

The first real memory I have is in that flat. Yes.

In the front room.

We must have just moved in – because there are bin bags of clothes and toys everywhere. I think it is late – unless time has distorted the recollection – and Mum is typing on her laptop.

At the time, she was starting a diploma in administration – an online course – because she didn't have a degree. She was applying to jobs and needed to be more employable. She was always so stressed. In Birmingham, she didn't have a job. She didn't need one. Dad was wealthy.

Until he wasn't.

In the memory, Mum is sat in the front room. There is a faint smell of cigarettes.

She would smoke out of the kitchen window – we were on the twelfth floor – but pretend she didn't.

In this memory, I start crying, and Mum tells me not to.

We don't do that.

It's not useful.

She then hugs me and takes me back to bed, into the room Nick and I shared. Nick talks to me. And makes me laugh.

He laughs, too.

His laugh.

A year after we arrived in Tottenham, my mother became a PA to a very wealthy banker in the city. She was now working for people she once had dinner parties with – but at least she was there, on the periphery of a world that she loved and longed for. That Christmas her boss, the banker, bought her a Tiffany's bracelet. This was the only time I have ever seen her on the brink of tears.

Mum always said one day she would own a house. And now she does. In Cheshire. In a town called Macclesfield. It has a little garden, where she has potted plants and two deck chairs. A little sun trap, she calls it.

I shove the mints and tissue back into her pocket, trying to push an unidentifiable nausea that has arisen into it with them.

When I re-enter the kitchen, Mum is sat at the island, and Ronan is gesticulating wildly – performing, mid-flow – telling his story about meeting Ralph Fiennes. I watch her smiling, dipping a bread stick into guacamole. She looks so happy. She always does around him. I can tell the stool is a little high for her, but she would hate for me to suggest we move somewhere more comfortable, would hate for me to assume she was struggling.

'Oh, I'm so glad he was nice. Sometimes you hear about these celebrities, that they aren't.'

'Oh – I have more stories for you. Maybe when the whiskey kicks in. But you'll have to promise not to tell anyone.'

Her eyes bulge as she draws her fingers across her lips, as if zipping them shut. 'Your secrets are safe with me.'

'Any holidays coming up?' he asks her. I am not sure if they have noticed me return.

'Yes – I've booked one in Greece at Easter.'

'Oh lovely.'

'That's nice, Mum.'

'Are you taking anyone?' he says. 'Any lucky man?'

'Oh, no.' She waves her hand, batting him off. 'No, no, *no*.'

'What?' he retorts. 'Don't you want to?'

'I think the question is would anyone want to come with me?' She does seem older. More fragile.

Ronan puts his hands up. 'Well, you know what I think – anyone would be lucky to have you. You're a total catch, Stace.'

If I was writing this as a scene in *The Air Between Us*, I'd be highlighting the dialogue in red and putting a note next to it saying: *CHANGE!!! TOO CLICHÉ!!!*

Ronan takes a gulp of his whiskey, winking at me now to let me know he is joking. He is just making her feel better.

'Thank you, Ronan.'

'How's the school, Mum?' I ask, as I join them at the table. And as we sit and talk – through smiles and nodding heads and topped up glasses – I feel myself begin to warm. It is as if my extremities thaw. Ronan takes my hand in his, squeezing it, and I let him. I see Mum's eyes noticing, smiling, laughing. More stories. More wine. And the air stills. A calm begins to take hold. Even the lighting in the kitchen starts to feel different. More golden.

'So.' Mum looks at me. 'How *are* you, Mallory?' There is a slight shift in her tone.

Ronan leans across the table and takes my hand in his. 'She's doing brilliantly, Stace.'

Mum nods. 'That's good to hear. Ronan told me you've been having a tough time again.'

Again.

I glance at him. He nods, approvingly. *Go on. It's OK.* 'I'm OK,' I say. 'I had a little *wobble*.' I hear myself say the word, and want to take the glass of tomato juice in my hand and smash it into my own forehead. 'But I'm doing OK now.'

'That's good. I'm glad. You're very thin.'

'Mallory is writing a new book,' Ronan says. 'Aren't you, Mal?'

'I am.'

I smile at Mum.

She flashes her eyes at Ronan. A look of half empathy, half concern. 'Oh, that's great, Mal,' she says.

'Why don't you tell her about it, Mal? While I take the suitcase up?'

Mum nods, a little anxiously.

When Ronan disappears back into the hall and up the stairs, we sit in silence, with only the noise of him above us, the wheels across the landing. Mum takes the bottle of wine and tops up her glass. I watch her take a few large gulps.

'So,' I say. 'Yes, I've been writing a romance.'

'A *romance*?' Mum repeats. *Is that scepticism?*

'Yes.'

'So, you've become *unblocked*?' *Is that sarcasm?*

'I guess that's one way of putting it,' I concede. 'Ronan and I were talking – he thinks it's a good avenue for me to go down.'

'Yes, he's very clever.'

'He is,' I say. 'Also, they say: write what you know.'

'Do they?' I can feel her staring at me. 'Well, then this should be great.'

'How's work going?'

'It's going well, thank you.'

I get up and go to the fridge to return the bottle of wine. It was better with Ronan here. Perhaps I should start cooking. I see the Ocado fish on its own shelf, its jelly eyes staring right at me. *How could you let me die? All for what? A dinner with the mother that hates you?* I nearly shush it. Instead, with a sudden rush of fervent desire to put it straight in the oven and grill it dead, I pick it up with my bare hands. 'I'm going to make us salmon en croûte – is that OK?'

'Sounds lovely.' I keep my back to her, but I can hear her thinking, sipping, thinking. Deciphering how to phrase what she is about to say. I don't want to hear it. I try to concoct a swift plan to stop it happening. Slap her with the fish? 'You know...' She hesitates. Here we go. 'I'm worried.'

'Oh?' I turn to face her, appearing nonchalant but also confused, as if this were a very ridiculous and very out of the blue thing to say. I close the fridge door with my elbow like a capable domestic wife does. 'Worried? What about?'

Confused, but relaxed.

Sane.

Holding a dead fish that just spoke to me.

'I always have been.'

'Mum, do you think I should use parsley—'

'I didn't bring you up to be someone people worry about.'

I look down at the fish. 'OK, maybe we should keep things—'

'But ever since you were a teenager – I have worried about you.'

'Right.'

'And when you met Ronan, it was a bit of an answered prayer, if I'm honest.'

'Oh, right.'

'Your book happened and it was wonderful. But I still knew, deep down – that it wouldn't be enough. I worried that despite this life you found – you wouldn't be happy. I thought once you were married, you would be OK. But then with the hospital admission seven years ago – I didn't want to pry or meddle, because you weren't my responsibility anymore. You were your own woman, and you had a husband. You were so erratic. He had to do everything for you.'

'Mum—'

'You going into the hospital was not nice for any of us.'

'*Mum—*'

'And then, over time, you got better. And I thought – maybe *this* is it. Maybe she's found a way to be settled now. You still had your *writer's block*, but you started your counselling course. And you seemed happy. You did. Calm. And you had *this* – this house. You have so much, Mal.'

'I know.'

She takes another large swig of her wine. I forgot how much of a lightweight she is. I watch her inhale, readying herself, like she has prepared this. Like it is written down on the back of one of her wilted tissues, and she has rehearsed it. 'I want to tell you this, and then I won't bring it up again. I think you use a generated perception of your past to justify your behaviour, Mallory. It is like you have told yourself a story over and over, and now believe it to be true. You need to get yourself together, accept what has happened, and move on. I know you, Mallory. I've known your desire for drama and your pull towards mess since you were a child. This needs to stop. This is a version of you that you must leave behind. It's childish. It's time to grow up – get in the real world. You're not a character from one of your books. You have responsibilities. You are a wife. And hopefully, soon, a mother. That is, if you get yourself together, before you miss your chance.'

'Mum – this is a bit much if I'm honest.'

'Is it? Ronan told me everything. The young man outside the house in the middle of the night. Following him. Using Ronan's pictures on a...' She pauses, stopping herself, then whispers, '*Gay app*,' like it is blasphemy. 'He could lose his *job*, Mallory. He is in a very brilliant and very powerful job – that is providing for *you*, no less – allowing you to do your counselling and write your books. And he could *lose it*. And then what would you do?' She doesn't give me time to answer. 'You need to grow up. No more of this childish fantasy world you live in. I know you justify this to yourself as *creative flare*. As *freedom*. But frankly, it's just a bit embarrassing.' She shakes her head. 'You need to be careful, or you will push him away.'

I stand still, staring at the marble counter top. My *Shallow Embers* book advance is buried in the stone. The weight of Mum's words pushes down on me. I feel the pressure like I'm miles underwater, like it's trying to drown me. I look at the dead salmon I am still holding in my hands. 'Well. That was quite the monologue.'

'Well. You needed to hear it.'

My brain feels like it has been put on spin-dry. This is the mother I know. The mother I remember. 'Thank you.'

'Don't get sarcastic with me. Don't get performative.'

'I'm not, Mum.'

'I would have killed for your life, Mallory. You don't know how easy you have it.' She gulps her wine, emptying her glass. 'Now, I'd love a top up, if that's OK? It's beautiful, is it Sauvignon Blanc?'

I keep staring at the jelly eyes of the fish. I thought that when things died, they felt peace. It doesn't look peaceful. More in complete shock. 'It's in the fridge,' I say.

She stands, opens the fridge door behind me and finds the bottle. 'It's lovely. Yes, from New Zealand – I thought so.' I can feel the scales of the fish beginning to peel off in my hands, sticking to my skin. She keeps pouring. 'You think you know so much, Mallory. You live in your own perceived reality of the world. But however you try to spin this to yourself, I am not to be blamed for your inability to participate in your own life.'

'What are you two nattering about?' I snap my head up to see Ronan stood in the kitchen doorway, now wearing an olive-green T-shirt and some loose-fitting joggers.

And Birkenstocks.

'Oh, nothing,' I reply. 'I was just telling Mum about *The Air Between Us*. I have an idea for the ending.'

'I can't wait to hear about it, darling,' he says, then looks at my mother. 'I opened the window in your bedroom, Stace. It was getting a bit stuffy up there.'

'Thank you, Ronan.' She nods, then takes a sip of her wine. 'Right. I'm starving. Do you need a hand with that salmon, Mal? You look like you're about to hit someone with it.'

39

Leo

It's dark now.

I can see them finishing their dinner through the glass doors at the back of the house. I'm figuring out how to get to her, to talk to her, but it's gonna be tricky. Cos of him, and this new lady. They've been taking their time – with their white wine and Smeg fridge and massive fucking fish – but time is now something I don't have much of. The shakes are getting bad, I feel like my brain is gonna splinter and I swear the devil from the gravy came into the shed with me. Which is why I relocated to the bush by the fence in the garden. I saw its little face watching me from the corner of the roof, all dusty now, and mean, whispering stupid shit. Laughing.

> *The police are gonna get you, Leo.*
> *I'll tell them the things you've done.*
> *Come. Into my arms.*
> *It's safe here, baby boy.*

I slept though. I fucking slept. Feel a bit more with it now. A bit clearer. If I can just tell her what's happening – tell her the truth – I might get a bed. Food. A shower. Tell her I just need to lay low for a few days. Talk about what's next. About what happened. Talk about getting to meetings. A sponsor. Maybe some proper therapy. That's what she said would work.

I'm fucking ready.

I am.

But this Ronan guy. There's something not right about him. I mean, I'm not exactly the best person to judge, but there's something in him that I recognise. I know this kind of man. I do. He's got this power. This fucking charm. I can see it through the glass. It's so bright. A gravitational pull that's covering something. I know it, cos I feel it draw me in. I wanna know what's there. Underneath. Danger. It spikes my brain.

Takes one to know one, I suppose.

The way he looked at her, on the porch, two weeks ago. I keep remembering it.

I need to get her on her own. I need to do it soon. It's getting fucking freezing.

I watch them cleaning up the kitchen. At first I thought this new woman was *his* mum – cos of the way she looked at him, all lovingly, throwing her head back and laughing at everything he says. Then I saw her face properly – and she is Mallory but older.

It's her mum.

I'm watching Ronan. Watching him pour himself a massive glass of whiskey, then kiss Mallory on the back of the head. She turns to him and smiles, then he takes the glass of whiskey and leaves the kitchen. After a minute, the light goes on in the window up in the roof. Must be their bedroom. I can see him through it, texting on his phone. He pulls the blind down.

That's him out of the way. Just the other one now. Then I can get Mallory's attention. She keeps washing up, and her mother is sat at the little kitchen table behind her, staring into the fruit bowl. She keeps looking up at Mallory, but it's dead weird, cos every time Mallory turns round, she pretends she's not and looks back at the bowl, picking at a pineapple.

Then she moves. She stands and comes to the window-doors. *Shit.* I pull myself back a bit, further behind the bush, as she stares out into the garden. Then the shutters close.

I wait. Dunno what to do now.

That's not good. I can't detox in the shed on my own. I'll be fucked.

Come to me. I'll look after you.

Nope. Not you, you fucker.

I look up at the back of the house, squinting through the dark. There's a window open. Up on the second floor. That could work.

Come back to me.

No.

I move – fast – along the garden, hugging the bushes, across the patio, past the chair and table set and a weird bird bath.

I pause at the wall. Wait. Listen.

Drainpipe.

I start to pull myself up it. Feel like my stomach is gonna fall out my arse, crawling up the side of a house to escape the devil, but I'm at the window pretty quick – woah, it's fucking high! I'm gonna vom – can't vom from here... *Just get inside!* I put my foot onto the window ledge and pull myself across, holding onto the wooden frame, and look through the glass.

A light is on. A bed is made. An unopened suitcase is on top of it. Flowers are on the bedside table.

This is where the mum is staying.

Gonna have to be quick. I lift my leg and yank myself through the gap. *Can't be loud, can't be loud.* OK, this angle's not great, not great at all. Head first, it seems – yep – down into the room – slow, *slowly* – sliding forward – ow, fuck – the fucking window latch cutting into my stomach. Hands out, down, and I'm onto the floor, in a little heap.

I stop.

It was not exactly balletic. But there was no noise.

I feel a bit buzzy. Might vomit.

I wait again.

Pause.

Listen. I can hear Ronan pacing around on the floor above me. A low murmur from down below in the kitchen. I stand and walk to the door, then clock the suitcase again.

Could be something in it. Something useful.

I unzip the side of it, and slowly lift it open. Loads of folded clothes. I start rooting through – *nope, nope, nope* – then see a little wash-bag. She might be nuts in the head too. Let's see what she's got. I open it: tissues, toothbrush, toothpaste… And then, the meds. Bingo. God, she's got a right fucking collection here. Pill salad. Amlodipine. No. Calcium. No. Vitamin D. No. Citalopram. Hell, no. Omeprazole. No. No benzos. Fuck.

Take the whole fucking lot, Leo.

'Fuck off.'
Nope. Don't speak. Do not speak to the devil.
I zip everything back up, making sure it looks as neat as I remember, and go to the door. I open it as quietly as is humanly fucking possible. I wait, listening. Massive hallway. I look up and down it. Hanging glass lights that look like something from a Dickens book. The coving by the roof is all twirly. It starts to spin and twist, like snakes.
Jesus.
I blink, to stop it. I see the door at the bottom of the hall, on the left. A bathroom? I creep along the hall, trying not to make any creaks, then open the door.
I fucking knew it. She does have one of those massive stand-alone baths with feet.
I kind of want to get in it.

Drown yourself.

Nope, nope, nope.
I push the door shut gently behind me and go to the sink. I look at myself in the mirror. Takes me a second to recognise the reflection. Holy fucking shit, I do not look good. I suddenly see little horn marks, burning into my forehead. I blink. They disappear. I nearly instinctively punch the glass, then I see it is a cabinet. A mirror cabinet. I push it so it clicks and swings open. The first thing I see is the mouthwash. Listerine Total Care. *Total care.* I pick it up and look at the back: 21.6% alcohol.

Do it.

No.

Do it.

I quickly sift through tooth picks, hand wash, soap, cotton wool, razors, fluoxetine, mirtazapine, and then see what I am looking for. A packet. Prescription.
Lorazepam. 1 mg. Mallory Maddox.
For use when experiencing anxiety and panic attacks.
This'll do it. In the detox places, they gave me one an hour, to help me come down safe.
I place two on my tongue, and swallow.
A noise.
I spin my head to the door.
Footsteps.
On the stairs.
Shit. *Shit.*
Mallory, or her mum, or both, coming up. My brain stalls. Fucking *come on. Get it together.* I can't go out the window in here. It's locked. Then I see it in the reflection, behind my head. A massive cupboard. Double slatted doors. I put the sheet of tablets in my pocket and the Listerine bottle back in the cabinet, push its mirror-door shut, turn, tiptoe over the tiles and pull open the cupboard door. I'm hit with heat and the smell of something beautiful and clean, like a warm meadow. There is a boiler in the middle, towels and bedding all folded on a shelf above it, and below, a space. I kneel down, get in below the boiler, push myself to the back, pull the doors shut.
 I wait, listening. I can hear them.
'Night, Mum.'
'Goodnight, Mallory.'
Then Mallory's footsteps. Up to the attic. Shit. She's gone up – to him. Not good. Oh my God, it's really fucking toasty in here. I can hear her mum coming down the corridor, to the bathroom. To me. Shit. I hear the bathroom door open and hold my breath,

watching through the gaps in the slats. She goes to the mirror and looks at her reflection. Stands there, looking at herself. I know I've had a benzo but it feels like she's doing it for a really fucking long time. What she's doing?

Can she see me?

Can she fucking—

No. Wait.

She's crying.

She's actually crying.

She turns the tap on and starts washing her hands, scrubbing at them, then splashes the water over her face. It's all a bit swimmy, a bit blurry. She sniffs. Once. Twice. Turns towards me. Frowns. Looks directly at the slatted doors.

Shit.

Can she smell me? Is that what's happening?

Then she shakes her head. Turns away and wipes her hands on the towel hanging by the sink. She exhales slowly. Then leaves.

I sit under the boiler, blinking. The light from the hallway cuts through the slats. Every time I close my eyes it's still there, imprinted, white slices in the dark. OK. What now? Back to the shed?

The lorazepam is hitting.

I can feel it pulling at me. Can't stay here. Can I?

I start to drift. To slip. In and out. My head against the wall. It's so warm. The smell of the washing powder is nice. Makes me feel all safe. I start to see things. In my mind. A field. Flowers. I feel warmth, on my face. Can hear things, too. Birds. Waves. Fucking waves. The sea. Am I by the sea? Keep jolting awake, then back to sleep. I'm on a beach. It's fucking lovely.

I hear another noise.

A door opening.

It's all hazy. I look out through the slats. Dunno if I'm still dreaming. Dunno what's real. Because it's not her this time. It's him. Ronan. Topless. Just in his boxer shorts, standing in the middle of the bathroom, flexing his muscles in the cabinet mirror. He has something in his hand. His phone. He pulls his boxers down. Then he bends forward. I hear the sound of the camera on his phone. Clicking away. Then he leans forward again, pulling his kecks back up. All blurry. All swimmy. I watch him scanning through the photos he just took, smiling to himself. Then he sends it to someone.

I stare at his face in the mirror. His chiselled jaw. His freckles. Green eyes. He smiles to himself, like he thinks only the sink and the mirror will know. Bathrooms must have a lot of fucking secrets.

Then he's gone.

40

Mallory

I sit quietly on the closed toilet seat in the en suite of our bedroom, trying to stop my knees trembling, staring at the screen. Stan replied three hours ago, whilst the fish was baking at a solid 200 degrees.

I am only reading it now.

> Hi Mal,
>
> I've tried to call you, but the number I have seems to be switched off. Perhaps I have an old one? I have heard from the publishing house – they got back to me very quickly which usually means one of two things.
>
> Sadly, they didn't like what you proposed for the ending.

Shit.
Shit shit shit.

> Gina's note was: 'I am disappointed to say that M.M.'s proposed ending didn't quite have the emotional pull we were looking for – and some of the authenticity fell away. It didn't feel genuine to the journey Liam was on.'

Shit.

> I'm sorry, Mal. I rather liked it myself!

However, all is not lost. Gina was going to withdraw her offer (which can happen, it's not unusual!) but I have managed to convince her to give you another go. Are you able to do this? Would need it <u>asap</u>. By tomorrow.

I don't want to lose this deal for you. You've worked so hard!

Dig deep. Think about how to really throw the reader an emotional spanner. You know these characters, Mal.

Stan

No kisses.
No double words.
No *urgent*, *necessary* or *relevant*.
Just *disappointed*.

The image of the Vizsla on the beach fractures, slipping away through the folds in my brain, like shards of glass.

I hear the door of the bedroom shut.

Where's he been?

'Mal? What are you doing in there? I had to use the other bathroom.'

He sounds annoyed. Suspicious. 'Coming!' I call, pushing the flush. I can't have him hear my panic. I lean down and slide the laptop into the inch-tall gap beneath the cabinet and the floor.

I stand, wash my hands and exhale. *Box breathing*.

Regulate.

I can do this.

I can do this.

As I push open the en-suite door, the shaft of light spills out from behind me and illuminates Ronan lying in the bed under the covers, putting his phone on the bedside table.

'Hey – sorry,' I whisper. 'Needed to pee. Too much tomato juice.' I flick the light off behind me, making him disappear, tiptoe across the carpet, peel back the duvet and slide under it next to him. I lie still, feeling his presence, not looking at me, but probing.

Do I seem rattled?

Can he tell?

'Today went well,' I say quietly. An attempt to keep things *light*, to keep things *fun*. But then I remember what happened at the office and backpedal. 'With Mum, I mean. I know your day was hard. I'm really sorry about that, Ronan. I've been thinking about what you said, and you're right. I need to do better at looking after myself. And I'm going to prove to you I can.'

He's thinking. 'Mmhmm.' Is he still angry? 'She looks old now, doesn't she?'

'Sorry?'

He continues facing the ceiling. 'Your mum. She looks old. I actually worry she might be becoming a bit... Slow.'

'Slow?'

'She seems less sharp these days.' She still seems sharp to me. 'A little less switched on. When she showed us pictures of the house in Macclesfield... Jesus, I forgot how small it is. She's done it up nicely, I'll give her that. You couldn't swing a cat in it though, Jesus. It's a little embarrassing, don't you think? Bless her.'

'I think—'

'She's turning into a bit of a cliché. Mutton dressed as lamb.' He makes a little chuckle that has the quality of an invitation, an invitation for me to join him. 'You need to encourage her to buy some new clothes.'

I stare into the darkness above me. 'Maybe I'll take her shopping.'

'Not this week.'

'Well... No. Maybe next week.'

'Let's see,' he says. Then, in the dark, I feel him move. His hand on my arm. Gently this time. 'Come here.' He pulls me, drawing me across the sheets, into his body. Before I protest, his arms are around me, engulfing me. 'I'm here,' he says. 'I will always be here. If I seem frustrated, it's only because I love you, Mal. I want you to be OK. When you're not seeing clearly, I know you understand that I know what's best for you.'

'I'm OK, Ronan.'

'I don't want you ending up in hospital again. No one wants that.'

'No.'

As he squeezes me into him, our skin clammy and sticking together, nausea swirls. 'I love you so much. No one will love you the way I do. Do you know that? I would put everything on the line for you. I have.' He exhales slowly so his breath tickles the side of my face. I can smell the whiskey. 'I don't want you to end up like your mother.' His lips graze my neck. 'Alone. Bored. Nothing to show for yourself.'

'Ronan—'

'I want to show you how much I love you,' he whispers. 'Will you let me?'

I instinctively shift away from him slightly. Not much. But it stops him. He shifts back. His hands let go. We unstick. He sits up, placing his arms onto his knees. 'It's been weeks, Mal.'

'I know. I'm sorry. I think increasing the medication has messed with my libido.'

'Right.' While he runs his hand across his face, I wait for it. I know what's coming. 'I checked the fertility app. You start ovulating tomorrow.'

There it is. 'I don't...'

I don't want it.

I do not want it.

'We should try,' he says. 'I've been doing a lot of reading, and I wonder if some other things might help. The book says that women who are trying to conceive in the geriatric period should be as relaxed as possible. I want to give you that. Maybe we could come up with a list of more things that would help? What do you think?'

I think the word geriatric is horrendous. 'That sounds good.'

I see his eyes brighten through the dark. 'Yeah?'

'Yeah.'

'I can think of one thing.'

It is an odd thing to recognise just before intercourse, but he looks like a child.

While I lie back, watching him thrust, his eyes shut, I wonder who he is thinking about. Who he is picturing.

I picture the German Vizsla. But the whole thing lasts much longer than the few seconds it takes for my imaginary Vizsla to run along the beach, because Ronan is drunk. I always forget how vocal he can be. I want to tell him to try and say less, because he might wake my mother on the floor below. But I also want him to think this is a relaxing experience. So I decide to conjure up some more distractions. I intend to picture nice things – the future – my future – but my mind betrays me. With each thrust I seem to be lurched back in time.

'*Oh, yeah…*'

To the tiny flat we rented in Stoke Newington after six months of dating.

'*Mal…*'

Me, finishing *Shallow Embers* there, and reading it to him at night. His comments and notes.

The agent picking it up. Selling it in a week. The first British advance.

'*Oh, Mal…*'

The American advance. Nearly falling over at the sight of it in my account. His face when I told him. His disbelief.

'*Oh, yeah—*'

His jealousy.

'*Yeah…*'

The marriage proposal that came not long after it. The marriage itself, three months later. The field. The wellies. The sun in his eyes.

'*Mal…*'

The book sales. The royalties.

'*Mal…*'

His jealousy.

Me. Excited. Thinking of new book ideas.

'*Oh—*'

Him, telling me I could do better. That they weren't good. That they were awful.

'*Oh—*'

Telling me that the only reason *Shallow Embers* did so well must have been because of the notes he gave me. '*Jesus – I'm joking, Mal. Don't be so sensitive.*' Him, starting the joint account. Me, putting my book money into it.

'*Oh, fucking hell—*'

The pressure in my brain. We were married. It was fine. Him, bringing me the brochure for this house. Telling me he had put down a deposit. With my money. Me, agreeing it was a good idea. My brain hurting. The pressure.

'*Mal...*'

Him, interning, while my book paid the mortgage. Me, feeling like I was losing my mind in the house. Him, saying I was lucky. Many women would kill to have what I have.

'*I love you...*'

Me, saying I wanted to apply for a job in publishing. Him, telling me it would be too stressful for me. That I wouldn't be able to *hack it*.

My mind, slipping.

'*Oh, yeah...*'

More book ideas. Him, telling me they were juvenile – basic – that I would embarrass myself. Telling me that I would be a great mother, and should focus on that. '*Imagine our babies, they will be beautiful.*' His promotions.

'*That's it, baby...*'

The snap in my mind.

'*Yeah – yeah – yeah.*'

Snap. Snap. Snap.

'*That's it—*'

Me, telling him I didn't want this life anymore. That I felt trapped. By him. That I wanted to write what I wanted to write. And I wanted to leave.

'*Oh, baby, I love you so much.*'

Racing thoughts. Putting the money in the boat on the Gower. My money.

'*Oh, yeah—*'

Him, saying I couldn't be alone. That I needed him. Or I would ruin my life.

'*Oh, yeah—*'

Me, believing him.

'*Oh, yeah—*'

Him, questioning my sanity.

'Uh, baby—'

Me, questioning my sanity.

'Baby—'

My mind stalling.

'Are you close?'

The psychiatric ward. The blinking light of the fire alarm on the ceiling.

'Oh, Mal.'

The—

'Ugh! Fuck, yeah!' Oh. He's finished. 'Oh, my God. That was amazing.' He falls off me.

'Amazing,' I repeat.

'I love you,' he says, pulling the duvet over him.

'Love you too.'

I think of the Vizsla again, pulling the image of it running along the beach back into my consciousness. When Ronan is asleep, I get up and pull on my dressing gown.

41

Leo

THE WAVES

There's a beach
Somewhere
Where the wind blows a Fanta can across the pebbles.

The sea's not blue
It's like Tupperware
Cloudy
Streaked and stained
But it makes sense

The waves come in
The wind brings them in
Constant

They don't wash anything clean
But when they hit
They're so loud –
Louder than the hum
I carry in my ribs
Louder than the spin of it
The static
The ache
From trying too hard to feel nothing
Cos it's big that thing

It's big

But for a minute it's quiet
Not in the world
Not on the beach
Just in me.

And I want them forever –
I want the chaos of the waves
To slam into me
To keep it quiet
Forever.

Leo Fuller
Year 9

42

Mallory

I need fresh air.

I need space. I need to breathe. To *think*.

To plot out the end of the book. I decide the back patio is the best place for me to do this. Currently, there is no surveillance device monitoring the rear of the house, so I shouldn't be noticed. The keys for the Crittall doors in the kitchen remain in the fruit bowl. Ronan hasn't moved them yet. There are some Vogue menthols stashed somewhere in one of the old cooking pots in a drawer, behind the Jäger. I will also need these.

As I descend the staircase from the attic, past the first floor, I check my mother's bedroom door is shut. It is, but as I pass it, something prickles at the back of my neck, a warning – a sign to be quiet – making me move as lightly as I can. I avoid creaks from the floorboards beneath the chic woollen runner lining the stairs, and then I am safely on the tiles of the ground floor hallway. I move gently into the kitchen.

It's dark.

I should keep the lights off.

Feeling my way through the room, I become aware of the buzz in my brain – a soundless electrical charge. It seems to amplify each movement I make, putting me in a state of hyper-awareness. The pad of my feet on the herringbone floor. My breath moving in and out of my nostrils. The click of my knees as I kneel down next to the island to open the cupboard door. The clunk of the latch, reverberating into my body like a clap. I pause, holding my breath, waiting for it to pass through me, listening. When I am sure that no one else has heard, that no one has followed me down the stairs, I start gently sifting through the pots. The Vogues are at the bottom of an old Le Creuset casserole dish next to a matchbox. *Bingo.* I stand, take the keys from next to the pineapple that was delivered today by Ocado (for aesthetic reasons only – no one will eat it) and unlock the back door.

As I step out onto the cold porch slabs, the air hits. The sudden change in temperature does something to the back of my throat, my muscles and the fluid in my eyes – shocking me. I immediately feel like I might burst into tears.

No. Control it. *Box breathing. Reality checking. List four things you see in front of you.* I pull the doors closed and check off a list of things that enter my vision on our perfectly landscaped patio. The bay tree. The decidedly mismatched planters. The Nkuku outdoor table that can be set at two different heights. The porcelain bird bath.

I pause. Why did we get that? I don't think I've ever seen a bird go anywhere near the thing, let alone bathe in it. It would have more use as an ashtray.

This is it. This is my reality.

As I stare at the blue and white swirls of paint covering its shiny exterior, my mind feels like it might slip. Slip into a terrain I do not want it to enter.

I can't finish this book without Leo.
I will be in this house forever.

As I look down at the Vogue cigarette now resting between my fingers, something odd happens. I feel my consciousness move. It shifts, transporting me to outside of my own body. I see myself from above. A bird's eye view of a woman about to light a cigarette on her back patio. It's not just like I'm being filmed on a drone camera. I notice that I don't look like me. Or how I think I look. There is a certain grading to the image: a wistful and melancholic hue, like a scene from a low-budget but very cool indie film.

And it looks… kind of chic. Very: *Girl, Interrupted.* But more romantic. More *subtle.* It momentarily eases my nerves. Well, no – it doesn't – but it gives them some kind of… *Meaning.*

Importance. Profundity. The idea that someone might see them, that someone might say, *Yes – yes! I've felt like that too – oh my gosh, it's awful*, fills me with a strange warmth. And they would cry, because I am crying. A bond would form between me and that person.

I find myself wondering if Saoirse Ronan smokes. She would, in this scene. I have always felt some strange affinity with her.

I have.

I see the image of me smile.

I strike the match, stopping to allow the nostalgic sting of its fumes to seep into me, then touch the flame to the cigarette. I inhale deeply. Once. Twice. Three times. Like Saoirse might.

It does the opposite of what it is supposed to.

With each drag I am pulled back inside my body, and a deep unease rises. It's as if the menthol is smoking out the façade that I have attempted to generate over the past two weeks (fine, seven years), revealing only a well of raw and damaged nerves. My hands begin to shake as my mind more than slips. It tumbles. There is no camera. And no one is watching. *None of this means anything. That's the truth.*

Beneath it all, beneath everything we spend all our lives creating, are we all like this?

We are completely and utterly alone. The reality of it nearly winds me. Anxiety peaks.

We will never truly know anyone.

I lean forward, because I feel nauseous. I don't know if it's a symptom of the nicotine rush or the existential crisis, but it is so intense that I feel like I might vomit. When I was with Leo, I felt more in the world. Less in my brain. There was something about him, his energy, the way he moved and talked and experienced life that was urgent, and I had no space to consider. Just to be.

I feel a film of saliva coat the roof of my mouth, tasting bile at the back of my throat. I am going to be sick.

I open my mouth – expecting it to pour out of me. I wait, hunched over, for what must be minutes, but nothing comes. When I am sure it won't, I stand. I wipe my mouth with the back of my hand, feeling the faint air of disappointment that I haven't covered the porch in tonight's dinner. In the film version of this, I would have. But it would have still been, somehow, glamorous. Glamorous but real. A rare blend.

Am I insane?

I look into the bushes at the back wall, next to the shed, flanking the gate that opens out to the cobbled bin alley. A thought enters my mind.

Could he be…? I wouldn't put it past him.

'Leo?' I whisper into the dark. I pause, listening, stock still. '*Leo?*'

No response.

Nothing.

I was wrong. The awful realisation that Ronan and my mother are right takes form inside me. I *am* childish. I *am* unstable. What was I thinking? This book was never going to work. It was a fantasy. Something that never belonged to me.

I should be grateful. I have everything. I do. This is it.

Get into reality.

I inhale sharply.

I will leave the book. I will leave Liam and his story and tell Stan that this is not mine to tell. That I have lost the plot. Not literally, although possibly that also. I have no way forward. I will explain I have become blocked again. *Perhaps in the future, we could collaborate on something else. I have a romance that I'm working on…*

I look up – in some final plea for inspiration – following the trail of smoke into the air with my eyes. My mother's window is open, right above my head.

Shit. She will smell it.

I forgot she does that. Opens the window of any room she sleeps in. I tiptoe quickly to the bird bath and push the cigarette into the porcelain, stubbing it out dead, marking the paint with a grey smear. Then I make my way back into the kitchen, lock the door, put the packet in the Le Creuset casserole dish and place the keys back in the fruit bowl.

I stop, staring at the bowl.

That's odd.

There are flies. Tiny flies hovering around it. I didn't notice them before.

I wave my hand over the pineapple in an attempt to disperse them. They move, but immediately seem drawn back towards the fruit. I pick up the pineapple, inspecting it. Did they send me a mouldy one in the Ocado delivery? It seems fine. Firm.

I notice something at the bottom of the bowl.

A single tangerine.

But it is rotting. Half orange, half green with mould. There is a black welt in the middle of the green, oozing something that appears almost poisonous.

It looks like someone has punched it.

That shouldn't be there.

How did I miss that?

I stand still for a moment, my eyes following the flies as they attempt to re-land on its decaying flesh. The way they seem so intent, so unphased by what they are moving towards.

And then I stick my finger in it. It sinks right in.

I let the gloopy mess swallow it.

I close my eyes.

It is soft and warm.

What am I doing?

I gag. I pull my finger out, take a piece of kitchen roll from the countertop, use it to pick up the tangerine and quickly throw the thing in the bin. I find the bleach under the sink and spray the inside of the bowl. I wipe it down. I wash my hands, careful not to make too much noise with the water running out of the faucet, and use the Aesop Resurrection hand cream, inhaling the soothing scent of lavender. Wiping moisturiser residue on a towel, I glance around the kitchen – checking nothing is out of the ordinary – then make my way back into the hallway.

But before I begin to ascend the stairs, I stop.

The light is on in the living room.

That's odd. I never leave the light on. I am almost one hundred percent certain that I turned it off. When I open the door, I see Mum sat in my armchair in front of the bookcase, under the glow of the corner lamp. The TV is on, but muted. She is reading.

I squint. She is reading my book.

'Mum?'

'Jesus.' She jumps, startled. Pulls down her glasses. 'What are you doing?'

'I came down for a glass of water. What are *you* doing?'

'I couldn't sleep.'

I hover in the doorway for a moment, like one of the flies from the kitchen. Back in the flat in Tottenham, this same scenario would play out: I would hover in the doorway and she would tell me to go back to bed. I half expect her to do the same now. Why is she reading *Shallow Embers*? I almost don't want to know the answer.

She wrinkles her nose. 'Have you been smoking?'

'No.' I point to the book. 'A bit of nighttime reading?'

She looks down at her lap. 'Ah. Yes. I was just interested.'

'You've read it before.'

'A long time ago.'

'You're making headway, you're nearly halfway through.'

'I was looking for a certain part.'

I wish she *had* told me to go back to bed. 'Well, I'm getting some water, do you want anything?'

'No, thank you.'

I turn to the door.

'Mal, wait.'

'I'm tired, Mum, I think I'll—'

'I found the part.'

'Right.' I turn back to her but can't meet her eyes, so I stare at her legs. She does seem older, but Ronan was wrong. She is no less sharp in her mind.

'I wanted to ask you about it.' I see her motion towards the couch. A sign for me to sit.

'It's past one o'clock.'

'You have never slept well, Mallory. Five minutes won't change that.'

She's right. I don't have an excuse, and I don't want to start an argument.

But I also don't want to have this conversation.

I tentatively push the door shut.

I move to perch on the edge of the couch, making sure to find a position that will allow me to get up quickly and make a swift exit if necessary. Which it probably will be. A position that also – I realise – makes me feel like I am about to be reprimanded by a head teacher. It is an odd sensation to feel like I am a teenager again. And even odder that now my youth seems so close to the present moment. Far less than it did fourteen years ago. 'OK. What part have you found, Mum?'

I still don't know where to look. I glance at the silent TV. BBC London is on, with subtitles. Maybe this is a new thing she does. Watches things with the sound off. Maybe this is what happens when you live alone. When you want to feel less isolated. Maybe this is what Ronan meant when he said he didn't want me to end up like her.

Is she lonely? She's never said it.

She's never seemed it.

'I always found it interesting that *Shallow Embers* was marketed as a book about a girl who runs away from home,' she says. 'It just seemed to me to be a book about a girl who is running away from herself.'

Jesus. I didn't come downstairs for reviews. I could just as easily have pulled up my Goodreads page if I wanted to hear what my book is. 'I was young when I wrote it, Mum. I honestly can't even really remember it.'

She picks the copy up off her lap, with an air of *Let me remind you*. It's the first edition hardback. She must have taken it from the bookshelf behind her. I watch her push her glasses back up her nose and flick through the pages until she pauses about two thirds in. She runs her finger down the text until it stops, and she makes an *aha* noise. With it comes the realisation that my mother is about to read an excerpt of my book to me. One that I probably (most definitely) don't want to hear. 'Mum – why don't we just—'

'*Mia's mother appeared in the doorway*,' she cuts me off. Her voice becomes posher again, as she assumes the accent. It makes me uncomfortable, her reading my words in that affected voice.

'Neat as a pin, eyes sharp. The instinct to run had never been so strong. To leave the woman who had caused her so much pain was an act that felt fundamental to the trajectory of her life – one that she always knew would happen. Mia had fantasised about this moment over and over again – in the dead of night beneath her sheets, on the school bus, crying in the bathroom, alone. She had fantasised about the exact words she would say, and constructed numerous versions of how things would look, and depending on the pain she was feeling, the extremities of the interaction would shift. Sometimes she would visualise that there would be screaming and tears. Sometimes she would imagine the goodbye was achieved with only a look, and no words. In her darkest projections, the interaction would end with chunks of hair and blood on the carpet.

But tonight was different. It was at odds with every version Mia had imagined. Tonight was eerily calm, as if her mother had always known – always expected – that this would eventually happen. And what really made Mia falter was that it was as if her mother was prepared, ready and even willing. Her mother's willingness to say goodbye had never been a version Mia had considered. One where her own mother allowed it to happen. Her mother allowed her – or even wanted her – to leave, to be on her own, to fend for herself in the world. She was only fifteen.'

Mum stops.

I feel her look at me, waiting for a response, but I don't know what to say. I pick at the couch seam for what feels like an eternity, then opt for: 'I had actually forgotten that bit.'

'I see.'

'Mum...'

'Earlier, in the kitchen, you said you *write what you know*.'

'It's just a story, Mum.'

'You never told me that's how you were feeling.'

'It isn't real life.' I point at the book. 'That girl isn't me.'

'Isn't she?'

'No.'

Her eyes remain locked onto my face. Something about the awareness of her glare builds a pressure inside me.

'You think I wanted you to leave?'

'Mum, *seriously*, this is ridiculous – it's late—'

'I brought you up to be able to face the world.'

'The book *isn't about us*, Mu—'

'That's what's so interesting about first-person narratives – you only see things from one particular point of view.'

'Mum, please.'

'I personally would love to see a sequel, or a spin off, from the mother's point of view. Perhaps write that one next, instead of your romance novel.' She is angry, but the fury is not in the volume of her voice, rather, it is in the design of her words: the precision of each consonant, and the inflection of each sentence. Direct, but not forced, like she has rehearsed this. There is intent. And I am in no way ready. I am caught off guard. I feel my cheeks flushing. 'A story about how the mother sacrificed everything for her children.'

'Oh my God – really, Mum? You want to do this now?'

'One where she is left to fend for herself, and does it. One where a man leaves her with absolutely nothing. *Less* than nothing. I think I'd read that. It sounds good.'

'Can we please—'

'She is very determined. Very capable of seeing a way through. Proactive. Maybe she becomes a lawyer. She manages to fulfil her own dreams.'

I pause, staring at my feet, the pressure in my brain rising to fever pitch. 'You made your own choices, Mum. Please don't blame us for that.'

'I was surviving.'

'Is that what you call it? That's not what it felt like.'

She suddenly laughs. 'Wow.'

'Yeah. *Wow*.'

'It is remarkable how you manage to make everything about you.' She crosses one leg over the other. 'Do you remember when you were seven and you got sent home from school because you wanted to be in Nick's class, and they wouldn't let you, so you threw a pen at a teacher?' The mention of my brother's name feels like a wasp sting to my core. I haven't heard her say it in years. Hearing it come from her mouth, voiced so casually, makes me freeze, as if ice has been injected into my system. 'You've always found things harder than they need to be. You have found it hard to do things alone – to do things for yourself. Either myself or Nick – and now Ronan – have had to hold your hand. I tried to raise you to be self-sufficient.'

'Well, I'm sorry I was so needy.'

'Oh, come off it, you're not needy, Mallory, because you don't *need* anything. And you never have. You have always been looked after. You seem to place yourself in a position of pain – but I'm not sure you really know what it is to struggle. You like to think you do, but your life is enviable. Look around you. I know you miss Nick, and I know full well that you blame me for it – but you really need to start moving on. You're stuck.'

Her words slice like a knife. 'Wow, say what you really mean, why don't you, Mum.'

'Someone should.'

'Who said I blame *you*?'

'Sorry?'

'For Nick's death.'

'Oh, come off it, Mallory. The way you have acted with me for the past ten years – I know you see his death as a direct result of my parenting.'

'*What?*' Is she drunk? Or has she been wanting to say this for years? Did she come downstairs while I was outside and wait for me to have this conversation? She is so confident, so assured—

'Is that why you don't want to be a mother, Mallory? You're worried you'll mess your children up, like I did?'

'Jesus Christ, Mum.'

'You painted me as a monster in this book.' She holds up the *Shallow Embers* hardback. 'Is this what you're scared of becoming? A shitty mother?'

She never swears. Never. 'I'd like to leave this conversation now.'

'Are you ever honest?'

'Sorry?' Again, I freeze. I want to say, *You have no idea. You didn't know him like I did. You're the one who can't see the truth.* 'Fine. Yes. I think it was your fault. I think it was your fault Nick died.'

She narrows her eyes. 'There it is.'

'You weren't there for him when he needed you. You never were. You were obsessed with yourself. With being seen in a certain way.' She raises her eyebrows. *Go on. Keep going.* Is she enjoying this? 'I have often wondered what happened to him the night before he did it. I want to know if his decision was planned. If he had some very clear and rational understanding that his life should be over. Or if it was impulsive. I want to know what was going on inside him. It wasn't a mistake, I know that much. He wasn't asking for help – it was too intentional and too secret. He never asked me for help. Not once. I want to know what was inside that made him want to keep all that in. It was so unexpected – because he never told me. I want to know why him. Because let's face it, we both assumed I would be the one that would end up that way.'

'Finally, some honesty.' She pauses. 'I'm glad you didn't end up that way.' Her eyes glint, watery under the light of the corner lamp, but she looks at the floor. 'You're lucky to have Ronan. I'm glad you have him, Mal. He is good for you. I know you don't want to hear it, but you struggle on your own. You need him, and that's OK.' I feel like I might cry again. Or be sick. I can't tell the difference. 'We need to put this behind us now, Mallory. I am here to help you. Tomorrow you can show me some of your book, and we can talk about getting you back to work – doing your therapy. Doing what you need to do to be a part of the life you have created...'

I don't even excuse myself. I just leave the living room. I don't know how I get upstairs, but I do, my mind moving, firing, rapidly weaving something together. I tiptoe into the en suite and sit.

I pull the laptop out from under the sink cabinet and begin to type.

Hi Stan –

Here is the new version of the final third of the book. I hope the publisher finds this to be more aligned with what they are looking for.

The words pour out of me.

So much so that soon the laptop is about to die on me. I sneak back downstairs, plug it in at the kitchen table, pour myself a glass of wine and continue.

When I am done, it is 3 a.m.

In an exhausted post-creative haze, I stare at what I have written. At my future. It's good enough. I know it is. It's what they want.

I press send.

I go back up to bed, to my sleeping husband, and lie next to him. I stare at the ceiling and do something I haven't done for a long time. I pray.

Please let this work. Please let this end.

43

Leo

Mouth dry.
    Body wet.
    I was dreaming I was in the sea. Drenched.
    I'm still under the fucking boiler. Head spinning like someone stuck a drill into my actual ear hole and left it on – churning my brain into pulp. I fumble around the floor for the tablets, feel the foil sleeve and take another two. They won't go down. I crunch, the bitterness exploding across my tongue. I look out of the slatted wooden doors in front of me. What time is it? Not a fucking clue. It's still dark. Isn't it?
    Did Ronan come in and take dick pics? Did that happen? I dunno what's real. If he did, they weren't for her. I know that much. I push at the cupboard door so it opens with a click, cool air hitting me. I stand up quietly and see Mallory's mum's electric toothbrush on the sink. She must have come in at some point. I need to get out. Back to the shed. I'll detox in it.
    I have the lorazepam.
    It's still dark.
    I go into the corridor, trying to move like a shadow, fast and quiet, down the stairs and into the hallway. The kitchen is to the left. I step down onto the wooden floor.
    This kitchen.
    Fucking mental how nice it is. I can kind of see her in it. All together. Perfectly placed, but a little bonkers. There's a warmth to it. I close my eyes and let it move into me. It's nice. I feel something. Excitement. Hope. It's weird.

I need to get out the back door, get myself together in the shed. Where's the key? I tiptoe round the kitchen island. There's a laptop on it.

It's open. Plugged in. It's on. The screen is unlocked.

I shouldn't look.

But I do.

An email thread is open. To a man named Stan.

Slay: A Novel.

I open it, and I begin to read a story. A story of a boy named Liam, and a woman named Mandy.

44

Mallory

'Shit.'

I pick up the piece of bacon that has landed right on top of my bare foot, noticing – but not immediately feeling – the red blotch left on my skin by the scalding oil. '*Shit.*'

'Careful, Mallory.'

'Sorry.'

Mum is watching me from a stool at the island, wearing her Jimmy Choo sheepskin slippers and a disapproving glare. Ronan gave her the slippers for her birthday three years ago. She was ecstatic when she opened the box – I've never seen so much joy related to discounted soft shoes. They still appear brand new: the wool remains completely white. How does she do it? She hasn't even mentioned last night. I assume she won't. We don't do that. We sweep these things under the carpet. We pretend. 'You don't need to apologise, Mallory, just be careful.'

I try to zone in on the radio to drown her out. The news. It's 08:30. Ronan is late for work. He hasn't come downstairs yet. I've decided to make him a bacon sandwich to take with him because he will be hungry and, more importantly, I need everything to be fine. Normal.

'You're shaking, Mallory. Did you sleep at all?'

'I did.' I didn't. Hardly. I pick up the fallen rasher and place it into the bin, slamming the lid shut, too hard. A giveaway of my anxiety. I say, '*Oopsy*,' as indifferently as possible, in a bid to offset any evidence that I am internally obsessing over last night's email.

Wait. Where's the laptop? Did I leave it upstairs, in the bathroom?

I swear I brought it down with me—

A voice on the radio.

'The body of a man has been found in Regent's Canal, in Camden, in the early hours of this morning.'

My fingers clench.

'The police have yet to identify the body. Wearing joggers and a hoodie, drugs found in his system...'

Oh my God.

'Mallory? Are you listening to me?'

The speed at which my mind moves leaves a metallic taste in my mouth. It can't be him. *He can't be dead.* There is no way. Can he? *High. Drunk. A young male. Hoodie. Joggers.*

I automatically flick the radio over. Classic FM. A dark and moody film score fills the kitchen, instantaneously making me visualise his body, face down in the canal, gently floating.

Like Virginia Woolf did.

I should go to prison. That would be the best place for me.

I should have helped him!

What have I done?

'Mallory, what are you doing?'

'Hmm?' I look down to see that at some point since binning the bacon, I have piled up the rest of it from the frying pan on top of a piece of bread, balancing the rashers together like I am creating an art installation. It is made up of six pieces arranged in the shape of a tent. 'Oh! Look at that!' I exclaim, as if I am both surprised and very proud of my ability to stack meat in this way. My mother doesn't seem convinced. 'Ronan loves bacon,' is all I can think to add. Again I feel like I am under water. My brain appears to have no ability to actually register what is in front of me, to connect me to reality. That this bacon teepee is my reality. All I can think about is Leo.

I try to add ketchup to the meat mound, but the bottle is nearly empty, so it suddenly sprays out a constellation of red splotches, like I am endeavouring to add some kind of Jackson Pollock-inspired flare to my creation.

'Does Ronan usually leave this late?'

'No.'

'Hmm. Maybe you kept him up.'

I'm sweating. Mum puts her fork into the scrambled eggs on the plate in front of her, picks up the smallest amount on the end of her prongs and nibbles like a tiny bird. I want to scream. I smile instead. It hurts to do it. 'Do you not want the toast, Mum?'

'You know I don't eat bread.'

I take a slice from the loaf on the counter and push it right on top of the bacon stack – collapsing it, squashing it with force into what I hope will be a more appropriate and edible state – and then wrap the whole thing in tin foil.

'Where is he?' I whisper to myself.

'Right here.' Ronan's voice, just behind me. I jolt with the shock of it and nearly scream. But I don't. I don't because, as I feel his arms loop round my waist, his lips on my neck, I immediately experience such an incredible sense of familiarity that instead, I want to burst into tears.

'Hi, darling,' I say.

'What is this?' He laughs, pointing at the tin foil sandwich – the size of a brick. The way his arms stay wrapped around my body sends a thrill into me, energising something deep in my bones. A sense of actuality. Of safety. Of protection. 'Is this for me?'

'I thought you might be hungry,' I say.

'Clearly,' he says, taking the sandwich. When he lifts it, he makes a groaning noise like it is weighing his arm down. I hear my mother laugh. I laugh. We all laugh. With the laughter, the tension in my body breaks, my nervous system settles. My anxiety around the news report dissipates. *Of course it wasn't Leo. There's no way it was him.*

'You look amazing this morning,' Ronan whispers in my ear.

I feel myself smiling. 'Thank you.'

'You're going to have a great day.'

'So are you.' I turn on the spot so I am facing him, greeted by his green eyes. His hair is pushed to the side, wire-rimmed glasses balancing on his nose. He is so professional. So effortless. So sexy. It is a difficult balance to achieve. And yet he does it. So brilliantly.

I can feel Mum staring. He must too, because he makes the smallest wink at me. A wink *for me*. It makes my stomach flutter – *our own in-joke, excluding everyone else, our own coded language*. He turns to her and says, 'Stace, do you need anything today?'

She keeps nibbling her eggs, not looking up. 'No – I'm fine, thank you, Ronan.'

'What's your plan?' he says, packing his tin foil brick into his bag.

'I have a few bits to do for work, and then Mal is going to show me some of her new book – aren't you, Mal?'

I nod. 'Yes.'

'We're going to talk about her getting back to her clients' – I wasn't aware of this part of the day, perhaps she has discussed this with Ronan… – 'and I thought we could make a quiche Lorraine for dinner. You like quiche?'

'I do,' he says brightly. 'It's a favourite.' He looks at his watch. 'Right. I am going to be horrendously late.' When he turns back to me, I notice a flicker of concern in his eyes. *What is it? What does he know?* 'Mal,' he says cautiously. *Oh, God.* 'Do you mind helping me choose a coat for today?'

'A coat?'

'Yes – I have an important meeting.' Oh. 'I need your fashion advice. I want to give off a certain *vibe*.'

I try to keep the relief out of my voice. 'Of course – you'd look great in anything.'

'What kind of vibe?' Mum asks.

'I think…' He pauses, placing a hand on his hip, in mock contemplation. 'Sensible and relaxed, but with a hint of the *unexpected*.' He makes a self-knowing, modest laugh, swiping his hand through the air – like he could never achieve such a thing.

'Oh, God, I don't know what I'm doing. This is why I need my beautiful wife.'

'Well. I think you're certainly giving off that vibe,' Mum says, still nibbling.

'That's very kind of you to say, Stace.' He nods, and picks up his bag. 'Right. See you later.'

'Hope it goes well today,' I say.

He is about to turn into the hallway, when he stops. 'Are the porch windows open?'

'What?' I turn and look. They are, just an inch. Did I leave them open last night? I can't remember. I must have.

'Look,' he's pointing to the floor in front of them. The keys. The keys are on the floor.

That's... Wait. *Did I do that?*

I can feel him glaring into the back of my head. 'Oh,' I say breezily. 'I just opened them this morning to let some air in. All the smoke from the bacon.'

I quickly pick up the keys and put them back into the fruit bowl. Was I a bit drunk last night?

'Mal, are you ready?'

'Huh?'

'Coat.'

'Yes!' I nod, wiping my hands on a tea towel, then follow him into the hallway. I pull the kitchen door behind me until it clicks shut. I expect him to stop halfway down the corridor and open the coat cupboard, but he walks straight past it.

'Ronan?' I say, but he keeps walking, only stopping at the very end by the front door. Now is as good a time as any. He's in a good mood. 'I was thinking, darling – it would be quite good if I could have my phone back – if I'm going to be looking at work stuff today.' He keeps his head down, eyes to the tiles. No answer. Odd. 'Ronan?'

I open the cupboard and take out the most relaxed but unexpected coat I can find: a camel bomber, from Cos. He will look cool. My husband is very cool. 'This one is cool—'

'I need to talk to you.'

His tone. A shift. Small but seismic. My nervous system instantly ignites.

'OK?' I say, approaching him with the coat. But he doesn't take it.

Instead, he holds out his hand. 'What's this?'

I look down.

Oh, God.

No.

A sheet of tablets.

My birth control pills.

Shit. 'Ronan…' I look up at him. His expression is blank. As I stare at him, trying to find my words, he remains completely still, until the muscle beneath his left eye flickers.

'How long have you been taking them?' His voice is low. Quiet. But determined.

'Ronan, wait…' *He must've been in my wash-bag. It was under the bed.*

'How long have you been taking them, Mal?' Louder. Forceful.

I turn to check back down the corridor – that the kitchen door is still closed. I lower my voice. 'Maybe we should talk about this late—'

'You're lying.'

He won't look at me. 'Ronan. I was going to talk to you about it – I just needed to find the right time. I take them to help regulate my mood, because—'

'I cannot believe you would do this to me.' He is shaking. 'If you lie to me, how can I know how to keep you safe?' He suddenly looks so small. Like a child. His voice trembles. 'I love you so much, Mal. I don't know what I'd do without you. I need you. I need you here with me. And I'm so scared…' His eyes fill with tears. 'I'm so scared of losing you. You're scaring me.'

'Ronan, I'm so sorry…'

'Do you understand how much you mean to me? Do you?' I can hear the desperation. The pain.

'Yes. Yes, I do. It's only been a recent thing – I promise. After everything that happened… I wanted to do all I could to keep my mood as steady as—'

'Don't give me that bullshit. Your mood is fine. You're playing games.'

'Games?'

'You have no capacity to understand how your actions affect other people. Everything is about you.' He keeps his eyes down, his voice flat. Emotionless. Factual. 'You're selfish. Playing with people's feelings. Your self-obsession makes me sick. You're a narcissist, Mallory – in sheep's clothing.'

'Ronan—'

He leans towards me, putting his lips right next to my ear, body pressed into mine. 'It's good that you reserve the real Mallory only for me. No one else would accept it. You're lucky I haven't thrown you out. No one else would put up with this level of manipulation. It's frankly disgusting.'

'Is everything all right?' Mum's voice at the end of the hallway.

Before I can turn to look, Ronan's body instantly softens. He pulls me into him, kisses my ear, closing his hand around the tablets and pushing them into his pocket. 'I love you,' he whispers – just loud enough – then kisses my cheek, smiles and turns to Mum. 'Everything is great! Now I *must* go!' He takes the camel bomber from my hand, slings it over his shoulder, makes a pose like a model and says, for Mum, 'Sensible, relaxed and unexpected. Nailed it.' He turns and leaves. As the door shuts behind him, Mum stays where she is, arms folded.

'Everything OK?' she repeats.

'Yes,' I say, blowing the hair out of my face that has fallen from my bun. 'All good. Right, I must get my laptop and make a start.' How long was she stood there?

I move quickly past her, up both flights of stairs and into the attic. In the bedroom I stop for a moment, allowing my breath, the unease in my chest, to settle. To regulate. *The birth control pills*. How could I be so *stupid*?

I need my phone.

Where would Ronan put it?

My body moves me before I can think, round the bed towards the inbuilt wardrobe in the opposite wall. I pull open the doors on the left, his side, and stare at the perfectly hanging clothes. He will know if anything has been moved. I have to be careful. I gently run my hands across the pockets of the jackets and trousers.

But nothing. I kneel down on the floor, to where his collection of shoes are, stacked below the clothes, still in their boxes, all perfectly lined up. Methodically I begin to open each one, take each shoe out and check inside. When satisfied that they are empty, I place the lids back and make sure the boxes are aligned exactly as I found them. *Nothing.* Where would he put it?

At the back of the wardrobe I see a single sock, wedged between two boxes. I pull it out to see something the shape of an iPhone inside. I am stock-still for a moment, wondering if there is some kind of security seal he will notice has been broken, but there isn't. It is just a sock.

I carefully lift out my phone.

I push the side button, praying that it has battery. The white apple appears on the black glass.

I look back behind me, as if Ronan might suddenly reappear. I can feel my heart against my ribcage. *Stop it. He's gone. He's at work.*

I glance down to see the phone asking for my passcode.

I type it in.

Error.

He's changed it.

Shit.

I pause, my fingers hovering over the screen.

It won't be my birthday. Or his. Maybe our wedding date? No.

I type in the date he got his promotion. The phone opens.

Of course.

Immediately I see four missed calls from the same 020 number flash up. I don't know it. Could that have been Stanley – trying to get in touch? I navigate straight to WhatsApp to see three unread messages. None of them are from Leo. I scroll down, searching for my message stream with him, only to see it is not there. It has been deleted. I open up my contacts and type in his name. Nothing. He's gone.

He's gone from my phone.

No way of contacting him.

Of checking—

A sickening feeling erupts in my stomach, making a film of sweat break out across my skin. I try to swallow the rising panic. Is he alive?

I quickly go back to my unread messages to see the top one is from Joanie. I open it and read back over a conversation that appears to have taken place yesterday. A conversation I had no part in, but apparently there I am, chatting in the message stream.

> Hey Mal xxx
> Just checking everything is OK
> Not heard from you in a while
> Was good to see you the other week
> That boy was crazy I hope the police got him
> That poor old lady
> We are having a dinner on Friday – everyone is coming
> Please join!
> Xx

Hey gorge
I'm actually not free this weekend
Been feeling a bit low lately
I'm OK though – Ronan is looking after me. I'm sure I'll be back to myself soon xxxx

> Oh sweetie I'm so sorry to hear that
> Glad he's helping – let me know if you need anything?
> You got this. You're incredibly strong
> I LOVE YOU!

Thanks
I'm doing better. Actually writing a new book!
Ronan thinks it's great and useful to keep me stable so I'm going to keep going with it
He's been great

> Omg Mal that's amazing!!!
> I'm so glad you're writing again!!

> You are SUCH A GOOD WRITER!!! AHH!
> Fancy a coffee soon to discuss (gossip)?

I'm in a proper flow with writing at the moment – shall I message you when I have some free time?
Don't worry about me – if I go quiet it's just because I'm in the zone
And thanks – I think it's a lot to do with Ronan's encouragement – but I'm excited
It's a romance! <3 <3 <3

> Oooh a romance
> Sounds amazing. Can't wait to hear all about it
> I'll tell the others you said hi on Friday
> Xxxx ☺
> You sure I can't pop round?
> Just to say hi?

No no – I'm doing fine
Speak soon xx

I stare at the messages I didn't write. He's been replying as me. My fingers begin to move.

Joanie – this is Mal
I didn't write those messages – it was

But I stop, because I realise the first thing she will do is message him and ask. I remember the night of the party. Seeing her message on Ronan's phone. *Hope Meek Mal gave you some fun in the end.* She goes to him now. He is where she finds her truth. Not me.

And Ronan will check this phone, too.

I need to keep things the way they are. Just for now.

I delete the words that I have typed to Joanie and quickly scan through the other unread messages. One is from Mum about train times, sent three days ago, and the other from a client saying they hope I get better soon. I glance above the client's message to see that Ronan has messaged them too, saying that I won't be available for a couple of weeks because I am recovering from a *short illness*, like something from a Jane Austen novel. Like I have consumption.

I turn the phone off, put it back in the sock and place it meticulously where I found it – making sure the material of the heel is poking out the exact same amount as before. I check the shoe boxes are precisely as they were, and when I am certain, I close the cupboard.

A memory surfaces. This time, it's not about my mother, but about Nick. I am stood at a bar with him, visiting him at university in Leeds. The floor is sticky and the whole place smells like Red Bull. We are ordering drinks and a boy sidles up next to him. They glance at each other. It is only a brief moment, but I notice the look between them. The smiles they exchange. Coy, understanding, flirtatious. I realise there is something in this second that I can't understand. An understanding born from a history, a history I do not know, a history of the forbidden, that appears to make the exchange all the more exciting. They both know, in their bones, that the look between them is theirs only.

I feel the heat of tears down my cheeks at the realisation that I will never meet that person. I will never know him. The life he could have led. The person he could have been. The smile he shared with that boy at the bar… He never introduced me to that person. Because for some reason… For some reason he felt that he could not be that person.

I don't blame my mother.

I don't. But she was so desperate for her children to appear a certain way. Living vicariously through us. He might have felt the weight of that pressure.

My father. Could it have been his fault? But he was absent. He barely knew Nick – and Nick never seemed to care. Can someone's lack of presence cause that amount of pain? Nick never mentioned him. It seems so unlikely that it would be the thing to send him over the edge. Perhaps something happened? Something he was ashamed of? Something he felt he couldn't speak about. A date gone wrong. A sex party. Like the T-Party.

I wonder if Nick was on Grindr. And if he was, what his profile name would have been. *Polite, quiet, shy*? Did he have fun? Or did he meet someone, someone like Mo?

And *was* it a mistake, what he did?

Was he not in his right mind?

Does it matter?

I would have been there for him. I would have. I hope he knew that. But perhaps I was too busy thinking about myself, my own problems, to ever notice him fully.

I think perhaps I was.

I do. I am angry at the spots of tears falling onto the tiles – I feel pathetic.

Ronan called me a narcissist.

Maybe this is true.

I will never know Nick's story. I will never know what happened. All that can be done now is to try to fill in the gaps. It doesn't seem fair. It doesn't seem OK that he is not here to tell it to us.

I quickly make my way to the en suite, to get the laptop. To see if Stan has replied.

Wait.

It's not here.

If it's not here, it should be in the kitchen. And it wasn't in the kitchen.

I feel like I'm losing my mind.

Ronan. He must have taken it. The one person who cannot see what is on it.

45

Leo

HEAVEN – A BALLAD

Kissed a boy once.
Kissed many boys.
But this one
This one
Was out of this world.
I'm not going to heaven,
Buggery and all that.
But this guy
This guy was kind.
Dunno why, but I could taste it.
The kindness.
His kindness was the heaven.
Because it made me feel
Like I wanted to stay here,
On earth.

@Alias22

46

Mallory

I can't find it.

It's not here. I've searched the house all day, while avoiding my mother and intermittently pretending I've been writing in my room, on a laptop that no longer seems to exist. If he finds it, I'm done.

And Leo... That news report...

What have I done?

'Mal?' Mum, from downstairs.

'Yes?'

'There's someone at the door!'

Oh, shit. *Shit.*

I need to stop my hands from shaking. I've been wanting a lorazepam, but I seem to have taken them all. Which is odd, because I just got a new prescription. Unless Ronan hid them. With the laptop. Is he trying to make me feel crazy? He's done this before. Get me looking like a lunatic in front of my mother.

'*Mal!*'

'Coming!'

I hesitate. Arrange my face. Present a smile. Pull open the door.

'Mal!' Joanie says. She stays back a bit, on the porch.

'Hey! Joanie! How are you – what are you doing here? It's so nice to see you!'

'I thought I'd make an impromptu drop-in!' she says. 'I wanted to bring you this.' She holds out her hand. In it, I see a glass jar.

'Oh! Jam!'

'Yes – it's damson. I thought you might like it. Lovely on toast. Might inspire you to get up in the mornings. Oh...' She pulls a face. A grimace of regret. 'Sorry – I didn't mean—'

'No – you're right! Great motivation. It's great. Thank you so much.' I take it from her and inspect the label. 'Lovely,' I say. 'Looks delicious.'

We stand in silence for a moment. It's almost uncomfortable, but it has been this way for so long now that we are both fully trained in negotiating it. We smile simultaneously. I lean on the door frame, folding my arms. She pushes her hands into the pockets of her jeans.

'You look great,' she says.

'Thanks,' I offer. We do this. We say what we think the other person wants to hear. We act like we are the kind of women who grow rose bushes in their back gardens and own Ottolenghi cookbooks. OK, we are those women. But at fourteen we would ride our bikes together from Crouch End to Tottenham, swigging alcopops – screaming bloody murder at each other, swerving in and out of the cars – thinking we were the most rebellious and carefree girls in the whole of London.

Now look.

An impulse inside me wants to tell her about the texts.

To tell her everything.

We will both be dead in fifty years, I want to say. *Why are we doing this? We both hate it.*

It is so easy to lie.

'How's the writing going?' she says. 'It's so good to hear you're doing it again.'

'Thanks, yeah. I'm enjoying it.' I pause. 'It's a *romance*.' I pull a face: *I know, how wild*.

'Yeah, you said.' No – I didn't say. Ronan said. Those messages were from my husband. 'I was interested to hear that – I thought you always hated romance. You always seemed more driven to write things that are *gritty*.' She says the final word with an element of excitement – a thrill. Then I notice a sadness that moves over her features.

'Yes, well. I think that's in the past now,' I tell her earnestly. It always interests me that we often talk like we are being watched by other people, even when we are alone together. How mannered we are. 'I want to tap into a new genre. It's good for me. It's more uplifting. More hopeful.'

'That's good,' she says. 'That's nice.'

'They say, write what you know.'

'They do.' She raises her eyebrows. 'Are you sure everything's OK?'

'What makes you say that?'

'Well, I know you've been struggling – and I'm sorry. You just seem...'

'What?'

'Quite resolved, really. Level.'

Should I be acting differently? I presume so. 'Oh, right. Yes. I feel that way.'

'That's really good.'

The performance remains. Joanie. My friend who I do not know. She narrows her eyes.

Is she willing to break it? The pretence?

Am I? 'Well. Actually. There is something.'

'Yes?' Her eyes widen. *Hope?* Does she hate this as much as I do? Is she dying for the truth as much as everyone else, behind their shuttered glass windows and Chardonnay-blurred eyes? Or can she not face it? She looks conflicted. Unsure. Unsafe.

'You know the messages we exchanged?'

'Um... Yeah?'

I lower my voice. 'I didn't actually send them.'

She cocks her head, shocked. Shocked because she believes me, or shocked because I sound insane? 'What do you mean, Mal?'

'Yes, what *do* you mean?' A figure emerges behind her, walking down the pathway towards us. Ronan. *Shit.* Swinging a bunch of flowers. '*Jojo!*' He kisses her on the cheek.

'Ronan!' she says. 'God, you smell good – what is that?'

'Hard work and probably a dose of exhaustion.' He flashes me a look. A warning. One that she doesn't see. 'What are you doing here, Jojo?'

She stands differently now. Shifting on her feet. Trying to appear relaxed. Effortless. Breezy. 'I just wanted to bring Mal some jam. I would have bought Jäger but – maybe not the time.' She laughs.

He laughs.

I laugh.

Ha ha ha.

'There's always time for Jäger,' Ronan says, and then he hands me the flowers. 'Here, these are for you.'

'Oh!' I say, taking them from him. 'They're beautiful.' They are. Then, for some reason that I cannot control, I ask, 'Why?' It just slips out of my mouth.

'*Why?*' he repeats, then makes a snort, as if this is the most ridiculous question he has ever been asked. 'Because I love you and you are wonderful.'

Joanie looks enviously at them, or at me. I can't fully decipher which.

'Oh! Well, thanks, darling.'

I look down to see his hand on my arm. Gentle. But there. 'I can smell dinner,' he says. 'I'm famished.'

I stop, considering, then look at Joanie and ask her, 'Do you want to come in for food?'

Ronan's fingers tighten their grip, ever so slightly. I watch Joanie's lips part, then she stalls, not knowing the answer. She looks to Ronan, like he might have the correct one. I sense him give the subtlest shake of his head. One he does not think I can see. One imbued with melancholy. One that says, *She's still not ready.*

She's still unwell.

Joanie's eyes widen with understanding. She nods conspiratorially and turns to me. 'I'd love to, Mal, but I've got to get back to the kids. I'll come over next week. If you're not too busy with the writing.'

It's clever, how he does this.

How he's done this over years and years.

Taken her.

'That'd be great,' I reply.

'Night, Jojo,' Ronan says. 'Thanks for popping by.'

He's in a hurry, but Joanie won't notice – his smile is too bright for her to see past it to his hand pulling my arm. Just before I turn with him into the doorway, she says, 'Wait – Mal?'

'Yes?'

'Do you remember when we used to do that reading group?'

That's odd. A memory I had in fact forgotten, until now. 'I do.'

'Maybe we could restart it. Come over to mine one night? Read some trashy fantasy book and bitch about the characters?'

I feel a warmth inside me suddenly build. 'I—'

'I think she's a bit tired, aren't you, Mal,' Ronan cuts me off. 'What with the new medication.'

'Oh – right…' Joanie takes a step back, like she has just been moved into uncharted territory – territory she does not belong in. Territory that frightens her. 'Well – you get back to you, and then maybe we can plan something.'

'Well…' I say. 'I'm actually not that tired – I'd love to come over, Joanie.' Ronan's grip tightens. 'Let's make it happen.'

Then I do something I didn't expect.

He took my phone, I mouth at her.

She cocks her head. Momentarily confused. As if perhaps it didn't happen. Her eyes narrow. There is a brief moment where I see her. *Her*. The Joanie I have known for twenty years, peering out from behind the façade we have all created.

I do it again. *He took my phone.*

Her eyes narrow. 'Mal?'

I feel Ronan turn to me, his gaze lingering on my face.

'What?' I say, and shrug.

'You just…' She stops. 'What did you just say?'

'I didn't say anything.' I shrug again and make a confused laugh, like I am deeply perplexed. But Ronan is properly gripping my arm now, and it is starting to hurt. 'Is everything OK, Joanie? Maybe you need some of my meds!' I laugh again.

Ronan joins me this time: laughing. It's all very funny. But Joanie doesn't. She begins to, half a smile appearing on her lips, but then it is overtaken by complete bewilderment. Like I am insane. 'Sorry – I just thought you whispered something.'

Shit. 'No?' I say. 'I didn't.'

Ronan's finger nails dig in. 'Right – let's not leave your mother waiting, Mal. Night, Jojo.' I see his eyes try to communicate with a look. *Ignore Mal.*

She's unwell.

'Your mother's here?' Joanie says. 'Oh, God. Good luck.'

She narrows her eyes at me. *Why didn't you tell me?*

But before I can reply, Ronan has pulled me inside and closed the door behind us. He doesn't stop, yanking me down the corridor towards the kitchen with him, not saying a word. Before we enter it, he abruptly stops. He turns me to face him.

'Ow – Ronan—'

'What did you say to her?' he hisses.

'What? Nothing.'

'You said something.' He puts his face in mine. 'Was it about me?'

'I don't know what you're talking about...'

'You're lying.'

'I'm not.'

'I can't trust you. Do you want me to speak to the doctor again? Is that best? You're acting oddly.'

'I'm not, Ronan.'

He flinches, as if holding something in – the muscles in his neck tightening. 'You can't be kept safe if you keep lying.'

He snatches the flowers from my hand, not looking at me, opens the kitchen door, walks straight towards my mother and hands them to her. 'Stace! Oh my God that quiche looks incredible.'

She takes them, eyes wide with glee. 'Are these for me?'

'Of course.'

'Oh, they're *stunning*. Thank you, Ronan.'

I enter behind as Ronan opens a drawer in the island and takes out a bottle of whiskey. He moves effortlessly, pouring himself a glass. 'Are you having wine, Stace?'

'I...' She falters. And something odd happens. She glances at him, then rubs her hand on her chin and says, 'No. I'm just going to have water tonight, thank you.' Her eyes flick towards me, for the smallest of moments. There is something in them – something that I cannot interpret.

Ronan pauses, looks at her, then pulls a face is if to say, *Kill-Joy*. 'Oh, don't be a bore!' I hear the faintest trace of annoyance in his tone. My mother wouldn't notice it, but it is there. He is angry. He takes a wine glass from the rack and opens the fridge. 'Just one, I insist.'

'I...'

He takes it to her. 'I want you to relax. We all need to relax a bit, and this is very good wine that I don't want to go to waste.'

She takes it. 'Fine, just one.'

He winks.

'Do you want to help me serve, Mal?' she asks.

'Yep, sure,' I say.

She nods.

Ronan kicks off his shoes, and as I serve the vegetables onto the three plates my mother has lined up, I hear the glug of the whiskey entering his glass. He's pouring a large one tonight.

'How did you get on with your word count, Mal?' he says.

I place carrots and broccoli next to each other, taking my time to neatly line them up. 'I did OK,' I say.

From behind me, I hear his glass hit the table. A little harder than usual. With a little more vigour. 'Did you read it, Stace? How was it?'

Mum cuts her knife through the quiche. 'No, I didn't. Not yet.'

'I think you'd really like it,' he says. There is, again, something in his tone that I can read, that she won't. He is mocking me. 'You're the perfect readership for it, you should give Mal notes.' He is mocking both of us. 'You'd like that, wouldn't you, Mal?'

'I don't mind,' I say. 'Shall I do the mash, Mum?'

'Mash?' Ronan queries. 'Pub-grub style.' The glug of the whiskey again.

'Do you not like mash, Ronan?' my mother says. 'I can do you without.'

'No, I *love* it.' Sarcasm. He is so good at it. So convincingly real.

'Oh, great,' my mother says.

I watch her neatly place a piece of quiche on each plate, and then an extra one on the third. She takes the heavier portion and hands it to him. 'Oh, cutlery,' she remembers.

He nods.

While we eat, Ronan makes jokes. I watch my mother watching him, as he spins his web. It is so enticing. So intoxicating. The way he holds her eye contact. The way he compliments her. The way he makes her feel like she is the only person in the room. He has an instinct for her vulnerabilities. He is able to use them to bolster her. He tells her she looks young. That she deserves someone wonderful, but that she should be picky. 'You only deserve the best. I cannot believe the wonderful life you have carved for yourself.' He keeps topping up her wine. She keeps drinking it. He compliments me, too, but through her. He says all my good traits have come from her. My tenacity. My strength.

It is such a skill.

As I eat my broccoli, chewing absently, I imagine myself clawing at his face, pulling it off his skull, holding it up to Mum and saying, *Look – this is him*, while his blood cascades over my hand and he groans on the floor in agony.

My thoughts go to Leo.

'Why don't you read us what you've written today?' Ronan requests. I suddenly realise he is talking to me.

Shit. 'What – now?' I say. 'No one wants to hear that now.'

'I'd love to hear it.' He smiles at me.

'My laptop's upstairs,' I say, tentatively. I can't tell if he's playing games. Does he want to derail me.

'No, it's not. It's here,' Mum tells me, and I turn to see her holding it up.

'Wait – where did you get that?'

'It was just here.' She pats the stool next to her. 'Are you OK?'

'Yes, yes. Of course.'

She passes it to me.

When I put my finger on the mouse pad, the screen lights up. Shit. Why didn't I close *Slay*? And the email chain…!

I quickly, and as calmly as possible, pull up *The Air Between Us* to cover them up. Was the laptop here the whole time?

It might have been.

Or did Mum take it?

I glance at her from under my eyelids.

'Come on, Mal!' Ronan huffs.

Mum looks none the wiser. Well, that's good.

'Are you sure you want to do this?' I ask. 'It's getting late, and it might be a bit... I don't know, boring?'

'No. It's the opposite of *boring*,' Ronan says. 'It's going to be very fun. I love your writing.'

'OK,' I reply.

'Maybe go back a bit,' he says. 'There was something you wrote the other day that I really loved. Show your mum how good you are.'

'Which bit?'

'The bit where they meet.'

'At the party?'

'Yes – that's it. It's really brilliant.' He looks up to see my mother is clearing the plates, taking them to the sink, her back turned, then takes another large gulp of his whiskey. While he pours another one, I scan back through the story until I am at the beginning of the chapter he is referring to.

'Are you sure?'

'We're sure.'

I look at Mum. She doesn't answer.

'*The morning of the party, Jessica had no idea she would be going.*' I clear my throat. My voice sounds hoarse and quiet.

This is horrendous.

'Skip on a bit,' Ronan says. 'Nearer to where they meet.'

I scan down through the document.

'*She was done. There was nothing more here for her, and she knew it – so she headed to the bar.*'

'Yes, this bit,' he says. 'This bit is really good.' He looks at Mum. 'Are you listening, Stace?'

'Yes! I'm all ears.'

He nods at me. *Continue.*

'*There was nothing more here for her, and she knew it – so she headed to the bar. After what felt like hours of trying to convince* the older generation at the production company that she had something important to say, she felt exhausted. A little part of her died inside as she ordered her third glass of cheap white wine.'

I stop, because I can feel Mum looking at me.

She knows it's bad.

She knows it's awful.

'Ronan, maybe we should leave it,' I say, feeling my cheeks begin to go hot. 'It doesn't sound right when I read it out loud – I'll probably need another pass on it—'

'Keep going,' he instructs. 'I'm really enjoying it.' He smiles, encouragingly.

I can't look at her. I can't look at Mum.

I stare at the screen and carry on.

'Jessica had – earlier in the evening, while deciding what to wear – put on her "confident" dress.' I stop again. 'Ronan…'

'It's great!' He is smiling. 'It reminds me of *One Day*. Or *Normal People*.'

I swallow hard.

'The green one she couldn't fit into after university. She had been on a diet for a month in a bid to squeeze herself into it. She didn't want to become a cliché – the young temp having to put her breasts on display to be noticed – she wanted her talent to be noticed. But no one was listening to her. "Thank you," she said to the bartender as he passed her the lukewarm glass of wine. As she did, their fingers touched. "Oh, sorry," he said, smiling toothily. There was no electricity. No spark. He wasn't awful to look at: he had a few spots across his cheeks, but his eyes were kind. He seemed quite… Young was the only word she could use to describe him. "How much?" she said. Perhaps it was time to start flirting. "I'll get it." Jessica turned to see a man stood behind her. She had noticed him earlier, amongst the melee, making a crowd of people laugh. She had watched them, enthralled by his every word. But here, now – up close – he took her breath away. He was, in short, beautiful. There was something rugged about his features, but the way he held himself was almost ethereal. Otherworldly. His eyes were like two pools of light.'

I want to disappear. There is nowhere to go. The kitchen remains silent – so silent that I cannot bear it. I keep reading.

'The man's voice was warm and inviting. "What brings you here?" he asked. "I am here to lose all dignity, apparently," Jessica mumbled. She didn't think he had heard her, but he laughed. "God, it's bleak, isn't it?" he said, tapping his phone on the card reader that the bartender was holding out. There was a look of embarrassment and awe in the barkeep's eyes. Not jealousy. This poor boy was so much the opposite of his current punter he couldn't be jealous. "Yes," Jessica said. The man continued, "So what is it you are losing your dignity over... Sorry – what was your name?" "Jessica." "Jessica. That's lovely." "I always thought it was kind of basic." "It depends on who's wearing it, I guess," he said. He then looked down at the floor, sheepishly. There were equal amounts of confidence and modesty in this man, Jessica thought, that made her feel slightly off balance. A rare blend. The thing she noticed was that she did not feel anything but pure joy. She felt alive again. The pain was gone. Here he was. This man. Her anaesthetic.' I look up. Silence. 'That's it,' I say.

Ronan starts to clap slowly. 'Well done, Mal. It's genius.'

I want to throw the laptop at him. I feel my cheeks burning and my eyes stinging. I minimise the document on the desktop, to see my email thread with Stanley, and the attachment of *Slay*. I quickly push the laptop shut.

I can't look at Mum. I don't want to see her face.

'What do you think, Stace?' Ronan says, eyes wide. I can see the laughter in them.

'Very intriguing,' she replies quietly, her back to us, still wiping the dishes. 'Very good.'

I want to scream.

Ronan's eyes bore into me. 'You're getting back to yourself. It's so nice to see.'

'Thanks,' I mumble.

'I love you,' he whispers. 'I really do.' I look down at the top of the island, attempting to disappear inside it. 'Right. One of the shows I worked on premieres on Netflix tonight. Maybe we could put on the first couple of episodes? Would you like that, Stace?'

'Oh, that sounds *exciting*.' She's tipsy now. I can hear it in her voice. 'What is it?'

'It's a family drama. A dark thriller. We adapted it from a memoir – no one has really heard of it – but we bought the rights years ago. Added to it. It's about a man who is murdered, but it's more of a whodunnit – which member of his family killed him. It's got a cracking cast.'

'Oh, I *love* a family-drama thriller.'

'We all do. Shall we go through?'

I leave the laptop and go with them into the living room in a dreamlike state. Once again, I feel like I am underwater.

I sit on the couch next to him as Mum takes the armchair. My writing chair.

Ronan takes the controller and turns on the TV, bringing up the news channel that Mum was watching last night. Still on mute, with subtitles.

'Go on, then, Ronan,' Mum says, making herself comfortable. 'Give us your pitch.'

'Netflix wanted something gritty, brutal, but something real, truthful, so it's shot in a handheld form. It feels almost like a documentary.'

As he talks, I squint at the TV.

I can see the subtitles.

The newsreader talking.

Words flashing beneath her on the screen.

An update on the body found in Regent's Canal earlier today...

Oh my God.

The man has been identified as Monty Jackson – known to his friends and family as Mo.

It wasn't Leo.
Thank God.
Leo is alive –
Wait.
Mo?

The police are looking for a young man who was with him that night, and anyone who might have any information about his whereabouts.

It disappears. Turns into the Netflix symbol.
'Wait...'
'Are we all ready?' Ronan says, pointing the controller at the TV. He sounds so excited.

And as he presses play, and the opening scene begins – aerial shots of a crime scene with police tape – I feel myself slip. Again.

What did he do?
Where is he?

47

Leo

THE LIFE OF AN ORANGE – *A BALLAD*

When my skin
Rots
Away
From
Me
You'll see the pieces underneath and think –
They were sweet once.
How did they go black?
Who let that happen?
And then stick your finger in me
Because you can't help yourself.
You wanna know what it feels like.

@Alias22

48

Mallory

'So?' Ronan says, turning to us, eyes wide. 'What did you think?'

We have sat through the first two episodes – a whole hour each. My brain hurts.

Netflix would have loved *Slay*.

'Very tense,' Mum says, now next to him on the couch. 'Very real. The stabbing scene was horrendous.'

'Thanks, Stace.' He looks at me. 'Mal?'

I have attempted to spend the last two hours keeping my face and body as still as possible. How many people are called *Mo*? That could live around that area? Surely more than one. Mo is a common enough name. It really is. But Monty. *Monty.* 'Yes, I thought it was brilliant,' I say, trying to instil excitement into my voice. 'Scary how real it was.' He nods, a little stoically, contemplatively, as if he is thinking. *I hate it when he thinks.* I can't tell what he's thinking *about*. Is he thinking about the show, or whether my limited review has anything of worth to be considered. I decide to dig deeper, to keep him from probing. 'I love the way they paint the characters. The way the show drip feeds their back stories – it's really great. Keeps the audience guessing. I could learn from that.'

His face relaxes. I've done enough to appease him. 'Yes,' he says. 'See, in the book – the characters were a little too naive to justify their actions. We felt we needed deeper back stories. That's the problem with so many books these days. Not enough from the characters' pasts. We need to see their trauma. What motivates them. What drives them.'

'Can't wait to see what happens next,' Mum says.

'Me neither,' I agree. 'You should be really proud.'

'There will be a meeting tomorrow about viewing figures. So I'd better look spritely. I'm going to head to bed,' Ronan says. He stands from the couch, stretching. Swaying slightly. He's drunk now. He isn't slurring yet, but I can tell because his eyes are glazing over. He begins to cross the room towards the door when Mum says, 'Would you ever make Mal's book into a show, since you love it so much?'

He stops.

There is something in the way she says this that makes a pang of something bittersweet erupt in my stomach. There is an edge to it. An edge of defensiveness that feels bold. Daring. I haven't heard from this side of Mum in a long time. As Ronan turns to her, I see in his eyes a flash – a momentary flicker – of what is clearly *annoyance*. She sees. He hasn't been able to hide it. It immediately sucks the air out of the room. But Mum doesn't move. She just keeps looking back at him, her hands folded on her lap, a little like she has been in church for the past two hours.

Where did that come from?

He stares at her.

She stares back.

Something passes between them.

Then, he smiles. But it is a little strained – effortful – like he is resisting something. 'Stace,' he says quietly. 'Because Mal hasn't been sleeping great, I thought it might be good for you to be somewhere more comfortable?'

She blinks. 'Sorry?'

'I was thinking – perhaps a hotel? I'd pay of course.'

'Oh!' She sounds surprised. She glances at me. I smile, because I do not know what else to do. Perhaps it would be best. Perhaps it would be best for her to be somewhere else. 'Why?'

Ronan shrugs. 'I think it'll be best for Mal.'

'Is that best for you?' she says, looking at me.

'I don't mind, Mum. Let's talk about it tomorrow.'

Ronan is on edge. 'Don't be late,' he says to me, although he doesn't meet my eyes.

'I won't,' I reply. Then, 'I'll turn the kitchen off. Need to get my laptop.'

He nods and pulls the door shut behind him.

As my mother and I sit together in silence, we listen to the pad of his feet up the stairs – one flight, two flights – then the low thud of the attic bedroom door closing. We both stare at the television screen, paused on the credits of the TV show.

His name is there.

EXECUTIVE PRODUCER – RONAN MCSWEENY

'Strange,' I hear Mum say gently.

I turn to her. She is still in exactly the same position. 'What is?' I ask.

She looks up at me. 'Hmm? Oh, nothing.'

'Do you want some space?'

A beat. 'Do you think that's best?'

I feel like we are in some kind of meeting.

'I don't mind, Mum.'

'Is he...' She stops. 'Where's your phone?'

'My phone?'

'Yes.'

'It's upstairs. Why do you ask?'

She bites her lip, then shakes her head. 'No reason. Right, I'll see you in the morning.'

As she stands, I hear her knees crack. 'I liked that book you are writing, Mal. But you are better than that. I don't mean that in a harsh way – it just doesn't really feel like you.'

Jesus. Here we go. I nod. 'Right.'

'Yes,' she says quietly. She picks up her empty cup of tea.

'I'll wash it, Mum,' I say.

'Are you sure?'

'I'm sure. See you tomorrow.'

And she leaves.

I wait to hear that she has gone into her room, sitting and staring at the Pooky lamp in the corner. I pick up her cup, turn off the lights and head into the kitchen. The candles are still lit, so it smells pleasantly of oranges.

I do love this kitchen. I inhale slowly and take the cup to the sink. Instead of putting it in the dishwasher, I add it to the half-submerged pile.

I pause for a moment, staring at the soap suds on my fingers. Something is different.

Something in this room is different.

I turn to the island.

Where's my laptop? Again? I swear—

'Hey, Mandy.'

My body instantly freezes. At the far end of the room – stood in front of the Crittall-glass French doors – is the shadow of a man. He's got my laptop in one hand and the Sakuto knife in the other.

'Leo?'

He steps into the light. He looks awful. Like he has been awake for a year. 'Was gonna ask for your help, but then I found this' – he thrusts the laptop forward – 'last night.' He keeps moving until he sits at one of the stools by the island. 'I've been reading it. The whole thing. In the shed. I like your shed.' He places the laptop down on the counter, and I see next to it a half-empty bottle of vodka. Grey Goose. Ronan's. Leo points to the laptop screen with the knife. Turns it to face me. I see the email chain from Stan, open. 'It's good news. You got the deal. They love it. They love the new ending.'

'What?'

'One-hundred-thousand-pound advance.'

'Leo...'

'I thought you wanted to help me.' His eyes go black. 'Is this really how you think it will end for me?'

49

Leo

The vodka burns, right into my soul.

I forgot how much I love it. Her mouth hangs open. I can see her shaking from here. She puts her finger to her lips. *Shh. Please. Don't make any noise.* 'I'll ask again. Is this what you wanted for me?' She's not answering. Her hand goes over her mouth. She looks at the door. 'He's asleep,' I say. 'Don't worry. Loves the whiskey, that one, doesn't he? Oh, and your mum is fine.'

She stares. Eyes bulging. 'How did you get in here?' she whispers.

'I've been here for a while.'

'But—'

'*One-hundred thousand pounds.* Shitting hell. Mandy, Mandy, Mandy. Aren't you pleased?'

She doesn't answer. She's shaking. I think she's pleased. 'That's a lot of fucking money. For a fucking book. Jesus. You should be proud of yourself. Well done.'

'Listen… Leo. You can't be here.' She steps towards me.

I lift up the knife. 'Just – stay where you are.' My voice is steady. I'm not even shaking. Sometimes when I get mad as fuck, everything goes calm.

'Can we talk another time, Leo?'

'Who's Leo?'

'What?'

'Do you not mean *Liam*?' I dunno what I'm expecting this absolute nut job to do right now, but she looks like she's about to cry. She can't look at me.

'You don't understand.'

'You're fucking right I don't.'

'Please keep your voice down…'

'I was so wrong. I actually thought you wanted to help me. And I was ready. I was. I was gonna ask. But…' I hold up the vodka. *Cheers.* 'This is so much better. And we should fucking celebrate.'

'Leo—'

'Love the name. *Slay.* Love the irony. Funny, too. Some of the book is really funny. But also sad. A great balance. I mean, I know you've not totally done the ending yet – but the proposed ending is fucking horrendous.' She frowns. 'What? You look surprised. Oh, I see. Did you not think I could read?'

'Leo – I…'

'Cos there's this scene where Liam can't, so I assumed maybe you thought the same of me?'

She looks back to the door. She is fucking terrified. 'You're drunk.'

'Yeah, I am. That mad bit where he gets bullied at school cos he can't tell the time. Bless him. He's a very interesting character, isn't he? Fucking madhead, this guy. It's sad, isn't it? What happens to him?'

'I want to explain, Leo, but let's do it when you're sober.'

'I'm never sober.' I tap the screen with the knife again. 'You know that.'

'I don't think now is the right time.'

'I think now is a great time. You've just got a fuckton of money for this book and I for one am very proud of you. Pour yourself a drink.'

'Leo – no—'

'Pour yourself a fucking drink, Mandy. Some wine?' I get up and move to the fridge. She flinches. I pull open the door. There's the carcass of a fish on the bottom shelf. Fucking mental. It's eyes just staring at me. 'Do you drink white?' I say, trying to make my voice all posh. It makes me laugh a bit. I pick up one of the bottles from inside the fridge door. 'A little *Sauvignon Blanc*?' I pop the cork.

Fun.

I see the glasses hanging upside down from below a shelf that has a load of herbs on it. I take two. Put one down in front of her. She flinches again. I pour the wine into it, right up to the top – glug, glug. Love a posh wine glass, me.

'Here you go.' She takes it. 'Brilliant. A toast?' I take the vodka bottle and hold it up. 'To you, Mallory Mandy Maddox.' I glug. Glug till the thing is almost empty. It's so good. 'Now. I just want to know a few things – as a fan of your work. If that's OK? So – let's talk about Liam. Do you want to sit? You look like you're about to fall over.' She puts her hand on the sink. Then moves towards the counter thing where I'm sat back down. Think they call it an island. She definitely looks like she's drowning. 'You gonna sit?'

'No.'

'OK. Right, let's dig in. Christ, Mandy. His mother abusing him like that. How fucking horrible. No wonder he's such an addict. Makes sense, doesn't it? I mean – you should know, shouldn't you – what with you being sober for so long. Oh wait – look.' I point to her glass of wine. 'Oh well. I won't tell if you don't. Now – let me just find the bit that really got me...' I start scanning back through the document, up to near the beginning. There are all these comments in the side bar from Stan. Stan the man.

Oh this bit is brilliant – Mallory!
This gave me chills.
I love this!
It's darkly beautiful.
You have me in tears here.
Why are you putting me through this!!
I just need to know what happens!!!

What a fucking lightweight.

'Here it is...?' I squint at the screen. 'Yeah. When he gets battered by his mum. I mean he's only, what? Six? And then she dies. And he gets passed around all these people who seem to fucking hate him. And all that abuse – sends him a bit crazy. Really harrowing stuff. And then he starts to get mad, doesn't he. Like – he starts to realise what has happened to him and that it's not really his fault and he wants justice, I suppose. Trying to find the men that hurt him. Fuck me, this shit is dark. It's really dark, isn't it? I kind of get it, though. He just wants to take the pain away. He wants redemption.' She looks at me, baffled. 'What – did you not think I'd know words like that? I did good in English you know. At school. The thing that's weird – there's not that much plot in *Slay*. He just sort of goes around getting abused, doesn't he?'

'Leo, please—'

'Just sit, Mandy, just fucking *sit*.' She flinches. Perches on one of the stools opposite me. She looks like she's about to vom. 'That's it. Nice. Perfect.'

She whispers something. Sounds like, 'My husband.'

'He's not gonna hear us – he's out of it, Mandy. And I think your mum is just minding her own business. She's a bit doddery isn't she, bless her. She fucking loves *him*.'

'Have you been watching us?'

'Ha! That's funny. You're funny.'

'Please can you—'

'Right, there's another bit that I wanted to discuss.' I look up at her and smile. 'It's like a book club, this, isn't it? Very civilised.' She's shaking. 'Never been invited to a book club before. I feel very important.' I pull the laptop towards me. 'This is fun, isn't it?'

'Leo.'

'I saw your emails with Stan. Stan the man. Let's talk about that new *proposed ending*. Jesus Christ. Brutal. You know – I liked the other one too. The ending where Liam and Mandy make their little therapy centre. Very cute. But Gina – is it Gina? The lady from the publisher? Yeah. She was right. It's just not believable. I agree with her. Think killing Liam off was the best route. Now let's talk about his death, cos *fuck me*, Mandy… What an ending.' Now I'm shaking. 'Suicide is fucking bleak, isn't it. I mean, I almost cried reading that proposal. Just so fucking sad, isn't it? The description got me feeling sick in my stomach. I know it's just an outline, but Jesus. This poor lad had nothing, didn't he? He had absolutely nothing, got abused his whole life, then he fucking ended it and no one gave a shit.' I squint at the screen, taking a swig of my wine. Tastes fucking rank. 'Let's see what you wrote. *No one will remember him.* Yeah – that's mad that. Fucking sad. So fucking sad...'

Fuck.

Fuck me.

I'm really shaking now.

She wipes her nose on the back of her hand. Is she pretending to be sad? I can't tell. I never know anymore. I never know if people are actually sad or trying to do the right thing. She's just fucking staring at me.

'Can I ask you a question?' she says. She sounds so meek.

'Please.'

'How did Mo die?'

Oh. I see. 'Do you want it for your book? Mark doesn't die in *Slay*, does he? Which is odd, now I come to think of it.'

She's looking at the knife in my hand. 'I mean it. What happened to him, Leo? How did he end up in the canal?'

'Lots of people end up in that canal, Mallory. For lots of different reasons. Use your imagination. You seem to have a good one.'

'Was it you?'

'Ha. Course you'd think that. Nah. He slipped.'

'He slipped?'

'Yeah.'

'I was actually pretty sad myself that night. Was gonna get in the canal. End it. Then I thought, actually, nah. I like being high. I'll stay high. Forever. Easier that way. Just keep running. I'm good at it. So I called Mo. Went to his place. Then got him to come down to the bridge.'

'Did you see him slip? Did you see him fall in?'

'Yes.'

'Didn't you help him? Call the police?'

'No. Anyway let's get back to this wonderful work of fiction you've created.'

'Leo...'

'I always knew you were fucking nuts. But this is some next-level shit. I knew you were watching me. I wondered why you thought my life was so interesting. Lots of people do. Like my mum's mate, Jean. You're a bit like her. Thing is though, Mandy – you've got it all a bit wrong.'

'What do you mean?'

'See – I lie. A *lot*. I make a lot of shit up – to get what I want. So – maybe we could talk about some changes you could make to the book – so it's really real. I'll give you some truth. Firstly, my mum isn't dead. She's actually totally alive. She lives in Essex in a pretty normal house. She's absolutely sick of me – been trying to help me for a fucking age. She's always been dead nice. Tried to help me. Paid for treatment. My parents remortgaged their house once, to help me. Feel bad about that one. When I was little, she tried to protect me. I was bullied a little bit but nothing bad. Nothing bad ever really happened. She never fucking beat me up – no way. Neither did my dad. Yup, I have two whole parents. They're just sick of me. And I don't answer my phone to them – they never know where I am. I prefer it that way. I dunno why I'm like this, Mal, but I think it's something to do with this world. I just hate the world. I've always had a lot of emotions, Mandy. I have. I was called sensitive a lot as a kid, so I just tried to stop that. Is that dramatic enough, though? Do you think people would give a shit? Now, I'm no author, but I don't think they would. Not to the level of chaos that I've caused. Doesn't seem proportionate, does it? But honestly, think it all started when someone told me I was *wet*, cos I cried. But you've made it so much better. You've really run with it, haven't you?'

'I want to explain.'

'Please do.'

She shakes her head. Leaves her wine where it is. She hasn't touched it. 'When I started this – I was trying to find a way out.'

Can she hear herself? 'A way out of what?'

She looks at the door. Lowers her voice. 'This life.'

I actually laugh. She sounds so fucking *earnest*. Like a character herself. 'You want to get out of *this* life?' I point at her massive fucking kitchen.

'Yes.'

'So you thought you'd leech onto mine?'

'Yes.'

'And you enjoyed it? It give you the thrill you wanted?'

'It did. Yes.'

'You're insane.'

'I've been told that.'

'Are you just fucking bored? The mad thing is, to me – right – even my lies weren't enough for your book. For the thrill. You made it worse. Liam and his HIV. That bit was a curveball.'

'That wasn't my idea.'

'No?'

'No. It wasn't.'

'Do you even know anything about it?'

'What do you mean?'

'It felt a bit *under-researched*. Is that a term you writers use? Don't take this personally. It's just a note. From me. A fan.'

'Listen…'

'And the therapist. She's a well interesting character. I mean – I get it. Saviour complex. Trying to help the poor guy. But Mandy. She's *you*. You even put us meeting in the café. But Mandy felt so bad for him that guess what? She started to care about him. That's so sweet.'

'I do care.'

'Bullshit. Then this bit in the proposal.' I find what I am looking for. *'No one will remember him. Except Mandy – the therapist. He will have a lasting impact on her life.'*

'Leo…'

'I love a bit of guilt appeasing. I do it. It's great. We all do it – don't we?'

'Listen—'

'I know I've fucked my life up – but Jesus. Is this really what people see? I… Wait – are you crying?'

'I'm going to say no to the book deal. I don't want it.'

Why does she get to cry? I've not cried in years. I want to fucking cry. 'No, no, no. You don't get to take the moral high ground now.' She frowns. 'Yes, I know what the moral high ground is, Mandy. Is this how you see me? All the *shit*. Is that what makes me so interesting? I am a fucking person, you know. *I am a fucking person.*'

I think I'm shouting. I am.

She's proper crying. Her face isn't moving but tears are falling right down it.

Then I see him. Coming into the kitchen through the door. 'What's going on?'

He stares at me. At the knife in my hand.

I point the knife at him. 'All right, Ronan. Story time. You joining in?'

50

Mallory

A child
Frozen
In time.
I bring her with me
Everywhere.
She is not seeable.
Not knowable.
But she is here with me
Moving within my shadow.
And all she ever wanted
Was to be close to someone
Close enough to feel safe.

@Malmaddoxwriter

51

Leo

'Take a seat,' I tell him.

'Put that knife down.' He seems pretty fucking mad. Just in his boxers again. Jesus, this guy.

'No.'

'What's going on?'

'Mandy's gonna tell you.'

'Mandy? Who's Mandy?'

I look at her. 'Wait… Doesn't he know?'

He looks at her. 'Know what?'

'Oh, another curveball.'

'Know what, Mal?' he repeats.

He seems stressed. Let's calm him down a bit. 'Do you want some wine, Ronan? Or vodka. She's drinking wine and I'm drinking vodka. It's all chill. It's a book club. See?' I point to the screen. 'This is the book we're reading.'

'Why is he here, Mal? Did you let him in?'

Can she talk? She seems to have forgotten how to. I'll help. 'I've been here for a while, Ronan. You have good cupboard space in this house. You sure I can't get you some wine?'

'Get out of my house.'

'You gonna call the police again?' He doesn't have his phone. Unless he's hiding it in his kecks, but it doesn't seem that way. 'Just sit down and join our book group.' He doesn't. 'Sit down, Ronan. Sit the fuck down.' I tap the tabletop with the knife. 'We were discussing the topic of redemption.' Mandy looks at me funny. 'A good story – from what I remember at school – needs some redemption at the end.'

'What the hell are you talking about?' He's still not sitting.

Fine. 'Sit the fuck down, Ronan. I like this knife. Looks sharp.' He looks a bit conflicted, hesitant (I like these words, good words for a book group). Then he nods. Sits at one of the stools. Does not look happy about it. 'That's better. Here we all are. The meeting can resume. So. What do we think of redemption?'

'OK. Leo, is it?'

'No.'

'No?'

'My name is Liam.'

He frowns. Puts his hand out towards me, like he's trying to calm me down. But I feel pretty fucking calm. 'Well, Liam. Put the knife down, and we can talk. I'm not talking to you with that. We don't want an accident to happen.'

'You're a liar, you.'

'Excuse me?'

'I know what you are.' I keep the knife in my hand. 'So let's go back a bit. To Mandy's book deal.'

His eyebrows raise. Surprise. 'What book deal?'

'She got a one-hundred-thousand-pound book deal.'

The way he looks at her actually makes me feel weird. He loathes her. 'What? The *romance*?'

I laugh. '*Slay* is definitely not a fucking romance, Ronan.'

'*Slay*?' He pulls a face. Like, fucking fuming. He can't hold it in. This is a mad conversation. I need more wine. I take a big fuck-off glug as he turns to her. 'I thought you'd deleted it, Mal? I saw you delete it.'

She's still not speaking. I'll answer for her. 'It's definitely not been deleted.' I point to the screen. 'It's right here.'

He stares at me. I shrug. He stares at the screen. I can see him itching to lean over the table and grab the laptop. He won't though. He looks a bit stupid, actually. A bit pathetic. Smaller now he's sat down. I reckon he was blonde once. I feel drunk. On the voddy. But also the power. I like this knife. It's good.

'Leo...' Oh, she *does* speak. Very quiet though. 'Please can you just give me and my husband—'

'No fucking way. All members of book club should be present when discussing important book club-related topics.' I smile, because I want to seem like a willing participant.

I am willing.

I like it here.

And there are still some things I need to know.

'Leo, please, just put down the knife and pass me the laptop—'

'So when you followed me, Mandy – and you came to the AA meeting...' I hold up the vodka bottle again. *Cheers*. 'You were so nice to me. What I wanna know is, if I'm the inspiration for Liam, is there something like copyright I can get? Is that what it's called? Or is it royalties? Asking cos I'm skint, and some of that money would go a long, long way for me. You know, this poor little drug addict sex worker over here needs to pay his way. Although – I'm not really a sex worker. I suppose I am a bit. But I never meant to be. Anyway. Whatever. I want some money.'

I smile.

'We don't have any money for you, Leo.'

Ronan can fuck off. 'Liam.'

'Fine – Liam—'

'What were you gonna do with it anyway? You're minted. Look at this place. Help a poor boy out,' I say. I clasp my hands together like Oliver Fucking Twist. 'Please, sir, I need some more.' I don't even know why I'm having to ask, if I'm honest. 'Should I email this Stan guy, ask him what he thinks?' I stab at a laptop key to activate the screen. 'He might love that. Meeting me. He might offer more. Maybe we could do like a joint interview.' I see her face. 'Oh. I see. He doesn't know about me.'

I get the email chain up.

She flinches. 'It's not you, Leo. It's not about you.'

'Why are you lying? I wanted to talk about the love interest. *Mark*. It's mad, this stuff. So let's just go through it, my fellow book-clubbers. Liam is gay – which is very cool, isn't it. He gets raped by a teacher at school a few times, and then when he gets older, he meets this man, Mark, who pays him for sex but also abuses him – but Mark loves him really – so it's kinda like OK because Mark has his own shit. He's a well-rounded human so we feel a bit sorry for him. Which is really nice. He's a real human being with his own faults and stuff. I think Stanley said it was brave of you to do that. Yeah, *brave*. That's what he said. It is. *Very brave, Mallory*. Making Liam keep going back to the man who's fucking him up because he just wants to be looked after, because he can't do it himself. Wait… Maybe Leo is actually you?' I stop. They don't look at each other. 'See, I think these characters are more similar than they know. And that's interesting to me, cos when I came back – to speak to you—' I can hear my voice crack. Fucking stop it. I down more voddy. 'I was never in *love* with Mo – you know that right? Just checking. And definitely did not want his protection. I just wanted his fucking money, like I want yours.' I take another gulp. It helps. I get *Slay* back up, start scrolling through the text again. 'I was in love once. A long time ago. His name was Sam. He was dead sweet and stuff but we were very boring together. It really wasn't very dark or interesting. But I do like that you made Liam insane for a man who fucks him over and drives him to the edge.' I stop talking, scrolling. Look up at her. 'Makes you feel sad for him, doesn't it. But I do love that you make him cool. He's like edgy-cool, Liam. Isn't he? Kinda doesn't really give a shit that his life is in fucking tatters. It's fun. Oh—Oh.' I find the bit I'm looking for. 'And he's sexy. I really love that. There's this bit where you talk about his muscles when Mark is doing something fucking awful to him. His… "*six pack gleaming with sweat*". I pull my top up. Show them my stomach. 'As you can see, I do *not* have one. So I liked that you put that in. Stanley loved that too, didn't he. He said it's no bad thing to make your lead character hot.'

They both look at me like I'm fucking bonkers.

I think *they* are.

'Leo, this is getting out of hand now,' Ronan says calmly. 'I want us all to be safe. I want you to be safe.'

'Do you?'

'We can sort you somewhere to stay tonight, and then figure out the help you need, OK?'

'The help I need?'

'Yes.'

'*You* need fucking help.'

'Leo—'

'Does that mean the money I'm owed?'

'Owed?'

'Yeah.'

'We don't owe you any money.'

'She does.' I point the knife at her. 'Lots of the stuff in her book came from my brain. I know they were lies, but they were *my* lies – and she made them way worse. I was lying, you know, for money. I wanted you to think I was really fucked up and sad then invite me here so I can nick your stuff. But isn't that what you've been doing? I genuinely want to know. It's OK – cos like I said, it means we are the same, you and I.' I stand.

'Leo—' she says again.

'Did I use the words correctly there? You and *I*. Not: you and *me*.' I start to move around the table towards her. I feel a bit… I dunno.

Out of control.

But not.

Fucking calm.

It's mad.

I move in front of her. 'Are we the same?' She looks up at me. Something in her eyes. Something terrified. I know it. I do. Makes me feel suddenly sick. 'What would Liam do?' I say to her. 'Right now?'

She shakes her head. 'Please, Leo – please just—'

'I think we have to give him a chance, don't we? Cos I dunno, I'm not the author or anything, but I think he would fight. Fight for himself. For his survival.' I am close enough now to see the mascara smudged down her face. 'Why are you crying?'

'You're scaring me.'

'I'm scaring you? That's a good thing, isn't it? Nice dramatic material.'

'Leo…' Ronan says.

I look up at him. 'What do you want?'

'I need you to calm down.'

'I'm very calm.'

'Move away from my wife.'

'You're running too,' I say to her. I feel all ballsy now. Feel like a madhead. 'You said when you started this you wanted to leave.' I point the knife at him. My hand is trembling now. 'Cos I love in the book how you really got stuck into the life of the therapist. I guess she's just trying to survive too, isn't she? She sees something in Liam – it gives her something back. A part of her she misses. It's dead nice that. And that thing she wants – he wants it too. Liam and Mandy actually want the same fucking thing. It's genius. That's what the book is saying. We are all just trying to survive. I was really hoping she would get out. Cos her husband' – I jab the knife through the air at him – 'is a fucking *cunt*.'

'Put the knife down, Leo.'

'No – Ronan. No.'

A noise.

From the kitchen door.

We all turn at once. There, in the doorway. The other woman. Her mum.

'What is going on?'

'Mum – please go back—'

'No!' I say. 'Definitely don't go back upstairs. Are you here to join book club?'

She looks fucking petrified. And half asleep. 'Who is this?'

'I'm Liam,' I say.

'Liam?'

I should clarify. 'Yeah. Liam. From Mandy's story. I'm him, in the flesh.'

Her eyes widen. 'What is happening—

'Stace, go back upstairs.'

'No, Stace, do not go back upstairs. We are having a very interesting discussion. Sit. Sit. Sit.'

She makes a small whimper. Then sits. Good. Easy. My hand is really shaking now. I can see it. 'Let's move onto the topic of endings. So in the ending, there is a death. Have you read it, Stace? No? Oh, OK. It's really good. But a bit *much*. I dunno if you like to read about bad things happening to other people but that's basically the gist of the book. Anyway, then he dies. Sad that, innit. He kills himself.' Her face has gone white. She looks absolutely fucking terrified. 'Mandy made me the focus of the book.' I do a little spin. I dunno why. Put a bit of gay flare into it. 'Yas, gawd. I actually won the award in high school for most likely to be famous – and here it is! I also won most likely to be dead before I'm twenty-seven – which… I mean, all bets are off for that one. But if Mandy's story is right – both things could be true.'

Stace stares at me.

'So – I was just clearing some stuff up for her. It's the first time I've been able to give feedback. I can tell she's a bit unsure – but I wanna give it anyway. And Ronan, here' – I point the knife at Ronan. I see him flinch – 'Ronan isn't really keen for me to be here, but I think it's fun. Do you have any voddy?'

'What?'

'Vodka. Get more vodka, Ronan.' Stace looks like she's gonna fall off her seat. 'Ronan, I said get the vodka.'

He stands slowly. Goes to the fridge. Opens the freezer compartment below. Takes out another bottle of Grey Goose. 'Yes,' I say. He takes a glass from the cabinet and starts to pour. 'More. More, Ronan, more.' He keeps glugging. When it is nearly full, he stops and hands it to me. 'Ta.' I do it in one. The burn is amazing.

'Right, Stace, so you haven't read it – but in the book Liam is the lead character. He's a nice guy – but a bit stupid. Gets himself into all sorts of bother. He gets abused a lot and gets sick and all that – and he can't read. That was interesting to me. Cos the thing is, I can read. I actually used to love reading. I went to uni to study English but I fucked that up – drugs. Yeah, drugs will do that. Had to drop out, went back to Essex. Pretty boring, really. Anyway – I read Charles Dickens when I was like fourteen and absolutely fucking loved it. Do you know why I loved it? I loved it cos it was funny. I found it well funny. I love a bit of humour. *Slay* doesn't have much humour. Actually, *Slay* is not funny at all.' I rotate the knife in my hand slowly. It feels good. Weighty. 'Also, I liked Shakespeare. Shakespeare loved killing people off, didn't he? Can I get a big gay book club *yas* to that one?' No one says anything. 'I think most of his main characters died. So makes sense that Liam dies at the end of *Slay*. He's a bit Shakespearean. A bit dramatic. Tortured. But I'm missing something. I'm just trying to get to the *reason*, Mandy – the reason *why* he does it. I mean, I might be wrong – and maybe we should open it up for discussion – but I think he dies cos he is *gay* and can't *cope*.' I look at Stace. Stace doesn't look like she should be called Stace. 'You haven't read it, so I'll just clarify. There was a version of the book where Liam got better and had a happy life – but people thought it wasn't realistic – and I agree. So he has to die. Liam has to die. Isn't that right, Mandy? Have I got that right? Liam has to die for people to buy it?'

She stares at me.

They all do.

Fucking well quiet in this kitchen when I'm not talking. Someone else should have a go. All I can hear is the hum of the fridge.

'In the *proposed outline*, you don't actually say *when* he does it. What do you think – should it be today? How about now?' I turn the knife to my stomach. 'It might help you. With writing it. If you *see* it. Know what I mean?'

She puts her hand to her mouth.

'Liam...' Mallory says.

The mum looks like she might drop dead. Don't think that was in the proposed ending.

I look down at the knife in my hand, facing my own tummy. I wanna cry. I really want to. I thought I would be by now. But I can't. I just feel nothing.

They're all crying though. Guess that's something.

Didn't really expect it to end like this. I am sad. Fucking gutted, actually.

That this is all it comes to.

How fucking bleak.

'Is this how you see me?' She still doesn't answer. None of them do. 'All I wanted was some warmth,' I say. 'A bit of your warmth.' Nothing. 'Right,' I continue. 'Since you know best. Goodbye then.'

52

Mallory

Hi Stan,

I have the ending of *Slay* here for you. I wanted to make sure I got it right. The publisher has paid a lot for this, so I really hope it meets their expectations. I think it will.
   See attached.
   For clarity: the edit begins just after Liam has turned up in Mandy's kitchen, having read all of her therapy notes about him. He is angry and upset (after he's tried to get clean) that she is privately predicting he's unlikely to make it. He has turned the kitchen knife on himself. I know you thought this was a lovely cliffhanger to end on, but I needed to add more, so the reader knows the full truth.
   Richard, Mandy's husband, has entered the scene. He is not aware that Liam has been watching them in the house, as Liam was seeking refuge in the airing cupboard. I have, as you know, also added Mandy's mother, Sarah, to the story. She is in the kitchen too.
   I'd like to push back on any changes the publisher might have for this – this is the final ending. This is the way the story finishes. I want to keep it as truthful to the characters as possible. Thank you, Stan. I will be going away for a while now. I need a bit of time. If you could give me a week for my final revisions of the text, that would be brilliant. I will be in touch soon.

Mal

Attached: *Slay*. Kitchen scene. Ending.

Mandy

'Right,' Liam said. 'Since you know best. Goodbye then.'
She watched him look down at the blade in his hand, pointed towards his stomach. For a moment, she wasn't sure if he meant it. If this was some cruel joke. But then she saw his eyes. The hopelessness in them. The vacant intent. And a small flicker of the muscles in his wrist. 'Stop,' she said. 'Please, Liam. Stop. Listen to me.' He looked up at her. 'You're right,' she said, putting her hand out tentatively towards him. 'You're right. We are the same.'
As he stared back at her, his lips parted, she saw in his expression the emergence of something she had long forgotten. A glimmer of lightness. Hope, perhaps, or gratitude. Yes, he was thankful. Thankful that she had stopped him. And in that moment, she knew he did want to live. That she had got it wrong. And so had he. 'Give me the knife, Liam,' she said. 'You don't want to do this. And I don't want you to do this.'
'What are you doing?' Richard hissed from behind her. 'He's dangerous, Mandy. Stay back.'
'Give me the knife, Liam,' she continued.
'He's testing you,' Richard said, harsher now, attempting to take her arm. But she resisted, pulling it from his grip. 'He's playing a game, Mandy. It's all for show. He's manipulating you.'
'Coming from you?' Liam said. 'That's funny. You're fucking funny, Richard.'
'Excuse me?'
Liam glared at him. 'I'm not the one sending naked

pictures of myself to other women from the second-floor bathroom.'

At this, Mandy turned to look at her husband. She saw her mother's eyes move to him too.

'What are you talking about?' Richard said, his glare remaining fixed on Liam.

'I was in the cupboard.'

Richard faltered. Momentarily. The mask slipped, a fraction. Just enough, enough to be seen. Behind is panic. 'What do you mean?'

'You took a lot of them. Sent a lot of them. Then stared at yourself in the mirror.'

'You were watching me?'

'Yes.'

'You're insane.'

'Just like your wife?' The room fell silent. 'That's what you want us to be, isn't it? Insane. Crazy. Unwell.'

'You are unwell.'

'Nah, mate. It's you,' Liam said. 'You're the reason she's so fucking nuts.' Mandy looked at Liam, and she felt something shift inside her. A glimmer of something. The same thing she had seen in him. Gratitude. 'You're a fucking phoney. I've seen the way you look at her. You hate her. And I've seen the way she looks at you. She's terrified of you. And you're just this pathetic, weak, insecure prick. You have nothing, you have absolutely nothing, so you want to take it from her too. You are actually just fucking boring. I've met so many men like you, and you're all just really, really fucking dull.' Liam's eyes were now wet. 'I don't even know you, and I fucking hate you. I hate you. I fucking, fucking hate you.' He spat on the floor, at Richard's feet.

Richard stepped towards him. 'Get out of my house,' he said, moving closer still. 'If you're going to kill yourself, just fucking do it.'

'Richard—' Mandy said, but before she could move to stop him, Richard had already begun.

What happened next was so strange, so unusual, that it took her a moment to register.
Her husband's hands clasped around Liam's, which were still holding the knife pointed towards his torso. He thrust. It was quick, and soundless.
The blade entered Liam's stomach.
He didn't yell. He didn't cry out.
'Richard!' Mandy screamed, but in an instant, Liam was on his back, on the kitchen tiles, and Richard was on top of him, pummelling his fists into his body. His face. His arms. His head. Over, and over, and over.
Mandy lunged forward and tried to pull Richard away, but he turned and threw his arm at her, sending her sprawling backwards. As she tried to stand, she saw her mother by the kitchen island, her hand over her mouth, staring, paralysed with shock.
'Mum! Help!' she screamed. Richard continued to throw his fists into Liam, his torso gleaming. Mandy slipped as she tried to stand. She looked down. Blood. Blood all over the kitchen floor.
The sound of something shattering made her look up. Her mother had taken the fruit bowl and brought it down onto the back of Richard's head. It was obliterated. Exploding into a spray of tiny pieces. The force of it made Richard's arms suddenly stop moving. His body swayed, then slumped sideways.
Her mother's face appeared before hers. 'Quick, Mandy,' she said. 'Try and stop the bleeding while I call an ambulance. Here – use this.' She thrust a tea towel into her daughter's hand. 'Now, Mandy. I need to get my phone.'
She saw her mother step over her husband's limp body and move out of the kitchen. Soon there was the sound of her footsteps on the floor above.
Move, Mandy, she thought.
And she was on her knees, next to Liam.
'I'm here,' she said. 'I'm here.' She could see her tears

falling onto him as she pushed the tea towel around the knife.

'Mandy...' he whispered. 'I didn't want to do it.'

'I know,' she said. 'I know you didn't.'

In that moment, staring at him, while her mother's voice spoke frantically to the ambulance operator out in the hall behind her, she saw something. She saw herself, lying in front of her, dying. The life seeping out of her body.

All he was ever trying to do was survive, she thought. To feel safe.

And she felt something so strong, so profound. Love was not what she had thought it to be. It was not what the books, the films, the poems or what our instincts tell us.

It was here, between them.

It always had been.

It just is. It exists.

We are all the same, *she thought.* Underneath, we are all connected. And that is love. That is the place where peace is found. It is in knowing that we are all the same.

Part 4

Thirteen months later

53

Mallory

COSMOPOLITAN MAGAZINE

Articles: AUTHOR PROFILES: MALLORY MADDOX
Written by Callie Harper

Before the publication of Mallory Maddox's *Slay* in August – her comeback novel after nearly eight years away from writing – she sat down with me to discuss her literary heroes, making a home for oneself and how her new book has reshaped her life.

We met in a quaint café in Crouch End, where she formerly resided.

'It'll be nice to go back,' she said over the phone when I pitched it to her. 'In many ways, I've missed it.'

To say that a lot has happened to Maddox this year would be a gross understatement, and she has remained, for the most part, absent from social media and the press. This, she tells me, was something she needed. But on this warm summer afternoon in June, in the quietness of a leafy back street in the north of London, tucked behind a gift shop, she decided to let her guard down.

As I poured a second sugar into my oat milk latte, I looked at my watch. Maddox was going to be late. I was a little frustrated, and momentarily I formed an opinion of her: that she had become a cliché, an author on the brink of something big, with a newly formed arrogance and little regard for the time frame of a busy journalist. Just as I was conjuring the image of a Miranda Priestly-style monster in my mind, I looked up to see her entering through the door. Immediately, I was stunned. I was wrong.

She appeared completely... Normal.

Sure, her hair was different to the photographs I had seen of her – now cut short into a neat little bob – but other than that, she was the opposite of severe. There was something so unassuming about her. With her Sweaty Betty leggings and tote bag slung over her shoulder, she could have been any of us. This was, I decided as our conversation went on, the appeal of her. Her ordinariness.

'How are you?' I asked, as she rolled up the sleeves of her cashmere sweater. I knew from first glance that the sweater was from Zara – I happen to own one myself – and it shocked me. I had heard rumours about the size of her American advance (yes, only rumours – but the publishing world loves to talk and often gets it right) and wondered, if it had been me in her position, if I would be wearing something more... expensive. It gave me pause for thought.

'Well...' she said, with a slight exhalation that said so much. 'I'm doing OK,' she continued, brushing a loose hair out her face, then taking a sip of her decaf latte. She was off caffeine. Off alcohol and cigarettes too, so she claimed. She said she had been going through a major reset. I was envious and nervously hid the two empty sugar sachets that I had loaded into my coffee. 'Oh, don't be silly,' she said, noticing. 'I'm still eating bloody sugar!' She leaned towards me conspiratorially. 'Let's order cake...'

I immediately warmed to her. We could be friends, I thought.

I could be friends with this woman.

The conversation began with us discussing her love of Virginia Woolf. I had read *Shallow Embers* as a teen (if you don't know it – you should) – a genre-defining YA coming-of-age story about a girl on the run from her family, and from herself – and was always a little surprised by the puff quote on the front of the book likening Maddox to Woolf. I understood the vague similarities, the stream of consciousness, the inner thoughts, the bleak outlook, but her words seemed so much fresher. 'Why do we have to keep likening authors to other authors?' I asked her.

'Sales,' she said frankly. And she was right. 'I don't mind the quote now,' she added, in a reflective haze. 'But at the time I just felt like such a charlatan.' She went on to tell me all about Woolf's home. 'She lived in Monk's House in East Sussex with her husband, Leonard, until the day she drowned herself in the River Ouse. Tragic, yes. But on a more positive note, Monk's House is the most beautiful house I have ever seen. Have you ever been?' she asked excitedly. Her flippancy was refreshing, and her enthusiasm infectious.

I was ashamed to say I hadn't been.

'You must go. The whole cottage exudes a creative energy. In the spring, the gardens sprawl, and roses climb the back of the exterior, reaching up to the slatted roof. There's something about the building that makes it look both solid and fragile at the same time, as if the heavy weatherboard could topple in a particularly strong gust of wind. It almost leans and creaks with the weight of the genius that lived inside it. Leonard designed the gardens himself.' She spoke so effortlessly. So beautifully. Again, I was envious.

'Tulips reach up through a sea of wild flowers in its borders, causing this incredible patchwork of colour that surrounds the lawn. There's an orchard, reachable via a cobbled pathway. There's also a vegetable patch. Inside the house, nothing is straight. Every line is curved or tilting. It is off, but it feels right. Correct in its imperfections. It is poky, but there is an expansiveness too as you weave your way through the rooms. The lounge is my favourite. The walls are a very particular shade of green – a shade that could very easily be the colour of bile, but the way the light hits it, it looks nothing less than chic. There are bookshelves. The brown spines, neatly lined up together, perfectly contrast with the mismatching armchairs. It is maximalism, but effortless. Gives new meaning to higgledy-piggledy. And the beams. Oh, the overhead beams. Dark wood that looks like treacle is coursing through the veins of the building. Virginia had her own bedroom. A Room of One's Own. It had a fireplace, surrounded by tiles that her sister Vanessa gave to her.'

At Cambridge University, where I studied English, I wrote a fairly unconventional essay called 'The Charm of the Bloomsbury Set'. Maddox had the same breezy, idealistic charm. A slight darkness underneath, haunting the beauty. She would fit right in with them, I thought. They would have loved her. 'I've taken inspiration for my new place,' she said.

'You've recently moved, haven't you?'

'I have,' she said. In respect for her privacy I agreed not to print the exact destination, but she now lives somewhere on the British coast, and it sounds utterly divine. Maddox said she doesn't want people knowing where she is now, for various obvious reasons. 'It's been so joyful doing the house up,' she said. 'Making a home for myself is so important. I really understand that now. Especially after...' She trailed off. I knew immediately what she was referring to.

'Your marriage ended...' I finished for her, tentatively. I had cleared with her publicist that we could mention it – it is relevant to the book in many ways, as you will see when you no doubt read it – but I was still nervous to ask.

'Yes,' she said, with an air of resolve that took me by surprise. 'My marriage ended.'

'Are you OK?' I asked again.

'I am,' she said. 'Yes. I really am. I am adjusting.'

She nodded her head in a way that let me know that was all I was going to get, and I respected her for it. It was enough to know she had been able to leave the marriage that had kept her caged for so long. I had wanted to ask Maddox if there was anything she wished the readers to know about her experience, but I knew the answer.

It's in the book.

The answers are in the book.

'So this book is about a woman trying to help someone, essentially. She is trying to find herself by helping another. What would you say to people out there who feel lost?' I asked her. 'Who are in need of that help, and feel completely stuck?'

The ending in the book is brutal. I won't give any spoilers, but be prepared.

'Oh, that's such a tricky one,' she said, looking out of the window. I noticed the evening sun getting low in the sky, and I realised that we had been talking for over two hours. It was like two old friends catching up. This is the magic of her words. Of her writing. You will see it in *Slay*. You will feel like you have known the characters forever. 'I think I would tell those people that there is always someone out there that you can connect to. Always. There are good people on this planet, and most of us, actually, are. We just lose it, the older we get.'

'Have you always written?' I asked.

'Yes,' she said. 'I've always loved to write. Since I was little.'

I imagined this ordinary woman sat before me as a child, much like the rest of us, and it is inspiring. We, too, can grow up to be like Mallory Maddox.

Because there are people in their Zara sweaters and their Sweaty Betty leggings everywhere. There are people just like Mallory Maddox everywhere.

54

Leo

TWATS: A POEM

There are twats
Everywhere.

@Alias22

55

Mallory

Today is a wonderful day.

In fact, it is so wonderful that I had to take a brief moment to myself – a breather. In what I think must be some kind of storeroom (but it is very dark, so I am not entirely sure). I thought I might pass out, I think from all the excitement. Everyone is very excited. But when I let myself in here, something strange started happening, because now I am surrounded by dragons.

I can't see them – it is too dark – but I know they are here, because their smoke is filling my nostrils and clogging my senses. I can taste it at the back of my throat. The bitterness. The danger. It is searing into my bloodstream, threatening to topple me. And the heat. *It is suddenly so hot in here.*

I don't know where these dragons are from, but what I do know is that I don't want to pass out. I can't. Not now. Definitely not today.

Because today is *exciting*.

It is a great day. *A wonderful day!*

I hear something. A movement at the back of the room. I try to remain still, but I am shaking. *Why am I shaking?* Maybe I should be nice to them. I should be nice to the dragons.

Yes.

Yes. Be nice to the dragons and they will go away.

'Hello?' I whisper.

Nothing.

Cut it out, Mallory. You're just overstimulated. Just get out of this room and—

But then I see them. Huge green eyes glaring back at me through the dark, flecked with yellow. With desire. I push the palms of my hands into my eye sockets and try to rub them away but when I open them, they are still there. In fact, there are more. So many more. And they are hungry. Desperate to breathe flames across my body. To scorch my flesh.

We have been waiting.

Oh, God.

The dragons just spoke.

And there are so many eyes. So many dragons. Hundreds of them. Thousands. Scales wet, talons razor sharp. I feel them prowling around me, hemming me in.

We have you now.

No. Please—!

We will tear you apart.

'Please don't,' I croak into the darkness. But my voice is tiny. Meek.

No. Not anymore.

'Please don't,' I assert myself. To the dragons.

You do not belong in here.

'I'm sorry.' My head is spinning. Panic is rising in my chest. I need to sit down. *There's nowhere to sit down.* I need to breathe. *I cannot breathe.* This room is unsafe. How did I get in here? I suddenly don't remember. How is this happening? *This room is not OK.* It is teeming with danger. I need to get out. I need to leave. 'Help me—!'

'Mal?' A voice I know, from the other side of the door. 'Mal, are you OK in there?'

There is something else in this room, though, as well as the dragons. I can sense it. It is small, barely a whisper. 'Mal?'

Then I realise.

Magic. *Magic* is in here. I feel my excitement flicker back awake. *This is so magical.* But, something is off. No. It is not the magic I want. Not the magic I wished for as a child. This magic is different.

'Seriously, Mal? Are you OK?'

It lacks something.

'Mal?'

Hope. It lacks hope.

'*Mallory?*'

'I'm OK, Meghan! Just give me a second!'

'Oh, thank God, babe. I thought I'd lost you for a moment.'

'I'm fine. Just a little nervous!'

This magic is dark. Threatening. But it is thrilling too. It is beautifully evil. I can feel it move towards me through the gloom, right into the darkest parts of me, then latch on. It tries to pull, to take hold wherever it can. It tugs at my shame, at the collar of my cashmere sweater, trying to draw me through the half-light and the fragments of dust, into oblivion.

'You're gonna smash it, babe.' And I cannot say no. I don't want to. I love it, the way it holds me. It is so powerful. The allure so strong. I want to go with it. 'Just do your breathing exercises like we said.'

'OK! Thanks Meghan!'

And I realise, it is endless. This room is completely endless. It is *incredible* in here.

Wait. Hold on. *What is that?*

There is a stench.

I try to place it. Rotten and bloody and dark. I know that smell.

Murder.

There is murder in here. I glance down, and gasp. Slain bodies lie scattered at my feet. There are so many. Throats slashed. Arrows protruding from chests. Men in bottle-green army uniforms with missing limbs, guts spilling across the floorboards. Women. Dead women in torn dresses, half naked, strangled and drowned and beaten, faces blotted blue and bruised.

Oh my God. My hand goes to my mouth. Children. Children lie at my feet. Dead children.

'I don't want to disturb you if you're doing your box breathing, hun, but we really don't have long now... Alice is asking for you.'

Something moves behind me. I spin round. It doesn't seem...

What is that?

Emerging from the shadows. So tall. So slender. So beautiful.

Oh my gosh.

I hold my breath, stunned.

An *elf*.

Gliding over the maimed bodies that are sprawled across the floor, not once looking down. Head up, tall and proud. There is a magnetism to it that is intoxicating. An arrogance, a stillness. It looks at me and I inhale sharply. In his eyes is a sexual desire so intense that my chest flutters. Something is written on his forehead.

Fantasy.

He speaks. It is so beautiful, like a song. His eyes burn with passion.

Does this elf want to have sex with me? In this storeroom? *Now?*

I'm not an elf, he sings.

I am a fairy.

'Sorry,' I say.

Sex. I suddenly notice the sex.

It is everywhere in here. Writhing in every corner. Pulsating in every nook and cranny, clogging the place with sweat and a throbbing heat. It drips between the floorboards and tangles itself within the cobwebs. Each droplet is laced with passion. And something else. Fear. I can hear the moans. The screams.

'Mal, they're saying three minutes. Have you got everything you need?'

Something else enters now, too.

A warmth. A glow.

It stills me, momentarily.

Love. Love is in here. I almost smile. I almost laugh. A whole abundance of it, in so many forms. I close my eyes and inhale. Love in all its glory. Tender. Bright. Naive. Pulsating. Confused. Twisted. Stagnant.

When I open them again, I startle. There is a man sitting cross-legged in the centre of the room. He is bald.

'Hello?' I say.

He smiles back at me.

I think he is a Buddhist. Some kind of monk. He lifts his eyes to me and places his hand on his chest. He exhales gently.

Warmly. *You will be OK, Mallory*, he mouths. There is something written on his forehead.

I squint.

Self-Help.

I shift on my feet, suddenly uneasy. There is something beneath the warmth. Something sinister. I shudder. His eyes turn red. *You are deeply fucked up*, he mouths. *You need to heal.*

'I will,' I say. 'I promise.'

'Mal, right... I'm starting to worry.' Shit. I can hear the anxiety in Meghan's voice from the other side of the door. I should reply. I should.

But I am distracted by the monk.

I did heal. I have *healed*, I want to tell him, but it gets lodged in my throat. He is still staring right at me. His kind gaze burning right into my soul. I feel sick. Is it nerves? I don't want to throw up on the monk. Not now.

Now is not the time to throw up on a—

'Seriously, Mal, I don't think we should be late for this, do you?' I hear the door handle turn. 'Hold on... Have you locked it?'

Oh. Yes. I did do that.

'I'm OK! I am, Meghan, I'm just—'

Others appear. So many people start to fill the room. People of all ages, all genders, all sexual orientations. I should not be able to tell by looking at them, but I can. I can because they have it literally written on their foreheads, stamped in ink, as if by a typewriter. The black ink bleeds down their foreheads. Gay. Lesbian. Trans. Young Adult.

Is that... Jennifer Lawrence?

And a random astronaut? Snogging another astronaut?

But... something feels...

There is something that threads this place together.

'Mal, what even is that room?' I don't know. I do not know, Meghan. 'Can you let me in?'

I stand still, looking. Everyone, everything, suddenly disappears.

And I am left, in the darkness. And I suddenly feel incredibly empty.

Sad.

'Right, that's it. Open the door now, Mal.'

All I have is stitched into pages. Immortalised, embalmed by the sweet, chemical smell of vanilla. Of nostalgic newness.

Of fresh paper.

Unread words.

New money.

I turn and open the door to see Meghan, my twenty-two-year-old publicist, in a beautiful black dress, hair slicked back, gripping onto her mobile phone for dear life, staring at me, wide-eyed. 'Mal, you look *unwell*.' She is very charming. 'Are you OK?'

'Yes.'

'Why are the lights off?'

'Oh…' I don't know how to answer that.

'Mal, have you been standing in this…' She looks at the tiny room I have been inside, and grimaces. '…this storeroom in the dark?'

'I'm fine,' I say. Because I am. 'I am.' I go to check my hair, my messy bun, only to remember I cut it off two months ago for the author photos into a neat, short bob. It startles me every time. They say I look professional. Like I mean business.

'How long have you been in here?'

'I just needed a place to focus.'

I just needed a second, to gather my thoughts.

'OK, babe. And are you?'

'Am I what?'

'Focused, Mallory!' She looks at me like I am either a complete fuckwit or a complete genius, and she has yet to decide which. She has always looked at me like that.

It makes me want to turn back round, into the endless wilderness. To keep going. To lose myself entirely.

'Alice asked if you want to run through anything?'

'Alice? Who's Alice?'

'Alice Fairfax? The head of Waterstones, Mal.' Meghan is getting impatient now. I can hear it.

'Oh! Right, no. Tell Alice I'm happy to wing it. I work better that way.'

She doesn't reply. It's not the response she wants to hear. Not now, anyway. Not today. Everything must go perfectly. I have been briefed so many times. I have practiced in the mirror. Relentless hours of saying the same sentences over and over again.

'I just can't believe this happened to me.'
'I thought I had only one book in me.'
'I am just overwhelmed by the response.'

It's a tricky balance, attempting to show both vulnerability and confidence in the same breath. To be shy, but not weak. To have conviction, but not superiority. To be relatable. To be authentic.

That's what they want, Stan told me.

'They just want to see you.'

A woman appears. Older than me, with pinched, stern features. Like she means business. 'Ah! There you are!'

I look at Meghan. She clearly sees the panic on my face and mouths, *Alice Fairfax*.

'Hi, Alice!' I say, brightly. *I am bubbly.*

My brain is fried.

How could I forget Alice Fairfax, the head of Waterstones? The woman who made this happen?

Or this event?

At their flagship store. Tonight.

Now.

'Are you OK?' she says, the faintest flicker of concern crossing her features.

'She's fine,' Meghan answers for me. 'She's going to be amazing.'

They both look at me for confirmation.

'I am,' I say. 'I'm ready.' Their faces relax.

'Could I get some water?' I ask.

'It's at your seat, on the stage,' Alice says. 'Still and sparkling. Paula requested elderflower, so she has that… She's sat on the left, you're sat on the right. That all OK?'

'I…' I do actually really like elderflower. 'Water is fine.'

'How is P.K.?' Meghan asks.

P.K.

I'm about to meet her.

Paula Kate.

Is about to interview me.

Alice nods. 'She's just arrived. All the guests are sat. And she cannot wait to meet you, Mal.'

'Oh, good,' I say. I immediately feel like I'm going to be sick again, and I'm not sure what's worse, throwing up on an imaginary monk, or the boss of Waterstones. 'Will I not meet her before?' I ask.

'Um... No. I think she's a little frazzled from the flight and said it might give off good energy to meet first in front of everyone.'

'Right. Yes. That's a good idea,' I say. But I don't know if it is. Is it a good idea? Why doesn't she want to meet me before?

'How many people are here?' Meghan asks.

'Two hundred,' Alice says. 'And people queuing for return tickets at the door!' She beams at me.

'Wow,' Meghan responds.

'Yes – wow.' Alice grins. 'We are so excited about this book, Mal.'

'Thank you.'

This woman is – both of these women are – vibrating with delight.

Alice peers behind me, through the door of the store cupboard. 'That shouldn't be open,' she says.

Meghan shoots me a look. *Best not to tell her.* 'What is it?' she says, before I open my mouth.

'This room?' Alice asks, going to pull the door closed. 'It's where we keep an overspill of the bestseller stock.'

'Oh!' Meghan says. 'Cool.' Her eyes light up as they dart around the stacks of books. I suddenly notice them – piles and piles of books I know. 'Oh my God, are there any *proofs* in here?'

Wait, were the dragons from *Fourth Wing*? The dead bodies from *In Memoriam*? I never read them, so potentially...

'Ha!' Alice says. 'I might have one or two at the back somewhere.'

Meghan looks like she has been slapped. 'For me?'

'Yes, of course!'

Wow, Meghan mouths.

Where was the monk from?

Alice turns to me. 'Did you see *Slay*?'

'Sorry?'

'*Slay*,' Meghan repeats, slower than Alice, like I'm becoming more stupid by the second. I notice her smile, attempting to cover her growing concern with faux confusion. 'Your book? The book you wrote, Mal? Your *Sunday Times* bestseller?!' She laughs.

We all do.

Ha ha ha.

'Right! Yes. That one.'

'Yes, that one.' Ha ha ha. 'No. I didn't see it.'

'That's because we've nearly sold out,' Alice says, then winks at me.

I wink back, but a split-second later I wonder why. Then Alice points to the floorspace in the cupboard just behind my feet. I turn to see the familiar neon green cover, my name emblazoned across the front, under the knife dripping with blood and the word *SLAY*. Three copies, all hardbacks, stacked on top of each other. Exclusive Waterstones editions with sprayed edges. 'Three left. Pre-sales were off the charts.'

'That's good,' I say.

'Good? Mal, it's *great*.'

'Ms Maddox?' We all turn to see a baby-faced man, dressed all in black, with an earpiece and a clip board. 'We're ready for you.'

And I realise. Pain.

Pain was the thread, in that room.

56

Leo

Some fucker is smoking a blunt on the seat behind me.

It's making my head spin out. Making my chest itch. Would have got a cab but can't fucking afford it, so bus it is.

I'm an honest man now, see. No running from cab drivers or hiding in the fuckin bogs. I never come into town anymore. Cos I fucking hate it.

I look out the window. See my reflection. Blonde hair. New hair, new me, 'n' all that. I pull my hood over my head. Someone in the street said I looked like Eminem the other day, and I wasn't mad about it.

Twitchy. Twitchy as fuck tonight.

Just gotta be quick. In and out.

Can see the lights of Soho through the glass. All the men getting ready to go out.

To dance.

To party.

These parts make me shudder. All the ghosts, lurking.

Don't wanna be seen anymore. Invisible works for me.

The smell of the weed nearly makes me drool. I never even used to like weed.

I feel weird. Lean down and put my fingers in my sock.

Pull it out and hold it in the palm of my hand. Squeeze it.

Picked up my six-month chip at NA last night. They made me a cake. Candles and all. I haven't let go of it since. It's just a little piece of plastic but I dunno – I don't fucking know – there's something about it that makes me feel lighter. Got it in my shoe right now. Dunno where else to put it. Don't wanna fucking lose it, so it stays in my sock. It's working. For now.

Cos I want it to.

I think I could. Live a life. That's what my sponsor said.

Her name's Debbie. She's sixty years old and fucking mental, but she said I could have a life if I wanted one. She said that no one is coming to save me. Not one fucker is coming and it's time I realised that. And I think I did.

I was always waiting.

I was.

Waiting for someone to come.

But they fucking haven't, and they fucking ain't.

And now I'm here.

Six months is the longest I've done since I was thirteen years old.

I cry a lot now. Cry most days. Debbie says that's about right.

Fucking love it, to be honest.

She told me there are three rules. Make my bed every morning. Don't use substances. Don't call anyone a cunt. Managed to stick to it so far. I wake in the night, craving still. Bag of Haribos and full-fat Coke by your bed, she told me.

Think it's working.

It's weird though. It's all very fucking new. Feel like I'm a tiny baby, wobbling through the streets. Like I don't really know myself yet, and never have.

That's the point, apparently.

But it scares me. Scare myself sometimes, still. Like I might do something. Something stupid.

But at least I feel it now, Debbie said. At least I fucking feel it.

It's good to be alive.

The pain is a gift. It's a window to yourself. I know how that sounds – I do – but I like it. There's a destination.

That's what Debbie said. '*The destination is you, you nutter. Stop running. It won't work.*'

Talking of destinations, I'm nearly at my stop now. Piccadilly Circus.

Nearly there.

It's good that I'm late.

I don't want her to see me. Just wanna hear what she has to say, that's all. And I wanna know how she ended it.

Not spoken to her since it happened. Since that letter she sent me.

Over a year now.

A long time.

A year is a very fucking long time.

57

Mallory

'Ready?' Meghan says.

I peer through the gap in the curtains. We have been told to wait here, just off to the side of the main function room, until we are given the go-ahead. I can see the last stragglers of the audience taking their seats, removing their bags, whispering to each other, apologising as people have to stand for them to shuffle along the rows. Eyes meeting, but with a look of approval rather than annoyance. *You're here, I'm here too! Congratulations!* Each with a copy of my book in their hands.

There are so many of them.

At the back of the audience, Alice makes her way to a seat next to Stan. When I see him, I feel like I might burst into tears. He is wearing a blazer and a crisp white shirt, and a look of complete wonder on his face. His eyes are wide, beaming as he takes in the room, tears glinting. He told me in the card that came with the flowers he sent me that this would be one of the happiest days of his life. He told me: *'This is why I do the job, for moments like this. You have made me so proud.'* When Alice taps him on the shoulder, he looks up to see her, and it's as though he might spill over with joy. *Alice, hi!* I see him say. *So, so good to see you. Isn't this all amazing?* He stands excitedly, nearly knocking his chair over. *Are you responsible for these?!* He holds something up between his fingers. I squint. The size of a matchbox, in bright neon green.

It is a biscuit. A biscuit with the cover of my book iced onto it. 'There are biscuits of my book,' I whisper, more to myself than anyone else, but Meghan replies, because apparently she hears everything.

'Oh, don't eat those,' she says. 'They taste like cardboard. They're just for Insta, really.'

'Right.'

'Talking of Insta,' she adds, pulling on my shoulder and turning me to face her. 'Can I just get a snap of you here, nervously waiting to go on stage?'

I wait to see her laugh, or eyeroll – any sign of irony – but then I realise she is being deadly serious.

'Really?' I ask. 'Now?'

'Yes, it'll be so *cute*.'

'Cute?'

'Yeah! Very on brand.'

'On brand?'

I can hear the confusion in my voice, which clearly ignites some profound awe in her as she looks at me again. *Who is this stupid, old, bumbling genius?* 'Yes, Mal. Your brand is kind of, *unassuming* and, *I'm not sure how all this happened to me...*' She waves her hands about and makes her eyes bulge in a naive, silly, vulnerable way. I assume, imitating me. Or the way she wants me to be. Meghan should be an actress. She really should. 'A nervy pic will work perfectly for that. And you look super adorbs in that cardy.' She tugs at my sleeve.

'Oh, thanks.'

She starts moving me, turning my body, doing something to my hair, realigning my necklace, then she opens the gap in the curtain behind me a little more. 'Just so we can see the size of the audience...' she says, then holds her phone up to my face. 'Right. Look scared.'

Again, no irony.

I try to pull the face she's pulled. I wonder if I should stick my tongue out and make a peace sign.

I don't.

'This is perfect...' she says, smiling. 'Oh my God, you look terrified. *Brilliant*.' She moves the camera down to find the best shot, and starts furiously pressing her screen. '*To filter or not to filter...?*'

'Sorry, are you asking me?'

'No. Hmm. I think... No filter. Yes. Authenticity is key. OK.' She exhales slowly, then pushes the screen hard with her index finger, like she is sending the code to ignite a nuclear bomb. 'Posted!'

'Great!'

She watches the screen. 'OK... twenty-four likes so far...'

'Amazing,' I say, but her face doesn't change, so I start to panic. 'Isn't it? Isn't it amazing?'

'It'll do,' she replies, then looks up at me. 'Babe, don't look so scared!'

'You just told me—'

'This isn't for you to worry about. That's what *I'm* here for. *You* need to focus!' She takes my shoulders and turns me back to face the curtain. 'Zone in.'

Zone in.

Through the gap I see the members of the audience begin to shush each other. Something is happening. The lights dim, with one left illuminating the stage. Two chairs are visible, a single table between them, with a single copy of my book displayed on top.

I suddenly see my mother.

My mother on the front row. Beaming.

'OK, everyone!' someone says. It is the baby-faced boy with the earpiece, now appearing on the stage, hovering half in, half out of the light, a little awkwardly, like he doesn't want to be stealing the spotlight. 'My name is Brad, I'm the manager of Waterstones Piccadilly – welcome.' A short round of applause for Brad. 'Just a few ground rules before we get started,' he says. I notice his tone has the right blend of modest and confident. I need that. I need to do what Brad is doing. 'Fire exits are here and here.' He points to the back of the room. 'And, I have been asked to inform you that tonight's discussion will delve into sensitive topics, so if you need to step out, please do so quietly.' He pauses sombrely. The slightest bow of his head. Brad is very good at this. 'I have also been told by the publisher to make you aware that should this discussion stir things up for you, the details of a support hotline you can text, should you wish, will be given out at the end.' The audience shuffle about in their seats, suddenly a little terrified, but also a little thrilled. *What will be said that will make us need to text a support hotline?* 'Now, it is time.' Oh, God. 'Before we bring out the author in question, as you all know, we have an incredibly special guest who has agreed to interview her. And we couldn't be more delighted, as their work so clearly aligns. If you could put your hands together, this author has flown in especially from California for tonight's event. The incredible, the prolific, P.K. Anderson!' He holds his hand out, to the front row, where I see she is sat.

She is sat next to my mother.

My mother met P.K. Anderson before I did.

The actual Paula Kate. She looks so... *Correct*. Exactly how you would imagine an author to look. Warm and kind at first glance, but there's a shrewdness to her. An intensity. An intelligence that feels almost above the rest of us. She continues to carry herself this way as she walks up the three steps into the spotlight and the crowd cheer.

She has an aura about her.

A stoic glow.

I try to align my expression with hers.

'Mal?'

Meghan, behind me, on her phone, not once looking up at Paula Kate.

'One minute...' I say. I don't mean to be rude, but Paula Kate is about to speak. To introduce me and—

'Can I just tell you something, before you go up there,' Meghan whispers. I really want to say *Not really, no*, and I nearly do, but stop myself, because when I look at her I can see she actually looks upset. Which is unexpected.

'Of course,' I whisper back, simultaneously trying to hear what superlatives Paula Kate is using to describe my book.

'I just wanted to say, I'm so proud of you.' Oh.

That's sweet. She's sweet. 'Thanks, Meghan, that's really kind.' I go to turn back to the gap in the curtain, to Paula, but Meghan holds my arm, gripping tightly.

'I know how much you've been through and I just want you to know...' she says, '...you deserve all this. And I haven't told anyone this before but... I had a bit of difficult time with my ex, he was quite emotionally' – she lowers her voice even further, to a barely audible whisper – '*abusive* – and the way you touched on that in *Slay* – with Mandy and Richard – I just wanted to say, it really resonated.'

I pause. 'Really?'

'Really. It meant a lot, to read it.'

'Oh, Meghan. I'm so sorry you went through that.'

'You're really brave.'

'I don't know about that...' I suddenly feel myself. 'It's just a book.'

'No, not to write the book. You're really brave for leaving him.' Twenty-two-year-old Meghan squeezes my arm. I look at her, and in the silence between us I see someone I hadn't seen before. Someone beneath the PR façade. Someone gentle, someone kind, someone who has built up an armour – a Gen-Z armour – whose purpose is fundamentally identical to my own, but looks incredibly different. And there is a sadness in her eyes, a deep sadness that I feel inside myself, and—

'Mal, what the hell are you staring at? You need to be on stage, *now*.' She turns me around and pushes me through the curtain.

The whole room erupts with applause.

58

Leo

I need a fag before I go in.

It's all I got now. Cigs and coffee.

Never been here before. It's big. Didn't think it would be this fucking massive. There's a man at the door staring at me. Since when do places like this have bouncers?

'We're shut,' he says. His eyes scan my body up and down. 'Can you smoke that away from the door, please?'

'Isn't there an event on tonight?' I say, taking a drag.

He frowns. 'It's ticketed,' he replies, a bit pissy, a bit like I'm wasting his time.

'Yeah,' I say. 'I know. I've got one.'

I hold up my phone screen towards him. He takes a second, like he's checking if it's a fake. He looks at his watch. 'Well, you need to get up there,' he says. 'It's started. They might not let you in.'

'Huh? I'm sure they will.'

'Oh yeah?' he says. 'And why's that?'

'Cos it's about me.'

He looks at me like I'm high. Which is ironic, considering everything. 'What are you talking about?'

'The book. Mallory Maddox's book. It's about me. I'm Liam.'

He shrugs, like he couldn't care less. 'Haven't read it, mate. Now put that fag out. It's on the fifth floor.'

59

Mallory

I only half hear the question because I'm too busy looking at her teeth.

'Where did the inspiration for this incredible story come from?'

She has such perfect, Malibu teeth. It feels odd because she has an accent still, from the UK. I think it's Brummie – somewhere in the midlands definitely – but it is being overruled by a lot of Californian rhotic Rs and vocal fry. I was thinking of getting Invisalign myself, but I'm waiting for the publication payment to come through. The book sold in the USA for five times the amount it sold here, so I know I'm going to be OK, but it just doesn't feel quite real yet. Like the money won't hit my account. Like someone will do something to prevent it from happening.

But it *is* real.

I am here.

I am answering all of her questions perfectly. And people are laughing. People are hanging onto my every word. A little like when I was in that AA meeting all that time ago, but this is different. This is *my* AA meeting, with *my* people.

Bookaholics.

Yes!

I'm a little giddy. The adrenaline is coursing through me, as if I am in a film on fast forward. They are filming this, actually. I was told by the publishers. They are filming it so they can use snippets of it for their awards promotion.

'That's a great question,' I say. I have practiced this answer, so many times. Thankfully the publisher gave me a list of points P.K. would bring up, and this was point number one. I had recurring intrusive thoughts of me spontaneously saying, *I googled it drunk in the bathroom,* and *Reddit told me what to do,* which put the fear of God into me. So I prepared the answer to a tee. 'Inspiration is such an interesting thing. I have written books before and friends have read them and said, *Oh my gosh, Mal, that character is so like you.* But at the time of writing it, I had no idea. I genuinely couldn't see myself in them. In fact, I could have sworn the *opposite.* So what I've come to realise is that the inspiration, I think, for all my characters, goes back to my own childhood. Often to my own shadow.'

I did a bit of reading around shadow work for my counselling course. It ties in nicely here.

I have been waiting to say that bit for so long.

And when I ran it past Stan and Meghan and Gina and the team, they all loved it.

And seemingly, so does Paula. Because she is earnestly nodding. 'So interesting that writing these books is an act of therapy in itself,' she says. 'Eking out the subconscious.'

Someone in the audience makes an *mm* sound, which, unexpectedly, creates a pang of what I can only interpret as jealousy inside me.

Paula got an *mm*. I'm not sure I have got one of those yet. Unless I didn't hear it...

'So...' she goes on, and I can see in her eyes that the *mm* has buoyed her. 'If this goes back to your childhood...' She smiles knowingly, this new confidence turning her out to face the audience in a way that says, *Don't worry – I'm not letting her off the hook with that answer!* which elicits a pre-emptive laugh from a few of the more astute audience members. Damn, she's good. *She's so good.* They love her. 'Let's go back to your younger years, if that's OK with you?'

'I don't mind at all,' I say. I keep my eyes on Paula, noticing the shade of lipstick she is wearing is some kind of orange, which frankly is a little bold. But also, somehow, on her, very chic. I ready my voice, to be assertive and vulnerable all at once. 'I think there is this pain in me, this pain that has been there for a very long time. And I have spent so much of my life trying to avoid that pain.' I pause, for a fraction of a second, just long enough to hear an *mm*. An *mm* for me this time. 'Whether it be through relationships, work—'

'Writing,' Paula cuts me off.

'Right!' I say, pulling it back to myself. *I was going to get there, Paula.* 'Writing. Literally avoiding myself by escaping into a fantasy world.'

'But so much of this *isn't* fantasy, isn't that right?'

I pause. Not because I'm thrown, but because I want to appear considered. Next to her. Who is so considered. I want to be the underdog of considered. I want to surprise people with how considered I come across, next to her. 'No. A lot of it is based on real life.'

'I mean, it's needless to say that the therapist – Mandy – is based on you.'

'Yes,' I say. 'That's a given.'

'Because you are a therapist.'

'I am. Well, I was. I'm a little busy now.'

Laughter. People laugh. At me. Well, *with* me.

'And Mandy is a searcher. Desperate for a way out.'

'Yes. She is. She has that compass within her.'

'It's incredibly brave, what she does. She goes through a lot, throughout the book. And it's almost overshadowed by the pain of the other characters. Almost. But it remains, a haunting undercurrent. It is the thread that ties it all together. Her pain.' Wait. Didn't I… didn't I think that in the cupboard? 'The way the dynamic between her and Richard is written is incredibly chilling.'

My brain suddenly wobbles.

I feel… odd.

A little off, all of a sudden.

Like I am momentarily freefalling.

I blink a few times.

No. I'm fine. *I'm completely fine.*

'Thank you,' I say, but my brain is hesitating, lingering on what she just said: *the pain is the thread*. And then I hear something. A chair screeching against the floor, somewhere at the back of the room. A latecomer, perhaps. I squint into the audience. I can just make out their faces, all glaring back at me, hopeful, ready to be inspired, to learn – from me.

'And you have been quite forthcoming that the nature of the relationship between Richard and Mandy is something you have experienced yourself.'

I go immediately cold.

Not because of what she said. But because—

Oh my God.

Is that…?

He's here.

Oh, God.

When I wrote to him, I told him we shouldn't see each other—!

Paula is looking at me oddly. Because I am not answering her. But I can't – I can't remember what she said… *Why is he here?*

'And what about the other characters?'

My hands have gone completely numb.

I can't quite see his face. It's too dark.

God, I hope…

I hope he's… I'm not—

'Mal?'

It might not be him. *Is it him?* Perhaps it's the stress. The stress of everything. I have been stressed. This whole thing has been incredibly stressful, come to think of it. And I have just spent a concerning amount of time in a store cupboard hallucinating dragons and dead people, so it could just be— He moves, and I catch a better glimpse.

It's *not* him. This person's hair is a totally different colour. This person is blonde. Leo is not blonde. And this person is chunkier. He has more weight on his bones. Leo was a skeleton.

Thank God.

Thank God.

I'm safe.

Aren't I?

They look very similar.

I rub my eyes.

My head. It hurts.

'I think many people would be interested to know who the character of Liam is based on,' Paula says, as if she is living directly in the centre of my mind.

'I...' I look back at Paula, and something inside me stalls. I want to stand up. To stand up and walk down the centre aisle, out of this building, and disappear.

What am I doing here?

I feel my face flush. It is incredibly hot – like it was in the cupboard with the dragons. A burning, erupting inside me. I realise, I think I'm about to burst into tears. There is a flicker of something in Paula's eyes. She can see I'm struggling, and that it's from more than the emotional weight of our performance. That something is happening to me that feels off script. She suddenly looks nervous.

'I don't know if I can...' I say, and glance back at the boy.

It is undeniable.

It's him.

He's here.

He's dyed his hair.

Paula can tell something's gone very wrong. I see her eyes flash down to the prompt card in her hand, wondering if she should help me. Wondering if this silence, this stalling, is all part of the narration. The story.

'He's based on your brother, isn't he?'

The silence that follows feels like it might eat me alive. It is a 'Yes' that I finally say. I try to go on, to search for the rehearsed response. But I can't find the words. They have completely escaped me. Dried up. I pick up the glass of water and take a sip, as if it will replenish them, but nothing comes.

He has his arms folded.

I can see his eyes now.

Go on, they say. *I dare you.*

'I know this is difficult,' Paula begins again, trepidation in her voice. 'Your brother really struggled, didn't he?'

My mother. My mother is staring at her feet. 'I...'

Saying this was fine, in the bathroom mirror.

Saying this was fine, with my flat white in the park.
Saying this was fine, in the letter I wrote to Leo.
After everything.
But now.
This.
Now.
Here.
It all feels incredibly real.
'My brother...'

But he *did* struggle. Nick did struggle. And I have spent my life avoiding myself. I have spent my life avoiding my own pain. I'm not lying, not at all. 'Yes,' I say, but it sounds thin. He did. *This is not a lie.* 'Yes,' I repeat, with more conviction. 'He struggled a lot. With being gay, and the shame that brought him. With drugs. He struggled a lot with drugs. And with himself. His story deserves to be told, and the pain of what he went through deserves to be shared. I wrote this book for him.' I look directly at Leo. 'And for anyone else that can relate to that struggle.'

'Of which...' Paula says gently, 'There are so many. In fact, what struck me most when reading this story, was that Liam is an *everyman. He is all of us.*' She stops, to allow the profundity of her words to land. 'Like Mandy, his inner world is so rich, so deeply raw, that you can't help but relate.'

'I hope so,' I say. 'I really do.'

'And – as you so shrewdly write in the closing scenes...' She turns out to the audience, pre-empting their collective groan. 'Don't worry!' she says, putting her hands up like a thief caught with their loot. 'I promise – no spoilers will be given...' I hear the collective, grateful sigh. 'But one of the overarching messages of the book is so simple, yet so important. *We are all the same,*' she says. 'And we are. Underneath all the behaviours we have individually built up to remove ourselves from feeling – we are all *pain*, we are all *shame*, we are all *guilt*, we are all deeply and honestly *human*—'

'We are all scared,' I add.

'Yes,' Paula says, almost excitedly now. 'Yes. We are all *petrified*, and trying not to look it.' She looks out to the audience.

'Who can relate to that?' People shuffle about nervously. 'Show of hands, please.' A few eager ones dart straight up. But then, one after the other, more are raised, until the whole audience has a hand in the air. 'I rest my case,' Paula says. Except the boy's. The boy's hand is not in the air. I want to ask Paula if she can see him. To make sure. To make sure he is real. 'You tap into something in all of us.'

'I just wanted to write what people are scared to talk about – the deepest parts of ourselves – and I think – well, I hope… that that's why readers are connecting to the story.'

Paula turns to them again. 'For those of you reading it, or those who have finished: are you? Are you connecting?'

There is applause.

Applause for me.

'I'm glad you're connecting to Mal and Leo,' I say, when it dies down.

Silence. I glance at Paula. She's pulling a face. She looks a little confused. A little shocked. 'Sorry?'

'What?'

'Who are Leo and Mal?'

Oh wait. Oh God. 'Oh! No. Liam and Mandy.' *Oh, God. Quick. Quick – think.* 'Those are just nicknames. Ignore me.' She pulls another face. Shit. What was it that Meghan said? *If all goes to shit, go to the reading.* 'Maybe I should read an excerpt?' I hear a few mutters. I turn towards the sound and face the crowd. 'Would you like that?' I ask. And they all say yes at once. I pick up the book. I can see how much my hands are shaking. I wanted to do a part from the middle, but I'm struggling with the pages, fumbling with them, and I can hardly see the words… 'Oh, I think just the opening bit, if that's OK with everyone?'

'Of course it's OK,' Paula says gently, then, very quietly, so only I can hear, 'Take your time, Mal. We're all here for you.'

I exhale slowly and nod. 'I just wanted to say, for anyone who hasn't read it, that ultimately, this book is a story of survival.'

I begin to read.

And when I am done, and I look back up, he is no longer there.

60

Leo

I'm out the front, eating one of those mad fucking book biscuits.

It's nasty as fuck. Tastes of absolutely nothing. I want to spit it out, but I've been cornered by a man in a yellow corduroy shirt called Julian who came out to smoke. It's mad, cos if someone asked me to draw a book in human form, I'd actually draw Julian. And I'd call him Julien.

He's talking a lot. In fact, he won't shut up. About himself. There's not much else. He hasn't come up for air in about four whole minutes. He's an editor at the same publishing house that did *Slay*, but he works with crime fiction. He has just had a very stressful situation pushing the publication of a book by some famous fucking author that I've never fucking heard of that the industry has projected to be a hit. He's worried it's going to be shit.

Fucking well fascinating how much he thinks I care.

'Have you had one of these?' I ask, holding up the biscuit.

'Sorry?' he says.

'These biscuits.'

'Oh, are they good?'

'Yeah. Have one.'

I dunno if he heard me, cos he just launches into something else, about a book-prize shortlist. I could probably just turn around and leave. There's a big chance he wouldn't even notice. But I realise I might need Julien and his yellow corduroy shirt. Need him to answer some things I wanna know, then I can fuck off.

'Have you read it?'

Oh, would you look at that. I think Julien just asked me a question.

'*Slay*?'

'Yes!'

I haven't. 'I have, yeah.'

'Isn't it just marvellous. *So* dark.'

'So dark.'

'You know…' Julian glances around himself quickly, then leans towards me as if he's about to pass me intel on a terrorist attack. 'I think some people are wondering if Mark – you know, Mark, the man who was abusing Liam and was pushed in the canal…?'

'Yeah, I know Mark.'

'Well, apparently, she was inspired by a story on the news. A man fell in Camden canal.'

'Oh right?'

'Yes.'

'Interesting that.'

'Very fucking interesting.'

He looks a bit taken aback, then thrilled. That I swore. 'Fucking interesting indeed,' he repeats, with delight, like I gave him the permission to do it.

I didn't push Mo.

I went to speak to the police after the body was found. I spoke it through with my sponsor, cos it was eating me up. I did secretly hope that he had fallen in.

But I didn't push him, and I do remember the whole thing even though I was high as a fucking kite. He just left me under the bridge, stumbled away and never came back.

'Fucking insane, the whole book!' Julien says, still giddy with the swearing.

I wonder if I can find out. 'And that ending…' I say.

'Oh my God…' he agrees. 'Leo's death. Brutal.'

He dies.

She killed him.

She fucking killed him.

I feel a tug in my stomach, like a hook behind my ribs, rupturing my insides. 'Yeah,' I say. 'Brutal.' It burns. She wrote me off the page, and out of her life. She fucking got rid of me in every way she could. That's all she saw me as. A walking fucking wound.

'Are you OK?' Julien says. 'You look shocked. I thought you said you'd read it?' He stops and looks at me like he is properly noticing me for the first time. 'Sorry, who did you say you are again?'

'Just a fan.'

'Oh, one of those BookTokers?'

'Yeah. One of those.'

'Jesus, you guys have a lot of sway with the sales. It was never like that in my time.' He pauses. 'Well, I mean. No. She did catch the zeitgeist. I can't give you all the credit.'

You fucking should Julien. 'The zeitgeist, yeah?'

'Yes.'

'I guess a lot of your job is predicting that.'

'Well, we are only editors, we can't tell the future,' he says, in a way that looks like he thinks he actually can. 'But we get an idea of what people are looking for.'

'And what is that?'

'Next?'

'Yeah,' I say.

'Well, horror is about to come back around, in a big way.' He gives me a look, like he has just let me into a massive secret.

'Oh, cool.'

'Do you like horror?'

'Depends.'

'I think more… rural horror is going to be in.' His eyes widen, surprised at his own choice of words, like he has just coined the next literary trend. 'People are looking for spooky, psychological horror. That kind of thing.'

'Spooky horror. Is that right?'

He makes a little shrug. 'Who knows. It's what Stan thinks. Have you met Stan?'

'No.' I haven't, but I have spoken to him. Not that he would know.

'Do you write… erm… Sorry I've forgotten your name?'

'Luke. I write a bit, I'm a poet.'

'Ah, wonderful. So, Poet Luke… Is your writing sort of…' He eyes me up and down. 'Edgy?'

'I wanna write something else now.'

'Good idea. Poetry is a hard sell.'

I know. Stanley told me, when I sent him my poems under a pseudonym, before I relapsed, six months ago. I wanted money, and I was done with the men. Couldn't fucking stand them any longer. And I'd taken his email address from Mallory's laptop in the kitchen that night. He replied. He said his LGBT list was full, and he was only really being drawn to the proper authentic stuff. That mine was a bit too scrappy and forced. He said to come back with something better. That he liked that I was working class.

'Well, we're always looking for new voices. It's a big part of our ethos here. Championing new and underrepresented voices.' His eyes move up and down me again.

'Yeah? OK.' He looks like he wants to get away from me now. Maybe my working-class anger, bubbling up under the surface, is too much for him.

'Oh, speak of the proverbial devil!' Julien says, turning to a small man in a suit. 'Stan!'

'Jules!' the small man says. They kiss each other on each cheek.

'Stan, *I heard*,' Jules tells him.

Stan raises his eyebrows. 'Heard what?'

'Half-a-mil deal in America?'

Stan looks behind him. '*Shhh…*'

Half a mil.

Half a fucking mil.

Julien shakes his head. 'The book isn't even that good, Stan. Don't know how the hell you pulled that one off.'

Stan winks. 'It's all about positioning. About timing.'

'Well. You're a pro.'

Stan suddenly sees me watching.

'Oh, sorry,' Julien says. 'This is…' He pauses.

'Luke, I'm Luke.'

'Luke! Yes.'

'Hello, Luke. Have you been at the event?'

'Yeah. I was in there.'

'He's a BookToker,' Julian whispers into Stan's ear.

'Ah! Well, we love what you do,' Stan says. 'You are so important to getting stories out there. Thank you, Luke. It's great to meet you.'

'I'm also a writer. Well, a poet.'

Silence.

'Well,' Stan eventually says. 'I hope you've learnt something this evening, Luke. You never know, it could be you up there one day!'

'Nice to meet you both.'

I turn, and I am fucking gone.

61

Mallory

The pub down the road from Waterstones is quiet and dimly lit, with a few suits dotted around after a day of corporate exertion. Gina, Stan, Meghan and a whole host of other people from the publisher, who I have never met before (or have, and can't remember), are all huddled around a table in the corner.

'It was such a success, Mal.'
'*Such* a success.'
'You were amazing.'
'*So* amazing.'
'I nearly cried at one point.'
'Oh, I was silently *sobbing*...'

They all look at me, waiting for me to say something. 'Did anyone speak to someone called Leo tonight?'

They frown, confused.
'Leo?'
'No.'
'I don't remember a Leo.'
'Never mind,' I say.
 'Sorry, Mal.'
'Why?'
'It doesn't matter. I'm not very with it, I'm just frazzled.'
'You must be exhausted.'
'Of course you are, Mal. You don't have to say a thing. Just sit there and drink your wine.'

I can't think straight. Did he dye his hair? Or am I imagining things? *Was he even there?* 'Did you manage to speak to Paula, afterwards, Mal?'

'I didn't.' I didn't speak to her at all, other than when we were on stage. I watched her signing autographs and then taking photographs outside the front of the building. I overheard her publicist beside her say she should get to the hotel, because she has a big day tomorrow. She's going to Paris, for the launch of her next book. I tried to catch her eye, but she either didn't *see*, or she—'

'She's so lovely.'

'So lovely.'

'It was so kind of her to come.'

'She's so brilliant. So insightful.'

'Yes,' I say. 'She is.'

'You handled the questions so well, Mal.'

'Thanks, Gina.' *Was it Leo? Was it him?*

'Are you sure you're OK, Mal? You don't look great.'

It can't have been him.

I stopped sleeping. For so many months I couldn't sleep, worrying about him. I got a therapist. A proper therapist. And I separated from Ronan.

Part of me thought that one day I'd see Leo on the news.

I dreamt I would.

And that I wouldn't be able to cope.

'Look at this, Mal.' Meghan shoves her phone across the table-top so the screen lands directly in front of me. 'This tweet will cheer you up.'

I GOT TO MEET MALLORY MADDOX TONIGHT
SHE WAS SOOOO NICEEEEEE
WAAAAA
HER BOOK THOUGH! THIS BOOOOOOOOK
IS SO BLEAK
YOU WILL DIE
YOU ARE NOT READDDYYYYY!!
I HAVE BEEN FKIN TRAUMATISED SINCE I READ IT
WHHUTTT !!!

'Oh, wow,' I say. I look at the name of the person who posted it. @kellyannreads. 'Yeah, that's great.'

'So what's your plan for the rest of the week, Mal?' someone asks.

'We have a big schedule,' Meghan says. 'She needs to rest tonight and then after this week' – she looks at me – 'you can have your break.'

I smile at her. 'Yes.'

'How is the house coming on, Mal?' Stan asks. 'The pictures look stunning. White walls. Plants climbing up it. Right by the sea. Glorious.'

'It's great, yeah. I mean, I still have a lot of work to do to it, but it's taking shape.' I pause. 'The air is fresh. It gives me mental space. I feel peace there.'

They all stare at me longingly. 'Oh, Mal. You deserve it.'

'You really do.'

'Maybe you should go back to your hotel… I think you're just overwhelmed.'

'Yes, I think I need to get to bed.'

As I rise from the table, and I'm given hug after hug after hug, things blur. Stan tells me he is so excited for the next one. He says the American money will be coming soon. Gina tells me to rest, then for me to pitch her the next book idea in the coming weeks. They ideally want to publish the follow-up next year, off the back of the success of this one. Meghan tells me that she will meet me in the morning, by the entrance to Foyles, where we will do a signing. The next two weeks will be spent with booksellers and podcasters and interviewers and photographers.

As I wind my way through the quiet London streets, to the hotel in Piccadilly, I keep stopping.

Turning.

Looking.

I hear…

I swear…

'Hello?' I swear… I swear I keep seeing him. 'Leo?'

No.

It can't be. It's me. It's my mind.

When I get back to the hotel room, I sit on the bed. Safe.

I am safe.

I put on my meditation app and do my breathing exercises, as I've been told to do.

I am safe now.

I am.

When I am done, I sit on the bed, and I stare at the book in my hand.

SLAY
A NOVEL
By Mallory Maddox

I open the front page.

To the dedication.

> *For one person in particular.*
> *Who helped me more than he will ever know.*

A droplet of water appears on the page. I wipe my eyes.

I was going to pay for him to go to rehab, but my therapist told me it was a bad idea. She told me no one could help him but himself.

And that I needed to put distance between us.

I think about him every night.

Every single night.

I open the notes app on my phone, where I composed the letter that I wrote to him, last year. I read it occasionally, to comfort myself.

Dear Leo,

I am so, so sorry that I cannot be a part of your life anymore. I was sincerely hoping that we could be friends, and that I could help you.

I wanted to – in whatever way I could.

But now I have learnt that the best way for us both to move forward is to separate our paths. You have changed me in such a wonderful way. Your strength of character has inspired me. I really hope you manage to find happiness, and peace.

I hope that life brings you everything you've ever wanted.

All the best,

Mal

But this time there is no comfort. This time, I cringe. I feel sick.

I delete the note and get into bed. Every time I am about to drift off, I see the dragons' eyes, watching from the darkness.

I take a pill.

It helps.

*

Over the next two weeks, the publicity tour is a haze. So many people. So many questions. The same ones, over and over again. And I keep seeing glimpses of him. His ghost. His shadow.

Just behind me.

Just out of reach.

In the periphery of the half-light.

And now I am home – this place I have made a home – where I am safe, I see him in the waves. When I am walking across the beach. In the pages of the books I try to read. Out of the window, late at night, when I cannot sleep.

Part of this comforts me.

To know he is still there. Moving forward.

I hope he is.

I hope he gets the life he deserves.

62

Three weeks later

Leo

I've learnt a lot about resentments over the past year.

I've been told they're like drinking poison and hoping the other person will die. I get that, I do. But I have also learnt that they can be useful. They can make you want to change your fucking life. I think, without them, without their toxic fucking potency, I would have let myself disappear.

But now I feel awake. More alive than ever.

Because I'm fucking angry.

And desperate.

The gift of desperation.

And I don't want a drink. I don't want sex. Not anymore.

I've spent the last few weeks going to the library, where the computers are free. They have Microsoft Word and all. Been dead nice, actually. Nice and quiet. Thought my brain would hate it, but I've done all right. Got into a bit of a flow state. Felt fucking incredible.

And then, in the evenings, after the library writing seshes, I've been sat outside the M&S in Crouch End. Sat on the floor with my fingerless gloves – works a fucking charm. Got talking to a few rich people with a guilt complex who took pity on me. Over three weeks, managed to make a few hundred quid. People love a sob story.

So now, I've decided to come away for a bit.

The hostel here is all right. Basic. Cheap. Nice view. Quiet.

Got a top bunk. I've seen a lot of randoms come and go in the bed beneath me, but I keep myself to myself. And no one really asks questions.

I'm here for a whole month.

'*To clear my head,*' I told Debbie.

'*Make sure you're checking in, and getting to online meetings,*' she said.

Would have told Mum and Dad, but they don't wanna know me.

It fucking hurts.

All of it.

But at least I feel it.

And I'm looking into the void, like I've been told to.

And there's some clarity that has come with the anger. With the desperation.

It's fucking cold tonight.

I pull my coat around me and look down at my phone, at the email reply from Stan that he sent two days ago.

Hi Luke,

It's a pleasure to e-meet you!!

Thank you for sending me through the first three chapters of your book, *The Poet Acts*. It's really quite something. I have to say, I was really, really blown away. The premise is EXACTLY what I'm looking for. It's like you read my mind. A dark, spooky psych horror set on the coast in rural Wales? Count me in.

I would love to see more. Could you send me the rest of the book, please?

I have a few pointers, if I may be so bold?

I love our protagonist. He is a very interesting character. His anger at his therapist is understandable, after she discards him; the way her neglect affects him is truly believable.

I love the plot development... That he decides to get revenge and drive her insane (what a clever idea!) by following her around London, and when she moves to the countryside, his leaving the notes and odd little poems on her doorstep is a brilliant way to begin with this. I'm thinking the story can continue with him creeping into her house, moving things, etc., making her feel like she is really losing her mind. I just really want things to escalate. Are you able to make him a real threat to her? Make him become… *obsessive*? This is such a great word, one that's really been circulating around the publishing world recently. He could actually become enamoured with her, too.

And, I know you weren't sure, but I think it would be really, really impactful if it ended with her death. Ending a book with a dead therapist: this will *certainly* get people talking. It asks some wider questions. How safe is therapy nowadays, in this world of overexposure to wellness? *Everyone* seems to be a therapist now. Is this *dangerous*? Dangerous for whom? And how?

I love the conversation it opens up.

I think the concept could be a real winner. I was speaking with a few editors at some leading publishing houses at an event only a couple of weeks ago, and there is a real thirst for danger. For horror. But horror that feels as if it could happen to you. That's the key. It needs to feel *real*.

I look forward to reading more from you, Luke. There is an anger in your writing that really propels it. It's very exciting to read.

Remember, authenticity sells. Make these characters as real as you can. Do some research. Find the voices of the characters, their inner worlds. Make people scared. If people are scared that it could happen to them, we are winning.

Go for it. Go dark.

There is an appetite for dark.

All my best (for now!),

Stan

It's dark now.

I look up at the house.

It's nice, this place. Small. White walls. Plants growing up the sides.

When I reach the porch, I can see there is a light on in a downstairs room.

A little light. On a writing desk.

There she is. Sat at the bureau. A big cardigan wrapped around her, glass of wine in hand.

My lead character.

A new story begins now.

ACKNOWLEDGEMENTS

First and foremost, thank you to my agent, Clare Wallace. Meeting you and working on this book together has been such a joy. Your kindness, creativity and openness have meant a lot. This book wouldn't exist without you, and I'll always be grateful. To the whole team at Darley Anderson. To Kat Lenahan. Your early take, fresh eyes and exciting notes really helped shape this. Thank you.

To my editor, Wayne Brookes. Thank you for your insight, enthusiasm and brilliant instinct. I couldn't have done it without you. And Kobe Grant. Your energy and encouragement have been incredible. I've felt fortunate to work with you both, and I hope we get to do more together. Hayley Warnham – you are insanely talented and a genius wizard. The whole team at Oneworld – Mark Rusher, Shadi Doostdar, Juliet Mabey, Lucy Cooper, Matilda Warner, Katie Jennings, Paul Nash – you feel like family. I'm grateful to be part of it. To my brilliant copy editor, Maddy Hamey-Thomas – thank you so much.

To my friends.

To my family.

To the Gower coast.

To the sea that cleared my head right up.

To the staff at Gran T's Coffee House in Ancoats, your kindness meant a lot.

To the quote from *Dune*: 'Fear is the mind-killer.'

To the void.

JOSH SILVER grew up on a farm in the Lake District, before moving to Manchester with his family, where he spent his teenage years loving the city. He trained as an actor at the prestigious Royal Academy of Dramatic Art in London and went on to perform in the West End and on Broadway. After deciding to change careers, he now works as a mental health nurse. Josh lives in Manchester.

@smudgecotton